# To Enchant a Wicked Duke
## The Brethren Series

For more information about the author:
www.christicaldwellauthor.com
christicaldwellauthor@gmail.com
Twitter: @ChristiCaldwell
Or on Facebook at: Christi Caldwell Author

For first glimpse at covers, excerpts, and free bonus material, be sure to sign up for my monthly newsletter!
Printed in the USA.

Cover Design and Interior Format

# To Enchant a Wicked Duke

Heart
of a
Duke

THE
SERIES

*USA Today* BESTSELLER
# CHRISTI CALDWELL

# ~Other Titles by
# Christi Caldwell

**THE HEART OF A SCANDAL**
In Need of a Knight—Prequel Novella
Schooling the Duke
Heart of a Duke
In Need of a Duke—Prequel Novella
For Love of the Duke
More than a Duke
The Love of a Rogue
Loved by a Duke
To Love a Lord
The Heart of a Scoundrel
To Wed His Christmas Lady
To Trust a Rogue
The Lure of a Rake
To Woo a Widow

**LORDS OF HONOR**
Seduced by a Lady's Heart
Captivated by a Lady's Charm
Rescued by a Lady's Love
Tempted by a Lady's Smile

**SCANDALOUS SEASONS**
Forever Betrothed, Never the Bride
Never Courted, Suddenly Wed
Always Proper, Suddenly Scandalous
Always a Rogue, Forever Her Love
A Marquess for Christmas
Once a Wallflower, at Last His Love

**SINFUL BRIDES**
The Rogue's Wager
The Scoundrel's Honor

**THE THEODOSIA SWORD**
Only for His Lady

**DANBY**
A Season of Hope
Winning a Lady's Heart

**BRETHREN OF THE LORDS**
My Lady of Deception
Memoir: Non-Fiction
Uninterrupted Joy

# DEDICATION

*To Sandra Sookoo. My amazing editor.*
*Thank you for being there since the inception of this story*
*and being a remarkable sounding board throughout.*

# PROLOGUE

*Suffolk, England*
*1807*

THE DEVIL HAD COME TO claim his due.

The rhythmic click of that very Devil's cane on the hardwood floors and the slow shuffle of his right leg echoed in the absolute still the shadows wouldn't brave. From where he stood at the end of the hall, Dominick Tallings clutched his copy of *Evelina* close to his chest. He ducked his head around the corner and frowned. *This is him?* He removed his reading spectacles and squinting, tucked them inside his jacket.

*This* was the man who had Father sobbing from sunup to sundown? Who had Mother shut away in her rooms with the curtains drawn? This was the man who'd ultimately seen Dominick's time at Harrow ended, and had him called back to Suffolk? All hint of strength his impressive height and broad-shouldered form conveyed, shattered by that limp.

Yet, the stranger walked these halls as though he owned them. Without benefit of the servant, whose escort he'd turned away.

The floorboard under Dominick's feet groaned in protest, shattering the quiet. The Devil spun with such speed, Dominick froze, immobile. Even with the length of the darkened hall, the soullessness of those dark brown eyes shone bright, glittering with gold—the color of greed and wealth.

The Marquess of Rutland flicked a cold, disinterested stare over his shaking person. Then with precise steps, he continued forward, until he disappeared around the corner. The faint *click* of Papa's office door opening and closing signified the late night meeting had commenced.

Heart knocking against his ribcage, Dominick picked his way quickly down the hall, overstepping the worn floorboards given to creaking. Holding his breath, he came to a stop outside Papa's office.

"You are officially out of time, Tallings." The marquess' deadened tones befit the Devil he was purported to be.

"I have a family. A son, a daughter, a wife." Did that weak, threadbare plea belong to his once joyous papa? "You'll destroy us."

"Your family isn't my responsibility," the marquess drawled. Ice skittered along Dominick's spine and he dug his fingers into his book. "Your failings are."

"Why are you doing this?" Papa begged.

Lord Rutland's menacing whisper pierced the quiet. "You have until the end of the week to pay your debt."

The *click-clack-click-clack* of the marquess' cane indicated the man moved. Dominick hastily backed away, tripping over himself. He stumbled and the book flew from his hands, sailing through the air, as he landed hard on his buttocks. Pain shot up his spine. The door opened. Ignoring his discomfort, he glanced frantically about as Lord Rutland stepped into the hall and pulled the wood panel shut behind him. The marquess limped closer and closer. And then stopped, towering over him.

Dominick's mouth went dry.

The marquess flicked a frosty stare over his trembling form. Then, stepped around him. As if he didn't matter. As if he wasn't worth the effort to waste a "pardon me" on.

Dominick stared unblinking at the man's retreating form. "You're a monster." Those childlike words echoed off the walls and he cringed as the marquess wheeled back to face him. Fighting for courage, Dominick pressed on. "My father has devoted his *life* to Tallings Iron and you come here," he slashed the air with his hand, "and bankrupt my father. Leave us destitute. Without so much as an apology?" Tears filled his eyes. *Then, what good would an apology do?*

A hard grin split Lord Rutland's lips. "If you learn nothing else, know this: *never* make apologies for who you are or what you have done. You may despise me, for actions that your father is guilty of, but I own who I am. Your father has not." And then with an infuriating dismissiveness, the marquess continued his slow walk down the hall.

A tear streaked down Dominick's cheek and he angrily swiped at it. "Someday, I'll destroy the people you love," he vowed. His voice shook with the force of his loathing. Where had that bold threat come from? Where, when fear rolled through him in waves?

The marquess merely glanced over his shoulder. Pain briefly flickered in the man's eyes and then it was gone, so Dominick was left to wonder if he'd merely imagined it. "I love no one. You would do well to learn now that revenge and hatred will make you far stronger than love," Lord Rutland said, jerking his chin at him. "You see, I will leave this house and your family and not ever think of you again, and *that* is where strength comes from."

With that, the gentleman left.

Dominick remained sprawled on the floor. Afraid to move. Afraid to breathe. He sat with the clock ticking away the seconds.

*We have nothing—*

From within the cottage, his mother's quiet weeping penetrated the thin walls of their home. Crying. She was always crying. *Had* been since he'd arrived home a fortnight ago. Abandoning his book, he shoved to his feet, drawn toward the sound of his mother's despair. He stopped outside her rooms. Door cracked, the faint glow of a candle spilled into the hall. Seated on the edge of the bed, her back to him, Mama shook like a frail reed caught in a windstorm.

Worry knotted his insides and he cast a look down the hall in the direction of his father's office. What would happen to her when she discovered Lord Rutland's demands on Papa? Backing away from her room, he paused outside his sister's chambers. He pressed the handle and stuck his head inside. Just a year older than himself, Cecily had taken on more responsibilities these past days than any girl ought to ever know.

*Mama said we will lose all, Dominick, and Grandfather will have no choice but to take us in.*

Her quiet, even breathing indicated she slept, sheltered in this moment from their mother's sadness. For now, untouched. Dominick pulled the oak panel shut behind him.

An eerie chill lingered in the midnight air. Hesitating, he cast a glance at his chamber door, wanting nothing more than to seek out his rooms and forget about his father's failing business and his mother's misery and Cecily's fears. He wanted to bury his head in Byron's work and remember how everything had once been…but there was Papa.

With a sigh, he started back down the hall. Dominick rapped once. "Papa?" Silence rang loudly. He knocked again. "Papa?" He pressed the door handle and stepped inside the dimly lit office. He blinked, bringing the room into focus. *DripDripDrip.* Dominick squinted, his gaze going to the upended bottle of brandy trailing the remnants of the bottle onto the floor. His mouth went dry and he took another hesitant step forward.

Then froze. He stood transfixed in an unending moment of horror.

"Papa," he whispered, his stomach heaving. The glow of a lone candle cast shadows upon his father's lifeless body—mouth opened in a silent scream, his eyes bulging—as it swung from a makeshift noose from the rafters. Dominick stumbled inside and then pulled the door closed, locking it behind him. As he leaned against it, borrowing support, he fought to draw in a breath.

Dominick pressed his eyes closed. *Don't look. Don't look.* Because if he looked, it would make it true. His panic mounted, threatening to pull him under.

*Stop!*

For Cecily and Mama he would have to be strong. He forced his eyes open. Taking pains to avoid his father's frame as it twisted in the silence, Dominick stalked over to the cluttered desk. His shoulders shook under the force of his tears. He sucked in a shuddery sob and pulled a drawer open. Fishing around inside, his fingers collided with cold metal.

He placed the blade between his teeth and righted the upended chair underneath his father's dangling body. Scrambling atop the oak chair, he forced himself to look. His eyes met his father's bulging, lifeless ones. A moan spilled from Dominick's lips and he quickly snatched the knife. He proceeded to saw the velvet strap used as a makeshift noose.

He'd destroyed Mama's curtains. Sweat beaded on his brow. As his arms strained under the efforts, he focused on the pain. Anything but the streaks of tears still left on his father's once-smiling cheeks. The stench of spirits slapped at Dominick's face. Papa rarely indulged in spirits. Now, it would be the last scent he wore on his person. The cord snapped and Dominick stumbled. With a grunt, he fell over, landing hard on his back. His body muted the fall of his father's prone form as it came down over him.

A humming filled Dominick's ears as he stared at the rafters overhead. *He is still warm.* When did a body begin to go cold? He didn't know how long he lay there. Mayhap moments. Mayhap minutes. Mayhap longer. He rolled his father's dead body off and began dragging him over to his beloved leather chair. Sweat stung Dominick's eyes and blended with tears. His arms strained under the effort of hefting his father's lifeless frame, and he focused on the hatred that blazed to life. Fueling him. Making him stronger.

Numb, Dominick stared several moments at his once-great hero. With fingers that shook, he closed his father's eyes.

And as he slipped away from Papa's now-tidied office, his father's garments and cravat properly arranged and evidence of his cowardly act largely hidden, Dominick found the Marquess of Rutland was correct. Revenge and hatred would make him far stronger.

He steeled his jaw. And for Papa, he would, one day, have revenge.

# CHAPTER 1

*Just outside London*
*England 1820*

THERE WERE DIFFERENT LEVELS OF evil.

Some men bore that transparent blackness with their every deed, every word. Other men had contaminated souls only the Devil himself could see and know.

Sated and now bored from an endless night of sex, Nick Tallings, the Duke of Huntly, contemplated the cherubs in the mural overhead with jaded eyes. Those plump, winged creatures danced amidst a pale blue sky. Only one foolish fat-cheeked angel hovered too close to the earth, a serpent near its feet. It spoke to the rose-cheeked, smiling cherub's ultimate finish. He grinned coldly. It was the unsuspecting who were ultimately always ruined. His father had been proof of that. Nick's smile withered and he swung his legs over the side of the enormous four-poster bed.

Two cream white arms wrapped about his waist. The sultry owner of them pressed her breasts against his back. "Never tell me you're leaving already," she breathed against his ear. She flicked her tongue over his lobe. "You are all that is keeping me sane in the country, darling." There was a faintly desperate entreaty there. Lady Marianne Carew, a lady once heralded as a Diamond of the First Water. How quickly a person fell.

Then, he well knew that.

Nick shoved away her hand. "I'd hardly call East Grinstead the country," he drawled in frosty tones. He grabbed his breeches and stuffed one leg in and then the other.

The lady flopped onto her back and stretched catlike in her supple grace. Her red-tipped breasts bobbed with that slight movement. "Oh, poo, Huntly," she pouted. "You know I cannot return to London."

He did. It enhanced the overall convenience of dealing with a viper like her. Not that he'd any qualms in dealing with sinners whose souls were as black as his own. She had proven a lusty diversion and, more, invaluable in terms of information she'd handed over about the Marquess of Rutland. The man who'd destroyed her family. A shared enemy was a powerful thing. Nick grinned coldly. Apparently, Rutland had missed that particular lesson. "We are done here," he said, bluntly.

All traces of sleep vanished from her voice. "Done?" she squeaked. The bed creaked with her sudden movement as she shoved upright, a display of carnality in all her lush nakedness.

"We both received what we desired in a partnership," he said coolly, pulling his shirt on. "And were well pleasured for it."

The siren, unhappily married to an ancient baron, had provided countless nights of pleasurable diversion. Her usefulness, however, had come to an end. "I have more information about him." All earlier vestiges of desperation gone, the husky promise there brought him slowly around.

"Do you?" he asked in deliberately neutral tones. Long ago, he'd learned to reveal little in the way of one's thoughts or feelings. To give little away. He'd spent years expertly crafting a mask, so that at seven and twenty years of age, it was the only skin he knew.

Marianne climbed from the bed and stalked over with long, languid steps that artfully displayed her well-rounded form. "Lady Rutland delivered her third babe."

There it was. The information he'd been awaiting. Nick snapped his cravat and set to loosely tying it in a sloppy arrangement that would have had his valet in tears. "Did she?" The marchioness' most recent pregnancy was what had allowed him to set his plan into motion.

"Ah, but that is not all," she teased.

"Oh?"

"It was a very difficult delivery. The papers say she almost died in childbirth. And the babe is weak." A sick desire sparked in the lady's eyes. As she stroked a hand over her breast, her breath caught.

Her depravity would have repelled a more honorable man. Nick hadn't been that weak-willed fool in many, many years. "Your information is reliable?" he demanded, impatiently.

"*Very,*" she purred.

He picked his way around the garments haphazardly thrown about the night prior and grabbed his jacket.

"Surely that excites you as much as it does me," she wheedled.

It did. But not for the same reasons that drove her madness. Again, she wrapped a pair of long, slender arms about his waist and caressed her clever fingers down to the front of his breeches. His shaft jumped reflexively under her ministrations.

"I see that it does." Her low, throaty laugh spilled past her lips but ended on a sharp gasp as he gripped her wrist and thrust it away.

"I have matters to attend." He softened that by pulling out a purse and tossing it to her. Coin always kept her happy.

The lady easily caught it in her greedy fingers. "I'm no whore." Her lips formed a soft moue of displeasure. Then, she yanked open the purse and roved her gaze hungrily over the contents, showing the depth of her avarice.

"We're all whores one way or another, madam," he said tersely.

The baroness pulled her bag close to her chest and eyed him. "When will I see you again?"

Nick didn't deal in clingy females. He took his pleasure when and where he wished, and be damned with emotional entanglements. Silently, he stalked over to the shellback chair and rescued his cloak. "Never."

"Never," she parroted. The velvet sack slipped from her fingers and clattered to the floor in a noisy jingle. "But…"

"Do not make any more of what we shared than it was," he said, ruthless in his honesty. He fastened his cloak at his neck and started for the door. With his plans, he couldn't afford to be linked to a mistress.

Her gasp exploded around the room and, with a catlike speed, she sprinted across the floor and placed herself between him and the doorway, barring his retreat. "But you need me," she rasped.

"You cannot see this plan through without me." He firmed his mouth, repulsed by her desperation. Desperation was what had started Nick on this journey. It had ended his father's life and left the Tallings' broken.

"See this through without you, madam?" he repeated. His dry humor raised furious color to her cheeks.

"But—but, I was the one who told you about Miss Barrett's love of silly gothic novels and her fascination with bonnets. If it weren't for me, you'd know nothing about her."

"You think I require any further help from you to seduce Rutland's sister-in-law?" His plan now must be set in motion. By the reports in the gossip columns, Miss Barrett was an empty-headed ice princess who was holding out for the most powerful title. He grinned. Fortunately, he now had one of the oldest, wealthiest titles to tempt the lady "I have, at best, a fortnight to make the lady fall in love with me, and you'd rather I stay here, tupping you?" Rage flashed in Marianne's eyes. He stepped around her.

"I will tell him," she called, her voice a frantic pitch as he reached for the door. "I will tell Rutland what you've done."

He paused, fingers on the handle. "Tell him what, my lady? That *we* plotted his family's demise," he reminded her, turning back. A cold, mirthless grin tipped his lips at the corners. "He ran your brother off to the Continent. Do you think the faithless maid in his employ will not gladly sing the tune of your treachery when presented with an inquisition from Rutland? And what will a man like him do to a woman who plotted to destroy his family?"

The color leeched from her cheeks.

"Madam," he said on a steely whisper. "I intend to bring Rutland to his knees. Will your hungering to have me between your legs blind you to the hell you now live because of that man?"

His words kindled the embers of hatred in her brown eyes. "Tell me what we shall do to them," she rasped, desire glazing those depths.

"I will bankrupt the father-in-law," he whispered, feeding her what she wanted, reminding her of what had united them. "So he is as poor as Rutland left your family. I'll strip his fool of a brother-in-law of all his wealth and future properties." For there was no doubt with the Barretts' love of the tables, they'd gamble away all that was not entailed. "All those Rutland's wife loves will be devastated. Their families in shambles." Just as he had done to Nick. Just as he'd done to this viper's family.

A hungry moan spilled past the baroness' lips and her lashes fluttered. "And the girl," she panted. "Tell me how you'll destroy that chit." As one of Society's Incomparables, Lady Carew had demonstrated a vitriolic loathing for Miss Justina Barrett; a woman she'd never met and yet hated because the lady had taken her place as the Diamond of the Season.

"I'll woo her," he said on a husky whisper. "Seduce her." She bit her lower lip, hunger clouding her eyes. "I'll win her heart. Trap her. Make her my wife and then shatter her."

"You needn't wed her," she protested.

"Of course I do," he said impatiently. Since he'd shared that particular part of the Barretts' ruin, Marianne Carew had been tenacious in trying to alter it. The lady was too blinded by her own lust for him. "Otherwise, her father can sell her over to another and have his debts paid," he reminded her.

"Will you think of me every time you have that mealy-mouthed virgin in your bed?"

"How could I not?" he countered, giving her the words she wished to hear. Even though he'd not give her another thought when he stepped outside these chamber doors. It was safer to feed this woman's vanity.

"Then you'll come back to me," she rasped as he opened the door. "You'll need a real woman in your arms, Huntly. In your bed."

Nick gave his head a disgusted shake. "I've already said we are through." He'd long ago tired of her. Theirs had been a relationship based on lust and hatred for a mutual enemy. Nothing more bound them.

"I shan't let you go," she said, a panicky tremor to her husky contralto.

"You've no choice, madam. And lest you again fill your fool head with the idea of sharing all with Rutland, remember, he is the man responsible for you selling your soul and body to an old baron who keeps you on a tight purse string."

Hatred contorted her features, turning her into something ugly on the outside that matched the inside.

"Would you humble yourself before the man who owned your

brother's debt and turned it over to another?"

Shock marred her features. Yes, Nick knew all. He knew of the vowels Rutland turned over to the Viscount Wessex; a fortune that had Lady Carew's brother facing debtor's prison. He had since been run off to the Continent. The lady, with no prospects, had sold herself cheap on the Marriage Mart, getting herself a doddering husband in the process. The man had one foot in the grave and the other gleefully tapping a rhythm of life that promised to make her a widow no time soon.

He smirked coldly. "I did not think so, my lady."

"But we are joined in our hatred of him and our plotting," she entreated.

"The loathing we share for Rutland is hardly a bond that ties us." Nick fished another sack of coins from his pocket and tossed it over.

The lady immediately folded greedy fingers around it. Indecision warred in her eyes and then lust won out. "I want more of you, Huntly. You have made me feel things I've never felt."

A low, humorless chuckle rumbled from deep in his chest. "You've had more men in your bed than a doxy on a Dials' street corner."

With a growl, she closed the space between them and wrapped her palm around his neck. Dragging his face down for a kiss, she mated her mouth to his with a roughness that had fueled his ardor in the past. Now, he felt a bored numbness with her. He'd been enlivened by the only thing that had brought them together. "Have some pride, my lady," he whispered, pulling back.

"Bastard," she hissed. Leaning up, she bit his lower lip.

He winced and set her away from him hard. "Show yourself out within the hour," he said, bored by her display.

With the lady's furious shrieks trailing after him, he yanked the door open and stepped out into the hall. He drew the door closed and a loud thump sounded in the hall. Followed by another. And then a spray of glass.

Lady Carew forgotten, Nick pulled a white, embroidered kerchief from inside his front pocket and pressed it to his bleeding lip. He made his way through the halls. Some other man's ancestors, people whose blood he only distantly shared, stared back in their pompous, frozen glory.

He reached the foyer and his butler, Thoms, rushed forward. "I've had your horse readied, Your Grace."

Nick inclined his head in thanks. When the remaining two servants had scurried off and prattled to the world about the telling marks of suicide on the Baronet Tallings' neck, this man had remained loyal. He'd stayed alongside their family as everything was stripped away and until Nick and Cecily had been carted off to their miserable grandfather's property. On his meteoric rise from the once-forgotten fourteen-year-old son of a shamed baronet to the suddenly-minted duke of a distant, childless relative, the first business he'd undertaken had been seeking out and rehiring Thoms.

The man, who'd remained silent on the darkness of that day and stood by his family, had demonstrated an ability to maintain a property where Nick's illicit dealings were conducted. "I want the household closed," he said, adjusting the collar of his cloak.

The graying servant nodded. "As you wish, Your Grace."

He jerked his head toward the opposite hall. "If she's not gone within the hour, see that she's removed."

Thoms again nodded and rushed to open the door.

Nick bounded down the steps and made for the servant waiting with his mount, Thunder. After he swung into the saddle, the midnight black stallion with the white streak between its eyes danced skittishly about and he adjusted the reins, until his horse settled. He urged the stallion down the graveled drive, leaving dirt and dust in his wake, until they reached the old Roman road that stretched toward Charring Cross.

While he rode, the early morn breeze slapped at his cheeks, invigorating, and he swallowed deeply of the cool air.

As a boy, he'd despised London. A man who'd climbed from the ashes of life, he'd slipped easily into the ugly filth of the London streets and the people who called that place home. Now, a duke, recently come to London with matchmaking mamas eager for the title duchess for their daughters, he'd been welcomed within Society's fold in ways he'd never been accepted as a boy who'd spent three fleeting weeks at Harrow.

Those eager matchmaking mamas and papas were content to see precisely what he affected on the surface. Charming. Affable rogue. Never a rake. Moderate at the gaming tables. In short, a paragon of the *ton*.

In sum, the apple dangled before unsuspecting sinners. None cared to delve into the past of a now duke, to see the life he'd lived prior to striking a rich chord at the expense of his late father's fourth cousin twice removed.

There was but one who could see, perhaps. A like-minded serpent who spied the evil under the surface because he carried it as a mark upon his worthless soul—Rutland. If Nick had slithered before his feet, the man would have looked. Closer. Because he knew. Knew never to trust a smile. Never trust the good in a man. Always question it. After all, Rutland had made him this way. Had shaped him in ways not even Nick's own father had.

For after his father had put a noose around his own neck and ended his life, Nick had learned a lesson delivered in blood—the fallibility of man. His father hadn't truly loved them. Not enough to stay behind and fight. Nick, however, was not, nor would ever be his father. He would have vengeance for not only himself, but for Cecily and her daughter, Felicity. And for Mother, whose spirit had flickered out, and then been forever extinguished not even six months after her husband had ended himself. Cecily, in her romanticism, had said their mother had died of a broken heart. Nick knew better. It had been the games of the Devil, Rutland, that had weakened her heart until that frail organ had attacked her.

That had always been one sharp, definable difference between him and Rutland. He had people who he loved. People who depended on him—his sister and her daughter. And Rutland? Well, he may as well have been sprung from Satan's side without a single person to his name. It was a fact Nick had spent thirteen years resenting.

Nudging Thunder with his knees, he slowed the mount to a canter. But every person had a weakness. For Nick, his would always and only ever be Cecily and Felicity. Theirs was a bond forged by blood. As such, he'd long ago given up hope that Rutland would ever willingly commit to the emotion that made a man vulnerable. Then it happened. His patience had been rewarded. The Devil had fallen in love.

Lord Rutland, long without attachments beyond the material, had tied himself to another and, in doing so, he'd found himself an entire family. A mother-in-law who wore a perpetual smile that did nothing to conceal the heartache in her too-kind eyes. A rake of a brother-in-law who'd lost, and would continue to lose, countless coin the way he'd been schooled at his pudgy father's knee.

Then there was the sister-in-law. The ever-cheerful creature he'd caught but a glimpse of weeks earlier hadn't fit with the reports of her being an ice princess. When others had been engrossed in the gossip and the performance unfolding at the Drury Lane Theatre, he'd watched boldly the young lady who would serve as the ultimate chess piece in his game of revenge. Naïve. Stars in her eyes. And hope in her heart. Miss Justina Barrett would be his pawn. And with one tiny, insignificant and powerless pawn, he would maneuver Rutland into the ultimate checkmate.

Then there could at last be peace. A like destruction that would never ease their suffering, but would equalize the world, filling Rutland's existence with a similar misery.

Training his gaze on the distance, where the sun, a crimson and burnt orange orb, just peeked over the horizon, he nudged Thunder onward.

NEARLY TWO HOURS LATER, WHEN the sun was climbing in the morning sky, Nick reached a pink stucco townhouse. He dismounted and handed the reins over to a waiting street urchin. "There will be more," he promised, turning a small purse over to the boy's dirty fingers.

The lad nodded eagerly and stood in wait. After bounding up the steps, Nick knocked several times on the front door. A moment later, the young, familiar butler pulled it open. "Your Grace," the man greeted. With surprise apparent in his gaze, he stepped aside and granted Nick entry. The man wrinkled his nose.

Yes, at this fashionable hour it was hardly a time for receiving visitors, particularly ducal guests that stank of horseflesh and sweat. Pleasantries and morning ablutions, however, mattered little when presented with the information he'd obtained a short while ago. Nick pulled off his gloves and glanced about. "Is my sis—?"

An excited child's cry cut across his question. He looked up just as a small girl rushed forward and launched herself into his legs.

He immediately settled his hands around his niece's shoulders and hefted her into his arms. With her pale blue eyes and blonde ringlets, she was a mirror of Cecily as she'd been in her innocence. A forever reminder of innocence destroyed. He forced aside the always-present hatred brewing under the surface and peered at her for a long moment. "Forgive me. For a moment, I believed you were my niece, Felicity, and yet..." He put his face close to hers and squinted. "And yet, when last I saw her, she was a sprout. Surely, she could not have grown so, and so quickly."

His niece giggled. "You just saw me a fortnight ago, Uncle Dominick," she scolded, slapping at his arm.

Nick flared his eyes. "By goodness...it *is* you, Felicity!" He staggered back under the weight of pretend shock, earning another round of healthy laughter from the girl.

"You, my dear, should be in your nursery seeing to your lessons."

Nick and Felicity looked as one to the owner of that gently chiding voice. His sister, Cecily, stood there, pale and solemn in ways she'd never been as a girl. Just a year older than his seven and twenty years, she bore the same hardship of life in the sad lines at the corners of her eyes. Pain stuck in his gut. There had been a time when she'd been garrulous and always smiling.

"Must I go?" Felicity pleaded with her mother, sparing him from having to formulate words past his tight throat. "Uncle Dominick has only just arrived." The girl looked hopefully to Nick, her saucer-wide eyes meeting his. "Did you bring me anything?"

He tweaked her nose. "I've been a rotted uncle, this time," he said in conciliatory tones.

"A game of chess?" she bartered.

He dropped his voice to a whisper. "I must speak to your mother, now."

She scrunched her mouth up. "Promise to return?" Since she'd been a babe just stringing together words into sentences, those three had become the ones she uttered at their every parting.

"Later in the week, I'll meet you for chess and then take you both for a ride in Hyde Park, with a bag of peppermints."

A girlish squeal trilled from Felicity's lips as she pressed a kiss to his cheek. "Permission to leave granted." Reluctantly, Nick set her down and she scampered off.

His sister spoke without preamble. "There are whispers about your intentions for the Season."

"It is lovely to see you, as well," he drawled. Doffing his hat, he turned it over to an attentive footman. Nick unfastened his cloak and the butler accepted it in his gloved hands.

Cecily stood, her gaunt face stretched in a solemn mask. Then she gave him a smile, an empty rendition of the ones that had creased her lips as a young girl. "You smell horrid, Dominick," she chided, the same little mother she'd always been to him.

He offered a half-grin. "That is hardly a welcome to receive after riding hard to London to see you and my favorite niece."

This time, her smile widened and, for the sliver of a moment, it reached her eyes. "She is your only niece," she needlessly reminded him and then motioned him forward. Nick fell into step alongside her. "It does not escape me that you did not answer my question," she observed as their footsteps fell in a matched staccato.

"Oh, was there a question?" he asked, stealing a sideways look.

She snorted. "You may be a man grown and the most sought after rogue in London, but you're as transparent now as you were as boy poring over a volume of poetry."

That beloved verse, buried and forgotten until now, whispered around his mind. God, what a callow fool he'd been. Poring over verses. Penning his own pathetic drivel.

They reached a vibrant parlor with sunlight streaming through the drawn curtains. "Well?" she prodded as soon as they were seated. "Has the Darling Duke set aside his reckless ways?" That droll inquiry sent heat rushing up his neck. It was one thing to be a rogue. It was an altogether different matter discussing it openly with one's sister.

His shoulders tight from the continuous hours in the saddle and his erect posturing, Nick rolled the stiff muscles. "I have."

Cecily surged forward in her Louis XIV floral upholstered seat. "Why?" she demanded, narrowing her blue eyes.

In a bid for nonchalance, Nick stretched his legs out. "I daresay you'd approve of me settling down in my…" He winged an eyebrow up. "What did you call them? My reckless ways?"

"Why are you here, Dominick?" she asked with her usual gravity.

He flexed his jaw. "Have I ever been a disloyal brother that you'd question my visiting?"

"No," she said calmly, folding her hands primly on her lap. "You visit every week you are in London with guilt stamped on your features. I do question your arriving with scruff on your face and smelling as though you've wrestled a horse."

He ignored the latter part of that admission as her words struck him like a fist to the belly. "It is my fault."

"Pfft," Cecily scoffed, settling back in her chair. "You gentlemen with your misbegotten sense of guilt and honor. You would hold yourself accountable for allowing me to be bullied into marriage by Grandfather? If that is what drives your visits, I'd rather you not come. It merely serves to remind me of my own mistakes."

*Her mistakes.* Marriage at just fifteen to an ancient bounder of an earl, who refused to die and make her a widow. And Nick had failed to protect her. Failed her when they'd been failed by so many.

His sister waved a hand about, slashing through his musings. "Do not distract me with talk about my own circumstances. It is your sudden changing ones that give me concern."

She'd always seen too much. Nick held her gaze directly. "There is nothing to worry about," he said quietly, offering her the only hint of truth he could. He'd see her protected. Nor could he tell her more, for reasons that had everything to do with her need for absolution of any knowledge of what he intended.

Cecily thinned her eyes into narrow slits. "This is about *him*, isn't it?"

*Him.* The unspoken name that they never breathed. "This is about me," Nick countered. He layered his arm along the back of the sofa.

"Do not," she commanded like a stern governess who'd never brook "no" for an answer.

"I've said nothing."

"You didn't need to," she shot back. "I *know* you." Cecily glanced to the doorway and then scooted to the edge of her chair. She tugged the large piece closer to Nick, scraping the seat noisily along the hardwood. "You have let him turn you into a shell of the person you were."

They were both empty caricatures of the people they'd been. Determined to not remind her of the misery of her marriage, he buried that profession. "I want you in the country," he said in hushed tones.

Understanding dawned in her eyes. "So, that is why you are

here." She shook her head slowly. "I'm not running to the countryside. And I'm certainly not taking Felicity to where the earl is."

He balled his hands. "Do you expect I'd ask you to go off with your husband?" He could not banish the disappointment that her doubts roused. "Go to Suffolk."

"To our old home?" Another sad little smile hovered on her lips. His purchase and restoration of that small cottage had begun out of his bid to eradicate the demons that dwelled there and had laid conquest to his past. "Oh, Dominick, you still do not see that nothing can right the past. Nothing can bring Papa and Mama back. Nothing can erase Grandfather's verbal assaults. Or undo my…" *Marriage.*

The word hung unfinished and as real as if she'd uttered it. "But there can be justice."

As soon as that whisper left Nick's lips, worry flooded his sister's eyes. "You will let him turn you into a version of him."

He'd already become that man. Only Cecily and his niece saw good in him, still. He'd not waste his breath trying to convince his sister of the contrary. Nick tugged out his watch fob and consulted the timepiece. "I must go," he said with finality. "I am meeting Chilton shortly." He snapped the gold trinket closed.

Cecily fluttered a hand about her chest and let her fingers fall to her lap. "He has always been a friend to you." There was something sad and contradictory in that quiet pronouncement. They three had been inseparable as children and Chilton had developed the same apathy for the peerage as Nick himself. She climbed to her feet. "Let your hatred go. It will destroy you."

As a boy who'd sustained himself on hatred and survived the hell of, first, his father's death, then his mother's, and then the misery of residing with his grandfather, it had been the hope of seeing Rutland love and ultimately lose, the way Nick's family had.

This would be an act of vengeance that lived not just for him, but for Cecily, as well. For all *they* as a family had lost on that dark night.

He started for the door and had his hand on the doorknob. Nick paused and glanced back. "I'll ask you again to please leave—"

"I am not leaving London, Dominick." Censure laced her reply. "This is where I belong. If you believe something you intend to do will have ramifications on mine or Felicity's well-being, then you should rethink your course." A curse stung his lips, but she quelled him with a look. "I. Am. Not. Leaving."

Nick dragged a hand through his hair and at her stony expression, the fight withered on his lips. She was as stubborn as he himself. He gave a curt nod.

"Please, be careful, Dominick." Her softly-spoken plea rang like a shot in the quiet room.

"I will do nothing to cause you any more pain," he vowed.

His sister held his gaze. "I'm not worried for me."

Forcing a grin for her benefit, Nick offered another reassurance and then took his leave.

# CHAPTER 2

MISS JUSTINA BARRETT HAD NEVER understood the fascination with diamonds.

They were clear, colorless, and, in short, dull. And yet, everyone wished to possess them. It was the stone to which all others were held in a comparative failing against. And it was also precisely as the *ton* had come to see her, six weeks earlier, when she'd made her Come Out.

Clutching the small book of Shelley's poems in hand, she ducked her head around the aisle and did a rapid search of The Circulating Library and Reading Room. Her gaze collided with the very figure responsible for her now hiding amidst the aisle of poetry.

"Is he still here?" Lady Gillian Farendale whispered.

Justina angled back and pressed her fingertips against her lips.

"Of course, he is," Honoria Fairfax said, with far greater discretion than the other lady. "He is *always* here."

Always here. In short, wherever Justina happened to be, so too went the gentleman. None other than the Marquess of Tennyson. He'd presented himself as a suitor at her first ball and had shown unswerving attentions since.

"I asked my sister to find information about the gentleman," Gillian whispered. It was no secret the lady's sister, Genevieve, had wed one of the most notorious rakes in London. As such, Lord Tennyson was the very manner of man the gentleman would have once kept company with.

"Well?" Honoria quietly demanded.

"They say he has…wicked proclivities." Gillian paused. "Behind the chambers' doors," she added on a hushed whisper that barely reached Justina's ears.

Honoria gasped. "Gillian!"

The gentleman stopped suddenly and his sapphire cloak swirled about his ankles. Heart racing, Justina layered herself against the row of books.

*Will you leave, already?*

She peeked her head around once more, just as the marquess disappeared down another aisle. Good. Now she could at least withdraw her book—

Honoria leaned around her and assessed the library. Then she took Justina by her spare hand. "Go," she whispered.

"But…" Justina looked forlornly down at the copy of Shelley's poems.

"Before he returns," Honoria urged, that reminder springing her into movement. Regret filling her, Justina stuck the volume onto the shelf and with Gillian trailing behind, they rushed through The Circulating Library.

With every step, her pulse pounded loudly in her ears as she waited for Lord Tennyson to step into their path and halt her retreat.

Honoria grabbed the door handle and shoved the door open; that movement setting the tinny bell a-jingle. The trio hurried outside into the bustling streets of Lambeth. Justina and the two ladies now at her side, well knew of the marquess' tenacity. As such, they continued their quickened pace along the crowded pavement, weaving between gypsy caravans, until they reached Honoria's family carriage.

The driver stood in wait beside the opened door and immediately handed them inside. A moment later, the carriage dipped under his weight as he reclaimed his perch atop, and then the conveyance lurched forward.

Justina released the breath she'd been holding and peeled back the edge of the red velvet curtain to look outside into the busy streets. Hardly the fashionable end of London, Lord Tennyson belonged in the streets of Gipsy Hill as much as King George himself did.

"He is making more of a nuisance of himself," Gillian said, echoing Justina's very thoughts.

"All gentlemen are nuisances," Honoria countered with her usual jaded cynicism toward the motives of young lords. Though, in the reflection of the crystal windowpane, worry marred the young lady's features.

Justina didn't know all the details surrounding the young woman's scandalous childhood, as the daughter of a publicly gossiped about mother, but she had to believe decency remained. What was the alternative? To find that they lived in a world where a man had no use for a lady beyond a pretty face and the babes she would give him? "That is not the case," she said softly, letting the curtain fall back into place. Even if her own father was a rotted bounder with a black soul. "My sister's husband is proof to the contrary."

Edmund Deering, the Marquess of Rutland, had proven more loyal and devoted to every Barrett sibling than even their own father.

Honoria pursed her lips. "Between Gillian and me," she said, motioning to the pale-blonde beauty on the opposite bench. "In all of our Seasons, how many honorable suitors have *we* had?"

Given their cleverness and spirit, they *should* have had countless.

Honoria formed a circle with her fingers.

"You make it sound even worse when you present it *that* way," Gillian muttered.

Ignoring the other woman, Honoria directed her next question to Justina. "And how many honorable suitors have you had who genuinely care to hear your opinions and share your thoughts?"

She wrinkled her mouth. Her silence stood as a damning confirmation to the other woman's correctness. Since she'd set foot in Almack's and been labeled a Diamond, she'd been swarmed by suitors. Not a single one of them had complimented anything more than her hair, smile, and even, on occasion, her teeth. Which had only fueled her annoyance with Society. She'd been relentlessly pursued by gentlemen who knew nothing about her…and who only wished to possess her. *Then, when have I ever freely spoken my mind?* Mayhap if she had, men would treat her as more than an object.

"Precisely my point," Honoria said gently.

Justina angled her head up. "Yes, well, just because we haven't *found* an honorable gentleman, doesn't mean he doesn't exist." For if there was no one out there who fit with every dream she'd long carried of her future suitor and husband, what was there? Men such as her father, Chester Barrett, Viscount Waters, who her poor mother found herself tied to until she drew her last breath? A man who'd never allowed his wife a free opinion. A cold chill stole through her, leaving an empty bleakness at the possibility. *I will not be my mother.*

Gillian held a hand up. "Before we debate the merits of all gentlemen, I expect we should give proper focus to just the one." *Lord Tennyson.* He was becoming increasingly bold in his pursuit. Tenaciously so. "You must send word to Lord Rutland," Gillian insisted.

Honoria and Gillian exchanged a look. "Though it does pain me," Honoria said in somber tones. "I do agree with Gillian."

"Phoebe only just had her babe." Justina frowned. "I will not burden them," she said quietly.

The pair on the opposite bench fell silent and a somber pall descended over the carriage. With the exception of Justina's family and the two women before her, no one knew the details surrounding Phoebe's confinement. After a difficult pregnancy, by her mother's missives, Phoebe was perilously weak. God himself with the Devil aiding, could not pull Edmund away from her side. Nor would Justina dare ask or expect that.

Her mouth tightened involuntarily. She was strong enough to hold off her father and any scheming suitors. Though, if she were being honest with herself, she did miss the support of her fearless sister and brother-in-law.

"We're here." Gillian's quiet pronouncement cut across Justina's thoughts. Both friends stared back at her, their eyes radiating concern.

Fixed in her seat, Justina again looked out the window at the white stucco façade of her townhouse. The front door stood open as two strangers stepped outside, a trunk in their arms, carting off her family's belongings. Her throat worked.

"I'm sorry, Justina," Honoria said softly, a remarkable crack in the young lady's always-present strength. Yes, because it did not take much figuring to ascertain precisely what the gentlemen in their formal cloaks and monocles were doing here.

She managed a nod, and continued staring as two familiar creditors streamed out into the street with smaller trunks in their arms. Which books had her father sold off now? Works by the Great Bard? The gothic novels she'd once favored above all other literary works? Her gut clenched. How many years had she failed to appreciate that room?

"If he knew, Lord Rutland would never allow this," Gillian said passionately.

"No, he would not," Justina murmured. He'd already come countless times to her wastrel father's rescue. Only… "Threats will not change a man," she said, more to herself. "And with Edmund away, Father is who he has always been." And who he would always be. A drunkard, who craved gambling almost as much as those disgusting spirits. "I must go," she said quietly and reached for the handle.

Honoria settled a hand on Justina's knee, staying her movements. "I'm delaying my visit with Phoebe until later in the Season," she began. "I will remain with you. She would rather I be at your side."

Given Honoria's rightful loathing for London, it was a testament to the other woman's goodness as a friend that she'd offer to remain here on her behalf. They may have begun as friends of Phoebe merely looking after the youngest Barrett, yet in such a short time, they'd become so much more. "Thank you," Justina said quietly. She held her friend's gaze. "When you do leave, I would have you say nothing to Phoebe." She held the other woman's gaze. Tight white lines formed at the corners of Honoria's mouth. "My sister needn't worry about me." Not when she was still weak from the sudden, complicated delivery of her latest babe.

Gillian clapped her hands. "Nor will she have to worry. We are both here with you, and then when Honoria leaves, I will still be here. As such, you'll be in splendid hands." A mischievous glimmer lit the lady's pretty green eyes, earning a groan from Honoria. "I'll help you avoid unwanted suitors." She winked. "And help you sneak off to steal time alone with the *wanted* ones," she whispered, startling a laugh from Justina.

"You will do no such thing," Honoria said, swiping a hand over her eyes.

"Oh, never," Gillian vowed with deep solemnity. Then ruined that show with a wink.

To the ladies' bickering, Justina pushed the door open and

accepted the hand of the waiting servant with a murmur of thanks. Tossing a wave over her shoulder for her friends, she rushed along the pavement, up the steps. Their loyal family butler, Manfred, pulled the door open.

She shrugged out of her cloak and turned it over to a waiting footman. "Manfred," she directed at the wizened butler.

"The viscount wishes to see you in his office, Miss Barrett."

Dread took root in her belly. Inevitably, there was only one matter of business her father cared to discuss—her marital state and, more importantly, how it served him.

The old butler gave her a pitying look.

Feeling much the way Joan of Arc no doubt felt being marched up to that dreaded pyre, Justina mustered a smile and strode down the corridors. The heel of her boots clicked quietly on the wood floor as she moved deeper down the halls until she, at last, reached the dreaded office. She rapped once.

"Enter," her father boomed.

Taking a deep breath, she plastered the expected smile on her face and stepped inside. "Fath—"

"Close the door, gel," he barked from where he stood at his sideboard.

Justina pulled the panel closed and started across the room. As a young girl, she'd often wondered if her father called her "gel" and "girl" because he couldn't be bothered with remembering her name. To him, she and Phoebe had only ever served one purpose—to make a match that would save him from debtor's prison. The pain of that truth had eventually dulled, leaving a marked numbness for this man who'd given her life. With stiff footsteps, she came forward. Before she'd even fully sat, her father spoke.

"I've had another bad turn at the gaming tables," he said swiftly, unexpectedly.

He always had bad luck at the gaming tables. He did not, however, bother speaking to his daughter about such matters. "Father?"

"Been losing of late," he muttered and waved a hand.

*Of late.* In short, since Edmund, the son-in-law he feared above all others, had left for the country with Phoebe. With Rutland gone, there was no one to keep the wastrel viscount in check. Not that anyone could truly keep him in check. Not with his hungering to sit at those gaming tables. "Never had much interest from the gents with your sister," he mumbled, more to himself with a brutal candidness that made her curl her fingers into the palms of her hands. "But you, pretty face and skill enough on the dance floor, caught the Marquess of Tennyson's notice."

An icy chill rolled along her spine. *This is what he intends.* To maneuver her into a match with some fat-in-the-pockets lord, who'd forgive her father's debt. In an interesting reversal of events, Lord Tennyson had been in search of a fat dowry but a positive turn at the tables had boosted the gentleman's fortunes.

"The Marquess of Tennyson wants to properly court you," he went on.

"A man who'd brush his hand over my buttocks during a dancing set is about as proper as a pig in church," she muttered under her breath. A selfish, horrible part of her soul hated her mother for leaving her here with her sire, who, with his machinations, was far worse than any determined matchmaking mama in the realm. And a small, horribly selfish part of her wished Phoebe was here, still. And more, Edmund. Their presence had deterred the viscount in his ruthless attempts at selling her off to the highest bidder.

Her father ambled his corpulent form over to his desk. "Promised me he'd forgive my debt."

Short, pudgy, and balding, the coldness in the viscount's eyes was only rivaled by the greed in his heart. Justina had spent so many hours searching for a glimpse of the man who'd somehow won her mother's hand. Loathing burned her tongue like vinegar on an open wound. "I hardly know Lord Tennyson," she said slowly in even tones meant to drum logic into a man who'd never loved, or even cared for his family. Nor, despite what her father might wish, would she ever wed a man who'd have any dealings with her reprobate father.

"Bah, doesn't matter if you know him." He settled his sizeable girth in the worn leather seat. "You will *know* him." He laughed as though he'd delivered a witty jest; his heavy form shaking with his hilarity so that liquid droplets tumbled over the rim of his glass and smattered the top of his hand. He pressed his fleshy lips to the moisture much like a starving man with his first taste of food. "Anyway, it is time you make a match." Her father peered at her down the length of his bulbous nose, with assessing eyes that counted her inherent value.

She attempted to reason with him. "It is *just* the beginning of the Season," she began.

"It's been six weeks," he snapped, all traces of his earlier humor gone. "No reason for you to be unwed, gel."

Not according to him and the ruthless *ton*. Her debut had seen her *praised* as an Incomparable. Her *golden* beauty was compared to that da Vinci painting, *La Belle Ferronniere*. Only Justina seemed to realize the irony in comparing a blonde debutante to a woman of not only dark coloring, but one who was also reputed to be a king's mistress.

Her father grunted. "You had a successful launching, but there'll be other girls, younger and prettier than you, next year. Must take advantage of your beauty before it fades."

Launched. *Like a bloody ship.* At his second cold likening that transformed her from a woman with hopes, dreams, and emotions into a vessel meant to serve, Justina dug her fingers so hard into her palms that they left crescent marks upon her flesh. Why couldn't she be more like Phoebe? In control, in command of her every exchange with their father. Where she had always been stammering and bumbling.

"You're a Diamond of the First Water," her father snapped, in tones better fitting a condescending instructor handing lessons down to an inferior pupil. He banged the desk again. "But even those stones eventually fade."

She curled her toes into the soles of her slippers until her feet arched. God, how she despised his comparing her to a cold, unfeeling stone for which no real emotion could ever be shown. It represented the material. A creation to be possessed but never truly loved. In short, how too many gentlemen viewed a lady. It was on the tip of her tongue to point out that true diamonds never lost their clarity. "I'll marry a man who loves me and who sees more than an ornament for his arm." A thrill went through her at that blatant show of defiance. Mayhap she had more of Phoebe's spirit than she'd ever believed.

"Come, gel," her father scoffed. "You haven't a brain in your head. Haven't since you were a girl." That same charge wielded when she was a girl by a hateful governess struck sharper now, coming from the man who'd sired her. "Which is good. No man wants a clever bluestocking for a wife."

She bit the inside of her cheek. Of course, Phoebe had always been seen as the bookish, clever one and Justina the lady with her head in the clouds, more interested in a bonnet than a book. "Phoebe—"

"Bah, your sister was fortunate Rutland wanted her." He waved his spare hand. "No gent wants anything more than a pretty face. It's bad enough your damned brother-in-law wouldn't fund a Season until you reached your twentieth year. But now I can turn you over to someone else." There was an edge of finality to that matter-of-fact pronouncement.

Her heart thumped at a slow, panicked rhythm. *I will not become my mother.* A woman forever bound to a worthless lord who wagered too much and carried on with other women. "If I am..." She grimaced. "An Incomparable, a Diamond," she amended, using that hated language in a desperate bid to dissuade him from his goals. "Surely you would be better served in not rushing me to accept an offer." Justina held her breath, using the ruthless logic her father lived by as a means of retaining her freedom.

"He's measured your worth, and the offer is right," he said, as though they discussed the sale of a mare.

*My worth.* Her character and body measured out the way a clerk counted his coins. Revulsion snaked through her and Justina forced her gaze to her father's repugnant face. "Would he also care to see my teeth?" she asked in modulated tones. "I've been told I possess remarkably even teeth." She displayed them for his perusal.

"Don't be silly," he barked. "Fortunate for you, the gent cares more about your other attributes."

Nausea churned low and deep in her belly. *I am going to be ill.*

"Tennyson's coming to call at noon," he said with finality.

She shot her gaze to the long-case clock. *Thirty minutes.* Her panic mounted.

Her father waved her off. "We're done here, gel." He picked up his previously discarded glass and dipped the empty snifter upside down over his mouth. With her eyes, she followed the trail of several amber drops as they slid onto his tongue.

By God, she'd see a drunkard like him in hell before she abandoned the dreams she had of a loving marriage. Not attempting to keep the disgust from her face, Justina stood and snapped her skirts before taking her leave.

Once free of his office, she quickened her steps. Her hem whipped noisily about her ankles. So, her father was determined to sell her off—and not even to the highest bidder—only to the most convenient one. He would sell her body and soul to that man.

Justina rushed around the corner and, not breaking stride, shoved open the door of the billiards room. She closed the door quietly behind her and opened her mouth to speak, but words died on her lips. Her brother stood, poised over the edge of the table, with a silly grin on his face. His faraway, dreamy gaze lingered on the untouched balls. The urgency of her father's intentions for her momentarily slipped to the corner of her mind as she stared at him. "What is the matter with you, Andrew?"

He jumped and his cue stick skidded across the table, scratching the surface. A crimson blush stained his cheeks. "Justina." He glowered. "Hardly the thing interrupting a fellow when he's—"

"Woolgathering?" Despite the direness of her own situation, a small smile pulled at her lips.

His cheeks flamed apple red. "Playing billiards." He yanked at his immaculate cravat. "What do you want?" he asked with a bluntness that raised a frown…and also brought her back to her reason for seeking him out.

She spoke on a rush. "I require an escort."

Andrew returned his attention to the two balls remaining on the table. "You always require an escort," he mumbled as he released his cue.

The crack of his stick striking the object ball filled the space.

Justina folded her arms at her chest. "You are my brother. It is your role to escort me about Town when I need to be accompanied."

"That is Mother's role," he said, walking about the table and assessing his next shot.

"Mother is with Phoebe and I'm here." She paused. "With *you*."

"And I just accompanied you shopping last week." Of course, with her visits to Gipsy Hill, he'd drawn the same flawed conclusion that any male might—that her sole reason for visiting that unfashionable end of London was for some fine frippery or another. "Besides, I am meeting someone."

Justina eyed him skeptically. "Who?" She knew every last friend

Andrew had. Men who were more acquaintances, with shared interests in gaming and drink.

Her brother flushed. "None of your affair," he mumbled, studiously avoiding her eyes. "A chap shouldn't have to explain who he's seeing and when."

She drummed her foot. At any other time, she'd press him on his red cheeks and lovesick look. "Father has a *visitor* coming shortly," she said, advancing deeper into the room. She'd not remain and be sized up by Tennyson like the Christmastide hog.

"'Fraid I cannot." Andrew leaned over the table once more and positioned his stick. He took his next shot. It sailed wide, missing his target.

With a frown, she captured the end of his cue.

"What—?"

"I have to leave, Andrew. Father wishes me to see Lord Tennyson." Releasing his cue, she stuck a finger in his chest. "You may believe yourself wholly removed from my circumstances, but if Father succeeds in marrying me off, then *you* will be next." He picked his head up and his eyes flared wide with panic. Now she had his attention. "You will be expected to find a lady with a fat dowry," she continued, playing on any young gentleman's greatest fears. "So, muster some fraternal devotion and accompany me."

Worry danced in Andrew's eyes. "I cannot go marrying another w—" He promptly pressed his lips closed, cutting off those telling words.

So, there was a lady who'd garnered her brother's notice.

"Furthermore," her brother groused. "It's not in good form to take a jab at a man whose dibs not in tune."

Dibs not in tune? "First, I do not know what that means," she said, positioning herself between him and the table once more, and earning another scowl. "Second, I require your help."

"No," he said, restoring his attention to his single-player game.

"Here." Justina fished around inside the clever pocket sewn into the front of her ivory velvet gown and drew out a small sack. She hurled it onto the table. Andrew looked between her and the velvet purse, and scrabbled for it. "We leave in ten minutes" she said, starting for the door. She paused, with her fingers on the door handle. "And if you care to speak of bad form, Andrew, requiring your sister to pay for your help is certainly the veriest form of low."

Her brother had the good grace to flush. "You know I *would* help you, anyway. You don't *need* to pay for my assistance."

Justina looked back at him. "I know," she said softly. And she did. She also knew that the same disease that led their father to those gaming tables night after night, and plunged their family further into debt, plagued her brother. Not for the first time, worry settled in her chest about Andrew and who he might one day become.

"Not that I'll reject your gift, either," Andrew spoke on a rush and tugged at his robin-egg blue satin cravat. "Bad form and all to reject a gift, *especially* from a sister."

Her lips pulled at the corners. "Ten minutes," she reminded him.

A short while later, Justina, with her reluctant brother in tow, made her way through the crowded London streets, onward to Gipsy Hill. Andrew whistled a discordant tune and drummed his fingertips in time to the rumble of the carriage wheels.

Chin in hand, she stared out at the passing scenery as the aged black barouche drew them farther and farther away from the townhouse. There, her father would meet with a gentleman and attempt to sell her off like some prized broodmare. The muscles of her stomach knotted. That was the manner of man her father was. One who'd trade his soul for a sack of silver, and release his daughter to a stranger without a thought of her happiness. Or her hopes. Or dreams.

With his avaricious heart that beat for nothing but those gaming tables, he could never see, nor care that she was a woman who longed for so much more than the gloomy existence her own mother knew. Justina wanted more than even a respectable, honorable husband who carried on a life separate from her own. She wanted a loving husband, loyal and devoted to her and their someday babes. And more, she wanted to be free to read whatever books she wished, write, and be a woman with control of her life…and thoughts.

And she would have it. Despicable father be damned.

"Why can you not be content with staying to Bond Street?" Her brother called her back to the moment. There wasn't a single Circulating Library on Bond Street. "All the thing, you know? Splendid tailor over there where I find all my jackets."

From the corner of her eye, she took in his shockingly bright, burnt orange cloak and the canary yellow satin breeches revealed through the crack in that garment. "Oh, I expect you might find an even better tailor at Gipsy Hill." She bit the inside of her cheek to keep from laughing.

"Gipsy Hill?" her brother parroted. "Egads, would you have me don garments fit for a gypsy?"

The reminder that his vibrant garments would be the envy of any true gypsy hovered on her lips, but she quelled it. As long as her mother remained in the country with Phoebe, Justina was still in need of his assistance. It would hardly do to offend him.

"Well, regardless," Andrew persisted, stretching his legs out and knocking her knees. "You'd be better served by finding your fripperies at Bond Street. All the crack, you know?"

"I like Gipsy Hill." At the junction of South Croxton Road and Westow Hill, the bustling streets lined with gypsy wares and carts didn't have the same crush of proper lords and ladies one found in the fashionable end of London. She'd discovered, merely by a matter of chance in those streets, The Circulating Library.

The carriage rocked to a slow halt, and Andrew grabbed his leather gloves from the bench and pulled them on. "At last. Will you pledge to at least keep this visit short? Meeting someone." He puffed out his chest like the prized rooster that used to dance outside Meadow Manor. The memory ushered in that place where she, Phoebe, and Andrew had known so much laughter.

Their driver drew the door open, yanking her from her reverie. Andrew jumped out and skimmed his gaze over the crowded streets. The servant, Stevens, reached inside for her. As her booted feet touched the ground, Justina flashed him a smile. "Thank you, Stevens."

"Come along," Andrew urged, smoothing the lapels of his cloak. "You were eager to shop, let's not tarry."

She pinched his forearm through his cloak, earning a wince. "Oh, hush." She dropped her voice. "You know very well, you're just as excited to be here as I am." The dull flush on his cheeks confirmed the supposition she'd long known. Nearly a foot shorter than Andrew's six-foot, two-inch figure, Justina went up on tiptoe and added on a conspiratorial whisper, "I promise I shan't shatter your reputation as a flawless dandy with the truth."

His color deepened. "I don't know what you're talking about," he mumbled, darting his gaze about. His eyes landed on a wide wagon littered with vibrant-hued kerchiefs.

Justina laughed. "You are free to go look. I wanted to select a book," the book she'd had to leave behind earlier that morn, "and then—"

"You're certain?" Andrew asked, his feet already carrying him several carts over to the toothless Rom. The young peddler held up a peacock blue fabric and her brother reached for it with reverent hands.

Andrew otherwise occupied, Justina strode purposefully along the pavement until she reached The Circulating Library. After she'd entered she moved quickly through the establishment and found the copy of Shelley's work. Collecting it, she made her way to the front and checked out the volume.

Prize in hand, she hurried outside. A blast of wind whipped at her face and tugged at her skirts as she started back down the street to where Andrew was engrossed with a purchase. Even with the length of distance between them, the burnt orange kerchief held up for his inspection stood out. Her brother eagerly grabbed the bright scrap. Justina fought back a grin. Though she'd long teased him for his garish fashion, she appreciated that he, at the very least, knew his mind and made no apologies for his interests or choices.

She picked her way around the crude table set out with bonnets, gloves, fans, and other colorful fripperies and stopped. Drawn over, Justina set her borrowed book down and trailed her fingertips over a straw bonnet with green satin ribbons.

A bemused smile tugged at her lips. How many years had she spent collecting nothing more than pretty bonnets and ribbons? As a girl, she'd spent countless hours trying on her mother's hats. Then, as a young woman, she had reveled in the power to at last select *something* of her own. She fiddled with the green ribbon, running it between her thumb and forefinger. The *ton* believed a lady incapable of having more than singular interests. By Society's narrow-minded standards, one who appreciated lovely bonnets could never also enjoy books.

"White gloves, my lady?" A gypsy with stringy, graying hair held the long, white cotton, embroidered pair aloft.

Setting down the bonnet, Justina shook her head and continued her perusal.

"Mayhap, a book then?" This time the woman held out a small

leather tome.

Unwittingly, Justina stretched her hands out and the Rom turned it over for her inspection.

The cacophony of the riotous street sounds grew distant as she stared at the faded gold title: *Evelina*. Justina fanned the pages of the old, musty-smelling volume. Of all the baubles or fripperies the gypsy should hold forth a copy of Frances Burney's work. Transfixed, she snapped the book closed and ran her gloved palm over the cover with reverent awe for the female author who'd challenged her father and Society's disapproval to publish the once well-received work under her own name.

Which only raised the reminders of her own miserable circumstances. She'd her pin-money from Edmund and a membership to The Circulating Library. There were little funds for the purchase of books. With regret, Justina made to set the book down when a shadow fell over her shoulder.

"Ah, the tale of *Evelina*," a deep baritone, smooth like warmed chocolate in the winter, sounded over her shoulder. It rang a gasp from her.

She spun about. The book slipped from her fingers and landed at her feet as her gaze climbed the well over six-foot figure of the gentleman before her. The spring breeze whipped at his midnight cloak. The fabric clung to his thickly muscled thighs and broad chest. The olive hue of his skin and aquiline nose hinted at his Roman roots. His noble jaw, with the faintest cleft and sharp, angular cheekbones, may as well have been carved by one of those great Italian sculptors, and this man their final masterpiece. He possessed the manner of beauty that would find him on the pages of any romantic tale. Justina's heart tripped a beat.

The stranger's lips turned up in an easy half-grin revealing two even rows of pearl white teeth. "My lady." He doffed his hat revealing an unfashionable crop of loose golden curls the Archangel Michael would have dueled him for. "Forgive me. It was not my intention to startle you," he murmured, jerking her back from the momentary spell he'd cast.

"It is fine," she blurted. "You did not startle me. Well, you did," she acknowledged and earned another one of those smiles that sent her heart into double time. "But it is fine. Was fine. It is *still* fine." *Stop prattling, Justina.*

He studied her with piercing intensity in his cerulean blue eyes. Like the sky on a cloudless summer day. No mere mortal had a right to such a captivating gaze. "I could not keep from noticing..." Her heart knocked hard against her chest. "...your book." *My book?* She blinked slowly. Of course. *You silly ninnyhammer. Did you truly believe a gloriously golden stranger would be spouting on about you amidst Gipsy Hill?* Then his words registered. *Evelina.* She gasped and glanced down. The stranger followed her gaze.

They dropped to their haunches as one and the street above disappeared so that only they remained. "Here," he murmured and collected the aged leather tome. "Allow me."

Justina stared wide-eyed as he dusted bits of gravel and dirt from the back of the book. "A lovely tale, is it not?"

This man knew *Evelina?* "You have read it, then?" she asked, unable to keep the surprise from creeping into her question.

"The story of Evelina and her Lord Norville? Indeed." The stranger, who she truly had no place speaking with, and certainly not without the benefit of introductions or a chaperone, returned his attention to the book, flipping through the pages and scanning the sentences.

Her own father and brother were too consumed by drink and women to ever notice something as insignificant to them as a book. "My governess once called the heroine an empty-headed fool." Just as she and so many saw her.

"And what do *you* think of *Evelina?*" he asked, picking his head up.

Her breath hitched. No one asked for her opinion. Even the sister and brother that she loved, and who loved her in return, saw her more as a child to be taken care of. "Evelina is young and, in many ways, unknowing of the world, but I believe she is also remarkably clever and perceptive when it comes to making judgments about those around her." His gaze bore deep with such a piercing intensity, it was as though he could reach inside and pluck the thoughts from her very head.

"Beautiful," he murmured in hushed tones, muted by the loud cries of vendors hawking their wares.

Warmth unfurled in her belly. In a moment that defied logic and all sense, she wanted to remain down here with him, this man whose name she did not know. *Say something, Justina. Say anything.*

"It is." *That is what I'd say?*

He cocked his head at an angle that sent a loose golden curl falling over his eye. Her fingers ached to brush it back.

"Beautiful," she clarified. "It is a beautiful tale." The story of a lady, of shameful origins, who ultimately found the love of a distinguished and honorable nobleman.

"Yes." He leaned close, his lips nearly brushing her ear. "But I was not speaking about the tale," he said on a husky whisper that lodged the breath in her lungs. He shoved to his feet and held a hand out.

Without hesitation, Justina placed her fingertips in his large palm. He folded it over hers, dwarfing her smaller one. Even through the fabric of their gloves, a searing heat penetrated and sent delicious tingles radiating up her arm, and then he released her. He sketched a bow. "My lady," he murmured, handing over the book. Then as quickly as he'd slipped into her life, he turned around and slipped out.

Heart racing, Justina stared after his retreating form until he'd disappeared in the distance. All the air left her on a slow exhale. How utterly silly to be so singularly captivated by a too-handsome stranger. And yet... She nibbled her lower lip. There had been something so wholly captivating about him. A man whose eyes conveyed a depth of feeling and emotion and who spoke so freely about literature...literature written by a female author, no less.

"Would you like it then, my lady?"

She whirled about. The old Rom gestured to her fingers. "Yes!" Justina exclaimed. "I will take it." After her meeting with the glorious stranger on the street, how could she not?

As the gypsy neatly packaged the copy, she stole a glance about the streets for a hint of the gentleman, but he may as well have been nothing more than a whisper of a dream. *Who is he?*

The quality of his cloak and gleaming Hessians bespoke of a man of power and wealth. She searched her mind for a hint of having met him and, yet, had she seen him at a *ton* event, she'd not have forgotten. What had brought a man such as him, here? As her brother pointed out, lords and ladies didn't spend their time in the southern end of London.

Exchanging several coins that brought the other woman's eyes flying wide, with a word of thanks Justina collected her borrowed volume of Shelley and her newly purchased *Evelina*. Questions swirling through her mind about the man whose name she did not know, she resumed her walk through the vendors' stalls.

# CHAPTER 3

ꟾT WAS TOO EASY.

If it had been any other woman, Nick would have, mayhap, felt more than this tiny, unwanted pebble of guilt. But it *was* this woman. She was linked by marriage and now family to the Marquess of Rutland. For that, her fate was sealed through her connection, just as his own family had thirteen years past.

As such, Miss Justina Barrett served as nothing more than the means to a proverbial end.

From the cart where he stood, concealed from the lady's direct line of vision, Nick studied her, without fear of notice. Near an age of nineteen or twenty, there was a youthful innocence to her heart-shaped face given to blushing. Her eyes revealed none of the world-wary cynicism that had invaded his own years earlier at the hands of her brother-in-law. After he'd freed his father from that self-made noose, Miss Justina Barrett's innocence was one he'd come to despise. It had served as a mockery to what he and his own sister had been denied. How did Justina, with the misery she'd known as Viscount Waters' daughter, manage it, still?

The young lady, even now stood, the wind whipping at her green velvet cloak, a dreamy smile on her lips, as she picked her way through the streets. Nick started after her, careful to keep distance between them. Occasionally, she stopped alongside a cart, sifted through the baubles there, and then continued at her unhurried pace. By the useful information he'd been handed by the Lady Carew, Justina Barrett was an empty-headed miss with a love for bonnets and not much more.

Yet what had held her enthralled hadn't been a silly frippery, but rather a book. Nay, not just any book. *Evelina.* His gut clenched painfully. The Devil had a sense of humor, indeed. That the leather tome Justina Barrett lovingly stroked, should also be the last he'd ever read.

He gave his head a hard shake and as the kernel of guilt vanished, Nick recalled his purpose. He glanced about for the phaeton. Chilton sat in wait, a hat pulled low over his brow and the high collar up around his neck. Yes, everything was set.

Nick looked to the lady, once more. And cursed under his breath. Where in blazes had she gone? Frowning, he skimmed his gaze quickly over the bustling pavement where men and women haggled with the Rom vendors. Then he found her. She hovered on the edge of the cobbled road, one booted foot poised to step, the other frozen as she battled back the strings of her bonnet that the wind whipped about her face.

Nick took a step forward, when a small, bent figure moved into his path, halting him in his tracks. "Care to have your palms read, my lord, and have your future told?"

He silently cursed the old gypsy. "A man makes his own future," he said curtly and made to step around her. But with a surprising agility, the aged figure intercepted his movements.

"Ah, we determine the paths, but our fate is already set for us," she said in haunting tones that sent an irrational chill skittering along his spine. "Come," she held her gnarled hands out and beckoned him forward. "Let Bunica see what lies in wait for you."

He didn't need a charlatan's false prophecy. He well knew what awaited him. *Vengeance.* "I—"

Loud shouts erupted around the busy street and, the old gypsy forgotten, Nick whipped his stare to the commotion that had garnered the crowd's notice. A screeching, bucking stallion galloped down the road, its rider dragged behind as the man frantically tried to shed his foot of his stirrup. Nick followed the path of the horse as it raced, making a beeline for a small beggar child who stood in the midst of the empty streets, frozen. A sharp cry went up and he followed the sound to Miss Barrett. Everything moved in a whir as the young lady bolted into the street for the boy, shoving him out of the way.

He cursed. *What is she thinking?* Nick bounded through the crowd, his heart pumping from his exertion. In one fluid movement, he knocked Justina Barrett down, startling a soft scream from her, just as the stallion's hooves pounded the ground where she had stood seconds ago.

The rider managed to wrestle himself free and then made a grab for the reins. The skittish beast reared on its back legs and pawed at the air. Heart thundering, Nick rolled himself and the young lady out of the way so that Miss Barrett briefly sprawled over his chest. He quickly shifted her under him. Shoving up on his elbows, he shielded her with his body.

Her loose curls tumbled free from her chignon and cascaded around her shoulders in a shimmery, golden waterfall. And at last, the young rider wrestled control of his mount. The small boy scrambled to his feet, stared wide-eyed at Miss Barrett and Nick, then darted off into the crowded street.

His chest heaving from the near brush with death, Nick looked down to unleash a tirade on the reckless chit's ears. What bloody lady risked her fool head with such abandon? Their eyes met. The young woman's mouth formed a small circle that matched her rounded eyes. "*You.*"

The stinging rebuke died on his lips. Adoration spilled from the lady's expressive cornflower blue eyes and all words and thoughts stuck inside his head. The vibrant depths of her gaze were not unlike the Suffolk sky at summertime.

"Are you all right?" Justina Barrett's question, rife with worry, brought him reeling to the moment.

What in blazes was he doing, staring at her like a lovesick swain? "Quite," he assured her. "I—"

"You saved me," she interrupted on a hushed whisper that barely reached his ears. But he heard it.

*...You'll destroy us...*

Justina Barrett's three words at odds with those ones uttered long ago by his father and, for it, bringing a greater satisfaction than the lady, soft in all the places a woman should be soft, now under him.

*A means to an end.* Nick shifted a hand between them.

"What...?"

"You have dirt, my lady," he murmured, brushing a trace of mud from her cheek. A charge raced from the point of contact.

Her breath caught on an audible inhalation.

"Are you hurt?" he asked, quickly lowering his hand.

She shook her head wildly on the cobblestones. "You saved me," she said softly. "And I do not even know your name."

"Nick Tallings, Duke of Huntly," he murmured.

"You are a duke," she blurted. He braced for the greed to fill her eyes. When he was a young man scrapping together wealth through hard work, a lady such as her wouldn't have given him a sideways glance. With the addition of his title and obscene wealth, every marriage-minded miss in the realm looked a little longer.

"Indeed," he drawled, unable to quell the cynicism in that affirmation.

The young lady tipped her head, the joy fading from her eyes. "It would not matter."

He furrowed his brow. What was she on about?

"Whether you were a duke or titleless gentleman." She angled her head up, shrinking the space between them, so close their lips nearly brushed. "I would be equally grateful for your rescue, Your Grace." Her breath, a delicate blend of apples and mint fanned his face and, unbidden, his gaze fell to her mouth. A potent surge of lust coursed through him, an unwanted sentiment, an unwelcome one for this woman.

"Justina!" That frantic shout from beyond Miss Barrett's head shattered the moment.

A gentleman in a revolting orange cloak staggered to a stop and dropped his hands to his knees. He'd spied the man countless times entering Forbidden Pleasures, tossing aside good coin. Dangling two whores on his lap. The man would be as easy to ruin as the sister, herself. "Justina," he rasped as he bent over, sucking in gasping breaths. "Are you…?" The young man's words trailed off as Nick stood, unfurling to his full six-foot, three-inch frame, nearly of a height with the dandy.

*Andrew Barrett.*

Sister forgotten, the younger man dropped a deep bow. "You're Huntly." The same awe to have filled the sister's eyes, matched this callow fool's similar stare.

Schooling his features so as to not reveal the disgust at the dandy's reaction, Nick bent and easily scooped the lady to her feet. A little sigh slipped from her lips as he lingered his hands on her generously flared hips. "None other," Nick drawled.

Mr. Barrett blinked wildly and then, widening his eyes, he looked to his sister. "Justina, are you hurt?"

She opened her mouth.

"I saw Huntly thundering through the crowd to reach you." The dandy stuck one of his bright pink leathered shoes out and swept his arms wide. "Not every day that one of the most sought after chaps in London rescues a man's sist—*oomph*." He shot an offended glance in the young lady's direction. "Did you *kick*—? *Oomph*."

Miss Barrett glared her brother into silence.

If Nick were a man intent on anything other than the ruin of the young lady, he would have been enthralled by her pluck. A silent battle stretched on between the siblings. With a sigh, Lord Andrew returned his focus to him. "Proper introductions, I expect, are in order, given your heroics this day, Your Grace."

Now, that would be beneficial, to continue this whole farce marching forward.

"My sister, Miss Justina Barrett. Justina, His Grace, the Duke of Huntly."

The lady sank into a flawless curtsy. With the wind tossing her long, golden tresses about her face and shoulders, she had the look of Botticelli's Venus. "Your Grace," she murmured in sweet, modulated tones. "Please, let me thank you for coming to my rescue."

Nothing could have been further from the truth where his actions toward this one were concerned. Nick sketched a deep bow, moving through the Social pleasantries expected of them. After all, the image he'd presented to Society, charming, affable rogue, had all been part of the scheme that led to this very meeting. "It was my honor, Miss Barrett." He held her gaze for a long moment, eliciting another audible intake of air from the lady.

Lord Andrew hooked his thumbs in the waist of his pants and looked back and forth between them, grinning like the village lackwit.

The lady worried at her lower lip, a question in her eyes. A question that asked if she'd see him again. A look that said she longed to.

And she would.

Nick retrieved his hat from the ground and snapped the flat brim back into shape. "Miss Barrett," he murmured again as he doffed his black Aylesbury. With that, he started down the street and left the Barrett siblings staring after him. A hard grin formed on his lips.

It had begun.

*That* WAS THE DUKE OF Huntly?

The rogue most sought after at every *ton* function? The man whose name was written about in the papers for the ease and charm he possessed. And he'd saved her. That was the manner of romance every young lady read romantic verse and fairy tales for.

Standing beside her brother, Justina watched after the young duke's retreating form. Nearly half a foot taller than the passersby on the street, he stood easily above the rest, moving with a sleek, panther-like grace. When he'd at last disappeared from view, her entire body sagged.

Years earlier, when she was just a girl, she'd read the tales of the Duke of Bainbridge's heroic rescue of the now Duchess of Bainbridge after she'd crashed through the ice at the Frost Fair. As a young child, she'd eyed those pages, wistfully, dreaming to know just that. The love. The romance.

Only to be rescued, four years later, by a duke who, with his smile and honorability, put lesser men to shame for things that had nothing to do with his rank.

"Not every day a young gel's saved by a duke, eh?" Andrew jabbed his elbow into her arm.

She winced and massaged the sore flesh. Having her feet literally and figuratively restored to the earth, she noted the details that had previously escaped her. The sharp ache of her lower back from where she'd slammed into the ground. The twinge in her hip. "No. It isn't," she said with a little smile playing about her lips.

Andrew jutted his elbow out. "I gather this was enough excitement for you today." He leaned down and whispered. "And everyone else," he said, waggling his eyebrows. Jolted to, she took in the people milling about the street staring at her.

Those onlookers held their hands up, shielding their mouths as they spoke. No doubt, tales of the duke's heroics were even now circulating the streets of London and would find their way into every parlor and ballroom.

Unbidden, Justina did another search for him.

"Wouldn't mind having a chap like that for a brother-in-law," he said too loudly and heat exploded in her cheeks.

"Hush," she said from the corner of her mouth.

"What?" He bristled. "I'm merely saying, you could certainly do worse than landing a man swimming in lard."

Justina groaned. "Can you not speak in the King's good English?" It should be a crime that these dandies corrupted speech in such a way that a person couldn't make heads or tails of what in the blazes they said.

"He's rich as Croesus," Andrew simplified. "Lucky fellow's distant cousin up and died, and he found himself a duke." He sighed. "Some men have all the luck."

What was it with lords and ladies and their dreams of wealth and power and nothing more? Even her brother. "Yes. To be so lucky as to find yourself with a title and wealth because some childless duke had the misfortune of dying."

"Exactly," Andrew muttered, failing to detect her subtle sarcasm.

They reached the carriage, with her brother still prattling on about the duke's horseflesh and townhouses and outrageous luck at the gaming tables. Followed by grousing on his part about his own ill-fortune at those same tables.

She accepted the servant's help, climbed inside the carriage, and settled herself on the bench. Andrew followed behind, taking the opposite bench. As much as she'd long abhorred his penchant for following the gossip in the scandal sheets, now she wished she'd paid a tad more attention herself.

Questions raced through her mind about Nick Tallings, the Duke of Huntly. What had he been doing at Gipsy Hill? A powerful peer, just below royalty, didn't come to these streets filled with gypsies. No, those predictable nobles didn't deviate from their fine clubs and their Bond Street shopping and their morning rides in Hyde Park.

Yet, this man had.

*Nick.* She silently rolled that name around her mind, testing it.

Strong. Powerful. Bold. Like warriors of old. How perfectly it suited him. Justina fiddled with the curtain and directed her attention outside the lead windowpane. *Be nonchalant.* "So, what do you know of the duke?" she asked, infusing a deliberate boredom into her query.

Andrew glanced over and his perplexed brow reflected back in the glass panel. "I just told you, he's a duke, fat in the pockets."

She swallowed a sigh. Of course, a young gentleman of one and twenty, he didn't see much of the world beyond those irrelevant details. Someday, there would be a young lady who set his world on its ear and she would quite delight in his befuddlement. Justina released the curtain and it fluttered into place. "Is there a lady who has earned his affections?"

Her brother scratched at his forehead. "I…I haven't heard mention of a lady." Then he flashed a smile. "A duke, with his choice of ladies, he could choose anyone. But he *could* choose you," he hurried to reassure. "After all, there is no accounting for the heart's desire."

She snorted. "Why, thank you."

He flushed. "That isn't to say you aren't a good match for some gentleman." In a show of brotherly devotion, he leaned over and patted her knee. "He'd do well to attach himself to you."

"I wasn't asking because of…" *Why else would I be asking?*

Andrew lifted an eyebrow.

"I was merely curious, is all," she finished lamely.

"Ah, of course." He nodded. "Well, as I said, you could do far worse than a gentleman like Huntly."

Yes, even only having met him but a handful of minutes on the street, she could say with certainty she could do far worse. Lord Tennyson's visage slithered around her mind. Yes, a bounder who'd keep company with her father would certainly never risk his neck, as the duke had, all to save her. A man who'd not been condescending of or toward a tale written by a female.

She gasped and glanced frantically about.

"What is it?" Andrew asked, looking back from the passing streets he'd been staring out at.

"I… my belongings," she yanked the curtain back once more and assessed the fashionable end of Mayfair they now journeyed through. "My book." That same volume she and the Duke of

Huntly had forged a slight bond over.

"Ah, well, just a reason for you to return shopping next week," he said with a wink.

Swallowing back her disappointment at the loss, she returned her thoughts to the young, golden-haired duke. Every last romance novel she'd ever read warned a lady of the perils of a rogue, rake, or scoundrel. And yet, never more had she truly understood the glorious appeal of those wicked men—until now.

As the carriage rumbled slowly through the clogged London streets, questions whirred around her mind about the man named Nick Tallings, the Duke of Huntly. The greatest wondering: would she see him again?

Some minutes later, their conveyance rolled to a stop outside the front of their stucco townhouse. The carriage dipped as the driver climbed from his perch, and then he opened the door.

"Thank you, my good man," Andrew called jovially.

Stevens returned the smile and offered a bow. "Mr. Barrett," he said, as he helped hand Justina down. As soon as her feet touched the hard pavement, a sharp jarring pain traveled from her lower back up to her shoulders. "Are you all right, Miss Barrett. From your fall?" Concern wreathed his wrinkled cheeks.

For his benefit, she smiled through the pain. "It will take more than a runaway horse to hurt me, Stevens," she said with a wink. And as she walked toward the townhouse, her skin still tingling from where the duke had held her, she rather believed herself incapable of feeling any hurt on this day.

# CHAPTER 4

"Whats the meaning of this, gel?"

The following morning, curled up on the windowseat overlooking the London streets, Justina glanced up from her book, and her heart sank. Her father stood in the doorway, brandishing a copy of *The Times*.

Ignoring the sharp twinge in her hip, she climbed to her feet. "Father."

His breath emerged as a rattling rasp from his exertions. The viscount waddled into the room and hurled the newspaper so it landed in a fluttery heap at her feet. Fury filled his beady blue eyes. "Yesterday, I told you Tennyson was coming. I was left making excuses for you." He grunted and hooked his thumbs into the waist of his blue satin breeches. "And now he and all of London find out about you and the Duke of Huntly in the scandal sheets?"

Justina retrieved the paper and her gaze snagged on her name paired with the duke's. Of course, the gossips would take that one meeting and weave it into something so much more. "Nothing happened with the Duke of Huntly," she said between tight lips. Even as she wished it had. "I was shopping," she said curtly. "And a horse nearly trampled me." It was a testament to the emptiness of her father's heart that he didn't bat even an eyelash at the possibility of her untimely demise. Once, that indifference had gutted her. Now, she'd found peace with who he was, and the understanding that he'd never, ever, no matter how many times she'd willed it or wished it or begged it from the stars overhead, be the father she wanted him to be.

Her father rubbed a palm over his mouth, contemplating her with a hard stare. "That's all?" he said at last.

*Indeed, it is beautiful. But I was not speaking of the book.*

It was so much more. "That is all," she snapped.

"Never sat down to a game with Huntly," he groused, his meaning clear. Unless a gentleman could forgive his debts, then he served little interest.

Her father was so very determined to see her enter into an advantageous marriage for him, loveless for her match. He'd have her be a pawn. Expected it. No doubt with good reason. She'd always been the weaker, more obedient of the Barrett girls. Well, she'd sooner lob off her right arm than sell her soul to settle her father's gaming debts. Justina firmed her lips. She'd have love…or nothing at all.

They remained locked in a silent battle, when footsteps sounded in the hall.

Manfred appeared in the entrance, bearing a silver tray.

"What is it?" her father barked.

"The Duke of Huntly has arrived to see Miss Barrett."

Her heart jumped a beat and she fluttered a hand to her chest. He'd come.

"Huntly?" he snapped, scratching at his paunch.

The butler looked back and forth between father and daughter. "I took the liberty of showing His Grace to the Blue Parlor. Should I tell him Miss Barrett is not receiving—"

"No!" Justina exclaimed and her father narrowed his bushy eyebrows.

*Think, Justina.* She schooled her features. "I expect it would make a *Diamond*," she curled her toes into the soles of her slippers, "even more sought after if a duke courted her favors."

Her father captured his chin between his thumb and forefinger. "Hmm." Then, he gave a slow nod. "I expect it would raise your value in Tennyson's eyes."

"Oh, undoubtedly," she said with a biting edge he either failed to hear or care about. "If you'll excuse me?" She forced her steps into a sedate pace. Then, as soon as she'd stepped into the hall, she hastened her step.

*He is here. Why is he here?*

Questions ran riotous through her mind as she reached the Blue Parlor. Justina pinched her cheeks and then taking a deep breath, stepped inside.

The Duke of Huntly stood at the floor-length window with his back to her, surveying the streets below. Through the drawn curtains, sunlight spilled into the room and cast a glow about his golden curls. With his broadly-muscled frame and towering height, how very different he was from the Marquess of Tennyson.

She'd wager her very life before another wild horse that Lord Tennyson would never risk his life and limb to save anyone other than himself. From within the crystal windowpane, her gaze collided with the duke's. Heat exploded on her cheeks at being caught staring.

He wheeled slowly around. "Miss Barrett," he greeted on a mellifluous baritone that set butterflies dancing in her belly.

"Your Grace," she returned softly.

Justina cleared her throat and motioned to the chairs. "Would you please sit?"

The young duke, who'd earned the *ton's* note and favor, waited until she'd claimed a chair. Then he strolled forward with a languid elegance that sent her heart beating into double time and sat beside her.

*Oh, saints in Heaven.* She stole a sideways peek at him. Of all the seats he might have taken—the King Louis chair directly opposite, the shellback chairs on the opposite ends of the rose-inlaid table— he'd sat next to her. He shifted slightly and his broad, oak-like thigh brushed her leg, crushing the fabric of her skirts in a noisy rustle of muslin.

"I trust you are well following your fall, madam?"

"Oh, quite," she lied. Her entire body throbbed and ached from her wicked tumble onto the cobbles. He reached inside the front of his jacket and Justina followed those precise movements. She gasped as he withdrew a small, tattered volume. "You rescued it." With her gaze, she briefly studied the now rippled and worn leather.

"I could not very well leave it," he murmured. "It needed to be restored." He handed the delicate piece over and Justina accepted it with trembling fingertips. She ran her index finger along the wrinkled spine.

So, this was why he was here. She couldn't battle down the disappointment.

"It is a shame that it has been marred."

Justina glanced up from that mark. "Oh, no. It's not been destroyed," she corrected. When he furrowed his brow, she explained. "You see," she flipped the pages, fanning through the book. "People expect a cover to be flawless leather, etched in gold." Just as Society expected of a lady. "But it hardly matters what is on the cover, but rather, what is on the inside," She turned the open volume toward him. "These words, they tell a tale." She closed it and indicated the marked spine. "As do the marks left that day in the street."

"And what tales do they tell?" he urged, shifting closer. His breath tickled the sensitive skin of her neck and she struggled to attend that question.

With tremulous fingers, Justina set the book down on a nearby side table "I expect it is a different one, depending on the person telling it."

SINCE HE WAS A BOY, he'd developed an innate ability to read the details around him.

It was how he'd known as a child of fourteen that his family had been steeped in financial ruin. How he'd known Lord Rutland, with that ruthless gaze, had come to wreck his family that night, long ago.

Nick assessed the cheerful space that showed the age of faded upholstery. The copies of aged poetry volumes scattered about a side table perfectly suiting a lady who made more of a timely rescue in the streets. It was how he also knew Justina Barrett was a hopeful dreamer, even with her family on the cusp of dun territory. He picked up a copy of *Camilla* from the side table and turned it over in his hands.

As a boy, he'd been voracious in his readings. There had been no work he'd left unread in his late father's once-vast library. What rot it had all been, poems and tales of love and works honoring nature.

All of it had proven meaningless diversions that could never truly detract from the ugliness that was life.

"Have you read that title, Your Grace?" Justina ventured hesitantly. He blinked, glancing up. She gestured to the volume in his hands.

His gaze involuntarily returned to the cover. There had been a time when he'd hungered for his days in the schoolrooms and longed for his days at Harrow. "I have," he said gruffly. All of that simplicity had been ripped from him. After his father's death, he'd discovered the uselessness of all those frivolities. Books and poems couldn't save a person. They could only distract one. "Many, many years ago," he added as a quiet reminder to himself.

There was no need to let this woman inside. His only goal was to shatter her defenses, capture her heart, and destroy her family. Then, he could finally be at peace, knowing he'd brought about the same destruction to all those Rutland loved, just as the marquess had wrought hell on Nick's own family.

Heart in her eyes, she scooted to the edge of her seat, coming nearer. Her contagious love of the literary word was an unwanted connection that made Justina Barrett real in ways that hadn't mattered. In ways he didn't want to matter. "You do not take exception to female authors?"

Guilt settled uncomfortably in his belly and he shoved it away. Had Rutland ever shown any such weakness to either Nick's father or anyone thereafter? His father's gap-mouthed body, limp upon that rope, flickered behind his mind's eye. Nausea turned in his belly. "On the contrary," he said truthfully and she glanced up with surprise in her blue eyes. "I'd not be so small-minded as to pass judgment on a literary work because of the author's gender." She touched a hand to her heart. "But neither do I read them anymore," he felt inclined to add, severing that thread between them.

"But why?" she asked, her delicate features wreathed in disappointment.

At her probing, he snapped. "Because life ultimately proves that those hopes for happiness are elusive dreams that children fill their heads with to usher them through the darkness of life."

Her mouth parted slightly. He forced the tension from his body and relaxed the muscles of his face. His skin flushed under the force of her stare. "I don't believe that," she said softly.

"That is because you still hope and dream," he countered. Why did he debate her on the merits of romance novels and poems? Bent on stealing her heart and ultimately shattering it, he should be filling her head with inanities and lauding the great romantic poets. Instead, he gave her the very real truths that had shaped him into the hardened man he'd become. Eventually, all dreams died. "What happens when your father loses all his wealth?" Which Nick would see carried out. As soon as the words left his mouth, he wished to call them back.

The lady recoiled as though he'd struck her and it spoke to his weakness since he wished to erase the evidence of her hurt; a hurt he'd inflicted. But she was fearless and that mark of strength momentarily alleviated his guilt. For, when he'd seen this through, Justina Barrett wouldn't be wholly wrecked. Not the way Cecily had been, relegated to the role of wife to an ancient, cold nobleman.

"What of the ladies in your family?" she pressed. He welcomed the reminder of his sister and niece who, when this was done, would be avenged. "Would you deter them from reading such books because it is nothing more than fanciful drivel?"

"I would not," he answered with an automaticity born of truth. His every move for thirteen years had been carefully measured with the purpose of ensuring what happiness and innocence he could for those two ladies.

A wistful smile hovered on Justina's plump lips. "Then they are very fortunate." What accounted for the sad glimmer in her expressive eyes?

He swallowed a sound of frustration. It mattered not what kind of existence, happy or otherwise the chit had known. It mattered that she was Rutland's naïve sister-in-law, beloved by Rutland's wife, and cared about by the demon marquess himself. She was destined to suffer and from that, break Rutland. The question slid forth, anyway. "Have your parents been less forgiving in your reading selections, then?"

"Oh, never." A golden curl fell over her eyebrow and his gaze went to the strand. Memories of those long tresses wrapped about them in the streets of Gipsy Hill thundered inside his mind and he hungered to see them fanned about his pillow. "Well, my father doesn't bother with what I read." Her lips twisted in an aberrantly cynical grin. "He so often doubts my intelligence he likely doesn't even trust I *can* read." The lady had more intelligence in her left littlest finger than Waters had in the whole of his body. "My mother would never dare limit what I read," she chatted, swatting at the curl. "She lives to see her children happy."

A mother who, even married to a reprobate like Waters, had not given up on life; who'd instead coaxed joy where she could from her children. Unlike his own mother who'd merely subsisted and then ultimately willed herself to death with her husband's passing. That juxtaposition should serve as a stark reminder of Nick's goals for the Barrett family and, yet, there was this unwitting and unwanted desire to hear more. For reasons he didn't understand. For reasons that had nothing to do with Rutland or revenge.

"My sister always read books of exploration and dreamed of travel," Justina said, opening the door further into her world. Letting him inside, the minds and dreams and hearts of her, as well as Rutland's wife. "My mother never demanded she abandon those dreams."

"What of your dreams?" he asked quietly, his inquiry born not of the seeds of revenge, but of a true need to know what a lady who wore her heart in her eyes yearned for. His belly knotted viciously and he hated himself for wanting those revelations from her.

Justina wetted her lips. For a long moment, he believed she'd ignore his question. Then, she stole a glance about. "I have always wanted to hold a salon within my own home, a place where young ladies can speak freely on literary works and exercise their minds without worry or recrimination." She blushed. "Of course, I don't think I'll be an Elizabeth Vesey, or an Elizabeth Montagu, but I do dream of having young ladies and gentlemen come to share ideas and works. As I share mine, Your Grace." Justina swiped the black leather journal from the table and looked at it for a moment. She held it out.

"Please, call me Nick," he responded.

Justina stared at him, confusion spreading across her features. "I beg your pardon, Your Grace?"

"Nick. That's my name. If we are to the point of discussing dreams, I think we can safely use our Christian names in private, don't you agree, Justina?" he replied.

"I...I suppose that would be acceptable," Justina stammered as she continued to hold the book out to him.

Nick stared blankly down at the book. How easily she turned over her intimate words for him. Had he embroiled a ruthless Societal lady with an empty head who hungered for nothing more than wealth and title, it would have been easier than this. A woman who lamented having an indifferent father. A woman of clever intellect who sought more in terms of her learning and her happiness. His gut clenched and he forced himself to take it with stiff fingers.

He flipped open the journal.

*A lofty title, a lady doth aspire.* Of course they did. Bitter cynicism pulled at his lips.

*But in time, she finds there are greater gifts to admire.*

*A lover's heart, and truthful lips those, forever inspire.*

He paused, his gaze transfixed on those words.

*…truthful lips…*

Guilt blazed a fiery path through his conscience, holding him silent. How could the lady retain that joy and belief in good when there were no true happy endings? *And I will destroy her. I will crush every last dream and hope of love and happiness.* A viselike pressure squeezed about his lungs cutting off air flow. And he didn't know what to do with this unwanted guilt or *any* sentiment that ran parallel to his thirst for revenge.

"It is incredibly rough," she said matter-of-factly, bringing his head up. "That is merely the beginning, but I thought how important it would be for young ladies to talk about the matches they make or are expected to make. And what we, as women, truly desire." She dropped her chin into a hand. "I visit the The Circulating Library and listen to countless discussions on romantics and the meaning of verses, but never do the speakers talk about challenging the cold, emotionless unions we're expected to enter in to." That made his planned rescue of her in those streets all the more vile for its cold-heartedness. His stomach turned. Who knew he, who'd prided himself on his indifference, was capable of feeling this shame? "No matter how many times I begin, I just cannot find the next part." She sighed. "I'm hopelessly stuck with nothing more than an idea and a handful of sentences."

Nick returned his gaze to the page. "Write your own words," he said quietly.

"What?"

"Do not search for inspiration within another poet or author's tales or verse." He captured her fingers and guided them to her breastbone. "Write from here." From that place where all great agony, love, and despair lived in a synchronistic harmony that left a man forever in tumult.

Her lips parted and she roved her gaze over his face. "I've never met anyone like—"

Nick cupped his other hand around her nape and claimed her lips under his, quelling words he didn't deserve from this woman, silencing her erroneous conclusion that he was in any way good. Justina stilled in his arms and he moved his mouth over hers in a gentle exploration, coaxing the tension from her, until a breathy sigh escaped her.

The women he'd taken to his bed over the years had been women whose souls were as wicked as his own. There was nothing tender in their words, thoughts, or kisses and caresses. As such, he'd engaged in violent matings of the mouth that had only served as a ruthless precursor to their inevitable sexual joining.

Nick continued to taste her and, abandoning her journal, he moved his hands down her waist. He caressed her lush hips, aching to sink his fingers into that flesh without the hindrance of her muslin skirts between them.

Fueled by the feel of her in his hands, he deepened the kiss, slanting his mouth over hers again and again, until she groaned and allowed him entry. He thrust his tongue inside and she touched hers to his in a tentative meeting. That innocence, so wholly unlike anything he'd known in any of the women before her, sent blood pumping to his shaft.

With an increasing boldness, Justina fiercely met his strokes, tangling her tongue with his in a primitive match that met the lusty joining of two bodies. She wrapped her hands about the back of his neck and pressed herself against him.

He groaned, the low sound swallowed in her mouth, and he worked his hands between them, searching her body. Discovering her. The ample swell of her breasts spilled over his palms and never more had he despised fabric than he did in this moment for impeding his exploration of her satiny soft skin.

Nick drew his mouth away, trailed kisses down her cheek and

lower, to the place where her pulse pounded in her throat. Growling, he sucked and nipped the flesh.

"Nick," she panted. That one-word plea, his name, fueled him.

He moved his lips in a slow, wicked path to her modest décolletage. He dropped a kiss atop the cream white mounds. The echo of footfalls in the corridor penetrated the mad haze of desire she'd cast. Struggling for breath, he swiftly slid to the opposite end of the sofa.

Her eyes clouded with passion, Justina blinked and glanced about.

Andrew Barrett burst into the room, panting. "H-Huntly, old chap," he rasped out, his chest heaving. "Just on my way to my clubs when I heard you'd paid me a visit." The man need but a single glance at his sister's swollen-kissed lips and rosy cheeks to glean what he and the delectable Justina Barrett had been doing. Instead, the fool remained fixed on him, oblivious.

Disgust coated Nick's tongue. The lady had been cursed with a ruthless father and an indifferent brother. "Barrett," he greeted.

The younger gentleman rushed over and inserted himself into the seat between Nick and Justina. "Thank you for entertaining him in my stead, Justina."

She rolled her eyes skyward and Nick found himself smiling. "My pleasure."

The future viscount was too consumed by his own self-importance to hear the sarcasm. "Care to join me at Forbidden Pleasures, Huntly, old friend?"

Having served in the role of father and elder brother to his own sister, Andrew Barrett's absolute disregard for the young woman before him defied fraternal logic. He snapped his eyebrows into an annoyed line and glanced pointedly at Justina. "I hardly believe such talk is proper discourse."

Befuddlement glazed the other man's eyes as he glanced from his sister to Nick. "Because of Justina?" he blurted. "Quite fine discussing it in front of her. She knows all about the gaming tables."

Intrigue replaced his earlier disgust with the man. "Does she?" Nick drawled, favoring the young lady with a long look. A bluestocking with a love of literature and who knew about the gaming tables.

A delicate, pink blush marred her cream white cheeks and she glared at her brother. "My brother is merely jesting—"

"No, I'm not." Andrew shook his head with such vigor that even with the thick pomade oil greasing his closely cropped Brutus curls, a strand fell loose. "In bad form to jest about the gaming tables, you know, Justina."

"It is also in bad form to discuss wagering in front of a lady," she muttered.

Despite himself, a low chuckle rumbled from Nick's chest; rough from ill-use, but raw and unjaded.

"In front of my chum, Huntly?" Shock rounded the dandy's eyes. "Quite safe to speak freely in front of one's friends."

Wheedling his way into Andrew Barrett's graces and lulling him into a sense of false friendship was going to be easier than snatching peppermint from an unsuspecting child. Far too easy to merit any *true* sense of triumph. In fact, both Barretts were making this too easy. It was the only reason to account for his restlessness.

Barrett continued his chattering. "Heard you were all the crack at the tables, but couldn't have ever predicted just how skilled." The dandy puffed out his chest and that slight movement stretched the pea green satin fabric of his jacket. "Granted, you've never sat down to a set of faro with me."

"Yes, all the *skill* required in that particular game," Justina drawled. Her brother broke from his pompous bragging to frown.

"Not just a game of chance like some might think."

Layering his arm to the ruffled edge along the back of the sofa, Nick leaned around the younger man and caught Justina's gaze. A little twinkle danced in her fathomless blue depths. *I'm sorry,* she silently mouthed.

He winked and her lush lips formed a smile that momentarily froze him. With her pale blonde curls and heart-shaped face, Justina Barrett would forever fit with all the standards of English ladylike perfection. That breathtaking grin transformed her into a captivating siren whose innocence he longed to peel back layer by layer and unveil the wantonly beautiful creature he'd tasted moments ago, whose passion was longing to be set free. He fixed a smoldering gaze on her.

Her lips parted ever so slightly and a whispery sigh slipped out. How free she was with even her silent thoughts; that unspoken desperation for a glimmer of romance. One which he'd exploit.

He tightened his jaw.

"My chum, Huntly, no doubt knows as much," Andrew went on. "I can show you all my greatest secrets to winning at faro. A visit to Forbi—er…the *clubs*?"

Nick forced his attention away from Justina and attended the man. "I am afraid I must politely decline." He quickly stood. "I've matters of business to attend." He couldn't stay here. Not with this woman who threw into tumult his well-ordered plans and dark revenge.

"Mayhap later, after?" Barrett persisted, wandering even further down the path to his own ruin.

Nick flashed his most charming grin. "I'm looking forward to it," he lied. Nick sketched a hasty bow. "If you'll excuse me, Miss Barrett?"

The two Barretts spoken in harmony. "You're leaving so soon?"

Justina brushed her palms over modest, dull ivory skirts. She searched her transparent gaze over his face. "That is, what I'd intended to say," if her blush turned any redder, her cheeks would catch fire, "is that it was a pleasure, Your Grace." Her breathless words stirred the embers of desire, once more.

"The pleasure was all mine," he murmured. Nick gathered her fingers and drew them to his mouth. He placed a lingering kiss on the inside of her wrist and thrilled at the hard pounding of her pulse there.

Andrew Barrett clapped his hands, effectively severing the charged moment. "Until later, then."

"Until later," Nick concurred. It was a certainty there would be a later. He was not here to make friends or connect emotionally with a woman, but rather to see justice done. Barrett's vowels, the viscount's, would all belong to him, so that not even the Marquess of Rutland's obscene wealth could salvage them.

He turned on his heel and left.

# CHAPTER 5

THE FOLLOWING AFTERNOON, NICK, IN the company of Vail Basingstoke, Baron Chilton, sat at the table in the back corner of Brooke's.

"Yesterday's turn of events was certainly convenient," Chilton drawled. The sardonically grinning man lifted his glass. "You hardly required my assistance at all."

Yes, everything had proven remarkably easy where Justina Barrett was concerned. He'd come to her rescue, albeit not in the way originally planned. Paid her the requisite visit, returning her silly book of poetry, and kissed her senseless. Yet, it was easy. Almost *too* easy.

That had to be the sole reason to account for this...restlessness inside.

With a snifter of brandy cradled between his hands, Nick took a slow swallow of his drink and looked beyond his friend's shoulder to the gentlemen boldly staring in his direction. The furious whispers filled the club.

And fruitful.

Word of his interest in the lady had already made the necessary rounds. The gossips were abuzz with the tale of the romantic meeting of a duke and a lady; the rescue of that damsel in distress.

Nick swirled the amber contents of his glass. Everything had been expertly set into motion. Everything down to the awestruck stars in the naïve lady's eyes. Why couldn't she be the avaricious, ruthless-in-her-own-right Diamond that Society purported she was? His fingers curled reflexively on his glass. *It doesn't matter what kind of woman she is.* It only mattered her connection to Rutland.

"What is the lady like?" Chilton asked with a bored edge to that inquiry. "As lovely as the papers make her out to be?"

*Lovelier.* He lifted one shoulder in a shrug. "It hardly matters what the lady looks like." Or how generously flared her buttocks were. Or how full those breasts that had pressed against his chest. Or that she'd thrown herself into the path of a wild horse to save a beggar child from the street. Nick took another stiff sip. For ultimately, she could be a heartless, toothless crone, and the result was all the same. *A means to an end.*

"I swear you are the only man who could set out on a path to ruin a lady and be so ruthlessly indifferent to her attributes," his friend said in dry tones.

Lust still burned through him with the remembered feel of Justina Barrett making a lie of his friend's erroneous supposition. Nick tipped his chair on its back legs. "Would you care to know about the lady?" he asked, lifting a hand in greeting to some pompous lord who needed some kind of affirmation from him. Bloody fools, the lot of them. And how he despised the pretense of the charming lord they all took him for. "She's blonde as any other English lady." With golden strands kissed by the sunlight. "Plump." Perfectly rounded with hips a man was meant to sink his fingers into. He gave his head a disgusted shake. *Enough. Your hunger for the lady hardly signifies.* "And short. Blue eyes," he thought to add. That glittered with flecks of silver in the light. "And she's in awe of a dukedom. Are you satisfied with that accounting?"

*It would not matter whether you were a duke or titleless gentleman…* Every single lady from debutante to ancient dowager sought his attention now that he had a title. Surely, she was no different.

"Hardly a scintillating creature to command your notice," Chilton agreed and then downed the remainder of his drink.

Nick shoved the bottle across the table and his friend promptly refilled his glass. "She needn't command anything. Her name alone does that," he said in a hushed whisper intended for the other man's ears.

"Ah, but it isn't her name," Chilton pointed out, with a waggle of his midnight eyebrows. "It is her brother-in-law's name."

He frowned at the ever-present disapproval. They fell into a tense silence, as Nick considered Miss Barrett's brother-in-law.

Rutland. The demon who'd shattered his family. A man whose only family was the woman he'd made wife. Nick gave his head a shake. Oh, the timing. If he had been in possession of the title duke and amidst Polite Society *then*, he could have robbed Rutland of the person who most mattered. He rolled his shoulders. As it was, he'd have to settle for destroying the man's sister-in-law. His father-in-law. His brother-in-law. And through that destruction, his wife's every happiness.

Then, the man would live with the misery of being crushed... without the finality of death, by which Nick's own family had been forever transformed.

He stared down into his half-empty glass. His mind slid back to a long-ago day. To a different bottle of brandy dripping on the floor. A crystal glass tipped on its side, as the amber brew spilled in a depressed puddle over the important papers scattered on that once-cluttered desk. Nick's hand trembled and sent liquid sloshing over the side, staining his fingers. He set the glass down hard with a loud *thunk*.

"You do not expect a man like him will not be abreast, even in the country, of his sister-in-law's well-being?" Chilton ventured, pulling him back to the moment.

"Hardly," Nick concurred. Rutland may have retired to the country, but the man, by nature of his evil existence, had made it nigh impossible to penetrate his world. "His wife's recent delivery and sick babe, however, will command all his notice for some time."

If it hadn't been for the baroness with one maid who'd slipped past the marquess' scrutiny, Nick would have been left with the same morsels thrown in those papers by the *ton*. But he now knew Rutland was fully focused on his own matters. He'd wager he had at most a month—mayhap less—by his figuring, to embroil the profligate Barrett males in enough wagers to cost them everything. All the while, he would dance the daughter down the aisle of ruin, without so much as a dowry to her name.

"Well, I will be damned." Chilton whistled softly through his teeth and Nick followed his stare.

The tall, slender young dandy in canary yellow satin breeches strode through the club. With his chest puffed out and his head tilted back, he had the look of a rooster pecking his way about the farm. *Lord Andrew.*

So, it truly *was* this easy. He thought of his late father's weakness. How very easily he'd stepped into Rutland's trap. How fitting that both Andrew Barrett and Justina should fall so neatly into a similar line.

The younger man came to a stop at his table. "Huntly, my friend." *My friend?* From the corner of his eye, he detected Chilton burying his grin behind a hand. "After all the excitement and your heroic rescue on my sister's behalf, I thought I would join you."

Nick plastered a smile on his lips and opened his mouth to speak, but Mr. Barrett had already yanked out a chair and claimed the seat between them. "Please, join us," he said dryly. The man either had arrogance to rival the king or was too much a bloody idiot to hear the sarcasm, for he sat back in his chair and grinned. "Barrett, allow me to introduce you to Chilton. Chilton, Barrett."

The younger man stretched an arm across the table and shook the baron's hand. "A pleasure." His gaze fell to the half-empty bottle and then he held his hand up motioning over a servant. "Another bottle of brandy and a glass." So, the gentleman intended to stay. "The least I can do to thank you properly for saving my sister."

Had he ever been this naïve? ...*I don't want to be a merchant someday, Papa. I want to be a poet...* His naïve child's voice of long ago, echoed around the chambers of his mind. Picking up his snifter, Nick finished the contents. *Fool.* They all started out as fools. He, Justina, and her brother, included.

A liveried footman rushed over with a new bottle and a glass. He set them on the table and, with a bow, rushed off. "A toast is in order," Barrett said, pouring himself a drink. He held it aloft. "To the beginning of a friendship."

Nick choked mid-swallow and Chilton, his shoulders shaking in silent mirth, leaned over and slapped him hard between the shoulder blades. "If you'll excuse me," his faithless friend managed to squeeze out as he shoved to a stand. "Let me leave you two to your budding relationship." Nick fixed a glower on the other man as he backed away.

And then he was left with Barrett.

"Really, rather good of you to save my sister and return her book," the younger man said, commanding his notice.

"It is nothing I wouldn't have done for anyone," he said, automatically. Well, mayhap one. Soulless, brown eyes flashed in his mind. With stiff, jerky movements, he swiped the bottle and poured himself another full snifter.

Barrett layered his arms on the table and drummed his fingertips on the smooth, mahogany surface. "I shouldn't say this," he said. Then he dropped his voice to a conspiratorial whisper. "Scandalous stuff, to speak of one's sister." Nick's ears pricked up and he went absolutely still. "But my sister did ask questions about you."

Ah. He repressed the cynical smile that would alert this man to the true darkness in his soul. "Did she?" he asked, leaning forward and erasing the space between them.

The other man nodded and then yanked his lapels. "As her elder brother, I've come to see whether or not you have honorable intentions toward the lady."

What would Barrett say to the absolute dishonorable ones he had for the whole of his family? "Given our...brief meeting, I cannot speak to any...feelings for the lady."

Barrett's face fell.

Nick leaned closer, still. "But I can say with a certainty, the lady has courage, wit, and beauty that any man would fight battles to win," he said. The young man's grin was back in place before the final word had left his mouth. He motioned to the felt tables about the club filled with men wagering away their fortunes. "A game of piquet, Barrett?"

The other man beamed and, downing his drink, shoved his chair back and promptly stood. "Splendid, Huntly."

Nick stood and fell into step beside the garrulous dandy content to carry the conversation for the both of them.

Splendid, indeed.

JUSTINA HAD SPENT THE PAST months lamenting the absence of her mother and Phoebe. She might not have a mother or protective older sister at hand, but what she did have, however, was a de facto mother. Or to be more precise…two. The pair of young women, contrasting images in every way, who right now stood at the front of the library with suspicious gazes and determinedly squared shoulders.

"We heard of your encounter on Lambeth Street," Honoria said without preamble, tugging off her gloves. With brown hair, brown eyes, and suspicious by nature, she could not be more different than the hauntingly beautiful Lady Gillian, who happened to share Justina's romantic spirit.

She opened her mouth, but Gillian glared at the other woman. "That is hardly the way to go about asking if she was at all hurt." Rushing over in a whir of pink skirts, she steered Justina to a seat and claimed the spot beside her. "Are you well?" Gillian asked on a rush. She wrung her hands. "I had it on the authority of my maid, who had it on the authority of Lady Jersey's footman that you were nearly trampled by a carriage—"

"A horse," Justina automatically corrected.

"And that you were rescued by the Darling Duke of Huntly."

"The rogue," Honoria muttered, coming over and settling herself into a nearby leather winged back chair. "We heard you were rescued by a rogue and that he paid you a visit."

Yes, she'd heard whispers of him being a rogue and not much more. As one whose family had long been gossiped about, she'd never bothered with the scandal sheets or the words of busybodies. After meeting the Duke of Huntly, she wished she'd paid just a bit more attention to the most sought after gentleman—beyond that unrevealing detail.

Thrusting aside the questions, she elucidated for the worried pair. "A horse charged toward me. When I pushed a small child from the horse's path, the duke knocked me out of the way." *And covered my body protectively with his own, like a warrior of old.* In what was the singularly most romantic moment of her twenty years.

Gillian glowered at Honoria. "Did you not hear what Justina said? She was nearly trampled by a horse. Phoebe would never forgive us if we allowed her sister to be trampled by a horse."

"A horse is far safer than a rogue, any day," Honoria muttered under her breath, earning another admonishing look from Gillian. "Phoebe would never forgive us if we allowed Justina to show interest in a rogue."

With the young woman's suspicious nature, she would put shame to any recalcitrant lady's watchful companion. And by the way she now studied her with narrowed, probing eyes, Justina would be that naughty charge. What would the other woman say if she knew the Duke of Huntly had passed his powerful hands searchingly over her? Or that he'd kissed her senseless? Justina's heart kicked up its rhythm and she sent a silent prayer skyward that the ladies would not detect her blush.

In a bid for nonchalance, Justina plucked at the fabric of her skirts; a hungering filled her to know more about the stranger in the streets. "Is he really a rogue, though? I trust Society cannot *truly* know that."

"The gentleman has acquired a reputation as a rogue, so Society can, in fact, know as much," Honoria said, earning a frown from Justina. The woman forced imaginings of other young ladies who'd earned the gentleman's favor.

Gillian waved her hand once more. "Well, according to my maid, that isn't altogether true. Not anymore. The Duke of Huntly *was* a rogue, but he's been quite…" She wrinkled her brow as though searching for her words. "Respectable," she settled for. "And there have been whispers that he's in the market for a wife."

Justina's heart jumped a beat. "Is he?" she squeaked.

"Not that I follow gossip," Gillian said on a rush. An uncharacteristically hard glint lit the young woman's eyes. "Nasty stuff." As a lady whose family had been mired in scandal following her eldest sister's failed wedding and then subsequent marriage years later to a notorious rake, the gossips had been as unkind to the Farendales as the Barretts.

Honoria scrunched up her mouth. "You are interested in the gentleman." Her words were stated in a matter-of-fact manner.

"Of course not," the lie tumbled easily from Justina's lips. "I barely know him." Beyond their shared, if brief, exchange over that copy of *Evelina*, and his rescue on the cobbles, and that dratted kiss.

"She's blushing," Honoria said, bringing her back to the moment. Planting her palms on her knees, she leaned forward to peer at Justina. "*Why* are you blushing?"

"I'm not blushing," she said quickly, her skin going ten shades hotter.

"I'm afraid you are," Gillian piped in with a nod. "As much as it pains me to agree with Honoria."

There was something so very comforting in the friendship of these two women who'd taken her under their proverbial wings. Even if they were more overprotective than her mama, they were loyal and concerned, and that was a welcome kindness she would have traded her pinky fingers for to know from her own father.

Honoria landed her ever-narrowing gaze on the empty spot beside Justina. She followed Honoria's stare to the faded black leather volume with its nearly indiscernible lettering. Nearly. Justina made a quick grab for the title. "And you are reading romance novels."

"Poetry," Justina amended. "I am reading poetry."

"She is always reading romance novels," Gillian correctly pointed out. She patted Justina on the knee. "Nothing wrong with a lovely romance novel."

"There is everything wrong with a romance novel," Honoria said tightly. "But," she continued, holding a hand up. "That is hardly the cause for concern, but rather the blush…" She paused and folded her arms. "And your visit from the duke."

"There is hardly anything to speak on," she assured. Justina's skin warmed all over again. Hugging her book close, she stole a glance at the doorway. "I dropped my book in the street and His Grace merely returned it," she said, giving them the safest truth that didn't reveal her personal hopes. The Duke of Huntly's visage slid forward in silent testament to the lie of the other woman's words. She bit the inside of her lower lip, willing her cheeks to remain cool. "Though, I thank you for your worrying," she directed that piece to Honoria. "Nothing untoward happened. If he was here, Andrew could even attest to that." Which he was not. For which she was immensely grateful. "Now can we please go?" she asked and made to rise. "I'll be late for my lecture."

"What could I attest to?"

The three ladies shrieked as the door swung open and revealed a grinning Andrew in the doorway.

Justina swallowed a groan. "Andrew," she muttered as Honoria and Gillian rushed to their feet and offered the requisite curtsies. "We were just—"

"Discussing Justina's perilous trip down Lambeth."

He dropped a sweeping bow and motioned the ladies to sit. "Please, please," he urged, closing the door behind him. "I expect you were *also* discussing a certain duke." He looped his hands at his back and strolled over with lazy movements.

Honoria gave her a pointed, more than faintly accusatory look.

Justina buried her head in her hands.

"I also would wager," Andrew ventured, "you were daydreaming of a certain duke."

*Bloody hell.* Justina held Andrew's gaze and willed him to silence.

Honoria and Gillian exchanged looks, and then urged the cocksure youth on with their stares.

At the attention trained on him, his grin widened, and he continued sauntering over. "But you did not deny it."

Her cheeks blazed. "I wasn't thinking of the duke," she gritted out, glancing over at Honoria who watched her closely. She resisted the urge to stamp her foot in a childlike display.

Andrew winked. "Oh, no?"

"No," she said in perfectly modulated tones that earned a snort from Gillian. Justina patted the back of her loose chignon. "I was attempting to leave so that I can visit my lecture which is vastly more entertaining than any tale you're telling," she said, shoving to her feet.

Alas, her two traitorous friends retained their seats.

Her brother stalked slowly around the sofa. "So, you wouldn't be at all interested if I told you," he lowered his hands quickly to the back of the chair and leaned close, "that I'd taken drinks with the gentleman?"

She gasped. Her mind racing… What…? Why…?

Andrew shoved away to a stand and strolled with an infuriating languor around to the leather winged back chair beside Honoria. He fell back in the seat. "Know a bit of a thing about love myself," he added, earning giggles from Honoria and Gillian.

And at any other moment, in any other time, Justina would be wholly fixed on the look of longing in her brother's eyes that indicated he very well did know about that grand emotion she'd desperately longed to experience. Alas, but a single mention made by her brother commanded her attention. Of the gentlemen whose company her brother kept, all fellow dandies he'd only mentioned in passing, never had she heard mention of him sitting down for drinks with the Duke of Huntly. Nor did the powerful, faintly roguish gentleman who'd rescued her in the streets strike her as a gentleman who'd be friends with her flashy brother.

"Why were *you* taking drinks with the duke?"

Gillian buried a laugh in her hand, quickly concealing it as a cough.

A slight, annoyed frown marred his lips. "Come, is it really such a surprise to learn Huntly and I are chums?"

"Yes," she said with an emphatic nod. "Yes, it is."

"Hmph," Andrew said with all the petulant annoyance of a troublesome child. "Very well, then." He released a long sigh and came slowly to his feet. "Then, I shan't tell you what the gentleman may have said about you."

Justina jumped to her feet and moved in a noisy rustle of skirts. "Don't you dare leave, Andrew Algernon Alistair Barrett," she warned. Grabbing his arm, she steered him into a seat. Her brother properly ensconced in his previously abandoned spot, she stood over him, hands on hips.

"Do back up." He gave a flick of his hand. "You are hovering."

Not allowing her already gloating brother further victory, she slid into the seat across from him.

"Well," Honoria urged, when Andrew stretched the silence.

"Lost a bit at the tables today," he said in an abrupt shift. "Not too much coin. But enough that a chap will certainly feel the pinch."

Gillian rounded her eyes like an owl startled from its perch. "Are you…is he…*bribing* you, Justina?"

Yes, he was utterly shameless.

He and Justina spoke at the same time.

"No."

"Yes," she said and he shifted in his seat the way he had when their mother had lectured him for his naughtiness. "Or he is attempting to, anyway."

Over in her seat, Honoria muttered something in low tones that sounded a good deal like, "You ladies refuse to believe that gentlemen are shameless…"

Andrew frowned at Honoria. "Hardly wrong to share coin with one's brother."

"Andrew." Justina's warning tone raised the color in his cheeks.

"I'm not giving you any additional coin." And certainly not as a bribe to obtain information about the dashing duke who'd rescued her at Gipsy Hill.

"You're certain you can't part with—"

Honoria and Gillian spoke in unison. "She's certain."

"Very well," he mumbled under his breath. He brushed a speck of imaginary lint from his shoulder. "As I was saying about my chum, Huntly." Justina rolled her eyes at that gross exaggeration. "Toasted the gentleman to his bravery, and he said…" Her breath froze in her chest. "…that he'd have done the same thing for anyone."

All the air left her on a swift exhale as disappointment flooded her being. "That is what he said?" she asked dumbly. *That's all? What did I think he would say?*

"See," Gillian offered far too cheerily to Honoria. "It is as Justina said, nothing untoward happened, and there is and was nothing more to their exchange." Nothing more. Justina's heart dipped. And yet, there had been something gloriously dizzying in his low-whispered words and his unwitting embrace.

"Honorable fellow," Andrew added.

Yes, a gentleman who'd so leap to the aid of anyone was to be commended and, yet, in the hours since his rescue, she'd allowed her whimsical musings to take root and grow. Tamping down her foolish regret, Justina sighed. "Now, may we go?" she asked the other two ladies.

And this time, they stood and made their way to the door.

"Oh, Justina?" Andrew called out when she reached for the handle.

*What now?* "Yes?" she asked, glancing around at him.

"I did want to mention the part where Huntly said you have courage and beauty that any man would fight battles to win."

Honoria gasped.

"He said…?" Justina fluttered her hands about her chest.

"I wager *that* information was worth a pence?" He winked.

"And certainly more interesting than a scholarly lecture," Gillian put in.

A hopeful glimmer lit Andrew's eyes. "If the information was more valuable—?"

"No, you may not have any additional coin," she said, marching from the room. Honoria and Gillian trailed close behind.

A smile pulled at Justina's lips. Mayhap there was more to hope for in terms of the Duke of Huntly, after all.

# CHAPTER 6

THE INFORMATION NICK HAD RECEIVED over the months during his assignations with the Baroness Carew had proven crucial in his plans for Lord Rutland.

He had learned Justina Barrett had a silly fascination with bonnets. She had a love of gothic novels and romantic tales. She was wistful and fanciful. And she'd taken to visiting The Circulating Library.

That *particular* detail about the lady's interests accounted for his presence at the back of said circulating room. Standing in the small lecture hall, Nick folded his arms and assessed the visitors scattered about the neatly arranged chairs. Five dandies, three ancient lords. He zeroed his gaze at the second to last row. And one *unattended* lady.

Miss Justina Barrett, to be precise.

The generously curved siren sat perched on the edge of her chair, hanging on the lecturer's words as though he were handing down a lesson on the meaning of life. Of course, the hopeless romantic, she'd be here listening to readings of those great poems. The same ones he'd once pored over in the dead of night until his candlelight flickered out.

Giving his head a cynical shake, Nick started quietly down the thin, makeshift aisle and paused at the second row. "May I claim this seat, Miss Barrett?"

The young lady shifted her attention from the reader to him. She flared her eyes.

Nick winged an eyebrow up.

"Of course," she said quickly, her words thundering in the quiet.

They earned reproachful stares from the reader, who stumbled over his verse, and the other poetry devotees. Justina blushed, her cheeks turning a stunning crimson hue.

Unapologetic, Nick slid into the vacant chair as the graying man with thick side-whiskers, resumed his reading. Justina sat stiffly at his side; her narrow shoulders tense. Tugging off his gloves, he stuffed them inside his jacket, and then deliberately pressed his thigh against her, crushing the fabric of her yellow satin skirts. The faintest intake of air escaped her lips and a surge of masculine triumph went through him at her body's natural awareness to him. "You are also an admirer of Shelley's work?" he asked softly.

The lady looked up, surprise stamped on her features. "*You* are a fan of Shelley's work?"

"Shh." The dandy in purple pantaloons shot a particularly nasty look in Justina's direction.

Nick inclined his head and then promptly dismissing the young gentleman, resumed speaking. "I am." A verse flickered in his mind. "'Life may change, but it may fly not; Hope may vanish, but can die not—'"

"'Truth be veiled, but still it burneth; Love repulsed—but it returneth,'" Justina interrupted with a smile. All the tension went out of the lady's shoulders as she shifted closer in her seat; her guards completely crumpled. "Most are admirers of Byron's work."

And he had once been, as a boy with his head in his books. Unnerved by that forgotten until now love of verse, he forced a grin. "Bah, Byron," he said with a little wave of a hand. After his father's death, he'd attempted to read those works once more, but the pointlessness of those words had made a mockery of his efforts. "I've often felt his work as overinflated as his ego."

If one could witness a person falling in love, then he would wager his ducal title that he captured a slice of Justina's heart in that moment. And all on a lie.

In truth, Nick hadn't thought of Byron's work since he'd been an eager student at Harrow, who'd excelled in his studies. The romantic works. Classical literature. With his father's death, he at last appreciated all those useless inanities had proven the rubbish people filled their life with to forget how miserable one's existence truly was.

The lecturer paused in his reading and, shoving his spectacles back on the bridge of his nose, glared at Justina and Nick. Then he continued his reading.

*"I arise from dreams of thee.*

*In the first sweet sleep of night, when the winds are breathing low, and the stars are shining bright…"*

"Shelley's poem, *I Arise From Dreams Of Thee,*" the lecture went on in nasally tones, "is far simpler than any written by Byron or Wordsworth…"

Once again, Justina stared, riveted by the gentleman speaking.

"I have thought of you since our last meeting," Nick whispered close against her ear, stirring a single golden curl artfully arranged over her shoulder.

She blinked slowly, and then shifted her attention over to him. "Did you, Your Grace?" Her hushed question barely reached his ears.

"Ah, but I thought we'd agreed to refer to one another by our Christian names." The fragrant scent of honeysuckle and lavender that clung to her skin wafted about his senses, flooding them with the rich, vibrant smells of summer. A wave of desire went through him and he forced himself to speak. "Would you not agree, Justina?" he asked on a husky whisper.

"How would you have me reply to that, in public?" she asked, giving the small crowd absorbed in the lecture at the front of the room a deliberate look. "*Given* the rules of propriety, most all Polite Society would disagree," she murmured, her bold challenge raised a faint grin. She held his gaze with an unexpected show of strength and boldness, which defied the reports he'd been handed by the baroness and gossip columns.

Surprise slammed into him. When he'd crafted his scheme, with the plans of using Justina, he'd resolved to suffer through her company in order to woo her and win her. Who could have imagined that he, Nick Tallings, a man shaped in Rutland's image, should actually enjoy being with her? "I daresay, a lady who'd take up a seat in a lecture hall about Shelley's work would not be overly impressed with Society's foolhardy opinions on what is proper."

Justina searched her gaze over his face. Did she seek an underlying hint of disapproval? If so, the lady would not find it. He gave two damns on Sunday what a single member of the peerage thought.

"Ahem." A loud coughing at the front of the hall drew their attention as one to the stern-faced lecturer.

Again, Nick lifted his head in acknowledgement. "I am surprised to see you here," he said when the older gentleman resumed his talk.

And where she'd once devoted her every attention to the words being recited by the portly gentleman at the front, Justina glanced up at him. "Are you of a mind of Lord Byron's and all others that I should not have an interest in poetry merely because I'm a female?"

"Hardly," he protested. "There is a difference between reading and reciting poetry, and…" He angled his head toward the man rambling on monotone at the front of the room, "…being lectured to on specific verse chosen by a pompous prig. Would you not agree?"

"I would not."

At that bold challenge, he angled his head. Who had been the baroness' contacts that they'd drawn such an erroneously empty sketch of the woman before him?

Justina tipped her chin up. "I expect, in contradicting you, I've either shocked or horrified you."

No one had noted Nick Tallings when he'd been a merchant, scrabbling to rebuild his family's wealth. As a duke, the world bowed and cowed before him. And they certainly did not challenge him. There was something so wholly refreshing in this woman's honesty. "Hardly," he said in a hushed tone, giving her the truest words he ever would. "You've intrigued me."

"Well," she went on, to clarify. "With the depth and wealth of meaning in a poem, a person connects emotionally to each stanza or verse. Ascribes feelings or thoughts to it, either deliberately or by the natural progression of one's wonderings. Do you not feel that way about it, Your…Nick?" she amended at his pointed look.

By rule, he was passionate about nothing beyond the goals that had driven him for thirteen years. His hatred, as Rutland had predicted all those years ago, had sustained him. Made him stronger.

But who was he, without it? Who would he be when he'd at last destroyed that man...and destroyed this woman with expectant eyes before him? "I believe we all connect with words in different ways," he settled for, unnerved by the questions she'd inadvertently roused.

"Precisely," she said too loudly, earning another reproachful look from the gentleman at the front of the room. "It is not this man's utterances," she gestured to the lecturer, "that move me. But rather, he makes me think about verses in a light I'd not previously considered, possibly opening up a new meaning that resonates in here." She tapped her fingers to the center of her chest, bringing his gaze downward, and then he forced his stare back to the passion in her eyes.

Despite his earlier-drawn conclusions based on the information he'd received on the lady, he'd expected her to be the same title-hungry miss as the next. Only to find, the truth so quickly at the front of an empty lecture hall. The lady was a free-spirit with powerful thoughts that moved beyond bonnets and baubles and, in that, unlike any other woman he'd known in thirteen years.

*And she will rightfully despise me when this is done.*

The nasally whine of the lecturer's recitation crept eerily into Nick's conflicted musings.

*Once, early in the morning, Beelzebub arose,*
*With care his sweet person adorning,*
*He put on his Sunday clothes.*
*He drew on a boot to hide his hoof,*
*He drew on a glove to hide his claw,*
*His horns were concealed by a Bras Chapeau,*
*And the Devil went forth as natty a Beau*
*As Bond-street ever saw.*

The older man picked his head up and his gaze landed on Nick, sending disquiet rolling through him. He then resumed his reading of those eerily accurate verses that Satan himself could not have better picked for him and his intentions.

"What is it?" Justina whispered, pulling him back to the moment, unguarded with her questions and her eyes.

*Remember who she is. Remember your goals for her family. And Rutland.* He battled down the unwanted stirrings of guilt. "What are the chances of all the women I could have met in the streets of Gipsy Hill that day was one who shared my love of Shelley's work?" Despising the pathetic guilt that pebbled at that lie, Nick dipped his head lower. "Though, I will be forthright in saying when I came today, I was unaware of the discussion taking place," he lied.

"You weren't?" Justina drew back, eyeing him with an unexpected and healthy modicum of wariness. Had the lady heard whispers of his reputation as a rogue? "Then, what brought you here this day, Your Grace? I expect you have a well-stocked library." Which suggested that she was not one of those peers whose family's library was as vast as their wealth.

"Nick," he reminded her. The lady followed his movements as he withdrew the book she'd gotten from The Circulating Library that he'd rescued from their first meeting. "I recovered this and merely came to return it when—"

Another young dandy swiveled in his chair. "Shh."

"—I saw you enter," he continued over the fuming man.

Justina accepted the book and their fingers brushed. Even through the fabric of their gloves, a sharp charge passed. Folding her arms around the leather volume, Justina looked to the front of the room once more. Nick could have returned both titles when he'd visited yesterday and yet he hadn't. It was a deliberate move on his part. Another carefully orchestrated meeting. Did the lady have the sense to wonder about it? Yes, his plans should be foremost in his mind and yet...

Unbidden, Nick's gaze went to that book she hugged close to her chest and his eyes went to the generous swell of her breasts that challenged her modest décolletage. An unexpected bolt of lust shot through him. The plan he devised had included wedding and eventually bedding this woman; and not necessarily in that respective order. Simpering, doe-eyed ladies had never held an appeal for him. He'd only sought women whose hearts were as empty as his own. As such, he'd not given thought to having Justina Barrett in his arms.

Until now.

Now, with the fool at the front of the room running on with the verses of Shelley's words, Nick stared at Justina with a potent need to lay her down and make her his for reasons beyond revenge, driven by a man's wanting. For the hunger raging through him, the lady attended the bewhiskered fellow at the front of the room with a singular attention that he was hard-pressed not to envy.

Despite the baroness' reports, Justina Barrett was not the pampered miss hungering for the highest title and fripperies. Rather, she had interests. Genuine interests that moved beyond the material; a rarity he'd believed didn't exist among the *ton*.

"Shelley, much as Byron, sees the perils in educating a woman." Ah, so they'd moved away from poetry and into a lecture on the poet himself. "Sees women rather," the older man looked pointedly at Justina, "as things of beauty to be revered and properly cared for, as all beautiful things are."

As those words resounded about the room, Nick attended Justina more closely while murmurings of agreement went around the scarce attendees present. The lady's lips tightened at the corner and if a woman could set fire with her eyes, the pompous bastard would be a pile of tinder at his podium.

"Shelley is *nothing* like Lord Byron," Justina challenged.

Silence rang in the small room and Nick looked to her. The wide-eyed young lady glanced about as though shocked by her own outburst.

And for the first time since Rutland had ruined his family, his lips twitched in an honest expression of mirth. The baroness and all the gossips in the whole of England had been wrong where Justina Barrett was concerned. There wasn't a thing fragile about her. No, she didn't fit with the words whispered in his ear by the baroness or written about in the papers. In crafting his scheme, it had been vastly easier to ruin a woman who didn't give a jot about anything beyond rank and wealth.

The lecturer opened and closed his mouth several times. "I beg your pardon?"

Justina's cheeks fired red and she glanced down at her tightly clasped fingers. "I…"

He'd been that hesitant person once. Silent, as Lord Rutland had infiltrated his home and Nick had stared at the heartless bastard, afraid to speak. Afraid to challenge. For the hatred he had and would always carry for that man, the marquess had liberated him in other ways that long-ago night. "Look at me," he commanded quietly and the lady shot her head up. "*Never* make apologies for who you are or what you have done," he said quietly.

Her breath hitched loudly. Such adoration spilled from her eyes that he was forced to look away. Something in this moment had become too real. For his encouragement hadn't been born of a desire to trap or trick, but rather a need to set her free from Society's constraints. He silently castigated himself for that dangerous slip that made more of their connection.

Justina looked to the lecturer and cleared her throat. "Mr. Shelley is a champion of Social justice for the lower classes. A man who once said, '*A husband and wife ought to continue united so long as they love each other. Any law which should bind them to cohabitation for one moment after the decay of their affection would be a most intolerable tyranny, and the most unworthy of toleration…*'" She turned her palms up. "As such, I believe Mr. Shelley would never dare speak against educating a woman." Her words were met with loud whisperings.

An unexpected appreciation for the lady he'd seen as nothing more than the Diamond the papers purported her to be gripped him. In this instance, he no longer knew what was game and what was real. "Brava, Miss Barrett," Nick whispered, in honest admiration for her clever retort.

The lecturer's gaunt cheeks flushed a mottled red. "Do you presume to know what Mr. Shelley believes about anything, my lady?"

At the condescending sneer on the man's lips, Nick narrowed his eyes and leveled him with a hard look. Rutland's relationship to the lady be damned. Before he'd landed the title duke, Nick himself had been the recipient of that same disdain. He'd not see this self-important prig cow this lady or anyone.

The man gulped audibly and glanced about.

Justina, however, tipped her chin up in an impressive display of spirit. "It is just… a man who is friends with a schoolmistress would certainly not look unkindly upon educated females." The lady required little help from him. And despite himself, she rose in his estimation.

"A schoolmistress?" the man repeated, his brow furrowed.

"Elizabeth Hitchener," she elucidated. "His confidant and the muse of his poem *Queen Mab*."

The lady was… a *bluestocking*. A new interest that moved beyond her relation to Lord Rutland awakened inside him. It stirred a long-forgotten, deeply-buried appreciation of learning and books. An appreciation he'd believed himself incapable of any longer for the course he'd charted in his life.

The old lecturer was unflinching in his debate. "Shelley's closest friend is, in fact, Lord Byron. And Lord Byron is quite clear on the roles of women, my lady." He looked to the other gentlemen scattered about the room, who nodded in a brotherly approval.

Justina's cheeks pinkened and she fell silent.

A muscle jumped at the corner of Nick's mouth.

With a pleased nod, the older man opened his mouth and proceeded to spew more nonsense.

By God, the stuffy prig at the podium wouldn't stifle her spirit. "Let us not forget," Nick called out loudly, interrupting the pompous fool. "Lord Byron also said those who will not reason are bigots, those who cannot are fools, and those who dare not are slaves. Lord Byron did not, however, differentiate men from women, lords from ladies or street urchins in his musings." His skin pricked with the heat of Justina's eyes on him.

Crimson color suffused the man's pale cheeks and he shuffled through his notes, mumbling to himself. With a thump on his podium, he adjourned his lecture to the polite applause of the attendees, and raced from the room as though his heels were on fire.

As the smattering of guests climbed to their feet and shuffled from the room, they cast annoyed looks at Justina. Then they left Nick and her—alone.

She fiddled with the book on her lap. "That was… You were…" she swiftly amended, "marvelous." A pleased smile turned her bow-shaped lips upward. "You *do* know Byron." A faint accusation rang there.

"I didn't claim to *not* know his work," he reminded her. "I merely claimed his poems were overinflated."

They shared a smile. And another kindred connection stirred for this woman who reminded him of a long-buried love of poetic works. Those he kept company with now were callow, empty shells of people, just as he'd allowed himself to become. He steeled his jaw. Nay, just as he'd been *forced* to become with the marquess' treachery.

Justina glanced back at the doorway. "I should leave," she said softly. She spoke as one who sought to talk herself into the action.

"You do not strike me, Justina, as a woman who does something simply because Society expects it of you." Nick stretched his legs out and looped them at the ankles.

"And yet, you are wrong," she said, fanning the pages of her book.

"Am I?" He propped his elbow on the back of her chair and angled himself so he stared directly at her. "Am I, when you went toe-to-toe with a pompous bastard who presumes to know more than you simply because of your gender?"

Most proper misses would have gasped and blushed at his frank speech. Instead, Justina Barrett proved herself remarkably different from those women, yet again. Setting her book down on the empty seat beside her, she put a question to him. "When did you begin reading poetry, Nick?"

Her sudden, unexpected inquiry held him momentarily frozen. How many days had he sat, a boy with reading spectacles perched on his nose, poring over poetry volumes, lost in the words on those pages? He couldn't even recall that level of innocence.

From the moment he'd sat down with his first tutor and been gifted Coleridge's works, he'd been lost to the power of words. "I was a boy." Had he ever been a child? Those days were so very long ago. "Eight," he murmured. A naïve lad, believing in the great capability of man and the power of love. Back when his family had been laughing and his sister smiling. "It was a poem by Coleridge." His gut clenched. How fleeting his happiness had been. "The happiness of life is made up of minute fractions…" he murmured in the quiet of the lecture room. The verse of Coleridge's work echoed around the chambers of his mind.

Why of all the damned women in the whole of the kingdom did Justina have to be bound to Rutland?

# CHAPTER 7

THERE WERE NO FEWER THAN three reasons that immediately sprang to mind as to why Justina should not be in this lecture hall, alone with Nick Tallings, the Duke of Huntly. One—they were alone without the benefit of a chaperone. Two—if they were discovered, there would be whispers and her eventual ruin. Three—he was a rogue.

And really only one reason that kept her fixed in her chair—she wanted to be here with him, now.

Wanted to be here, when logic and the rules laid out carefully by Society pointed to the folly in it, discussing poetry with him. When every last gentleman in this previously filled lecture room had listened to her talk and gawked at her as though she'd two heads and sprouted a third before their eyes, this man had not. Instead, he'd sat glaring at the lecturer at the front of the room and, with the faint glimmer in his blue eyes, urged her to freely share her mind.

In a world full of those who believed she was an empty-headed miss, Nick's approval was heady stuff, indeed. Yet... Justina glanced at the doorway that spilled out into the circulating room. Honoria and Gillian would be waiting. If they discovered her alone with Nick it would only fuel their suspicions of the man they called rogue.

Emotion darkened his eyes, filling those blue depths with such a bleak desolation that a chill went through her. All reason for her questioning escaped her. She fixed on that show of emotion. What caused that glimmer of darkness in a man who so easily wore a half-grin on his face?

Despite his open admiration, she did not often freely speak her opinions to all and, as such, perpetuated the same unimpressive opinions people had of her. She'd not been a particularly studious girl and hardly possessed the clear logic of her elder sister. Whereas Nick had been a boy of eight reading works she'd only discovered of late.

It was Nick who broke the easy, companionable silence, pulling her from her musings. "And when did you discover your love of literature, Justina?"

Her neck heated and she looked around the room, contemplating the great differences between her and Nick Tallings, the Duke of Huntly.

Justina picked up the volume of Shelley's poetry and held it out to him.

"I'm twenty," she began. What would he think when he discovered that they were less alike in this regard than he might believe?

Nick glanced at the copy a moment and then accepted it in his large, gloved fingers. He reached inside his jacket and withdrew a pair of spectacles. With one hand, he flicked them open and perched them on his nose.

Her heart caught. Those wire-rimmed frames added a realness to him. Oh, how easily she could imagine him seated beside her in a library, in a bucolic scene of husband and wife attending the same works.

He looked up from the book, questioningly, and her cheeks warmed.

Recalling her to the moment, Justina cleared her throat. "One day, I came here," she motioned about the room. "Well, not here, but the The Circulating Library because..." She grimaced. She'd not speak on the sorry state of her family's financial affairs. With her father's wastrel ways, there were no longer the funds for limitless purchases and certainly not the cost of a book.

"Because?" he quietly prodded, his penetrating stare one that threatened to pull out all the greatest hopes and darkest fears she carried.

"Because I sought a gothic novel," she substituted, offering him the truth of what had brought her here at the start of the little Season. "It is all I ever read."

"Do you believe there is shame in reading those works?" He spoke as one who tried to sort out the meaning behind her words. *Those works.* And a little piece of her heart slipped into his hands at the lack of condemnation in that inquiry.

Justina shook her head so quickly an ever-recalcitrant curl fell over her brow. She shoved it behind her ear. "Rather, it is the something that brought me here," she pointed to the floor. "To this room." Stealing a glance about and finding the hall was still their private sanctuary, she leaned closer. "There was a gentleman…" Though, with the exception of the Marquess of Tennyson's title and rank, there wasn't a thing gentlemanly about him. She tightened her mouth. A gentleman still hunting her, unyielding in his determination. Feeling Nick's gaze on her once more, she continued. "There is…*was* a gentleman pursuing me." He was always pursuing her. For reasons she did not understand, Lord Tennyson had set his sights upon her long before she'd even made her Come Out. When he knew nothing about her. He still knew nothing.

A low, primitive growl rumbled in Nick's chest and an odd lightness filled her at that protective response so unexpected in the males in her life. Her own father would throw her from Tower Bridge if the Marquess of Tennyson offered him the right amount. And her brother, though loving, didn't truly wish to be bothered with her. But for Edmund, there was no other…and his first priority was and always would be his wife.

"Who?" Nick gritted out.

She shook her head and dislodged the same curl. "It does not matter," she evaded, dodging his question. "But rather, it matters how I came to be here. My brother-in-law," *threatened my father*, "convinced my father I was not yet ready for a Season." Just like everyone else, Edmund had seen an empty-headed innocent in need of protecting. "While other ladies my age were making their Come Out, I was reading gothic novels." Those books she'd once lost sleep well into the night to read. "I'd come here and a…" She hardened her mouth. "*Gentleman* was pursuing me. In a bid to escape his attentions, I slipped into this room and sat over there." Justina pointed to the last seat in the far left corner; that spot she'd occupied all those months ago. "I was merely escaping." A coward in her actions that day. "I didn't come here to be enlightened or because of any keen intellect. And certainly not because I'm the spirited woman you took me for when I happened to speak my thoughts aloud." For she hadn't been. For nineteen years and a handful of months she'd been quite content to admire and long for nothing more than a bonnet or hat. "I went countless years," *too many*, "reading the same fairy tales and longing for pretty fripperies. I only stumbled upon Shelley by chance."

For a long while, Nick remained quiet. Then he shifted. The thin shellback chair groaned in protest of his broad, powerful frame. He dusted his knuckles down her cheek, eliciting delicious tingles at the point of contact. "It hardly matters how long it took for you to develop that appreciation, just that you did. Some of us are boys of eight, forever transformed," he said, brushing his hand back and forth in a whisper soft caress. Closing her eyes, she leaned into that seductive touch. "And some are young ladies just twenty." His words ran through her, lending a dangerous power to his touch.

Then he removed his hand and her eyes flew open as she mourned that loss. Except, he merely moved his attentions. Her lips parted on a whispered sigh as he captured her loose curl between his thumb and forefinger and gently rubbed. How was it possible for that action to warm her from the inside out, with the same heat of his caress?

She waded through the haze of desire. "Yet by your admission, you no longer read those works." What had led him to abandon his readings? Or had he, too, moved to a new interest that had taken the place of a once-great love? "You indicated that life killed the joy in those words."

A muscle ticked at the corner of his eye. "Is that a question?"

"Only if you answer."

He made an impatient sound and she thought he would not answer, but then he gave his head a shake. "Life intrudes. Oftentimes in different ways for different people. For you, it awakened you to a love of the poets and literary works. And for me, it intruded with responsibilities and expectations until there no longer exists time for such frivolities," he said, his voice hard with regret.

Justina leaned up, erasing the distance between them. "I do not believe a gentleman who knows Frances Burney's works and quotes Byron and Shelley with equal aplomb would ever dare believe literature is frivolous in nature." She braced for his rebuttal. Instead, the column of his throat worked, his eyes conveying a man at war with himself.

Footsteps sounded outside the room, followed by the sounds of two voices. Two familiar voices. Heart pounding, Justina jumped to her feet just as Gillian stepped inside.

"There you are…" Her words died as quickly as her smile as she moved her gaze from Justina to Nick as he unfurled to his full six-feet three-inches of raw masculinity. And then back to her. Gillian rounded her eyes.

Nick dropped a bow. "If you will excuse me?" He pocketed his spectacles. "I will leave you ladies to your pleasures."

A protest sprang to her lips and then withered. There was nothing proper in him being here. The rules of Society made his presence here not only an impossibility, but a dangerous one that could see her ruined. "Your Grace," she murmured, sinking into a curtsy. Justina rescued the volume. "You've forgotten your book," she murmured, holding it out.

He studied it for a long moment. And for an even longer one, she thought he'd reject that offering. Then with an in imperceptible nod, he accepted it in his long, graceful fingers, the same ones which only a moment ago had gently caressed her cheek. With long, powerful strides, Nick started for the door. The other lady hurriedly stepped out of his way and then he was gone.

When the two young ladies were alone, Justina wetted her lips. "He was merely here to select a book."

Gillian smiled. "I did not say anything." No, her eyes alone had conveyed the depth of her concern. "If Honoria did, however, note his presence here with you, then I expect she'd cancel her plans to visit your sister." Justina's stomach knotted. "Which is why," she said on a conspiratorial whisper, "it is best if we not mention anything to her." She followed her suggestion with a wink.

The words of thanks died on Justina's lips as Honoria rushed into the lecture room, breathless. "The Duke of Huntly was here."

"In here?" Gillian asked, puzzling her brow.

"Not in here." The lady threw her hands up in exasperation. "In the circulating room. I saw him taking his leave."

Justina nudged her chin up. "As a duke, I expect the gentleman can go anywhere." Even as she appreciated Honoria's loyalty, she did not appreciate being treated as though she did not know her own mind. She had lived with that low opinion since she was a girl with a frustrated governess.

"Gentlemen do not come to circulating libraries," Honoria snapped. "And most especially not dukes."

"Gentlemen are patrons, as well," Gillian pointed out helpfully.

For which Justina gave her a grateful smile.

"A duke would *not* come to a place that primarily offers gothic novels and romantic poetry."

Pity filled Justina. What had shaped Honoria into the cynical figure she'd become? "I believe it is a sad way to go through life, forming opinions and judgments on what a person should read, or where they should or should not visit, simply because of Society's perceptions," she said solemnly. After all, weren't those the same rigid constraints she herself had lived under as the label of Diamond she'd been hideously assigned? How often did the world expect her to act a certain way and be a certain thing just because Society's norms dictated it? "I will not pass judgment on a person simply because of what Society says of the gentleman, and most especially not when he's already only shown me the greatest kindness."

Honoria passed her gaze over Justina's face and then let out a long, slow sigh. "I do not want to see you hurt as your sister was."

"My sister is hopelessly in love with her husband," Justina pointed out, needing to remind the other woman that there was good in gentlemen, even if Honoria herself did not trust it or see it.

"Only after he hurt her," Honoria challenged, her words blanketing the room with tension.

"Honoria," Gillian chided, placing a hand on the other woman's arm.

"I am grateful to you and Gillian for taking me under your wings," Justina began.

"We are your friends," Gillian protested, a frown on her lips.

Justina gathered the other lady's hands. "I know. I also know Phoebe asked you to look after me, for which I am grateful. However, I will not allow myself to be hurt," she directed that pledge at Honoria.

Honoria worked her jaw. "You cannot control the actions of

others and, as such, you will not be able to protect yourself from hurt."

"Perhaps," Justina conceded. That lesson had, in fact, been handed down years earlier when she'd discovered just what manner of person her father was. "But neither will I build protective walls about my heart. Not when it would only deny me the possibility of knowing joy and love." For the ugliness in her father's soul, there was good in Andrew. And Phoebe. And Edmund.

And in Nick.

"Come," Gillian urged. Eager to be done defending her decisions, Justina started forward.

"Justina?" Honoria called out, staying her.

She glanced back.

"Mayhap the duke only came to return your book," Honoria conceded. "But what would he have been doing at Gipsy Hill when you were there?"

Justina frowned. Beyond the romanticism of his rescue and the chaos of that day, she'd not truly considered what had brought Nick to Lambeth.

Despite Honoria's wariness, only one question held her focus: would she see the gentleman again to find out?

TUGGING ON HIS GLOVES, NICK exited The Circulating Library and searched for his carriage.

His meeting with Justina Barrett had been a success in all the ways that mattered. The lady had been properly seduced with words and shared interests. Yet, instead of the thrill of victory, his body burned with the remembered hunger of her kiss. Locating his conveyance down the way on the opposite end of Lambeth, he started forward.

When he'd crafted his plan to break her heart and destroy all the Barretts, he'd been singularly fixed on his goals of revenge against Rutland. He'd not given thought to who Justina Barrett was. As such, he'd never expected to feel anything for the young lady.

Now, following their exchange in the library and all their previous encounters before, he was riddled with not only a desire for her, but intrigue. The self-centered girl, with a head for nothing more than bonnets and baubles as had been presented in the information he'd obtained about her, didn't fit with the woman he'd just left. A woman who wrote her own verses and attended lectures and challenged old, angry, and male scholars.

He frowned, despising the disquiet that came with that truth. It shouldn't matter what books she read or what dreams she might have. Only her connection to the Devil who'd destroyed all those he loved was relevant. Nick wound his way through the carts until they thinned and then reached his carriage.

His driver hovered at the edge of the door and he waved him off. "Your Grace," the servant said in gravelly tones. The man glanced about, nervousness in his eyes, and then tipped his chin toward the carriage door.

Nick followed the man's gaze and gave him a questioning look. The driver nodded. Tensing, Nick moved deliberately around the other side of the pavement and pulled the door open.

The baroness sat in the corner of the carriage in an elegant gold cloak. She pushed her hood further back and gave him a hard smile. "I've missed you, my love," she whispered.

By God, the lady was mad. Or tenacious. Mayhap both. Swallowing a curse, Nick climbed inside and quickly yanked the door closed. "What in blazes are you doing here?" he gritted out, assessing the red velvet curtains to ascertain they were properly drawn. One of the conveniences of his partnership with this viper had been her banishment to the countryside by her doddering husband.

The baroness pouted. "Oh, poo, Huntly. That is hardly a greeting for a lover." Given the furious glint in her brown eyes, this was not the moment to remind her he'd severed that connection.

Her presence in his carriage, if discovered, would prove calamitous to his goals. He rapped on the ceiling once and the conveyance lurched forward. "What do you want?" he demanded in clipped tones.

She narrowed her eyes and leaned forward. "I saw you with her."

Nick stilled. He took in the tense lines at the corners of her full mouth. The fury radiated from her expressive gaze. Frustration with his own carelessness gripped him. He'd been so fixed on Justina Barrett that he'd heard nothing and seen no one other than the lady. *And it was not your quest for revenge that held you captive.* He thrust back that taunting voice. "Then you saw me in the midst of our plan," he said at last.

The baroness scoffed. "You did not seem to be a gentleman pretending, Huntly," she spat. "I saw how you looked at her."

He folded his arms at his chest. "And just what do you believe you saw, madam?" he countered with deliberately bored tones. All the while, he remained coiled like a snake.

The baroness' lower lip trembled. "You care for her."

Care for her? Nick blinked slowly. He'd known Justina Barrett but a handful of meetings, and the baroness believed he cared for the young lady? Why it was…laughable. Or it would be, if the woman seated across from him wasn't burning him with the hatred in her eyes. "I do not care for anyone," he said tightly. It was a lie. He cared for his sister, his niece, and Chilton, but those were people whose lives had been joined to his and who would forever have his loyalty and regard.

"Then desire her," she challenged, with spirit restored in her previously dejected features.

He remained silent. With her blonde ringlets and always cheerfully smiling lips and eyes, Justina was unlike any woman he'd ever hungered for before. Now, he very much hungered after the young lady.

"You'll not deny it," the baroness cried softly.

"I owe you nothing," he reminded her sharply. "We have been joined for one purpose and that is the only bond that exists between us still."

"But there can be more," she promised him on a breathy whisper. In one fluid movement, she shrugged off her cloak, revealing a diaphanous gown. The dampened satin clung to her skin, revealing the outline of her generous breasts. Her rouged nipples peeked over the top, momentarily drawing his attention. "I want you to make love to me again," she beckoned, trailing a finger over her décolletage. "I want it so badly, I've braved London and discovery for it."

At one time, he would have been driven with lust by the sight of that offering. Now, after Justina's pure innocence and beauty, there was nothing but a repugnance for the desperate creature before him. "You've also braved ruining all our plans for Rutland. Cover yourself, madam," he ordered. "I'll not tell you again. We are through." Color flooded the lady's cheeks. "Are we clear, my lady?" he demanded.

She tightened her lips. "Abundantly. But let us be clear about something else, Huntly." The lady leaned forward and the pungent scent of roses slapped at his senses. "If you do not follow through on this plan, if you do not ruin Rutland's family, I will see *you* ruined."

By the fire snapping in her eyes, that pledge was driven by more than revenge… something more… something equally danger-ous—*jealousy*.

"You've no worries there," he coldly assured her. Had Lord Rut-land not have ruined his father and Nick's life had continued as it had, with him as the bookish boy with a love for the lecture room, he might have had something more with Justina Barrett. But her brother-in-law had shattered that pathetic child he'd been.

He firmed his jaw. Ultimately, he may desire Justina and have an unexpected appreciation for her mind, but there would never be anything more with her. Ever.

And he was glad for that reminder.

# CHAPTER 8

THE FOLLOWING AFTERNOON, NICK STUDIED the open ledgers before him. With a sigh, he removed his spectacles and set them aside. In truth, he'd been studying his books for the better part of the morn as well.

He squeezed the bridge of his nose. Having at last set into motion his plans for revenge against Rutland, the door to his past had been opened. Through the years, the marquess had never been far from his thoughts. However, that powerful peer had existed more as an amorphous demon than anything; a demon who'd shaped him. Molded him in his hardened image, so that he'd developed a strength to, at last, defeat the black-hearted Devil.

Never had vengeance been closer than it was now with the Barrett siblings. Yet, only one of those individuals commanded his focus—Miss Justina Barrett.

The baroness' accusations haunted him. Care for Justina Barrett. He hardly knew that lady. Except, a stolen exchange in a quiet lecture hall lingered in his thoughts. He'd not read a verse in thirteen years. More specifically, he'd not wanted to read a verse in thirteen years—until her.

Part of the plan he'd concocted had involved wooing Justina. Trapping her with pretty words and winning her heart with empty endearments. Yet, God help him, with every exchange, his attention to his plan faded as she forced him to think about and talk about things that had once mattered to him.

Books and poetry and literary works. Those useless pages that Rutland had sneered at him for reading, all those years ago. What joy or escape could those books bring, when he'd seen the ugliness that was life? When he'd witnessed the depth of evil and the absolute hopelessness.

That night had proven the single most formative moment of his existence, more so than all the thousands to come before it. It had marked the end of his and his sister's innocence; the death of dreams and happiness, and the beginning of reality.

Having borne witness to his sister's despair with her miserable marriage and Chilton's transformation on the battlefields of Europe, to his own shift in humanity, Nick had come to accept as fact the truth that innocence was inevitably shattered. It was what had made his involvement of Justina in his plans not only palpable but the obvious course.

What he'd not allowed himself to rationalize through, until his meeting with the lady, was that he would be the one to shatter it. After the reason for his courtship was discovered, would the lady, too, lose her love of the literary word and view the world with her own jaded eyes? For once his revenge had been enacted, she would hate him with the same vitriol he did Rutland.

Why had he not thought of that before? *Because she previously only existed as a name upon the scandal sheets.* Now, she was a young lady with wants and interests and desires that very much matched those he'd also once appreciated.

"Don't be a bloody fool," he muttered under his breath. Why should it matter whether her romantic spirit was crushed? That would only make the revenge against Rutland all the sweeter. *Wouldn't it?*

The small copy of Shelley's works she'd gifted him sat at the corner of his desk, a glaring, mocking reminder of her goodness against his evil. Tightening his mouth, he jammed his spectacles back on his nose and scoured the pages of his ledgers. All the while, he ignored the leather volume.

Or rather, attempted to.

The temptation to pick it up as great as an apple in the Devil's hand. Mayhap Rutland had been correct, after all, and Nick was, in fact, weak. With a curse, he swiped the small leather-bound

pocket book of poems and yanked open his desk drawer. He made
to throw it inside and then froze. Looking to the closed door, he
slowly returned the volume to his desktop and stared down at the
leather volume, warring with himself.

Drawing in a deep breath, he flipped through the old copy. Aged
by time, the pages having been dog-eared and bent, he fanned
through them. The sun's rays cut through the crack in the curtains
and cast a soft light on the yellowed pages.

He stopped fanning the pages and his gaze lingered on the verses
there. *"…A poet is a nightingale, who sits in darkness and sings to cheer
its own solitude with sweet sounds…"*

Rubbish and rot, the whole of it. Romantic words of dreamers
who gave people false hopes of life and love. And yet… he continued reading. Turning page after page, losing himself in verses he'd
never before read because Shelley's works had come long after he
had abandoned his love of literature.

He read until his neck ached and his eyes blurred. He read until
he was very much that boy of long ago, with a voracious hunger
that could only be quenched by the power of the written word.

A knock sounded at the door and he shot his head guiltily up
just as his butler opened it, admitting his sister.

"Her Ladyship, the Countess of Dunkirk," he announced and
then took his leave.

Neck heating, Nick hastily snapped the book closed and jumped
to his feet. "Cecily."

"Nick." She folded her arms at her chest and stared expectantly
at him.

Why was she here? She started forward and he rushed around
the desk, positioning himself between her line of vision and the
book.

Cecily stopped and eyed him suspiciously. "Is everything all
right?"

"Yes." No. He itched to drag his fingers through his hair. Nothing had been right since he'd knocked Justina out of the way of a
runaway horse. "Would you care to sit?" he asked, motioning to a
chair.

She made to sit, and he discreetly slid a ledger over Shelley's
works. Cecily sighed. "Dominick," she began. "First, do you truly
believe I didn't notice that you were reading a volume of poetry

when I entered?"

Of course, she'd noticed. He yanked at his cravat. To conceal the flush rushing up his neck and burning his cheeks, he strode around the desk and fetched himself a snifter. "Is that a question?"

*...Only if you answer...*

Justina's sweet, lyrical tones rang around his memory. He grabbed the nearest bottle and poured himself a glass of brandy. Thought better of it and filled it to the rim.

When he turned back, his sister stared on.

"I wouldn't begrudge you finding amusement in poems," Cecily said quietly, a faint accusation there. "Quite the opposite. The day you ceased reading, it was as though the person I knew as my brother ceased to be."

He ignored the pang those last words struck. "I was not finding enjoyment in it," he gritted out the lie. Poems and books were for young boys who'd not been scarred by life. They were not for heartless, soulless bastards such as him.

"Fine, then," she said. "At the very least reading it. You've been so consumed in amassing your great fortune and power, and triumphing over Lord Rutland, that you've lost who you once were."

He stared blankly down into the contents of his glass. He'd been lost for so very long there was no way back to who he'd been.

"I've read the reports about your meeting with Miss Barrett."

At her accusatory tone, Nick carefully schooled his features. He'd not debate this with her any further.

Cecily dragged her chair closer, scraping it along the hardwood floor. "Do you truly think I'm so naïve that I'd believe your heroic rescue and subsequent courtship of Lord Rutland's sister-in-law is a mere coincidence?" A courtship. A pretend one, at that. And yet, that was just how the world was *supposed* to see it.

It didn't matter what she believed. Or it shouldn't. Except, he glanced away, unable to meet the disappointment radiating from her eyes.

"I long ago accepted there is a darkness in Lord Rutland. But you are different, Nick. You were a studious boy. You enjoyed your books and your family..." She glanced pointedly down at the partially concealed copy of Shelley's work. "You still do."

"A boy."

She cocked her head.

"You are correct. I was a boy." He'd since grown into a man capable of dark deeds.

Cecily leaned back in her chair and layered her arms to the side. "I do not know what your intentions are toward Miss Barrett, but I do know, in coming upon you here and finding you reading again, mayhap it cannot be all bad, your meeting the lady."

His sister was wrong, proving a far greater naiveté than she'd earlier discredited. "Is that why you've come then? To inquire as to my intentions for Miss Barrett?" At stating her name aloud and his veiled plans for her to his sister, the muscles of his stomach contracted.

Her eyes twinkled. "If I thought you might truthfully answer me, then yes. You promised Felicity a ride in the park."

Nick flared his eyes and glanced to the clock.

"Nor do I ever recall you forgetting an appointment."

Because he didn't. He was precise and methodical and logical and never distracted, certainly not by maudlin thoughts of the past or by poetry books handed him by tempting sirens. He dragged a hand through his hair. "Forgive me. I…" Had no excuse that did not include Justina's name.

His sister slowly rose. "I trust you are incapable of truly hurting that young woman." She held his gaze squarely. "Or any other."

Five days ago, he would have sneered at her naïve faith.

Now, he remained silent and Cecily sighed. "Come," she said, the disappointment in her tone matching her eyes. "Felicity awaits with her nursemaid. There will be time enough later to speak about the lady who commands all your attentions."

Nick tried to tell himself his sister saw more than was there with hopeful eyes, he'd believed long ago jaded. He tried to tell himself that she saw good around her, still, and, as such, was blinded to who he, in fact, was. Only, as he followed her reluctantly from the room, he conceded, at least silently and only to himself, that Justina had woven some inexplicable spell over him.

IN THIS PRECISE MOMENT, JUSTINA could not write a single word.

And usually, she couldn't write a word because she was so fixed on selecting the right words, that nothing ever found its way onto the page. Today, she couldn't for entirely different reasons.

Seated on a blanket at the edge of the Serpentine River, her gaze snagged upon a pair in the distance, or more precisely, one gentleman. Setting aside her writing box, she scooted sideways on her buttocks to the shelter provided by an enormous boulder. She stretched out on her stomach and plucked the revealing blanket to safety.

"My lady?" her maid called out questioningly. Justina held a silencing finger to her lips, immediately quelling the concerned servant's words. Widening her eyes, Marisa hurriedly joined her. "Is everything all right, Miss Barrett?"

"Oh, quite," she said as conversationally as if they spoke about the fine spring weather they now enjoyed. Pressing herself tight to the boulder, she continued her study.

The Duke of Huntly came to a stop more than fifty paces away and snapped a blanket open. It caught briefly in the wind before settling upon the ground. His head came up and, with her heart racing, she quickly darted hers back behind the rock.

She was a debutante just out several months ago, but even she knew gentlemen did not visit Hyde Park at the early dawn hour for anything other than an early morning ride or a wicked assignation. And there was no horse about and one stunningly flawless blonde-haired beauty at his side.

Surely it didn't count as spying on a gentleman if she just happened to be at the same place, at the same time. And she just happened to *notice* him. Justina counted her rapid pulse beats and then peeked around the boulder, once more.

The pair stood, speaking.

She bit her lower lip hard. Who was the lovely woman? Gentlemen didn't meet women, alone, in Hyde Park. Not at this hour. Nor at any hour. And on the heel of that, an ugly kernel of jealousy knotted low in her belly. She hugged her writing box all the harder, so that the wood bit painfully into her chest.

A loud laugh echoed in the morning quiet. Shifting the burden in her arms, she leaned around once more...and her breath caught.

A small child hurtled through the grass, a nursemaid trailing at her heels. The young duke caught the girl with flaxen curls in his arms and hefted her high into the air.

His face, unguarded, revealed a tenderness and love that left her immobile. The sign of that devotion and easy teasing between them that Justina would have traded her soul on Sunday for. Was the girl an illegitimate child and the lovely woman Nick's mistress? Just then, the duke spun the child in a dizzying circle and from across the length dividing them, their eyes caught.

She jerked, feeling like one of those poor creatures her father and brother were forever hunting at their country estate and with the same amount of grace as those just-felled creatures. Justina pitched forward, coming down hard on her case with a loud grunt. Pain shot through her and she welcomed the stinging distraction. *Bloody hell.*

Mayhap he'd not seen her. Mayhap, the lovely lady at his side had failed to note—

"Oh, dear, Miss Barrett, are you all right?" Marisa cried.

Justina swallowed the inventive curse that her brother had imparted several years ago. For if the duke hadn't by some miracle from above witnessed her humiliation, he'd certainly hear it now.

"Miss…" her maid urged, frantically searching about.

The crunch of gravel on the empty walking path and fast-approaching heavy footfalls pierced her swiftly-growing horror. "Miss Barrett…"

They'd reverted once more to formalities, which was all a bit of a contradiction given Justina lay sprawled on her stomach with her buttocks jutting in the air. She stared at the crisp, green grass underneath her nose and, though she'd never been the praying sort, silently prayed for intervention from above.

"I believe she hit her head, Your Grace," Marisa's worried supposition earned a small groan. "She's not…"

"I've not hurt my head." *Only my pride.* Justina shoved away from the dratted box and into a kneel. "I assure you, I'm quite all—" Her words ended on a squeak as Nick captured her about her waist and guided her to her feet. She'd long mourned her plump form, but with Nick's effortless movements, he made her feel as dainty as those ladies she'd always wished to be. Too soon, he removed his hand from her person and the heat of his touch lingered. "Thank you," she said, wincing at the breathless quality of her words. Which was madness given his presence here with another woman. A fortunate other woman. "Please," she said on a rush. "Do not allow me to take you from your...company."

His company who even now walked this way, the flawless beauty and the golden child skipping at her side. Another vicious wave of jealousy gripped her.

"My company?" He followed Justina's gaze and then smiled. "What greater pleasure could there be than an unexpected meeting with you here today?" he put to her. He proved far more capable than any of the master poets combined, for his words stirred her heart even as her mind attempted to muddle through that boldness in the presence of the approaching pair.

They came upon her and Nick, and Justina's maid retreated several steps. "Miss Barrett, allow me to introduce you to my—"

"Hullo," the small girl interrupted with a gap-toothed smile. With her olive-hued coloring and the blindingly bright shade of her hair, the child may as well have been a girl-child replica of Nick. "I am Felicity."

Felicity. A name of happiness that conjured joy. With the girl's smile, it perfectly suited her. "Hullo," Justina returned quietly, attempting to puzzle through the pairing.

"—my niece, Felicity," Nick supplied.

She was a niece! Justina's heart jumped in her breast and she swung her gaze to the quiet woman at Nick's side. This must be...a sister. A giddy sense of relief danced in her chest.

"How do you know my uncle Dominick?" Felicity wondered, tugging at her hand.

The child widened the door of her connection to this man before her. *Uncle Dominick.* Justina's ownership of his whole name intensified the intimacy of their connection. "Your uncle..." She lifted her eyes briefly to Nick's. "Saved me from a runaway horse."

His niece gasped and shot an accusatory look at her uncle. "You did not tell me you had done anything heroic."

The duke ruffled the top of the girl's hair. "Hardly heroic, poppet. Just gentlemanly."

He was wrong. There had been a street filled with gentlemen and not a single one had rushed to the aid of her or that child.

Nick returned his attention to the lady at his side. "And my sister, Cecily, the Countess of Dunkirk. Cecily, may I present, Miss Barrett."

Justina sank into a belated curtsy. "My lady."

The woman smiled. "It is a pleasure." By the dimple in the lovely lady's cheek, she could almost believe it, and yet there was a strain to that grin that matched so many of the false smiles her own mother donned through life. What accounted for the lack of joy there? Disapproval?

"Were you playing hide and seek?" Felicity piped in. At her back, Marisa made a choking sound that sounded very nearly like a laugh.

Justina curled her toes into the soles of her boots.

"If so, I would dearly love to play. I've just Uncle Dominick to play with and he only comes but twice a week to visit." The duke visited his sister and niece twice weekly. All of Society took the gentleman as a rogue, but a chance meeting with a child who prattled like Justina herself had revealed that he was something else—a loving brother and uncle.

The warmth suffusing her heart spread.

Felicity frowned at her uncle. "Except he has been missing for nearly a fortnight, away—"

"I expect the lady was not playing hide and seek," Nick said abruptly.

His niece furrowed her brow. "She *might* have been, though. She was ducking behind the boulder."

*Oh, please let the earth open and swallow me whole.* "I was attempting to write," Justina said weakly. That was vastly safer than the whole I-was-watching-you-with-your-uncle business.

The countess gave her brother a pointed look that Justina would have to be blind not to see. "Then, we should allow the young lady to her writing."

CECILY'S DISAPPROVAL COULD NOT BE greater than had she climbed herself into the oak tree beside them and shouted the words into the empty park.

Concern had lit her eyes the moment she'd gleaned Miss Barrett's identity. Given his intentions to woo, win, and destroy the lady, his fortuitous meeting with Justina Barrett was surely the fates way of nudging him on to the path of victory over Rutland. But God help him, the minute he'd caught her peeking out from behind that boulder, he'd been transfixed, so that the last person or thought he'd had was of Lord Rutland...or anyone else.

"Would you care to join us, Miss Barrett?"

The lady flared her pretty blue eyes, and looked between him and Cecily. Had she detected his sister's disapproval? If so, she could not know that all disappointment was reserved for him. "Oh, I would not wish to intrude—"

"My uncle is a writer," Felicity happily announced.

Justina blinked wildly. "Is he?"

Nick tugged at his cravat. "I would hardly call myself a writer," he said truthfully. At one time, he'd aspired to it. Long ago, he'd abandoned his scholarly pursuits and traded them over for lessons and a life of treachery. The only verses or sentences he drafted now were ones for children—his only niece.

As though he'd not protested, Felicity nodded excitedly. "He is quite wonderful, isn't he, Mama?"

Justina's eyes went soft.

And with the unintended aid of his beloved niece, Nick would wager he'd earned another sliver of the lady's heart. And in this fleeting moment, a courtship built on deception felt all too real. He battled back the disquiet churning in his gut.

Cecily alternated her stare between him and Justina before settling on him. "Indeed," she said grudgingly, pleading with her eyes. "My brother once favored his books above all else."

Ignoring her silent appeal, he gathered Justina's writing case and held out an arm. The lady hesitated and then placed her fingertips on his sleeve. He guided her to the blanket he'd abandoned moments earlier.

Felicity broke the tension left by Cecily's annoyance. "What were you writing?" she asked as they reached the previously abandoned blanket.

"Felicity," his sister chided.

"No, it is quite all right," Justina urged. Disentangling her arm from Nick's, she fell to a knee beside the girl. "I was *attempting* to write a poem." She dropped her voice to an exaggerated whisper. "I'm rather rubbish at it." She lifted twinkling eyes to his and winked.

He blinked slowly at the unfettered lightness in their crystalline depths. Since he'd ascended to the title of duke, he'd had debutantes, dowagers, and ladies of the demimonde all throw themselves at his proverbial feet for nothing more than his title. Not a single one of them had ever had a smile reach their eyes.

"...Isn't that right, Uncle Dominick?" Felicity's inquiry yanked him back from the maddening spell Justina Barrett had weaved.

"I...uh..." Hadn't a single bloody idea what was right or wrong, in this moment.

Justina cocked her head.

"I *saiiiiid*," Felicity said in an exaggerated drawl, "since you are *friends* with the lady, that you could read her one of your verses." Friends with the lady? And with Justina Barrett blushing and his niece innocently believing his intentions could only ever be honorable, Nick felt something he didn't wish to feel, an unwanted, unpleasant emotion that only confused him—shame.

As his niece continued to sing his undeserved praise, he shifted, suddenly wishing he'd adhered to propriety and wanting distance between himself and Justina. Her sitting alongside his family, the people who mattered to him above all others, created this artificial bond that would never be. Could never be given his intentions for her own family. And what was more, there would be an additional bond he severed when he saw his plan through. It was a detail he'd not considered—until now. *What else did I not think through?* Nick balled his hands.

"Tell her one of the poems you wrote for me," Felicity implored, drawing him back from the tumult of his thoughts.

He coughed into his hand. "I'm certain Miss Barrett would rather not hear my paltry attempt at—"

"But I would," Justina blurted.

Felicity clapped. "Please, please. Tell her the one about night-time."

Grinning, Justina urged him on with her eyes.

"Oh, very well. I will tell you," Felicity groused with a roll of her eyes.

*"Shadows dancing, moon a'glowing. Nighttime creatures call.*

*Man is slumbering, and the earth is celebrating the peace that comes, only when darkness, at last falls."*

Justina clapped her hands. "That is lovely," she said softly, holding his gaze.

Disconcerted, Nick forced a grin. Other than for Felicity, he'd neither penned nor shared a single verse. Not since that day Rutland had paid a visit and his father had hanged himself for it. That stark reminder ushered in a familiar cold.

"Uncle Dominick wrote it for me," Felicity explained. "When I began having nightmares about—"

"A walk," Cecily squeaked, surging to her feet.

Three pairs of eyes went to her, Felicity's filled with confusion. "Mama?" Of course, as a child of seven, she had yet to learn not to bare secrets to anyone. In time, she would. Eventually, life jaded them all.

"Let us go pick flowers," his sister said, gentling her tone.

Excitement immediately replaced the child's befuddlement and she hopped up. With a final wave for Justina, mother and daughter walked off, leaving them alone.

Together, they stared after them. Justina drew her knees to her chest and looped her arms about them. "She is lovely."

She was an image of the person Cecily had been before life had left her broken. Unnerved by Justina's effortless move into his life, Nick turned his focus to the writing box. The sun's rays cast a soft light upon her heart-shaped face. "Most ladies sneaking about the parks only do so with scandalous intentions," he whispered temptingly, coming closer. His body burned at her nearness and he dropped his gaze to her lips. *I am going to kiss her. I am going to kiss her here in Hyde Park in view for everyone to see, in a move that has nothing to do with the Marquess of Rutland.* Where was the dread and panic that thought should bring?

Justina waggled her eyebrows. "I am not most ladies," she rejoined on a loud whisper that cut across this mad haze of desire.

His lips tugged at the corner and the tension went out of his broad shoulders. "No. You are not." In so many ways. Ways that had nothing to do with her status as Rutland's sister-in-law and everything to do with her spirit and wit. Fear over this inexplicable pull turned his mouth dry. Where was the strength he'd prided himself on these past thirteen years? In a bid for control, he turned the subject. "Tell me, what is the verse that has you so stumped, Miss Barrett?" he managed gruffly.

"Your niece indicated you are a poet," she countered.

Couldn't she be one of those ladies who only wished to speak about herself? She was clever. She was modest. She was a damned conundrum in every way. Unnerved, he patted his hand along the side of his leg. "I'm hardly a poet."

"But you write?" she pressed, unrelenting. Again with her questioning, proving the lies Marianne had gathered about the lady. Justina was no self-absorbed miss, eager to talk only of herself and her accomplishments.

He ceased his distracted tapping. Personal revelations about himself and his past had no place here. And yet… "I was," he murmured, looking out. As a boy he'd hovered at a dwindling flame into the early morn hours, capturing his own verses. "Not any longer," he said, feeling her gaze on him.

"Why did you stop?"

The wind whipped at his hat and he took it between his hands, beating it against his opposite palm. He stared into the distance where Felicity played alongside her mother, seeing in the child his sister as she'd been long ago. Before life interfered. Before their happiness had been shattered. "Because life happened," he said quietly, more to himself. "And eventually, the words just stopped coming." His skin pricked with the feel of her gaze on him.

"*What* happened—?"

"Uh-uh," he cut in, killing the question on her lips. He'd not allow her in, any more than he already had. It was too dangerous— for the both of them. "My turn. Which verse has you so stuck?"

Justina nibbled her lip as though she wished to say more. With a sigh, she layered her cheek atop her knees. "All of them," she muttered.

Setting aside his hat, Nick stretched his legs out before him and then hooked them at the ankles. He cast her a sideways look.

"I also haven't written anything," she conceded. "But where you were once able to write verse and can still manage them for your niece, I simply stare at the page and jot down ideas."

Since he'd been thrust into Polite Society two years earlier, he'd chafed at the falseness of the lords and ladies. Those same people that Nick and his family had been invisible to. The ladies were stilted and brittle. The lords, diffident and insincere. Then, there was this woman. He would have preferred Rutland's sister-in-law to be like everyone else. It would be easier to maintain a wall of indifference toward her.

*Alas…*

"It must be joy and you are making it work. As long as you see it as so, then you'll never have any words to write."

"Is that what it became for you?"

She was tenacious. "No more questions about why I stopped writing." Nick grabbed her writing box and flipped open the top. Withdrawing a sheet of parchment, a crystal inkwell, and a pen, he set up a makeshift desk.

Justina scooted closer to him, her eyes taking in his every movement. A light spring breeze pulled at the corner of the parchment and he layered it to the surface. Her fingers shot out to hold down the corners for him as she peered around his shoulder.

"What do you find joy in?" he asked.

"Reading," she said instantly.

*Books.* And here, everything he'd gleaned from the baroness had touted Justina Barrett as one with a love of pretty bonnets and ribbons. What else had they failed to correctly gather about the young woman? Shoving aside the worrying thought, he stared expectantly at her.

"My sister, Phoebe," she added. He froze. Rutland's wife. Ice shot through his veins as he forced his fingers to still and he wrote down that hated name. "As well as my brother, Andrew. My mother." It did not escape his notice that she carefully left her father off that list. Deservedly so.

Nick studied the concise but telling list, gathering one overwhelmingly clear truth about Justina—her family mattered to her. It was a bond between them that he didn't want. It had been far easier to plot their destruction when he'd seen them as nothing more than pieces upon a chessboard. Now, the Barretts were real. Too real. Loyal and loving, and about to be destroyed by him. *I should find a thrill at that thought.* Where was it? Why did it feel, then, like a boulder had been dropped on his chest and was weighting him down?

"There is also my brother-in-law, Edmund," Justina added. Nick unfurled his hands feeling burned by that page.

It was the Devil's reminder, a necessary one. "Look to the emotions your family evokes and write to that," he said, his voice coming harsher than he intended. Nick hurriedly retrieved her sheet and turned it over. Then he shifted the desk from his lap. With stiff, jerky movements, he returned the instruments to their proper place inside. "As my sister said, I should allow you to your writing, madam."

Did he imagine the flash of disappointment in her revealing eyes? Would she feel that same regret if she knew of his association with her beloved brother-in-law? "Of course," she murmured, and he helped her to her feet.

With Justina at his side, he carried her writing box back to the spot she'd previously occupied. "Miss Barrett," he murmured after he'd set her desk down on the spread blanket.

"Your Grace," she returned, sinking into a flawless curtsy.

He searched his gaze over her face a moment and regret tightened his chest; regret that life had ordained their future together long ago as one riddled with darkness.

With a final bow, he left her, hating that allegiance she carried for Lord Rutland.

# CHAPTER 9

AFTER JUSTINA'S ENTRANCE INTO SOCIETY, she'd found herself courted by gentlemen with little interest in her beyond the possible arm ornament she might make. From that moment, she had not looked forward to a single *ton* event—until now.

As her father's carriage slowly rolled through the crowded streets of London with her father and brother seated on the opposite bench, she stared out the window. Her mind was occupied by thoughts of Nick.

He was a poet. He was a gentleman who encouraged her to find her own words and speak her own mind. Her heartbeat sped up. No one, not even her beloved siblings, had seen more in her than a whimsical miss. Where Polite Society had very specific expectations of and for a lady, expectations that they embroider and paint stunningly boring floral arrangements, Nick had proven wholly unlike any other man she'd ever known.

Questions lingered in her mind about the enigmatic duke who'd once written...and then stopped. *...Life happened...* What had he meant—?

"Tennyson will be in attendance, gel," her father boomed from the opposite bench. Justina jumped as he slashed into her musings.

She was surely the only lady in the realm whose father was uninterested in the possibility of securing a duke for a son-in-law. "I'll not have you skirting the gentleman, this time," he went on, scratching at the paunch that bulged over his too-tight, purple pantaloons.

Andrew gave her a sympathetic look and she ignored it. She'd little use for his pitying glances. Actions and words were far more potent and she'd use them to save herself. "I've told you before, I've no interest in marrying Lord Tennyson," she informed him, proud of the steady rebuttal. All her life, she'd been meek and biddable. Nick had helped her find her voice.

Her sire flared his nostrils. "Is this because of your silly thoughts about Huntly?"

Her cheeks blazed. For a man who'd proven such a lackwit in so many ways, how very accurately he came to that supposition. "I don't know what you're talking about," she managed, weakly. She'd always been a rotted liar, incapable of artifice. "I'd never marry Lord Tennyson regardless of my exchange with the duke." That was, at the very least, steeped in truth.

"Your exchange?" He scoffed. "He pushed you out of the way of a runaway carriage—"

"Horse," she gritted out. A father who couldn't even be bothered with the details of her near death. "It was a horse." She'd not sully their last exchange in the park by sharing it with this man.

"It was more than that, Father," Andrew added helpfully from beside him. "Very heroic stuff."

"Bah, horse, carriage, it matters not." No, because, ultimately, she'd never truly mattered. *Ever*. Not beyond the match he might make with her. She hated the stabbing pain that reminder still had the power to inflict. Her father raked a methodical stare over her. "I don't owe Huntly a pence." And the gentleman rose all the more in her estimation for it. "The man cannot do a thing to erase my debt to Tennyson." Or any other man. The viscount mopped at his perspiring brow. "Either way," he barked, "rogues like Huntly don't wed chits like you. You want Huntly? Then make him your lover after you wed Tennyson."

"Father," Andrew said sharply over Justina's gasp.

"Mind your business, boy," their father snapped, earning a blush from his son. "Or I'll use you to make a match," he threatened. "Cut you off unless you find a lady with a fat dowry."

All the color leeched from Andrew's skin and his throat worked.

"That is better," Father said with a grunt. He nudged his chin so quickly in Justina's direction, his jowls jiggled. "I'll not speak to you again about Tennyson. Are we clear?"

A breathtaking hatred stole through her, gripping into her like vicious talons at the unneeded reminder of their father's ruthlessness. What manner of depraved father spoke so crudely to and about his own children? Mayhap five days ago, she would have given a weak nod. Mayhap looked to her brother for his intervention, once more. Looked to Edmund or her sister for help.

In a handful of days, however, it was as though she'd been set free from the gilded cage her father was so very determined to keep her trapped within. ...*Never make apologies for who you are or what you have done...* She seethed. "I will *never* marry a gentleman because you order it and certainly not to aid you in any way."

Andrew's mouth fell open and he alternated his wide-eyed stare between father and daughter.

After years of being the proper, demure daughter, she'd at last found her courage. And even with her father's vile words, a lightness filled her. It left her breathless with the power of her own strength.

The viscount sputtered, his fleshy lips flapping like he was a trout plucked from the river in search of water. "You'll do as you're told."

Justina tipped her chin up at a mutinous angle. "I'll not." For after she rejected Tennyson, there would be a countless stream of others that her father would seek to erase his debt with, using her as the pawn. And if she acquiesced, where would she be? Miserable as her mother, with little joy in life.

"Does your mother's happiness mean so little to you?"

And just like that, the argument was sucked from her, draining the air from her lungs. Her mother, another pawn in her father's schemes of life. "You'd dare speak to me about her happiness?" That shocked inquiry ripped from her lips. "You, who has brought her nothing but sad—"

He shot a hand out and she gasped as he squeezed her wrist in a punishing grip. Tears dotted her vision and she blinked them back. She'd be damned if she allowed him the satisfaction of a single one of those crystalline drops. "You've gotten mouthy, gel." he snapped. "Used to be biddable and obedient like your mother."

Yes, she had. Nick had helped her use her voice. "I will write Edmund," she lied, invoking the one name her father feared above all others. His son-in-law; the man who'd become protector and defender of the Barretts. He turned an ashen shade of gray and he released her suddenly. Justina rubbed the bruised flesh, reveling in her father's weakness. It fueled her. "I daresay, Edmund will not take kindly to your ruthless attempts at marrying me off," she continued warningly.

He scrunched his mouth up tight and then some of the tension left his broad shoulders. "Your sister nearly died giving Rutland a whelp." Her heart clenched at the reminder of her sister's near death. After a difficult childbirth that had nearly cost Phoebe her life and called their mother to her side, Justina could not be a burden to them. Not when there was her nephew, just born, still by her mother's report, fighting for his life. "You'd be so selfish and expect him to leave your sister?"

*Never.* She'd just not believed her father saw the special bond that existed between her and Phoebe, to know he could use it against her.

Triumph filled his bulging eyes. "You'll watch your sister this evening, Andrew. Make sure she's a good girl." While their miserable sire, no doubt, spent his night in the gaming room set up by their host.

Justina curled her fingers hard into the ripped edge of her seat. She'd come to at last accept the truth—nothing could be done to stop her father's descent into ruin. With his every action, he dragged his wife and her into that dark abyss of uncertainty. And she'd tired of it. Tired of his influence in her life. Wanted some control so she could be free of him.

After a seemingly endless carriage ride, their aged black barouche rocked to a halt outside the Viscount Wessex' townhouse; the white stucco awash in candlelight. As soon as the carriage door opened, she surged up from her seat, desperate to be out of the suffocating confines with her father.

She accepted the assistance of the liveried driver with a murmur of thanks. Squaring her shoulders, she marched quickly toward the fashionable entrance of the Mayfair residence.

"Justina," her brother called, hurrying after her. His longer-legged strides easily ate away the distance between them. She shot him a look from the corner of her eye. "I'm sorry," he blurted, his face a mottled red. "I should not have let him say those things or put his hands on you." He balled his gloved hands.

"It is fine," she assured him, some of the tension leaving her. "Just as Edmund cannot stop him from drinking and wagering, neither can you make him be kind."

His mouth tightened. "But you are my sister and I should have defended you."

Yes, he should have. Phoebe had stood up to their father. Justina had begun to challenge the wastrel viscount. At what point would Andrew find his voice? Or mayhap he never would? Regret pulled at her heart. They reached the inside of the ballroom and stood in the receiving line. Andrew took her by the arm. Justina lifted her gaze questioningly up to his.

"I won't let you marry Tennyson. No matter what Father wishes." He dropped his voice to a hushed whisper and she was struck by a solemnity she'd never before seen or known in her brother. "I know what it is to love…" The woolgathering… Of course. "And be unable to…act on that love." She'd been so consumed by her own dire circumstances she'd not allowed herself to truly think of Andrew.

"I'm sorry," she began softly.

He flicked a hand in a patently false dismissive gesture, eyeing the crowd as they moved closer to the front of the line. "If you care for him, then nothing should come between that."

A moment later, they were announced. From her vantage at the top of the floor, Justina skimmed her gaze over the crowd, searching for one gentleman.

"He's in the corner," Andrew said from the side of his mouth as they started down the stairs. "Staring at you."

Her heart kicked up a beat and she found him with her gaze. Their stares collided over the guests' heads, and all the world briefly melted away in a whir of distant music and the crowd's laughter.

What was he thinking?

HAVING ASCENDED TO HIS TITLE two years prior, Nick had found little pleasure in the mindlessness of *ton* functions. His presence at these same functions now served a purpose.

From where he stood on the edge of the ballroom, ladies from debutantes to dowagers to widows with wicked promises in their eyes stole glances in his direction. At another time, those sultry invitations would have beckoned, a welcome diversion from the tedium of these infernal affairs. Alas, his purpose in being inside Lord and Lady Wessex's ballroom was singular in nature and had everything to do with the lady surrounded by a crush of suitors.

The pale pink fabric of Justina's satin gown would have made any other lady with such cream white skin sallow. Instead, the chandelier cast a soft, ethereal glow upon the shimmery fabric that clung to her ample hips and curved buttocks. She had a body made for loving. *I want her.*

He'd only seen her as a means to an end in his game of revenge. Now, he looked at the lady with lust blazing through him and an eagerness filled him to lay claim to her for reasons that moved beyond vengeance. *Why don't you court her?* That tantalizing whisper slithered around his brain. He could simply twist his plans into something more honorable so that Justina never knew what he'd originally intended. Find another way to deal with Rutland. Then, he'd have both vengeance and also have Justina as his wife. The air lodged in his chest, staggering him with both the depth of his weakness and folly in his wanting to believe that both ends could be achieved.

"I expect if you intend to *woo* the lady, you would be better served by offering her a set." Chilton's voice laden with amusement sounded from over his shoulder and Nick snapped his attention sideways.

Entirely too smug, champagne flute in hand, Chilton positioned himself beside him. Nick quietly cursed. "Have a care," he bit out. Gossips lurked everywhere, hungry for an *on dit* to bandy about.

Unfazed by that admonishment, Chilton whistled slowly through his teeth. "You did the lady a disservice. She is lovely."

Such words did little justice to capture the effervescent beauty of the small, rounded-in-all-the-right-places siren. He'd sooner pledge allegiance to the Marquess of Rutland than openly admit he lusted after the lady who'd serve as just one pawn in his scheme. "It hardly matters what the lady looks like," he reminded his friend in hushed tones. Unease simmered in his belly. Was the reminder for him or Chilton?

"I expect it matters to some." Chilton tipped his chin toward the dance floor and Nick followed that movement.

He narrowed his eyes as one of Society's notorious rogues, the Earl of Bradburn, escorted Justina onto the dance floor. Even with the length of the ballroom between them, he caught the hungry glint in the gentleman's eyes. Another damned rogue.

Something dark and unpleasant slithered around his insides; something that felt remarkably like jealousy. As soon as the irrational idea slid in, he scoffed. His sole interest in the lady had to do with her name and nothing more. And yet... *Lord Tennyson? Or Lord Bradburn?* He expected the lady's father to be lax, but what in blazes was the lady's brother doing allowing either cad near her? Nick gritted his teeth as the haunting strains of a waltz filled the ballroom.

"Bradburn is known to be a rogue but a good deal better than that treacherous bastard Tennyson," his friend added, sipping too casually from his glass.

*Better than a treacherous bastard like myself.* He tamped down that nagging guilt and fixed on Bradburn's very precise, practiced movements as he guided Justina around the dance floor. The bloody bastard settled one hand low on her waist. Too low. A growl lodged in Nick's throat. It didn't matter the gentleman's interest. Or that he dipped his lips close to her ear and said something that raised one of those beguiling blushes—

The stem of Nick's champagne flute snapped under the weight of his hand and several liveried footmen rushed over to clean away the mess.

"Everything all right?" Chilton asked, furrowing his brow.

"Fine," he bit out, the lie coming easily. All the while, an unholy desire filled him to stalk across the room and rip the cocksure earl's wandering hands from her. By God, if the bastard moved his hands any lower...

"Tennyson has taken note," his friend murmured. Nick followed his pointed stare over to the marquess who stared on at Justina, like a vulture prepared to pick off its prey. "They say Bradburn's in need of a fortune and, as such, given the lady's own miserable circumstances, the gentleman poses no risk to your *plans.*"

Nick blinked slowly. His plans? Of course. Wooing her and ruining her and then breaking her heart. Distaste filled his mouth as he was presented so coolly and more accurately with his intentions.

Why should he feel this restlessness at discussing a scheme that had been so carefully crafted to make Rutland pay at last for his crimes?

"That gentleman, however," his friend went on, "*does* present a threat." Chilton gave another discreet wave toward the stone-faced Lord Tennyson on the fringe of the ballroom, deeply watching Justina's every movement.

The lady's story about that ruthless bastard surged to his memory. Yet, staring at Tennyson and the wholly removed way in which he studied her, there was something methodical and precise in how he sized her up. A frisson of unease dusted his spine. The orchestra concluded the set and he found Justina amongst the crowd. He dipped his eyebrows.

She moved quickly through the ballroom, skirting the edge of the dance floor. Periodically, she cast a look about. Where in blazes was she going? Then the ugly possibility slid forward like a venomous serpent poisoning his thoughts. Bradburn's whisper. Justina's crimson blush. Did the lady even now sneak off to meet the gentleman?

He growled. This rapidly spiraling rage only had to do with his plans for her. Nothing more. Not taking his gaze from the lady, Nick followed her movements as she weaved between guests and clung to the perimeter of the ballroom. Stealing one last look, Justina slipped out of the ballroom with a stealth a thief in the Dials would have been hard-pressed to find fault with.

"Most men would feel some compunction at how easy the lady is making this for you," Chilton said, clucking his tongue.

"I'm not most men," Nick reminded him. With that, he set chase. Quickening his steps, he kept his gaze trained forward, avoiding the lords and ladies seeking to capture his attention. They'd not bothered to so much as glance at an earl's untitled grandson. Now, they'd all sell their souls for a word of approval from him.

Nick reached the back of the ballroom and glanced back and forth down the empty corridors. He silently cursed. Bloody hell, the lady was quick. He did a small circle and then froze mid-movement.

A small, golden-haired child stared back at him with unabashed curiosity. "Hullo," she greeted.

*Bloody hell.* Discovered by a damned child. "Uh…" He glanced about.

"What is your name?"

His mind went blank at her inquiry. "Nick," he settled for.

"I am Marcia," she offered with no prompting. "My mama and papa are Lord and Lady Wessex."

The girl snagged his full attention. Her father was Lord Wessex. The man who'd owned the Marquess of Atbrooke's debt and run him out of England; an act that had earned this family a powerful enemy. The innocent child staring back through inquisitive brown eyes that made this family, who'd only been a name until now, real in ways he didn't want them to be. Just as he didn't wish for Justina Barrett to be anything more than Rutland's clever-minded, bluestocking sister-in-law. For it made them human. People who lived and laughed and loved, and not simply the pieces upon a chessboard he'd maneuvered from afar.

"Are you looking for the pretty blonde lady?" Marcia asked curiously. The girl drifted over and Nick froze. She was near in age to Felicity, a child born to his sister from a hateful marriage. A marriage that had been a product of Rutland's actions thirteen years earlier. His jaw clenched reflexively. "Are you angry?"

He flushed. How perceptive children were. They saw more than the adults of the world around them. "No," he said gruffly, desperately eager to be free of the girl so he might locate Justina.

She scrunched her brow up and continued coming closer with a fearlessness that would one day lead to her ruin. "Yes, well, you seem angry," she persisted. "You're frowning. And your eyes have gone cold."

All of him had gone ice cold long ago.

"Is it because you're looking for your lady?" she ventured, brightening. That innocent, whimsical supposition once again hinted at her dangerous innocence.

"I am," he said, gentling his tones.

Marcia cupped her hands around her mouth and whispered loudly. "She went to the end of the hall to my mother's gardens." Then, touching her fingertip to her nose, the child winked and rushed down the opposite hall in a rustle of white skirts.

Nick stared after her a moment and then gave his head a shake. The gardens. Once again, the whispering of jealousy slithered around and he increased his stride. Of course, she didn't go to secretly meet another. And yet...he sought her out. He'd be damned if Tennyson, Bradburn, or any other dared encroach on Justina Barrett.

# CHAPTER 10

AFTER FLEEING LADY WESSEX'S BALLROOM, Justina stole through the quiet corridors, desperate to be free of the oppressive suitors and drivel about the color of her eyes and hair—all of it. The allegations made by her father earlier in the carriage ride rang mockingly around the chambers of her mind, and she hated the vise that squeezed about her heart.

She reached the end of the hall and shoved the door open. A cold blast of night air sucked the breath from her lungs and she blinked, struggling to adjust her eyes to the unexpected garden sanctuary. Ignoring the bite of the late night chill, she stepped outside and closed the door quietly behind her. When presented with the demons in the ballroom or the cold of the night, she'd always seek the latter.

A night breeze tugged at the budding branches overhead and sent a handful of forgotten pink petals tumbling over the graveled path. Rubbing her hands back and forth over her arms, Justina willed warmth into her limbs. With each step that carried her deeper into the gardens, her slippers churned up bits of pebbles.

She stopped. The thick clouds drifted past the moon, opening a stream of light that bathed a stone rendering at the far back corner of the garden in a pale glow. That massive stone statue of a woman and man twined in one another's arms beckoned, urging her forward.

Lowering her arms to her sides, she strolled over to the now-barren cherry tree. Even in stone, the sculptor had masterfully crafted the unadulterated love coming from the man's eyes. With her back presented to anyone observing, the woman carved of stone fairly begged for the private intimacy of the moment with such a raw realness that Justina took a step away.

But something called her back. She peered at the couple. That motionless hero; both adoring and protective of the woman cradled in his arms. Justina wandered back to the statue, her breath catching. With his head bent toward his lover, there was something so gloriously breathtaking in his devotion, forever frozen for all to see, but somehow still shared between only them. It was madness to see the statue and imagine anything more. She stretched her hand out, brushing her fingertips down the rippled biceps of his arm, remembering another with arms that may as well have been carved of the same marble.

"We meet again."

She shrieked and, with her heart racing, spun about toward that deep baritone that had dogged her dreams and waking thoughts. Nick stood at the entrance of the garden, staring down the length of the brick, walled-in space. She followed his gaze to where her hand still rested on the statue. Cheeks warming, she quickly dropped her arm. "Your Grace, I was just…" How to admit to a stranger that she'd been envying the statue of a woman, who in this suspended moment, possessed everything her own heart desperately yearned for?

"Nick," he reminded, stalking forward with that sleek, elegant languor that drove her heart into a frenzy. The gravel crunched under his black boots, marking his path toward her. The moon's glow cast a ray of light upon his chiseled face, bathing his rugged jaw and hard lips in soft light. "Most ladies sneaking off during any ball do so with scandalous intentions," he whispered temptingly, coming closer.

Her heart quickened at his nearness. "Can a lady not just wish to escape the crush of a ballroom?" And the advances of improper suitors?

"Most would only escape *with* an eager suitor trailing," he countered.

A muscle jumped at the corner of his jaw and Justina widened her eyes. Why…he was jealous. Surely that meant he felt something for her. Butterflies danced in her belly. "I am not most ladies, Nick."

"No." His lips tugged at the corner and the tension went out of his broad shoulders. "You are not." Casting his gaze briefly up at the sky, he rocked back on his heels before returning his focus to her, robbing her of breath and thought. "Once more, we find ourselves together. Then, what did Virgil say? 'Fate will find a way'," he murmured, echoing those famous words of *The Aeneid*.

Who was this man who knew *Evelina* and read the poets and recited Virgil?

"I choose to believe our chance meetings," he murmured, "are merely the fates at play, Justina."

Butterflies danced wildly in her belly. How was it possible for a man to take nothing more than a name and wrap it in a husky whisper so that it felt like a lover's endearment? She closed her eyes. His breath, a delicious blend of brandy and chocolate, whispered upon her skin. Her body burned at his nearness. His words ran through her with the like harmony of their thoughts.

"Beautiful," he said softly. He let his arm fall to his side and she opened her eyes, bereft at the loss of him. Her gaze wandered to the stone masterpiece that now commanded his notice.

Regret pulled at her and she managed a nod. "It is," she concurred softly.

Nick ran his palm down the lady's curls and Justina took in that caress. How was it possible to so envy an inanimate piece of stone? Yet, he brushed his large, gloved palm over her with a tender regard she would have traded both her index fingers for. "What do you think the two lovers were thinking?" His hushed murmur brought her gaze away from that gentle touch and up to his face.

Justina wetted her lips, and glanced over her shoulder at the doorway. It was folly to be out here alone with this man. With any man. To be discovered with him would mean her ruin. Clenching and unclenching her fists, she looked to Nick once more.

He clasped his hands behind his back and retreated a step; his meaning clear. If she wished to leave, he'd not stop her.

And yet, if she did leave, she'd never forgive herself. All her life she'd dreamed of a romantic moment under the stars. Now, with the ugliness that her father held forth as her future, she'd steal her happiness when and where she could. In that decision, she'd own it and revel in that control, when her father was so determined to wrest it away.

Justina strolled over to the statue and ran her palm over the man's sculpted bicep; hard and unyielding under her hand. Her fingers twitched, recalling Nick's arm as he'd taken her body protectively under his. Not unlike that couple carved in stone. "If people were to look quickly, I expect they would see only lovers, wrapped in one another's arms." Her skin burned with the feel of his intense gaze on her every movement. "A couple in the throes of an embrace." She should be scandalized by the words tumbling from her lips and, yet, there was something freeing in speaking without recrimination with a person who truly wished to hear her opinion. With a person who didn't see her as a romantic who needed to be protected from herself.

"What do you see?" That hushed inquiry filled the nighttime quiet.

"I see a couple desperately in love." She lifted her gaze to his. "Two people who want nothing more than to shut the reality of the world out and live with only one another."

"You *are* a romantic," he murmured, drifting over so that her back was brought flush to his chest. He reached around her and her breath caught. But he merely trailed his hand in the same path her own had moved over the statue's arm.

Justina tipped her head back to search for the condescension that so often came with that admission. Instead, his gaze lingered on her face. Something hard glinted in his eyes that belied the gentle smile on his lips. There was something dark there. Something she could not identify or name. How could a man, so affable and charming, possess that fierce glitter? She rubbed her arms to ward off a sudden chill that had nothing to do with the night. "Yes," she conceded. Unnerved by the piercing intensity of his sapphire stare, she drifted around to the other side of the statue, placing it between them. "You never did say what brought you outside, Nick."

NOT FOR FIRST TIME SINCE Nick had met Justina, the lady's

eyes and words revealed a proper wariness. "What if I was to say it was you, Justina?" he murmured, strolling slowly around the tangled lovers. "What if I tell you that the moment you entered the ballroom, my gaze went to you, and followed you while those swains courted your favor, and then watched as you slipped away?" His words were the truest ones he had, or ever would give her. Until their marriage.

Her hands came to her chest, drawing his focus to the twin mounds that threatened her décolletage. "I would ask, why," she countered with a surprising boldness that raised the lady in his estimation.

For his first opinion that Justina Barrett could never see past her own dreams of grandeur to the truth of the ugly world before her, she now peppered him with questions of her own. "You do yourself a disservice if you fail to see why you've captivated me." Her eyes softened as his pretty profession restored her to innocent debutante. Why did he feel like the worst cad in the kingdom?

"Was it Tennyson?" he asked unexpectedly.

She cocked her head.

"The gentleman you evaded at The Circulating Library all those months ago?" Why did he ask such a question when it hardly mattered what Tennyson's goals were for her? Ultimately, this game of revenge would end with Justina as his bride.

Justina wetted her lips, and then gave a hesitant nod.

That confirmation sent a red bloodlust raging through him. "I despise Tennyson," he said with a quiet vehemence that rang from a place of peculiar truth.

"You know the marquess, then?" she asked, cautiously.

"I know he is a profligate gambler," he said, his every word deepening the adoration in her eyes. He hated himself as much as he abhorred Tennyson. Each word he uttered was an artful move on the path to wooing the lady before him and marked him more like that duplicitous rake than different. Both men with dishonorable intentions. "I know he's a man who makes his fortune on another man's misfortune and you deserve more than such a man as a suitor." Just as she deserved more than him. Far more. Shame needled at his suddenly, damnably alert conscience.

"You do not even know me," she said softly.

He came around the statue and cupped her face in his palm. "I know you have a clever mind that makes a person think. I know he would shut you away, crush your spirit, keep you in a gilded cage as nothing more than a pretty ornament he brought out to impress the *ton*." Nick lowered his brow to hers.

Her chest moved with the force of her breathing. "My father…" She grimaced. "Has very clear," her mouth tightened ever so slightly, "*hopes* for my future."

Nick knew as much. He knew the steps and moves the viscount would make, mayhap before the fat reprobate himself did. "Ah," he said with feigned understanding. "You have a devoted papa, then?"

"No." Her smile withered and died like a twinkling star that forever lost its light. It ushered in a cold. "It is not that." Justina's face set in a bitter mask, momentarily freezing him. The absence of her usual spirit and cheer raised gooseflesh on his arms. *The day she bears my name and learns the depth of my betrayal, she'll forever only wear this grim expression.* Such a truth did not matter. It could not. The profession ran as a hollow litany inside his head and he found himself more a coward than he ever credited. For he wanted to know those important pieces she offered like fragile gifts, not as a means to further ensnare, but to simply know more about her.

"My father is…" Justina plucked at her puffed sleeve. "Indifferent," she settled for. Her wry tone was at odds with the unadulterated innocence she'd shown since their first encounter on the cobbled streets of Gipsy Hill. "Most young ladies would, no doubt, be grateful for a father so removed from their lives that they could read as they wish and go where they wanted, when they wanted…"

The viscount was lax. Nick mentally stored that essential piece away. "Yet you did not wish that for yourself?" His was a bid to lull her into a false sense of his caring. To make her believe she mattered. And yet, waiting for her answer, why did it feel as though he lied to himself?

"I did not," she confirmed, lifting her gaze to his. How free the lady was with her words; unguarded. She didn't prevaricate or prattle about inanities the way the ladies of the *ton* did. "I wanted a father who loved me. Or who, at the very least, cared."

Her words went through him like well-placed arrows. For he *had* known the love she spoke of. As had Cecily. All gifts crushed with the brutal ruthlessness of one man's greed and cruelty. He attempted to steel his heart through her telling. To build up the desperately needed barriers, but her words continued coming, shattering all his efforts.

"Ultimately, I would have settled for a sire who saw me as more than a p…" She cleared her throat and looked away.

*A pawn.* A role she'd been born to as Waters' daughter and grown into as Rutland's sister-in-law. *A role she'd play as my wife.* Regret tasted like vinegar on his tongue, the bitterness of it making words impossible.

"Forgive me," she said, softly. And there was such a sadness etched on the heart-shaped planes of her cheeks that it drove home another damned dagger. "I've said too much." Yes, she had. So why did he wish to hear more? *Because she is the pawn she unwittingly speaks of.*

Liar. He ached to drive back that sorrow from her expressive eyes. "Does your father owe the man a debt, then?" he asked gruffly, ending the quizzing game to which he'd already possessed all the answers.

Justina hesitated and then nodded.

"Ah." He stretched that single, commiserative syllable out. "That is the way of our world, is it not?" he asked, strolling away from her, over to the wrought iron bench surrounded by a cluster of barren rose bushes. He settled his frame into the seat and laid his arms along the back, urging her over with his silent gaze.

Justina glanced again at the doorway. She darted the delicate pink tip of her tongue out and ran it over the seam of her lips with an innocence that was more erotic than any of the darker deeds he'd performed with jaded women. Like a moth to that fatal flame, she floated over to him, and then hesitated. Nick motioned to the seat beside him. Several moments passed and then she slid onto the bench. "I prefer to have a more favorable outlook on the world," she said, sitting thigh to thigh with him.

Her words held him motionless. "Even knowing your father's intentions for you and his disregard, you still have that optimism?" It was how, even now, she did not realize she kept company with the Devil.

She nodded, her gaze riveted on the marble lovers. "My father believes I'm an empty-headed girl. Naïve. I see more than he credits." Far less than she believed. "I'm not blinded to the ugliness that exists in the world. I just focus on the good. Otherwise, what is the alternative? To dwell in darkness?" Her gaze grew distant as she became lost in herself. "I choose not to. I choose the light."

What the lady failed to know and would soon realize was that, ultimately, darkness selected a person. There was no escaping it. It lived around them in the form of rotten men who'd ruined families and men bent on revenge who'd ruin in return. And for this woman, he would become the figure she came to hate with the same vitriolic intensity that he despised the Marquess of Rutland.

The truth of that pitted in his belly and he hated that even with the lesson handed him on that long-ago night, there was still this weakness inside him.

She lifted her face up to his and the moon's glow bathed the delicate planes in an ethereal glow that gave her the look of a siren at sea. "I expect I've shocked you with my honesty." There was no apology there. He admired her all the more for her strength. At their first meeting, he'd taken Justina Barrett to be a meek, blushing miss. He'd been wrong on so many scores.

"I'm unaccustomed to ladies who speak so candidly," he confessed. That admission did not come out as a way to wheedle himself into her graces, but rather from a need to try and make sense of this woman. A woman who reminded him of all those pleasures he'd once found joy in, and through her spirit and love of those same books, she'd sparked a long dormant part of his soul he'd trusted was dead. He recoiled; his palms growing moist in his gloves.

"And do you disapprove?" By the intensity of her direct stare, his answer mattered to her.

"What if I said I did?" he countered, in a bid to right his disordered thoughts. "Would you seek to make yourself into someone other than who you are?" *No, I'll do that all for her.* He curled his hands into tight balls.

"I wouldn't," Justina confessed. "I know no other way than to hope. My mother says I've always been her dreamer. My sister is one, as well." He stiffened as she yanked him out of this curious need to know more about her and doused him with the cool reminder of the woman whose blood she shared. "She had dreams of traveling to Wales." A wistful smile hovered on her lips. "And eventually, with Edmund, found her way there."

"And what of your brother-in-law?" he asked, dragging forth additional words about the man who'd ruined his family as a reminder to himself—he needed to remain dead to everything. Especially Justina Barrett. No good awaited their future together. "The one you spoke so fondly of at the park?" He fought back a sneer.

"Edmund?" Justina laughed. "Society once called him a scoundrel and moved with fear around him." She gave her head a shake. "No, he will never be a dreamer, but he is an honorable man who loves my sister and, for that, I will always love him."

A seething hatred snapped through him like fire, burning him with the force of his loathing. Obliterating all previous tenderness. How could a woman such as Justina so extol a beast like Rutland? *It is because she's a romantic who cannot see that which is right before her.* Wasn't the ease with which she'd stepped into his trap proof of that? What he'd never anticipated was caring one way or another how Justina Barrett came out at the end of this Devil's game.

A sharp crack split the quiet and they swung their gazes to the branch that snapped and tumbled from the cherry tree. It fell between the stone lovers, landing like a visible divide between them, caught in their arms.

"I should return," Justina murmured, climbing to her feet. She lingered and stared at him a moment.

Did she seek a protest on his part? Nick stood and gathered her fingers in his. He raised them to his mouth and placed a lingering kiss atop her gloved hand. "I do not know how to account for these chance meetings, Justina," he said quietly. "But I am glad for them." He retained his hold on her a moment. "I would like to call on you. If you are amenable to——?"

"Yes," she said quickly and then laughed, the clear, innocent tinkling like a bell. "I would like that very much," she said with such an unfettered smile, he rapidly released her fingers.

Justina dropped a curtsy and then rushed across the graveled path. She froze with her hand on the doorway and then looked back. "I am also glad for them, Nick." Her husky whisper stretched across the garden. "Our chance meetings."

Then, she left.

The lady now gone, Nick stared after her. In his quest for revenge, his hatred had fueled him. Edmund Deering, the Marquess of Rutland, had broken down his family. He'd made his mother a widow and his father's children, motherless. Because of his coward of a father and Rutland's evil, they'd been thrust into the care of their cruel grandfather who'd delighted in telling them just how worthless they were for the blood of their father that flowed through their veins. As much as Nick had despised his grandfather, he'd acknowledged the accuracy of his ill opinion of his son-in-law. The late baronet *had* been weak. He'd not had the strength to face his own demons. Unlike Nick, who'd long ago resolved to never be his father. Who'd committed to facing down Lord Rutland, when his pathetic sire hadn't had the backbone to do so.

Yet in his quest, he'd not given true thought to the people who'd be left in ruins, all to exact his due. Perhaps, in this, he was like his father after all. Failing to think about those he'd leave behind in his wake. That unwanted realization robbed him of breath and he pressed his fingertips into his temples to drive back the thought.

With every encounter, Justina became real. A woman who loved literature and spoke her mind. Nick swiped a hand down his face. *I am a weak fool.* Had Lord Rutland shown any compunction or regret in his vile deeds through the years? No, and as such he did not seek to destroy any other family than the one linked to the man who'd destroyed him.

If he abandoned a vow he'd made thirteen years ago, all because of a woman he'd known for a week's time, what did that say about him? It would prove he was that same, pathetic boy with a book of poetry clutched to his chest, quaking with fear as Rutland upended his world.

Steeling his heart and shoving his very real fear to the side, he started back for Lord Wessex's ballroom.

# CHAPTER 11

THE FOLLOWING EVENING AT A table in Forbidden Pleasures, one of the more wicked clubs in London, Nick stared into the contents of his brandy, feeling…empty. He'd hungered for revenge the way a starving man did food and drink. Only, to be handed over everything so easily left him strangely hollow.

Just days ago, all he had known about Justina Barrett was that the lady paid frequent visits to Gipsy Hill and had the misfortune of being sister-in-law to one of the vilest bastards in London. Now he knew she read poetry and visited circulating libraries to attend lectures. Dreamed of love and wished to write her own romantic verses.

And had a bloody bastard for a father who'd wagered away her future.

He tightened his hold on his drink, drawing forth the memories conjured when he looked into a glass of brandy; the bottle upended on his father's desk. The liquor stain upon those documents and the floor. Except, those memories would not come. Instead, in their place were the wistful blue eyes of a lady whose ruin couldn't have been easier had she been handed a script and given her lines.

With a curse, Nick tossed back his drink in a long, slow swallow, welcoming the fiery blaze as the liquid trailed down his throat. He set the empty glass down hard and the droplets clinging to the edge fell onto the table. Then, he refilled his glass, hoping to drive those eyes from his mind.

Seated across from him, Chilton shifted in his chair. "You're in a foul mood."

"I'm always in a foul mood," he muttered, skimming his restless stare about the club.

"Yes, that's true," his friend conceded with a grin.

Nick looked beyond Chilton's shoulder and froze; his gaze locked on the fat, foul, Viscount Waters. The sweaty lord, with a young beauty on his lap, bellowed with laughter, the sound muffled by the riotous noise of the club. The man buried his face in the voluptuous creature's ample bosom and bestowed his favor on her flesh.

Inked words penned inside a journal flitted through his mind. *…It sustains them through miserable childhoods with indifferent fathers, who betray the vows made to their wives…* He should be elated that Waters, with his failings, made his plans for revenge so bloody easy.

Waters wrapped his sausage-like fingers in the lady's blonde tresses and angled her face for a hard kiss. Nick peeled his lip back as revulsion snaked through him and he looked away from the loathsome tableau.

Chilton followed his stare. "I gather he is the reason for our visit this evening."

He gave a curt nod. The sole reason he'd taken up membership at the club and frequented it even now was to further drag the Barretts down the path to ruin by watching the man. With the wagers his own father had made in his business ventures, Nick had lauded and aspired to ruthless logic in every aspect of his life: from matters of business, to revenge, to the women he took to his bed.

He continued to assess Justina's father. The man drew his fleshy face out of the woman's neck, a woman of an age to Justina, and he gestured over a statuesque creature with midnight black hair and crimson lips. Bile stung the back of Nick's throat, as the old viscount bestowed his vile attentions on the two beauties.

"Are you certain you're set on this course?" Chilton asked stealing another peek at Waters. "I expect it's a punishment all in itself to have in-laws such as the Barretts." He gave a discreet wave and Nick followed his subtle gesture to the youngest Barrett sibling. Seated several tables over from his sire, Andrew Barrett tossed coins down at a hazard table.

These were the men Justina Barrett's security and well-being fell to—a treacherous father and a wastrel of a brother? While the young lady worried after her future and battled the pressures to marry a scoundrel who owned her father's debt, these two lords saw after their own pleasures, and not much more. And her sister had joined their family to the blackest scoundrel in London.

A muscle jumped at the corner of his eye. Mayhap the lady was better in his care, after all. He blinked slowly. Where in blazes had that thought come from?

"Have you yet considered," Chilton's quiet murmur brought him back to the moment, "when you marry the chit, you'll be forever bound to these reprobates?" The other man grimaced and took a sip of his drink.

Nick would be bound to her. Her family, he needn't see after the day he took those binding vows. He'd have his final say with Rutland and revel in the moment the man belatedly realized his sins had caught up with him.

Just as he needn't see Justina after their marriage. He didn't give a jot about an heir to a title that meant nothing to him. "It hardly matters," he said tightly. *Liar. It matters.* "I'll have no dealings with them beyond the day I call in those debts." And he would have his retribution. He'd not abandon thirteen years' worth of hatred for a short while of knowing a lady.

Chilton searched his eyes over Nick's face. "You will let your hatred destroy you."

Nick flattened his lips. He'd been destroyed long ago. What would life have been had he not been a victim of his father's failings and the marquess' evil? A bucolic image flitted in of he and Justina, poring over a copy of *Evelina*, discussing Burney's verses. How very real that tableau was.

*Too real.* He flexed his jaw. Any happiness belonging to him had been destroyed long ago by the lady's brother-in-law.

"And what of the lady when she is your wife?" his friend pressed. Nick went still as the quiet recrimination ran through him with an unwanted sharpness. "Will you expect her to so easily cut off all ties with her family because her husband ruined them?"

*...My mother would never dare limit what I read. She always lived to see her children happy...*

No, a mother who'd sought to fill her children's life with love and joy would not be a woman his wife would so easily cut from the fabric of her life. And yet, how much thought had he truly put into life with Justina Barrett after he'd destroyed her father, brother, and Rutland?

"It is not too late to alter your plan," Chilton said with a quiet insistence.

Did the other man sense his wavering? Not once had Edmund Deering, the Marquess of Rutland, deviated in his ruthless dismantling of Nick's father and, with that, the entire Tallings family.

"You are not a man who's rotted to the core," his friend persisted. "I know those men." The other man tugged his chair closer and dropped his elbows on the table. "I deal with men whose souls are beyond redemption. You are driven by revenge…and that is an entirely different matter. Very few can countenance a life of darkness. You are not one of them."

His friend did not know the blackness in Nick's soul. Chilton couldn't begin to understand the demons that haunted a man who'd cut his father's lifeless body down and who'd then been forced to perpetuate a lie to save his mother and sister. He flexed his jaw and, unable to meet the probing intensity of Chilton's stare, glanced around at the other lords present—unfaithful husbands, diffident fathers. Men who'd been nothing like his own loyal, loving sire.

He firmed his resolve. "My path was cemented long ago." Except… He glanced briefly at Waters embroiled in a game of faro with the Marquess of Tennyson, the man who sought to lay claim to Justina Barrett. A hard smile on his lips, he said something that made the Viscount Waters guffaw. This was the evil in Justina's life. She was a lady who'd somehow retained her glimmer of hope amongst the mire that was her actual circumstance, and he would be the one to ruin that. Nausea broiled in his gut.

"You're not a man to ruin an innocent," Chilton quietly pressed, following the direct path Nick's thoughts had traversed. "You can have your revenge without breaking her heart."

With his friend's arguing, he remained silent, an internal battle raging within him. He'd despaired of ever having retribution against Lord Rutland until the man had gone and married and, at last, shown a weakness to the world. That weakness was the woman he'd married—Lady Phoebe Deering and her family.

For two years, Nick had devoted his days to plotting that family's ruin. He'd failed to see them as people—until he'd slid into that damned lecture hall seat and witnessed the spirit of a young lady amidst a group of disapproving dandies and lords. Such a woman did not deserve to pay for Rutland's crimes.

With a curse, he tossed back the contents of his glass in a long, slow swallow that burned the back of his throat. He dragged over the bottle and poured himself another drink. Liquid droplets splashed over the top. Goddamn Chilton for being correct.

A serving woman sashayed over with a tray and, not taking his gaze from Nick, Chilton waved her off. With a pout, the lady shifted direction for another table of gentlemen. "*You* do not need to be the one to ruin this family. They," Chilton jerked his chin first toward Andrew Barrett and then to the father, "will continue down that path with someone ultimately destroying them."

"If I allow that, then I'm not the one to bring that fall. Where is the retribution against Rutland then?" he demanded.

His friend clung on like a dog with a bone. "Fine, destroy his reprobate father-in-law and wastrel brother. The lady will be sold to a gentleman who owns her father's debt and Rutland will watch them suffer, through actions that had nothing to do with you."

Nick curled his hands tight around his glass, draining the blood from his knuckles as Chilton's logic cracked through the wall of hatred he'd built about himself. Ultimately, she would be shattered by life, but it would not be at his hands. *I cannot do it. I cannot ruin her.* There would have to be another way. And a staggering shame and disgust at his own weakness swelled deep inside, bringing his eyes closed with the weight of his own failings. He'd spent thirteen years shaping himself in the Marquess of Rutland's image, only to find himself frail in ways the marquess never had been, nor ever would be.

He opened his eyes and stared blankly down at the smooth surface of the mahogany table. Yes, he could easily ruin the whole of the Barretts. But that did not require he steal Justina's heart and bind her to him with a lifetime reminder of her foolishness and his treachery.

Chilton jerked his chin across the room. "I take it you've seen your future father-in-law has company?"

Nick followed the gesture. The Marquess of Tennyson slapped the other man on the back. Then, lifting his arm, he motioned forward a lithe beauty carrying a silver tray. She sauntered over, hips swaying, with a full bottle of brandy. Setting down the decanter, she proceeded to pour the viscount a snifter full to the brim, and then leaned down to whisper something into his ear.

Waters angled back around, the two creatures on his lap momentarily forgotten as the serving woman brought the glass to his lips and held the crystal while he drank. A moment later, the viscount climbed to his feet and allowed himself to be tugged forward by the three lush beauties, stumbling over himself in his haste to leave.

Chilton followed Waters' departure and then looked back to Nick. "There have been whispers about the gentleman in the past. He takes an inordinate delight in shaming and breaking young ladies. Has no compunction about bedding an innocent." With his depravity and devotion to his wicked urges, Tennyson was a rake in every sense of the word.

Nick probed him with his stare.

"He's tried with little success to bed *La Belle Ferronniere.*" God, how Nick despised that cold, unfeeling moniker handed to Justina by a cold, unfeeling Society. "As such, Tennyson has moved in a different direction to capture the lady."

He followed Chilton's focus over to the Viscount Waters. The snifter nearly cracked under the weight of Nick's grip and he forced himself to loosen his hold. "Oh?" That single, meaningless utterance was all he could manage with fury licking at his senses.

"Waters owes him a vast sum." Nick tamped down a curse. Desperation made men do foolish things. His own father was proof of that. With a contrasting calm, Chilton dropped his elbows on the table and, leaning forward, spoke in hushed tones. "According to my same source, Waters has worked out a…deal of sorts with Tennyson."

*Don't ask. Tennyson's plans are not my own.* A potent surge of something dark and red, something that felt very much like jealousy, coiled tight in Nick's belly like a serpent poised to strike. "What?" he gritted out, damning himself for caring.

Chilton settled back in his chair and in an infuriatingly cool manner, swirled the contents of his glass in a small circle. "He'll bed her with no recompense of marriage expected." His friend smiled wryly. "And Waters will be free to wed her off to another who doesn't care for the absence of her virtue."

Bile stung his throat. Having abandoned his plans for Justina, what happened to the lady from here did not matter to him. Or it shouldn't. And yet, by God, the idea of her belonging to the notorious rake Tennyson in any way made him want to stalk over to the bastard like a feral beast and take him apart at the limbs.

Chilton shoved back his chair and, through his tumultuous musings, Nick glanced up. "See, if you simply let it all play out, the Barretts will be ruined through no effort on your part. Now, if you'll excuse me? I've matters of business to see to." Those matters of business invariably proved to be his half-siblings, bastard children of the Duke of Ravenscourt, that Chilton had taken under his wing, as though he were their true father. Siblings the other man had never failed, whereas Nick? He thrust aside thoughts of his sister. The other man finished his drink and set the glass down. "I merely thought I would try once more to deter you from bloodying your own hands."

Nick inclined his head. Treated with condescension by the whole of Society for his birthright, the other man had more honor than all the members of the peerage combined. That honor, only further proven by his heroics at Waterloo, had seen him titled for it.

After Chilton had taken his leave, Nick returned his attention to the Marquess of Tennyson, now fully occupied by a golden-haired beauty on his lap. With her broad hips and generous breasts, she was of like form to Justina. Tennyson shoved his hand up the woman's skirt, earning a squeal for his efforts, and he buried his face in the woman's ample cleavage.

An image assaulted Nick. An image of Justina in all her glorious innocence spread wide with the marquess rutting between her legs. The drink trembled in his hand and he set it down, splashing amber droplets upon the table. His gaze fixed on the pair locked in an embrace, Nick strode forward. He stopped beside the table.

The beauty with heavily rouged cheeks and crimson lips noted Nick first. She offered him a slow, seductive smile. "You've company, my lord." The marquess removed his attentions from the lady's breasts.

The marquess glanced up and his cold eyes registered surprise. He pushed the woman off his lap and she knocked into the table.

"Later, love," the man murmured, swatting her hard on the buttocks. The sharp crack of that blow earned a gasp from the lady and she quickly rushed off to another table. With the young whore gone, Tennyson spread his arms wide. "Huntly, to what do I owe this pleasure?"

It did not escape Nick's notice that the other man failed to rise. With a ducal arrogance Wellington himself would be hard-pressed to find fault with, he yanked out the vacant seat and claimed a chair. "I want Waters' vowels," he said when Tennyson raised his glass to his lips.

The marquess paused, his snifter halfway to his mouth. "Beg pardon?" he asked, dipping his eyebrows.

"What does the gentleman owe you?" Nick asked coolly, flicking a disgusted stare over him. "One thousand pounds? Two?"

Lord Tennyson looked back with shrewd eyes, finished his sip, and then set his glass down. "They aren't for sale." In short, it was the only power the man held over the viscount to bed Justina Barrett. When stripped away of that hold, the viscount no longer had use for him.

Nick leaned back in his seat and with slow, precise movements, tugged off his gloves. "Do you truly believe I cannot find out the amount owed?" he drawled, stuffing the pair inside his jacket.

The marquess ran his gaze searchingly over his face. "You'd own them so you can win the lady's hand from Waters?" he asked, his question laden with suspicion.

"If I was determined to own the vowels to win the lady's hand, I'd simply give the viscount the money as a settlement," he said in bored tones. That only increased the lines furrowed in the perplexed marquess' brow. "How much?" Nick repeated. "Three thousand?"

"Seven."

Long ago, he had become a master of dissembling. Even so, the staggering amount held him momentarily speechless.

"And the lady's dowry," Tennyson added and took another sip of his brandy.

Her dowry. The lady had not a pence attached to her name for a marriage settlement and, as such, her father had reduced her to one single purpose—settling those debts. A vitriolic hatred ran through him. "I want the vowels and the dowry," Nick said, at last. How very close he'd once been to conquering every part and parcel of the Barrett family, including Justina. Now, he'd have everything from them, anyway. Only in this, he could at least ensure she remained untouched by Tennyson and the reprobate father who'd sell her off.

"For what end, if you don't intend to marry her?"

Nick would give the depraved bastard credit for not cowering the way so many others did in his presence. Ignoring that bold question, he continued in frosty tones. "I'll offer you ten thousand and not a word more is said about this." The man choked on his swallow and Nick continued. "I'll have my man-of-affairs contact yours." His skin crawling at being in this man's presence, he stood.

"And you do not intend to wed the lady?"

"I'll not answer to you," Nick said with a ducal diffidence that sent color rushing to the marquess' cheeks. "Say nothing about our arrangement or the terms are off." With that threat, he started through the crowded club. Thick cheroot smoke hung heavy in the air, darkening the already dimly lit space. A place of sin and evil. As such, it was a place that men like he, Waters, and Tennyson belonged. Truly the Devil's own drawing room.

"Huntly! Huntly, my old chum!" Andrew Barrett's voice rang out among the din of the busy hell.

Goddamn it, could he not be free of a single Barrett? Was this to be his penance for his crimes and his failings? He could simply pretend he'd not heard the young man.

"Huntly," Justina's brother called again.

Swallowing down a curse, Nick forced a grin and adjusted his direction. The future viscount held his arms aloft and waved him over. As he walked the length of the crimson carpet to meet the younger man, Chilton's words echoed around his mind, bringing with them, an unwanted, needling guilt. He thrust it aside and came to a stop beside the young man. "Barrett," he drawled.

The younger gentleman glanced up. His eyes lit—Justina's eyes. Nick's stomach clenched.

"Huntly, my old friend." Barrett quickly shoved to his feet and sketched a bow. "Care to join?" He motioned to the empty seat.

*Old friend.* By his observations of Barrett at White's, Brooke's, and now this wicked hell, there was a shortage of *any* kind of friend for this man. Tugging out a chair, Nick slid into the seat.

Immediately, a beautiful creature with blonde curls strolled over with slow, languid footsteps. He eyed her a moment. With her trim waist, flared hips, and pale blonde hair, she was a veritable siren who'd tempt any. The woman, feeling his gaze, tipped her lips at the corners in an inviting smile as she leaned close. Only, her curls didn't possess the golden shades of sunlight and her lips were too thin. "Would you care for some company, Your Grace?" she whispered against his ear. Taking his silence for acquiescence, the whore slipped a palm inside his jacket and ran her fingers caressingly over his chest.

Aware of Barrett studying them, Nick drew back. "I'm afraid not."

With a pout, the blonde beauty sauntered over to Barrett, but the young man waved her away.

When he looked back at Justina's brother, the man wore a silly smile. "I understand that." Barrett grabbed the bottle and poured two glasses of brandy. He shoved one over. "When a lady slips inside your heart, she makes it impossible to think of another." The dandy gave a knowing wink.

Nick paused. The young man revealed too much. He collected the snifter. "You know something of that then?" he added non-committally.

Barrett's smile widened and he edged forward. "Quite." The other man's expression took a distant quality and he stared beyond Nick's shoulder. "Met a lady," he said, and then his cheeks fired color. "Never thought the day would come that a woman managed to win my heart."

The gentleman demonstrated the same lack of artifice as his trusting sister. Nick's belly knotted at that unwelcome connection between the siblings. Would that be their ultimate downfall?

Barrett hefted his glass up. "Then, they are sirens, aren't they? Change our thoughts. Make us forget anything but the need for them."

Those words, unerringly accurate, ran through Nick and he glanced down into his glass. For isn't that ultimately what Miss Justina Barrett had done? She'd shown herself to be a woman of intelligence, who longed for love, and, as such, she'd upset his plan—for her, anyway. He, however, could leave her dowry untouched, set aside so Barrett couldn't sell her off. Then with a clear conscience, he could ruin the rest of Rutland's kin.

With a shifting purpose, he returned his attention to Barrett. The other man sat sipping his drink, with that silly smile on his face. Nick could still have his revenge upon Rutland. *Would* still have it. It just didn't necessitate him wedding a twenty-year-old romantic with stars in her eyes.

The Barrett men, however, with their weakness for the gaming tables, were fair game. These were men of like darkness. Nick's lips turned up in a slow, triumphant grin.

"Justina is a good girl," the other man went on, not a confirmation required on Nick's part. How freely the man handed out intimate pieces about his sister to a man who was nothing more than a stranger. Mere moments ago, they would have been revelations he stored close with an aim to ruin her. "Bit of a bluestocking."

He well knew that. A memory of her slid in of her perched on the edge of her stiff, wood chair at The Circulating Library. *It is just, a man who is friends with a schoolmistress would certainly not look unkindly upon educated females.* "Is she?" A small smile pulled at his lips; the movement real and straining muscles unaccustomed to that free movement.

Barrett dropped his elbows on the table and leaned close. "Oh, yes. Wasn't always that way," he added with a casual shrug. "Nor would anyone expect it of her. Think she's an empty head, but she visits museums and bookshops."

How easily the man turned over the lady's secrets. Anger at Barrett gripped him and at himself for caring about Barrett's freeness with information about her.

Barrett chuckled. "Horrid places. Also enjoys the theatre," he added, the words more an afterthought than anything.

He'd not known that detail about the lady. Yet, beyond the information handed him by the baroness, he'd only truly known her a handful of days. That detail fit with the romantic lady who appreciated Tristan and Iseult and saw beauty in stone statues.

"Wants me to accompany her about," the future Viscount Waters prattled on, bringing Nick back to the moment. "Glad when she found friends, I was, but there is only so often a lady can accompany another lady." The careless dandy puffed up his chest. "Didn't really matter before giving up my time and all. I'm one of those devoted brothers."

Nick snorted and then quickly concealed it as a cough, covering his mouth with his palm.

"But now there is my lady and all and quite the chore trying to balance brotherly devotion with one's love."

"Ah, of course," Nick stretched out those syllables in long dry tones. "And this is the lady who's quite turned your world upside down?"

Barrett's eyes took on that far-off quality, once more. "There isn't another like her. Innocent. Good. Enjoys the violin. Used to play myself..." the gentleman's words trailed off.

With the other man lost in his own thought, Nick studied Barrett. A handful of days ago, he would have scoffed at that foolish naiveté. That youthful foolishness in which a man believed people capable of good. Outside of his own sister and niece, he'd not viewed a hint of that in another soul.

Until Justina Barrett. *Goddamn you, Justina.*

Apparently bored with that particular discourse, Justina's brother looked about the gaming hell. Then glanced back to Nick, his eyes bright. "Care for a game of cards?"

He bowed his head. "Whist or hazard?" And with a deck of cards and the fool Barrett, Nick traveled further down his path to no return.

# CHAPTER 12

¶IT HAD BEEN A WEEK.

Or six days if one wished to be truly precise. Which Justina certainly didn't. She didn't wish to think about how, for a handful of days, she'd found a gentleman who spoke to her of her thoughts as though they mattered, when the world saw nothing beyond the surface of who she was.

Seated on the neat row of chairs between Honoria and Gillian, Justina stared absently out at the couples twirling by in a violent explosion of vibrant fabrics. Hating that she searched the crowd for a hint of him. When he'd been quite clear in his disappearance that there was not anything there.

"It is no doubt for the best," Honoria said softly.

Justina didn't pretend to either mishear or misunderstand the other young woman's words. No doubt. On what did Honoria make that inaccurate claim? She firmed her lips. There was no doubt she'd laughed more, and spoken her mind freely and known the very real taste of passion with Nick.

"I expect there is probably a reason for the gentleman's absence," Gillian's quiet utterance, so full of her usual hope that she kindled the still-present embers of the hope Justina herself carried.

For surely there was a reason to explain why he'd simply…disappeared? "Do you believe so?" she asked, turning her full attention on the always-optimistic lady.

Gillian nodded emphatically. "Oh, yes. He could have…" She paused and creased her brow. "Or he could have…"

"You did not provide the first reason," Honoria pointed out absently as she devoted her attention to the crowd of guests.

Or mayhap she'd made more of a visit, a stolen embrace, and a private exchange in The Circulating Library than there was. Justina had attended inane affair after inane affair, all in the hopes of again seeing him. She had awakened each morning with the hope that he would call.

"Well, I would not have you with a gentleman who is inconstant," Gillian said, loyal all the way through. She patted Justina's hand. "You deserve a man who is honorable and good."

"And the duke was…*is* those things," Justina said softly. Just because he did not care for her, did not make him dishonorable. Her gaze caught on a couple moving through the intricate steps of a country reel. The unfamiliar gentleman dropped his hand lower on the back of his partner and such an intimate smile was shared between them, she had to look away. "He is a man who didn't simply wish to possess me." As Lord Tennyson and so many of the other suitors who'd come calling. She looked quickly about the room and found the marquess blessedly missing from the event, still. Relief assailed her. "The duke did not see me as the Diamond, but rather spoke to me about literature and free thought." Just as she'd always longed for in a gentleman and had begun to despair of such a man existing for her.

Gillian sighed and caught her chin atop her hand. "I am certain there is a reason to explain his defection."

"Ultimately, they always betray you," Honoria said with a stark somberness that served as a slight window into her past. "Our fathers. Suitors. Gentlemen who promise to love you, will fail."

"I do not believe that," Justina protested. "Yes, we've each witnessed the faithlessness of our fathers, but Phoebe found a gentleman who proved that a man is capable of love. That he can change."

"As did Cedric," Gillian piped in. Her brother-in-law, a notoriously reformed rake had disappeared to the country and now lived for only his wife.

"Nor did he profess to love me." A vise tightened about her chest. "It would be unfair to judge His Grace for not returning my affections," Justina continued.

Honoria eyed her sadly. "You will defend him, then?"

"Defend him?" she scoffed. "It would be a greater crime for the gentleman to have given me false assurances of affection." As it was, there had never been promises or requests for more. A pang struck. *Oh, but how I wish there had been.*

"I do not believe the gentleman is indifferent," Gillian murmured.

It was on the tip of Justina's tongue to point out that his absence spoke to the contrary, when Gillian motioned discreetly to the front of the room. She followed her friend's gesture and froze.

Nick stood at the top of the stairwell, exchanging words with their host, but his gaze remained firmly fixed over the tops of the heads of the guests on her. The piercing intensity of that volatile stare stretched across the distance between them and robbed her of breath.

"No gentleman can look at a lady as the duke is looking at you now and not feel something," Gillian said with a sly smile.

"Do not be silly." Justina's words emerged breathless. "He is not looking at me." She peeked about but when she returned her focus to the towering duke now descending the stairs, he stood at the side of the ballroom, surveying the crowd. And her heart dipped.

"Well, he is not looking at you *now*," Gillian pointed out. "But he was."

Disappointment blossomed again in her breast.

Honoria groaned, cutting across her pathetic musings, and she followed her stare. She sighed. Barreling past guests, Justina's father worked his way through the crowd.

"Do you wish us to secret you away before Honoria makes her leave on the morrow?" Gillian offered.

Despite Justina's fast approaching, matchmaking father, her lips pulled. What she wouldn't give to disappear to the country to visit Phoebe along with her. "No." Honoria had delayed her visit long enough on Justina's behalf. "I've learned he's better to meet up front and then distract him with talk of the gaming tables."

Her father came to a stop before her, panting from the rapid pace he'd set. The three ladies climbed to their feet with a matched reluctance. "Where have you been? Been looking for you, gel," he wheezed, ignoring the other ladies at her side. He swiped the back of his purple sleeve at his forehead. "You are not a wallflower," he griped.

Justina shot an apologetic look at her friends. Having proper nursemaids and governesses, the rules of Polite Society had been ingrained into her, just as they'd been into nearly every member of the peerage. How had her father remained so blind to proper decorum? "I was with Honoria and Gillian." She motioned pointedly to the ladies hovering at her side.

Her father scratched his wrinkled brow and then followed her gesturing. His bloodshot eyes lingered on Gillian and then moved over to Honoria, his gaze falling to the young lady's ample bosom.

"Lord Waters," her friends said in unison, matching distaste in their cold greetings.

Shame slapped at Justina. And hatred for this man who'd given her life sucked at her again. "You wanted something," she snapped and he blinked slowly.

Then, he gave his head a clearing shake. "Tennyson is looking for you," he gritted out.

Her stomach lurched and she quickly scanned the ballroom. "I didn't..." *Note his entry.*

"Come along," he muttered.

Like a mother tigress, Honoria stepped forward. By the fury flashing in her brown eyes, she'd go toe-to-toe with the viscount.

But she would not allow her friends to make a public display for her. Just as she'd not reach out to Edmund when he was attending his wife and new babe. For everyone's determination to see her protected, ultimately, since her mother and Phoebe's departure for the country, what her friends failed to realize is that she had been effectively taking care of herself and would continue to do so.

Panic mounted as her father motioned her ahead and Justina skittered her gaze about the ballroom in search of escape. When she'd been hiding from Lord Tennyson in the Royal Museum earlier in the Season, she'd sneaked into a lecture hall where the presenter had spoken of these magnificent displays of the earth's fury in which the ground shook and ripped apart. With her father determined to lead her on to Lord Tennyson, Justina found herself praying for one of those grand displays of the Lord's power.

Alas, life should have already proven the folly in seeking rescue from anyone but herself. Smiling for her friends' benefit, Justina started forward, when a long *riiiiip* cut through the loud noise of the ballroom. She glanced down with a giddy relief at the hopelessly torn lace hem of her gown dragging on the floor.

Her father furrowed his brow. "What's wrong with you, girl?"

She'd avoided that particular gentleman successfully for more than a fortnight and now her father would turn her over to him? "You tore my hem," she said quickly and pointed to the now blessedly tattered fabric. Saints in heaven. Who would have ever suspected her father was useful for something?

The viscount peered down at her skirts and scratched his head. "Then fix it," he barked, earning several curious stares from nearby guests. "And don't tarry."

Her friends held her eye for a long moment, a silent look of understanding passed between them. With Honoria standing as sentry at the edge of the ballroom, Gillian fell into quick step beside Justina.

They moved along the perimeter of the ballroom. "I do believe the duke was staring at you," Gillian said, those quiet words barely reaching her ears.

"Perhaps," she answered noncommittally, her gaze fixed on the back entrance of the ballroom. There had been a glimmer of a moment where his gaze had landed on her and the same potent hunger that had filled their blue depths when they'd met in Lady Wessex's garden had stretched across the ballroom. "But neither has he come to call." Or request a set. Her lips turned in a smile made of bitterness and regret. "Honoria should feel assured that those chance meetings between us were just that…chance meetings."

Gillian stopped suddenly and took Justina by the hand, halting their retreat. She looked quizzically at the other woman. "Honoria is wrong," she said quietly. "The duke has come to call and…" And that was all. But once, and only to return a book. "Honoria has been so hurt by her past that she fails to recognize there is still good in men. Even the rogues, the rakes, and scoundrels."

A kindred moment stretched between them as they shared a smile.

Gillian opened her mouth to speak when her gaze landed on someone beyond Justina's shoulder. She followed her gaze and swallowed down a curse.

The Marquess of Tennyson, his eyes fixed on her, wound his way through the crowd. "Go, see to your hem," Gillian murmured, giving her a nudge. "I will distract him."

Spinning on her heel, Justina lost herself in the crowd. As a young lady, she'd lamented her mere five-feet three-inches of height, now she gave thanks for the advantage it gave in escaping notice. She slipped out of the ballroom and rushed down the hall, her skirts rustling noisily in the quiet.

"Well, Miss Barrett, we meet again."

Those words, eerily familiar, uttered by Nick a week prior, now delivered coldly by another, brought her jerking to a stop. Justina wheeled around and fear iced her veins. "How…?" How had he found her so quickly?

An ugly, triumphant grin split the marquess' face. As he stalked slowly forward, it occurred to her that if it weren't for the soullessness of that stare, he would almost be described as handsome. But there was that emptiness. "Tsk, tsk. You do have a history of sneaking off. Quite scandalous," he teased and that frosty jeering snapped her back into movement.

Justina retreated several steps. "It isn't proper for us to be here, alone, my lord," she reminded him. Then, would a beast like the Marquess of Tennyson, who'd made it a point of stalking her whereabouts, be bothered with such trivialities as propriety? She continued retreating, not taking her gaze from him.

"No," he said in gleeful agreement that gave her momentary pause. "Particularly not with your torn gown." Involuntarily, her gaze fell to the floor and flew back to his. He smirked. The marquess continued coming. "Imagine the scandal if *La Belle Ferronniere* were discovered alone, with a gentleman?" Her back knocked hard against the wall. His grin expanded, revealing even white teeth in a cold smile the Devil would have envied, and then he continued advancing. "Do not flatter yourself, love. I've no intention of ruining you." He paused and smiled a slow, unfeeling grin. "Not anymore."

She held up a hand to ward him off. What was he on about? Her mind spun, trying to make sense of that cryptic assurance that wasn't much of an assurance. "Stop," she demanded in quiet tones.

With an infuriating calm, Lord Tennyson yanked off his gloves and stuffed them inside his jacket. "I've received a better offer than the one your father presented. That isn't why I'm here."

"My father is a fool," she said tersely and took a step to move around him.

He slid into her path. "I do not disagree there, Miss Barrett," he said, grinning. "Regardless, I'm not here to ruin you, as that tragic look in your eye worries over," he said casually. She remained tightly coiled, the mocking glint in his eyes fanning her wariness of this man. "I am here to warn you."

*Warn me?*

He reached inside his jacket and withdrew a single missive. Justina flicked her gaze between the scrap and Lord Tennyson's face. "Come, surely you'd care to know what's contained upon the page." He was the Devil in that original garden with an apple extended in his evil hands. And damn her for being as weak as the first woman for allowing him to toy with her.

Justina wetted her lips. Then she proved she had far more strength than Eve, for she snapped her skirts and wheeled about to leave.

"Aren't you curious about the gentleman who has you so captivated? Your precious Duke of Huntly?" he called out. Heat slapped at her cheeks. "Tell me, Miss Barrett," he went on, temptingly. "How well do you *truly* know the gentleman?"

Unease knotted her belly. She would not let him toy with her like the cat that had a mouse between its paws. A man such as Tennyson throwing aspersions upon Nick's character was like the Devil condemning God himself.

Except... She lingered.

"Ah, I see you are curious, Miss Barrett. Come, come," he taunted, waving the note. "Have a read."

She bit the inside of her cheek and, fool that she was, with stiff fingers, took it from him, and skimmed the elegantly scrawled letters.

*Miss Barrett,*

*If you were wise, you'd be wary of Huntly. Surely you are not so stupid, you believe in chance meetings?*

That is what the missive said? She was expected to trust this man who'd pursued her relentlessly since the start of the Season. Justina shoved it back into the marquess' hand. "I don't need your rubbish warnings," she said sharply. And not simply because Tennyson was a snake who kept company with her father. A man who, by his own words, had admitted to colluding with the viscount.

He frowned. "You will not give up on your girlish longing for Huntly and his title?"

Tennyson and whoever had penned his bloody note clearly had not gleaned that Nick Tallings, the Duke of Huntly, had tired of *her*. Nor did she give a jot about Nick's dukedom. "It is not about his title—" Justina promptly closed her mouth. She'd be damned ten times until Sunday before she spoke of her feelings with this man.

"So, you *do* care for the gentleman." The marquess sighed and stuffed the note inside his jacket, as though bored by their exchange. "You could not make this easy for me, Miss Barrett. Very well, you truly leave me no choice then."

Fear ran amok at the cryptic resignation to that statement. He took a step and she held a staying up. "What are you doing?" She prided herself on the steely strength of that deliverance.

"Why, I'm ruining you, of course." He started forward.

Her heart lurched. "But you said you didn't intend to ruin me."

"No," he corrected. "Alas, you now leave me no choice."

*Bloody hell.*

THIS WAS THE LAST NIGHT that he'd see Miss Justina Barrett. Oh, granted, given their statuses in the *ton*, they'd move through the same Social spheres. Yet, there was no need for their paths to cross with anything more meaningful.

Searching for her in the crowd, Nick sought to determine why that truth left him oddly…bereft. Hollow inside. His gaze landed on the pale-haired and brown-haired misses, so often with her, and he cursed himself for looking for Justina even now.

By God, he wanted to leave this infernal affair. Wanted to go to his home or his club, or ideally both, and get himself well and truly soused. The whole reason he was in attendance at Chilton's ball even now, was because it was at Nick's bequest that the formal affair had been thrown together, with the intentions of trapping Rutland's sister-in-law and ultimately forcing her hand. As such, he'd an obligation to at least suffer through the event.

But as he continued his systematic work seizing the Viscount

Waters' debt and the debt of that man's son, Justina had retained a tentacle-like hold on Nick's thoughts. Having convinced himself that poetry and any other piece of literature was nothing but rot, and that he'd not picked up a book of poetry in thirteen years—until her.

Nick stared over his glass of champagne at the tops of the heads of Chilton's guests and took care to avoid anyone's eyes. He didn't want bloody company. He didn't want to don the roguish smile the peerage had come to expect from the always affable Duke of Huntly, who inside had a soul as rotted as the scoundrel who'd been the scourge of London.

And he most certainly didn't wish to see Justina Barrett and all the gentlemen eyeing her with covetous stares, the way they might hunger for those shining gems that couldn't hold a flicker of actual light to the young lady's spirit.

With a sound of disgust, he downed his drink.

Chilton sidled next to him, a glass in his own fingers. "I'll have you remember this was entirely for your benefit," he pointed out with far too much relish.

"I recall," he bit out. And the misery of this affair was to be his punishment for embroiling Justina in his plans for Rutland.

The mirth faded from his friend's grin and the harsh planes of Chilton's face settled into a somber mask. "Other than the furtive glances you've been casting in the young lady's direction, you've made otherwise little move toward her."

Given the hushed quiet of that observation, Nick could very well pretend to fail to hear the words and question there. Yet, this man had been his friend since he'd been a youthful lad with a love of poetry to the then transformed boy who'd cut his father's dangling body from a rope. "I, of course, thought on your…advice," he said, stiffly. Chilton had always been remarkably clear in logic when Nick had been hotheaded with emotion. It was, no doubt, the reason for the baron's brilliant success upon the battlefields of Europe.

Goddamn the other man. Must he always be infernally correct? And more, goddamn himself for putting a young woman he'd known but a handful of days before a lifetime of hunger for revenge against Rutland.

His friend gave a brusque, approving nod. "It is the right decision."

"It is a weak one," Nick muttered. And here he'd spent years lauding himself a worthy opponent to Rutland.

The other man shifted closer and dropped his voice even lower. "Weak, because you will not ruin a young lady?" Chilton shook his head. "You are weaker if you see that end of your plan through," he said, motioning over a servant. He traded his empty glass for a full one. After the liveried servant walked off, he went on. "We do not ruin young ladies." That harsh, veiled, but still clear reminder of Nick's own sister, miserably wedded off with his grandfather's pressuring to a cruel bugger roused all the deepest hatred Nick had long carried for Rutland. He pressed his eyes closed a moment willing back the always-present guilt. "We only exact our revenge on other men, lest we become those men." Something dark flashed in the baron's eyes and then was quickly gone. "As I said, the lady's fate will be decided by her father, through actions you carried out, and you will not be bound to her."

*Wasn't that truly the same as if I had ruined her myself? It does not matter what happens to Justina Barrett from here. It does not matter.*

Nick searched his gaze over the floor for the lady who refused to relinquish her hold over his thoughts.

"She slipped away a short while ago," Chilton murmured, gesturing to the back entrance of his ballroom.

*…There was a gentleman pursuing me…*

He did a quick sweep of the ballroom seeking the relentless Marquess of Tennyson. Gone. He silently cursed. By God, he'd had the gentleman's word. Then, was there truly any value in the pledge given by a man who'd hunt a lady uninterested in his suit?

*She is not my responsibility. She is not my responsibility.*

Nick silently cursed and handed his glass over to his friend.

"What is it?"

Ignoring Chilton's question, he quickened his strides through the crowded ballroom. He kept his gaze forward, avoiding the stares of interested ladies and mamas eager for an introduction. He continued walking to the back of the hall, to the back entrance. Of course, it was madness to assume just because he'd been unable to locate Justina that she was at risk from Tennyson's advances. He'd purchased Waters' vowels and, through it, her dowry. There were more than two hundred guests present and countless reasons why he couldn't single-handedly identify either her or the marquess in the crowd.

*Do you truly trust the word of a man like Tennyson?* With his own black soul, he should know better.

The same knot of unease in his belly that had portended doom all those years ago with Lord Rutland's visit was now the same pit as he stalked through Chilton's townhouse. "Madness," he muttered. He was utterly—

"I said let me pass." Justina's voice ringing with spirited fury brought him jerking to an abrupt stop at the end of the hall. The lady stood in a breathtaking display of spirit; a bold, fearless energy radiating from her person.

Nick quickly worked his gaze over the scene—Tennyson in his shirtsleeves, his cravat loose, Justina's hem shredded. A primal fury better suited to the beasts of old surged through him. "Tennyson," he bit out and the pair at the end of the corridor whipped around to face him.

A staggering relief lit Justina's eyes. With the marquess distracted, she rushed out from behind the man and raced down the hall. Nick caught her by the arms and ran his gaze over her face. "Did he hurt you?" he demanded. By God, he'd shred the man with his bare hands and stuff his entrails down his throat.

She gave her head a tight shake.

"Huntly," the other man greeted calling Nick's attention. "Bad form to interrupt a tryst." Lord Tennyson smirked. "Then, invariably, the result will be the same as if we'd trysted."

Voices sounded in the distance, fast approaching. The smug grin on the marquess' face contained his triumph. The air left Nick on a hiss as he and Justina, as one, swiveled their gazes to the opposite end of the corridor. To the rapid footfalls. Her pink-tinged porcelain skin went a deathly white.

Nick's pulse pounded loudly. He'd believed, in purchasing Waters' vowels and holding control of Justina's dowry, that Tennyson would move on to a wealthy heiress. With his maneuverings, she would be bound to this man. Society would see her ruined and wed to a lecher like Tennyson. "Marry me?" he urged, the question tumbling out from a place of illogic.

Her eyes flared wide. "I don't un…" She followed his gaze to Tennyson and she gave a quick jerky nod.

He dipped his head and claimed her lips. She *deserved* far better than him or Tennyson or most of the other miserable blighters in London, but Tennyson would destroy her spirit. Having witnessed his own sister's demise into darkness, he could not live in the same Society and bear witness to that transformation. But with Justina's body close to him and her mouth pliant under his, the reasons for the kiss transformed so all he felt was her. He angled his head and further deepened his exploration of the soft contours of her flesh.

Great gasps and exclamations went up and doused the momentary madness that had gripped him.

Nick wrenched his head back, and quickly positioned himself between Justina and the small audience assembled in the corridor. Her father's mouth was opening and closing like a fish thrown ashore. The notorious gossip, Lady Jersey, nicknamed Silence, in the greatest irony for the leading matron could have talked Boney out of battle with the amount she prattled. Hope stirred. Though unpredictable and eccentric, the lady, however, had proven capable of great kindness amongst the *ton*. As soon as the thought slid in, he cast it out. No young lady could weather this gossip without being fully ruined and without Nick himself being forever labeled a blackguard.

*Then, isn't that what I have prided myself on secretly being?*

"I don't understand," the viscount whined, scratching his sweaty pate.

"I daresay, it does not take much to gather," the countess drawled. The respectable hostess looked to Nick with a glimmer in her eyes. "Tsk, tsk, Your Grace," she drawled, tapping her fan against her opposite palm. "Your reputation precedes you." Then, she flicked her gaze to where the Marquess of Tennyson hovered. "An evening for trysts, I see," she stretched out those syllables in an erroneous supposition. "You should run along, Tennyson, while this matter is settled." The marquess hesitated. The countess clapped her hands once. "Run along, Tennyson."

Then, like a child scolded by a stern tutor, he gathered his jacket, shrugged into it, and stalked off. Not before he withered Nick with a hard glare.

Chilton stepped forward. Disappointment steeped in his gaze, he took in the group assembled, lingering his stare briefly on Justina's rumpled gown. Then he politely averted his gaze. It looked damning. As he'd intended. But the motives that had first driven him to Justina Barrett were not the same motives that now saw him in this compromising position with her. This unexpected, but necessary act had not been intended to destroy, but rather to save.

*Will she still see it that way when I ruin her father and brother?*

"But…" Viscount Waters let out a small wail.

Lady Jersey patted him on the arm. "Rest assured, Huntly is a good boy. He'll do right by the gel," she assured. "Isn't that right, Huntly?" She winged a dark eyebrow up.

A thick, tense pall of silence fell over the gathering. His skin pricked with the heat of Justina's gaze and he looked down. Uncertainty filled their cornflower blue depths and she spoke in words that barely reached his ears. "You do not have to do this."

Nick told his brain to tell his head to move and he managed a semblance of a nod for the countess.

"It is settled then," the woman beamed. "He'll marry the girl. You've caught yourself a good one, Miss Barrett," she called loudly.

And standing there, with Lady Jersey's words ringing mockingly in the hallway, the older woman couldn't be more wrong.

He curled his hands tightly. With the treachery he'd originally intended for Justina and the revenge he still intended to have against Rutland, he was as much a spawn of Satan as Rutland himself.

# CHAPTER 13

THE FOLLOWING MORNING, NICK WAS shown through the corridors of Viscount Waters' townhouse. As he walked, he took in the fraying red carpets, the faded paint upon walls where portraits, now gone, had left the indelible mark of their presence. Paintings, that with his own machinations and his solicitor's efforts, had been carted off and sold part and parcel at auction. The peeled satin wallpaper stood as a stark testament to the Barrett family's circumstances.

This was the state the viscount had left his family in. Nick tightened his jaw. And soon, they'd be stripped of every last vestige of wealth they possessed. Justina, however, would be spared. *Would she wish to be spared if she knew what I intend for her family? What I have already done?*

He tamped down the taunting questions at the far corners of his mind. She'd be saved from a marriage to Tennyson. She'd live the life of a well-cared for duchess, with vast wealth at her fingertips so that there would be no need for those visits to circulating libraries. A life far safer, far more secure, than the hell his own sister knew.

With that always-present reminder of the wrongs Rutland had inflicted, the safe, familiar, and comforting hatred coursed through him, and Nick clenched his jaw. He continued following along behind the ancient butler, who moved with a shuffling slowness.

The servant brought them to a stop beside a heavy oak door and knocked once.

"Enter," Waters boomed. The butler pushed the door open. Seated behind his desk, Viscount Waters froze with his hand on a half-empty decanter of brandy.

"His Grace, the Duke of Huntly," the man announced and that introduction brought the viscount reluctantly to his feet.

"Bad luck you being in the hallway," the man said as soon as the servant backed out of the room, leaving him and Nick alone. Retaining a death-like grip on his decanter, the viscount sat and motioned to the empty seat opposite him. Nick crossed over and stiffly slid into the folds of the aged leather wing back chair. "Tennyson could have ruined the girl," Waters grunted, pouring the liquid to the brim. Several drops spilled over onto the man's short fingers and he sucked the liquor off the way a parched man might thirst for water.

"Yet, it was me," Nick said brusquely, removing his gloves and neatly placing them inside his jacket alongside the special license he'd obtained earlier that morn.

"Bah, my silly girl's fault," the viscount groused, waving his spare hand. "Not a brain in that one's head."

He stiffened as a desire to drag the other man across the desk and bury his fist in his face for that undeserved insult coursed through him. How could a man know his child so little? Nick's father had known precisely his children's interests and had nurtured them. When there had been limited funds, there had still been enough books to feed his love of them. "I've come to discuss the terms of the marriage."

Over the rim of his dusty snifter, the viscount frowned. "Did you take the girl's virginity?" How coolly he spoke of Justina. Nausea burned in his throat. The lady had deserved more in not only the man who'd be her husband, but in the father who'd given her life.

"No," he said quietly.

A grin formed on the viscount's fleshy lips. "Then there is no reason for the marriage. I can find another to take the girl, I expect." He expected. Not that he had any assurance from another *gentleman*. Yet, it was enough to throw over the security Nick now held out for Justina.

"Ah, but it hardly matters if you can find another," he said, infusing the hard ducal edge that shook the viscount's previous calm.

The man gulped audibly and his fingers quaked with such force, he set the glass down, spilling a healthy portion of his drink. "It matters that *I* am going to marry her." He paused. "With or without your permission."

And that had been part of his plan since its inception. Justina Barrett would have belonged to him—body, heart, and soul, forever merged, with her role of pawn for the Barrett family gone, and her happiness destroyed. With her whisperings in a lecture hall and in a midnight garden, she'd blasted a hole through his intentions for her like a cannonball through the wall of an old keep.

The viscount pursed his mouth. "The girl's dowry belongs to Tennyson."

Nick's patience snapped. "Justina." Four creases marred the nobleman's brow. "Her name is Justina. Not girl. Not gel. Use her bloody name," he bit out. A vise squeezed at his lungs as he imagined quick-witted, always-smiling Justina under this bastard's thumb. How had she remained so hopeful through life?

And would she maintain that same hope after her brother and father were made to pay for Rutland's sins?

The viscount scratched his paunch. "Doesn't matter what her name is, it matters what use she serves," he said with an uncharacteristic fearlessness.

"I've secured her dowry from Tennyson," Surprise lit the older man's face. "It will return and remain in Justina's name. Hers alone, as well as the family property you lost to him." Nick did not expect those gifts would ever earn her pardon when she discovered his actions against her family but they would be gifts so she had some control over her future.

Her father grunted. "I don't care if the gir—Justina," he swiftly amended when Nick narrowed his gaze, "is cared for. *I'm* in debt, Huntly," he said bluntly.

Hatred for this man burned all the stronger. And here he'd believed himself never abhorring anyone with the same vitriol as he did Rutland. How wrong he'd been. "To whom?" The reckless fool still did not know that even now he looked upon the largest holder. For the first time since he'd crafted his scheme, he found an unholy delight in destroying this bastard before him that had nothing to do with his connection to Rutland and everything to do with his treatment of Justina.

Waters waved a hand. "A little bit here. A little bit there. Tennyson owns the most and there are others. Men who'd be willing to pay the right price."

Bile stung the back of his throat. By God, Nick had resented his father for taking the coward's way and ending himself. But those sins and crimes paled when compared to Justina's father who'd sell her like a Covent Garden doxy. Smoothing his features into the cold, emotionless mask he'd perfected years ago, he settled a hard stare on her useless sire. "I've tired of this discussion." In a false show, he came to his feet and the viscount waved his hands frantically.

"No, no. Please, sit." That cocksure arrogance gone, Justina's father clasped his hands together. He was too much a lackwit to see that Nick would be damned ten more times to Sunday before he left without securing her hand. She could not remain here with this man. Not when he'd sell her off to a depraved rake. "I would be interested in…negotiating." Waters paused. "If you offer me the right amount, she can be yours."

Not even two days ago, the offer presented by Waters would have been the pinnacle of all Nick had dreamed of these thirteen years. Now, there was a bitter triumph that his revenge would come in this way, with Justina still used as a pawn. Only now…by the man who sired her and Nick an unintentional, but still voluntary player.

"I won't give you a pence as though she is some whore," he said, settling back in his chair.

Waters spread his arms wide. "Then we are done here."

Nick layered his arms to the sides of his chair and tapped his fingertips in a staccato rhythm. "There is another way…" He dangled that bait and the viscount instantly leaned forward.

"I'm listening."

"I'll buy up your vowels," he said and ceased his deliberate tapping. "You name anyone and everyone you owe funds to and I'll secure them."

Since he was a boy, Nick had appreciated how powerless those outside the peerage, in fact, were. He'd never, however, truly gleaned the extent of the power in the hands of noblemen, until he'd ascended to the rank of duke. Doors once closed, were opened. Ladies who'd once desired nothing more than a spot in his bed, vied for the role of duchess.

The irony was not lost to him in this moment. He now sat before the only man in the entire realm who'd rather have a fat purse than a cemented connection with a duke. "All of it?" Waters croaked. "You don't even know how much the amount is."

"The amount doesn't matter." Those were the truest words he'd ever given this reprobate. Nick had built his fortune in trade long before he'd inherited equally vast wealth from his dead relative. "Give me the names of the men who own your debt," he repeated. Feeling sullied for even sitting in the room with this man, he removed his gloves from his jacket and beat them together, eager for the end of the exchange.

Waters choked and shook his head. "You'd do that?"

He *had* done that. "I will." He'd own it all.

An unexpected wariness filled the man's blue eyes. Justina's eyes. Nick stared, riveted by those clear blue depths; that tangible reminder of her blood relation to this foul beast. "Why are you so determined to have the gel?"

"Would you talk me out of my decision?" he countered, deliberately evasive.

His response had the desired effect as the viscount shook his head frantically. "No. No. Beautiful girl. A Diamond. Prettiest in three Seasons, they say. Empty-headed, so you won't have one of those fishwives challenging you."

Justina Barrett possessed greater wit and intellect than the whole of the peerage combined. The stinging rebuke on his tongue burned, asking to be set free on this pompous, coldhearted bastard. "We'll wed on the morrow." Nick climbed to his feet. "Compile a list of those owning your vowels and see they are delivered to me." In doing so, he would have every last name and every last confirmation that he owned all this man possessed.

The viscount sprang to his feet. "An honor, Your Grace. Justina will make you a splendid bride," he said, quickly coming around the side of the desk. He wheezed as though he'd trekked across a countryside on foot.

Nick's lip peeled back in an involuntary sneer. The man did not give a jot, however, as to what manner of husband he would make Justina. "I'll show myself out." Before the viscount even crossed the room, Nick pulled the door open and started down the same corridors he'd marched a short while ago, eager to be free of this house and the vileness of Waters' soul. When he was a father, his own children would not know the selfishness of this man or even his own father, who'd taken his life and left their family in a quagmire of uncertainty. Which only conjured images of laying Justina down and knowing her in every way.

*She will be mine.*

Before, revenge had driven that need. Now, coupled with that, was a hungering for her; an irrational, inexplicable need that had proven his weakness.

He turned at the end of the corridor and slowed to a stop. All the tension eased from his taut frame. Justina hovered in the middle of the corridor. What power did she hold over him that she could, with her presence alone, dull the fury that had fueled his every thought and movement for thirteen years?

In her arms, she hugged a black leather book close. "Your Grace," she greeted softly.

A small smile hovered on his lips. "I think we've moved far beyond formalities, Justina," he said, quietly. After all, tomorrow they would be man and wife.

Her tongue darted out and traced the seam of her lips. "Why?"

Her question snapped him back from desirous musings. "Why?"

"Why would you offer to marry me?"

Images flitted forward. Justina on her back, arms outstretched. In his bed. "There was our meeting in the street," he began, drifting closer and erasing the space between them. Nick dusted his knuckles down the side of her cheek. He dipped his face lower and the scent of chocolate lingered on her breath, caressed his lips; tantalizing and sweet, so that he wanted to taste it on her. "Never tell me, you've forgotten our exchanges in the gardens and your parlor and—"

Justina gave her head a shake. "*I* did not forget," she interrupted. He'd have to be deafer than a post to fail to hear that slight emphasis. The lady stepped away and he mourned the loss of heat that had spilled onto his person at her body's nearness. She glanced about and then motioned to the open door beside her. "I would speak to you, away from the prying eyes of servants."

Nick hesitated and then followed her inside the cheerful parlor.

She spoke without preamble. "You've not come by in a week." Her words came out, not as an accusation, but as a statement of fact she sought to puzzle through. She slashed the air with a hand. "Last evening, you rescue me, yet again, and then you offer me marriage, saving me from ruin. Why would you do that?" She ran questioning eyes over his face.

How could the answer be both: to destroy and to save? And yet, that was the very real truth. He'd save her from being sold off by Waters, because if that were to happen, her spirit would wither and die. And he would be damned if he let anyone extinguish her effervescent light.

"You met my sister," he began quietly. He was letting her in, not to deceive or trick, but because he would have her know at least a part of who he was.

Since Justina returned from the ball last evening, she'd taken to her chambers where sleep eluded her. Instead, she'd been kept awake, riddled with regret for what would never be. But also, relief for what would not be—marriage to the Marquess of Tennyson.

And through that relief and regret, she'd sought to puzzle through Nick's rescue and offer of marriage as well as that cryptic warning issued by Tennyson before he'd attempted to ruin her. Why should Nick, a powerful duke who could have anyone he wished, who answered to none, and who'd disappeared from her life one week prior, save her as he'd done?

Standing outside while he'd met with her father, her ear pressed to the oak panel, she'd secretly hoped there would be an utterance of something—devotion. Affection. Even the simplest regard.

Oh, of course it could not be love. They'd known each other but a handful of days and, yet, nearly a fortnight earlier, she'd allowed herself to believe there could be that beautiful emotion she'd always dreamed of for herself.

Now, with but a handful of steps between them, Nick's unexpected admission, quashed that romantic sliver of hope she'd held.

Justina set her book down on the table with a soft thump. "Your sister?" she ventured, knowing she must sound like the greatest lackwit for echoing his words, which highlighted how little they knew of one another. "I do not understand how your sister has anything to do with your offering for me," she confessed in hesitant tones.

"I am trying to explain." *Explain.* As in why he should have ever asked for her hand. Her fingers came up reflexively to rub the dull ache in her chest and she caught herself, forcing her hand to her side.

Nick wandered over to a rose-inlaid table and picked up a porcelain figurine; the painted couple now chipped, it would hardly fetch a pence and, as such, was one of the few pieces her reprobate father had not sold off. "I was not born to be a duke," he murmured, more to himself, studying that porcelain couple as though they contained the answers to life. "My father was a merchant." At last, he picked his head up, leveling her with a piercing gaze.

"Do you expect I should judge you for having roots in trade?" she countered.

"It mattered very much to all of Society," he said with a wry grin. As a duke, she'd believed him incapable of knowing the same censure of Society's prying eyes. Only, with his revelation, he proved that he, too, had not always been immune to the judgmental *ton.*

Sadness suffused her heart. Yes, how little they knew one another. If he should even wonder, even think that of her, he knew her not at all. "I am not all of Society, Nick." Since she'd made her Come Out, she'd wanted to divorce herself in every way from those condescending lords and ladies who were content with the image on the surface; those shallow people who never looked deeper. "Do you believe I, whose father would sell me to the highest bidder, who would orchestrate my ruin to settle his debt, would find your father lacking simply because he was a merchant?" She was unable to keep the hurt from creeping into that query.

His gaze still fixed on her, Nick set down the figurine. "A fortnight ago, I would have said yes. I was invisible to the peerage for so long. I'd believed those people incapable of seeing anyone outside their respected sphere."

Justina drifted around the opposite side of the table and stopped across from him. She skimmed her fingers over the chipped surface. The whole of the *ton* saw in Nick Tallings, the Duke of Huntly, a rogue, in possession of one of the oldest titles. How many had truly given thought to who he was and who he'd been outside of that title? Including, her. Shame filled her. "It never mattered," she said softly. "To most it does. To me, it never did." To her, he'd been the man who'd thrown himself into the path of a wild horse to save her and who'd sat beside her in a lecture hall and encouraged her to speak her mind.

"I know that now." His gruff baritone washed over her. "I'm telling you so you might..." He paused and seemed to search his mind. "...understand," he settled for.

Understand the reason for his intervention last evening.

"When I was a boy, my father's business was failing. There was a..." Something dark filled his eyes and a chill ran through her. There was a depth of coldness that she'd not seen from him; an iciness that went against the man he'd shown himself to be since that day in Gipsy Hill. They all carried secrets. Which ones belonged to this man?

"There was a...?" She urged him on with her eyes and words.

"Nobleman." His lip peeled back in a sneer and Justina stared unblinkingly as that cynical glint in his eyes transformed him into more a stranger than when they'd met in the streets. "This gentleman called in my father's loans two years early. It mattered not that my father devoted his life to that business. Or that in calling in that debt, my father, my entire family would be ruined. He destroyed my family," he whispered. At the stark emptiness there, she took a step closer, wanting to drive back the pain he now spoke of.

"What happened to your family?" she encouraged when he fell quiet, filled with loathing for the nameless peer who'd destroyed a family.

He blinked and looked up. Had he forgotten her presence here until now? "My father died..." His expression darkened and the coldness there drove back all warmth from the room, leaving her chilled inside. "...soon after the debts were called in. We were forced to live with my grandfather, an earl who quite delighted in reminding my remaining family of our uselessness. My mother died not long after my father. My sister and I were..." Another hard grin formed on his lips. "left with my grandfather. I was determined to never be dependent on anyone, my grandfather included. I built one of the greatest steel companies in England."

She'd not even known of his mercantile roots. "*You* are a merchant?" Awe filled her for this man who would buck Social dictates and build his success and power with his own hands.

His lips twisted wryly. "I expect you find it scandalous to wed a man who works in trade, still."

"On the contrary," she said shaking her head. She found him inspiring. The *ton* looked down upon self-made men, and yet... "There is far greater honor in a man who'd work in trade to restore his family's wealth and honor, than a man who'd squander it all, and rely on nothing but the leniency of his creditors." As her father had done.

Surprise showed in his face.

They truly were strangers, in every way...he, a stranger who had stepped in to save her out of some misbegotten sense of honor. "What of your sister?" she asked softly, bringing him back to the tale of his family. Needing to know just who Nick Tallings, in fact, was.

"I was fourteen, Cecily fifteen, and my grandfather demanded she make a match," he spoke quickly, as though wanting the story told as fast as possible.

Her heart wrenched. At fifteen, Justina was still the naïve girl lost in her love of ribbons and bonnets, dreaming of love. She listened to his telling, torn between awe for what he'd managed to accomplish and regret for a boy who'd been forced to abandon his childhood because of some ruthless nobleman's disregard.

"I should have stopped it," he said and the muscles of his throat moved. "I should have prevented her from agreeing and I did not. And for it, she is wedded to an old, miserable lord who won't, at the very least, make a young widow of her." Fire glinted in his eyes. "You will never be like my mother or sister." *Or my own mother.* "Your dowry will belong to you. The manor your father lost, will belong to you. All of it." Her heart swelled to bursting, not at the material gifts he held out, but rather the intangible offering there. Self-control when Society would rob any woman of that gift.

He would give her freedom should she wish it, when his own sister was without. Another pang struck her chest, for Lady Cecily who'd been forced to grow up too soon, and for the hell she now knew, and for the guilt he carried. Justina stretched a hand across the table and touched his arm. His bicep jumped under her fingers and he met her gaze. "You were a boy. You will blame yourself for not intervening to save her and yet you were no different than her—a child, still." A child forced to grow up too soon. She forced her hand to her side and she smoothed her palms down the sides of her skirts. "Marrying me will not right an imagined wrong you've done your sister," she said quietly. He snapped his eyebrows into a line.

"Is that why you believe I offered for you?" he murmured, coming around the table.

"Is it not?" she countered, picking up her forgotten-until-now copy of Shelley's work.

"Do I wish to spare you from a life spent married to a man such as Tennyson?" He continued walking until he stood before her. Nick placed his lips close to her ear and her breath caught hard as a delicious tingle ran from her neck down her spine. "I do," he whispered. "I do not doubt your innocence would be forever shattered if you married him or any man like him."

She fought through the desirous haze he cast and tipped her chin up mutinously. "I'd not force a man to bind himself to me out of pity or—" He pressed his fingertips to her lips; the heat of his skin momentarily obliterating all thought and word.

"Not pity. I could only ever admire you, Justina," he whispered, angling her face to his. Her lashes fluttered as the intoxicating hint of sandalwood and brandy which clung to him invaded her senses. "I wanted to stay away from you because it was best." How could it ever be for the best? "Now, I would marry you because the thought of him, or anyone touching you, knowing you, in any way, drives me mad." He lowered his mouth and claimed hers in a searing kiss that scorched a quick path through her, setting her body afire with a fast-spreading conflagration that threatened to consume.

The book slipped from her fingers.

A shuddery moan spilled past her lips and he slid his tongue inside, stoking the fire all the more. Nick folded his hand about her nape and angled her head to better receive his kiss. Their mouths met in a fiery explosion. Where his previous kiss had been one of tender passion, there was nothing gentle in this embrace. With a groan, she turned in his arms and his mouth branded hers. He swept his tongue around to meet with hers and she boldly met his movements. Their tongues danced and mated, and with every stroke, desire for this man liquefied her. Her legs gave out, but he caught her to him, and guided her buttocks atop the table.

A soft cry escaped her when he drew his mouth away, but he merely trailed his lips down the curve of her cheek, lower to the sensitive place where her lobe met her neck. He darted his tongue out, tasting her, and she sank her teeth into her lower lip, wanting more of him. "I want to marry you," he whispered, between acts of worshiping her skin with his kisses. "Because I want to know you in every way. Because I want to have you in my bed and in my arms." She whimpered as he drew her earlobe into his mouth and suckled. "And I never want you to know another man but me."

"How could there ever be another but you?" she countered on a shuddery whisper.

Something powerful and unidentifiable darkened his eyes. He touched his lips to hers, once more, in a fleeting caress. "Never doubt why I'm marrying you," he said when he broke that contact. "I need you to know that. I need you to know, that since I saw you in the streets of Lambeth, you have captivated me. In ways I never wanted, nor understand. But my desire for you is real."

His desire. And yet, she wanted so much more.

Nick opened his mouth. There were words and questions in his eyes.

Justina cocked her head. "What is it?" she urged as an unwanted disquiet pulled at her.

"It is nothing," he said gruffly. "I have matters of business to attend before we are wed tomorrow." He gathered her fingers and raised them to his lips for a kiss. Little shivers radiated from the point of contact and traveled up her arm.

Except, as he left, Justina stood staring after him. For why, with his parting words sounding like the most beautiful of endearments had there been an ominous thread that stirred her unease? She gave her head a hard shake. He may not love her, but he'd laid a true foundation on which to build their marriage. She touched her fingertips to her lips where his kiss burned there still. And yet, for the excitement trilling through her, questions slid forward once more as to why he'd disappeared for a week.

# CHAPTER 14

THEY WERE MARRIED THE NEXT morning. By special license. In
her father's empty library. With just Lord Chilton as a witness and
Gillian and Andrew sitting on in support.

Seated at the leather button sofa alongside Justina's brother,
Gillian lifted her hand in a show of support and some of her mel-
ancholy lifted. Well, mayhap not all. She smiled and returned her
friend's wave. At her side, wearing his wire-rimmed spectacles,
Nick signed the final marriage documents laid out on her father's
desk. After he'd finished, the baron came over to speak quietly to
her husband and the vicar.

Gillian quickly took up a place at her side. Beaming as though
this had been a love match and not a marriage meant to save
Justina from ruin, her friend linked their arms. "You are happy? If
you aren't happy, Honoria and Phoebe will never forgive me," she
said in a bid for brevity.

Unbidden, Justina's eyes went over to her husband. "I am happy,"
she murmured.

*Her husband.* Hovering on the opposite side of her father's desk,
she rolled through that word in her head. He was her husband. A
man she'd now known a fortnight, whom she'd bound herself to
forever, with vows that would keep them until death did they part.

A silly grin on his lips, Andrew sprung to his feet. With a gaiety
in his footsteps better suited a child, he hurried over and nudged

Gillian out of the way.

She greeted him. "An—*oomph*."

He crushed her in a fierce hug and held her tight. "You made a good decision with Huntly." His was an observation from a brother who'd been more friend than anything; who knew her most times, better than even her elder sister. Where Phoebe had sought to protect, Andrew had treated her as an equal; a young woman who knew her mind and she would forever love him for that.

"I did," she agreed. Even as she'd longed for words of love from an honorable gentleman, she had been ultimately rescued from ruin by one of those good men.

Andrew cuffed her on the chin. "I know you wanted the courtship and marriage in those books you used to read," he said quietly. "But I also see you have the look of longing every time he enters a room."

Unbidden, Justina's gaze went to her husband, still speaking with the baron. When she was a girl with her nose buried in romance novels, she'd read of those long, piercing glances that passed between the characters. Until her sister had met and fallen in love with Edmund, that look had existed as nothing more than words on a page. Nick glanced over at her through thick hooded lashes that sucked the air from her chest. A charged energy passed between them and, with a little sigh, she smiled.

"And that is the look of longing," Andrew said, earning a laugh from Gillian.

"What do you know of the look of longing?" she teased. Justina nudged her brother in the side with her elbow. A crimson blush stained her brother's cheeks, diverting her attention momentarily over to him. "Who is the lady who has earned your heart?"

"Shh," Andrew commanded, a frown on his lips. Glancing about, he tugged at his cravat and then stared pointedly at Gillian.

She rolled her eyes. "I am Phoebe and Justina's dearest friend. You can trust I am the epitome of discretion."

Color splashed in his cheeks. "I'm not at liberty to say. It is a match that can never be," he spoke with the same dramatic flourish of those books she'd long favored.

The two ladies shared a small smile. With his self-absorption and love of the wicked—drink and gaming tables and the forbidden ladies at those clubs—Justina had never believed the time would come when Andrew could ever or would ever set aside his personal pleasures for another being. Most especially, not a young lady. At the troubled glint in his eyes, she took his hands in hers and squeezed. "If there is love, Andrew, it is a match that can be," she promised him.

"Indeed," Gillian concurred, with a firm nod. "My sister and her unlikely marriage to a former rake is proof of that."

A stark sadness glimmered in his like blue eyes. "It is not always that easy," he said with a forced half-grin. "We cannot all simply fall in love with a proper member of the peerage like Phoebe and Justina and your sister."

Fall in love? Justina gave her head a dizzying shake. Love Nick? They'd known one another but a fortnight, she could not love him. Yes, he'd rescued her—twice. And encouraged her reading. And made friends with her brother. And thought nothing of her attending scholarly lectures and—

A large, warm hand settled on her shoulder, bringing her spinning around.

Nick stared down with that same heated glimmer in his gaze that had the ever-present butterflies fluttering wildly in her belly. Something passed in his eyes and then, always a gentleman, he dropped a bow and exchanged pleasantries with Gillian and Andrew.

Justina observed him as he spoke, so casually and easily, nothing like the pompous, unfeeling sort a man of his station was purported to be. Did he regret the offer he'd made her? She worried the inside of her cheek. *I'll be a good wife to him.* And in time, mayhap there would be more.

"It is time," he murmured.

She forced herself to nod and turn back to Gillian. Gathering her hands, Justina gave them a gentle squeeze. "You may assure both Phoebe and Honoria that I am happy." Of course, this was not the romantic marriage she'd often dreamed of, but it was enough. It would have to be.

Tears filled Gillian's green eyes and she nodded.

Releasing her, Justina turned to her brother. "I will miss you, Andrew Algernon Alistair." She hurled herself into his arms and he staggered under the unexpected weight, then righted them.

With a grunt, he folded her in an embrace, burying his cheek

against the top of her hair. "I want you to be happy." He picked
his head up. "And I believe Huntly will make you happy." Then
with far more maturity than she'd ever remembered from him,
Andrew set her away and held out a hand to Nick. "Take care of
my sister." It was a gruff command that earned a slight frown from
her husband.

And then... Nick accepted the other man's hand. "I will see
her well-cared for." *What of love?* She bit the inside of her cheek.
Wanting that gift from him, when he'd already given her so much.
In time, it could come. Would come. She had to believe that.

Her father, nursing a drink, came over. "Father," she said tenta-
tively. He was the man who'd given her life. And yet, she had no
words for him. No feelings in leaving this place. There had been
far greater sadness the day her mother and sister had departed for
the countryside with Edmund than in leaving the home she'd
known the whole of her life with her father for company.

"You did good, gel," he grunted. "Not many gentlemen would
take a dowerless girl and buy off my vowels."

She swung her gaze up to Nick and found him staring on with
his face set in an unyielding mask. He had done this. He had saved
her father and, more importantly through that, her mother and
Andrew from certain financial ruin. She'd lost a little piece of her
heart to her husband.

"It is time," Nick said curtly and held out his arm.

It was time. She would set aside life inside this home that was a
threadbare shadow of the one it had been years earlier and go with
Nick. Justina hesitated a moment and then placed her fingertips
upon his coat sleeve. They walked the distance from her father's
office to the foyer in quiet. With every step, her gratitude for him
and all he'd done swelled.

*How can I not love such a man?*

They reached the marble foyer and a footman rushed forward
with their cloaks. As she shrugged into hers and fiddled with the
clasp at her throat, Justina murmured her thanks. The butler, Manfred, watched her through dewy eyes. "May I wish you all the
happiness you deserve, my lady?" he said, his voice hoarsened with
emotion better fitting a father than a loyal servant.

"You may," she said and went on tiptoe to place a kiss on his
cheek. "You must promise to look after A-Andrew." She wanted

the words to come out teasing. Wanted them to be lighthearted and carefree. The faint crack, however, belied all those futile attempts.

"Indeed, my lady," the old servant vowed and then swallowing loudly, he strode to the door and pulled it open.

She looped her hand in Nick's elbow, once again, and allowed him to guide her outside to his waiting carriage. Waving off his liveried servant, he handed her inside the massive black barouche. She blinked, adjusting her gaze to the dim space and assessed the elegant conveyance. The red velvet upholstery. The plush squabs. All signs of his wealth and power. A wealth she'd only just learned yesterday that came not solely from his rank, but by the work he'd done with his own hands.

His broad frame filled the carriage as he claimed a spot on the opposite bench.

A moment later, the servant closed the door and the carriage lurched forward.

Justina peeled back the thick, velvet curtain a moment and peered out at her family's townhouse until it faded from view and then was gone. Just like that, she was now a woman married. And she'd always longed for the day she'd find a gentleman and know love, only to now find herself married…as her sister and mother both were.

Had there ever been a time when her mother had been happy in her union?

"You are quiet," Nick observed, stretching his arm along the back of his seat.

She smiled wryly. "I believe that is the first I've ever been accused of that charge," she said, in a bid to end the nervousness at her new circumstances.

"What are you thinking?"

"I was thinking of my mother," she confided softly. "Wishing she could have been here. And Phoebe and Edmund," she added. His body went still. "My mother never speaks of her marriage to my father, but I wonder, the day she married him…what was she feeling? Was she ever happy?" And if so, when had her joy died? "She never wishes to speak of it." Him. Viscount Waters. "What of your parents?" she asked, desperately needing to shift the discourse away from her own private, troubled thoughts.

"My parents were very much in love." Her heart sang under

that additional proof of that very real sentiment. Some marriages were built of happiness and love and others....well, other couples became her parents. "It was hardly a match my grandfather approved of. He was a powerful earl, who'd plans for his daughter to marry another. In the end, she chose my father. He owned an iron factory. For as long as I recall, it was failing. My family, however, was happy regardless."

How alike and yet different they were. They had both known the love of a family. Justina's, however, had never known even a fleeting bit of happiness with her own father. "They were fortunate," she said quietly. Viscountess Waters had been cheated by life and the expectations of their Society.

He stitched his eyebrows together in a hard line.

"That your parents knew some happiness together." Her own mother's life had been remarkably devoid of any real affection, devotion, or even faithfulness from her miserable husband.

The carriage rocked to a halt.

A moment later, a servant opened the door and Nick leapt out. He turned back and helped her down. Justina climbed her gaze up the white stucco façade of the Mayfair townhouse. This was her home. So many of the memories of the previous townhouse she'd occupied had been filled with her and her siblings' attempts to make happiness where they could. Now, she looked on at this new residence; a grand one. The place where she would create memories with Nick. The home where their children would live.

"Justina?" There was a question in that quiet utterance.

Turning a smile on him, she accepted his hand and fell into step alongside him. The butler stood in wait with the door open. His cold eyes and wrinkled face set in a hard mask, stood as a stark contrast to the kind-eyed butler who'd been more friend than anything to the Barrett children.

With a murmured greeting for the servant, Justina proceeded ahead of her husband and then stopped. The soaring foyer with its sweeping ceilings featured a mural better suited to one of those Renaissance cathedrals. At the center hung a crystal chandelier lit with candles. Her mouth fell open at the extravagance of the ducal residence. She forced her lips together and snapped her attention downward to where an older woman stood in wait; her gaze averted. A little niggling of homesickness pebbled in her belly.

"Allow me to introduce you to Mrs. Benedict. She is the head housekeeper," Nick said at her back, and Justina jumped.

The woman of middling years came forward and sank into a deferential curtsy. "Your Grace," she greeted in austere tones far befitting a crusty member of the peerage.

"How do you do?" Justina said with a forced smile. How very different this household was to her former one, in every way. From the grand opulence that exuded ducal wealth and power, to the stern-faced servants hovering in the wings.

"This arrived earlier, Your Grace," the butler murmured. A footman came forward with a silver tray and a single letter atop.

Nick narrowed his gaze on the thick ivory velum and then with quick movements, grabbed it and stuffed it inside his jacket.

"And Mr. Stannis arrived a short while ago. I took the liberty of showing him to your office, as requested."

Her husband nodded curtly and then glanced briefly at her. "I've matters to discuss with my solicitor."

He would see to business on their wedding day? Of course, it was silly to believe there was anything romantic in the rushed affair brought about by her ruin two days earlier. Even sillier to hope for the romance they'd known in the gardens. "Of course," she said belatedly, when he continued to stare at her with an inscrutable gaze.

Her husband gathered her hands in his and a familiar thrill ran through her at the heat of his touch. "Mrs. Benedict will show you abovestairs until I've concluded my business." He drew her knuckles to his mouth and dragged a slow kiss along the skin where her wrist met her hand. Her pulse thundered hard under his lips. "And then I will come to you." His was a husky pledge that sent her heart tripling its beat and brought about a giddy nervousness.

And God help her, with his servants staring on, she should be scandalized by his promise and his lingering caress. Breathless, she managed a juddering nod.

Nick released her and she mourned the absence of his touch. Then with a purely male grin that held a promise for more, her husband stalked off. She stared after him a long while, until his retreating form disappeared down the long corridor.

"Your Grace?" the housekeeper urged. "Please, allow me to show you to your rooms." Without waiting to see if Justina followed, the expressionless woman started down the hall. She made it only three steps before noting Justina remained fixed in the foyer.

The last thing she cared to do was spend her morning sitting in wait for Nick to conclude his business, nervous with what would come. Why hadn't she had this conversation with her sister or her mother before? After Phoebe had wed? *Any* time? *Because I never imagined I would be married so quickly and certainly not with half of my family missing from those nuptials.* "Thank you, Mrs. Benedict, but I will explore a bit while His Grace holds his meeting."

The other woman frowned. "His Grace asked I escort you to your rooms, Your Grace." There was a determined glint in Mrs. Benedict's brown eyes better suited to a military commander leading his men on a charge.

"I'm not quite ready to retire." She mustered her most warming smile, but the mask of the stern-faced woman didn't crack in the slightest.

The servant remained rooted to the floor. "It is my duty to escort you to your chambers, Your Grace."

Justina hesitated. She'd not go toe-to-toe with the head of her new household, particularly when the woman sought to avoid displeasing her employer. Restoring her smile, she inclined her head and, wordlessly, the servant started through the halls, this time with Justina trailing behind. The tread of their footfalls was muted in the plush carpet. How vastly different than her family's now stained and threadbare carpets, most long ripped up, leaving only hardwood.

"Here we are, Your Grace," Mrs. Benedict murmured, bringing them to stop outside a room. She pushed the door open.

Justina stepped inside and the air left her on a slow exhale as she took in the extravagant wealth on display. Her husband's vast fortune shone in the porcelain vases atop mahogany Chippendale furniture. The thick gold, satin coverlet and matching brocade curtains were befitting royalty. Then, her husband, with his ancient title, was now a smidgeon below those exalted positions.

The servant spoke, recalling her attention. "Is there anything you require, Your Grace?"

"No," she said with a shake of her head. "That is all."

The woman dropped a curtsy and then retreated. As soon as she'd closed the door behind her, Justina did a circle around her room. Silence rang loud in the expansive space.

She counted the passing moments, long after the surly house-keeper left. This was her new home and she'd not be shut away because a servant sought to please her employer. As a married woman, there was no longer a need for the furtive sneaking.

A slow smile formed on her lips.

# CHAPTER 15

‌HIS MAN-OF-AFFAIRS, ‌STANNIS, OCCUPIED THE leather winged back chair opposite him. Ruthless. Accomplished. And dedicated, Stannis had served in his role with him since Nick had amassed a small fortune. Where Chilton had raised his reservations for his plans and intentions for the Barrett family, Stannis had demonstrated a ruthless ease for carrying out the destruction of that respective family.

"Sign here, Your Grace," said the man of middling years as he shoved a page across Nick's desk.

Nick stared through the lenses of his spectacles, his gaze lingered on the name inked in black so long, the letters blurred together. This afternoon represented every last goal he had dreamed of and at last attained. With stiff movements, he dipped his pen in the crystal inkwell and scratched his name to the page.

Silent, Stannis accepted the document and sprinkled drying powder on the fresh ink. Nick stared at that casual act as he set aside the sheet and withdrew another page. "This will call in the debt purchased from Lord Hertford," Stannis explained, pushing another page across Nick's desk.

He quickly scrawled his name. They continued through a stack of documents, with the official claims now made for Waters to make good on his debt.

Time had run out for the Marquess of Rutland's father-in-law, the hand on the proverbial clock being nudged along with Nick's clever machinations. The Barretts were effectively ruined. The man had long since pissed away his inheritance. His reckless gambling habits had left the viscount, his wife, his son, and his daughter with nothing more than their entailed properties.

He had seen to it that not a single merchant or bank would extend a shilling to the reprobate for the remainder of his days. Yes, today represented a victory.

And yet, how very hollow it felt.

His solicitor organized the neat stacks of ivory velum, placing them inside the brown leather folios. "It is done, Your Grace," the gentleman said in coolly emotionless tones.

"It is done," Nick murmured.

"I've drafted the letter, enumerating the expectations for the viscount's debt." Stannis withdrew a parchment and handed it over to him.

Flexing his jaw, he worked his gaze over the page. The moment Stannis delivered the official documents and notes bearing Nick's signatures and demands, his plans for the family would, at last, be clear. And revenge would be his.

Revenge which had sustained him for so very long.

"When would you have me deliver the note, Your Grace?"

The muscles of his stomach tightened. Goddamn, Justina Barrett had soured it all. Nay, Justina Tallings. She belonged to him now…in name, and this evening, she would become his wife in every sense of the word. He battled back guilt with the truth that through their match she would be spared the terror and uncertainty of her family's financial ruin. She'd never know the fear of debtors coming to collect. Or watching her every last possession marched out of the house and sold off. Only these items would go as payment to her father's sins. Nick's own father had labored through life, dedicating himself to his factory—and lost.

But he could not send the blood demands to the Barretts. Not yet. Soon. He pressed his eyes closed. Would Rutland have been this weak? Would he have waited? Had he waited with Nick's own father? He silently cursed. "Deliver it."

The man showed no outward reaction to that pronouncement. His face a cool mask, Stannis sketched a bow. "As you wish, Your Grace." Gathering his belongings, he filled his arms and then took his leave.

Nick stared at the closed door for a long while. It had begun. Destroying the Barretts today would be no different if he destroyed them tomorrow or a fortnight. The end result was destined to be the same. *And then my wife will forever hate me.* His gut clenched as his eyes fell to the missive that had arrived earlier.

The damning scrap enumerated his lies and marked his connection to the woman who wanted Rutland to fall as badly as Nick himself.

*My dearest love,*

*I've learned the silly chit enjoys poetry. Fill her ears with those pretty words you once spoke of and all the while dream of the wicked ones I've whispered in your ear.*

*Ever Yours,*

*M*

Despite their parting, the baroness still uncovered information on Justina and sent it along to him. Nearly a fortnight after he'd severed their arrangement and still she persisted. Self-loathing burned like acid on his tongue at ever having involved one such as her in his plans.

Then, she'd been the one to bring him to this very moment. If it hadn't been for the baroness, he would have never known the precise whereabouts of Lord Rutland. She'd allowed him to set his plan into motion without the other man rushing to London and coming to the aid of his family.

Now, where did that leave Justina? At one time, her role had been clear to him. She'd been just another prong in a multi-faceted attack on Lord Rutland. As Chilton had correctly put forward, Nick couldn't ruin a young lady. To have done so, would have made him no different than the bastard who'd destroyed his own sister's innocence.

He dropped his gaze to the note, again. Could Justina truly remain unscathed when his plan became clear to all? When her father and brother found themselves in the countryside working their entailed properties because nothing else remained?

Nick growled. Goddamn this niggling of guilt that grew whenever he thought of the inevitable outcome. Filled with a restlessness, he yanked open his drawer and stuffed the note from the baroness inside. He closed it with a firm click and pressed the intricate lock

that kept it sealed. Climbing to his feet, he started from his office
and set out for his wife's chambers.

He made his way through the corridors. The distant ancestors
memorialized in oil paintings glared down their ducal noses at
him. He passed the library and then stopped, retracing his footsteps to the entrance of the room. Justina stood in the center of
the library, her head tipped back, as she gazed at the floor-length
shelves filled with leather-bound volumes. He used her distraction
to study her. A reverent awe lined her features and, God help him,
as she crossed over and rescued a book from a nearby shelf, Nick
felt a wave of jealousy for the hunger in her eyes as she caressed
and studied that tome.

"Impressive, isn't it?" he called.

His wife gasped and the book tumbled to the floor at her feet,
the thin Aubusson carpet doing little to muffle the faint thud. She
stooped down in a rustle of satin skirts and retrieved the volume.
"It is," she agreed.

Pulling the door closed, Nick leaned against it. "As a boy, I would
have traded years off my life for such an accumulation of literature." He'd devoured books the way a person drew breath. "Which
title has you engrossed?" he asked, as he loosened his cravat and
removed the scrap.

She followed his casual movements.

"I was not really looking at any one title, but rather thinking of
my library," she explained, wandering over to a shelf. She trailed
her long fingertips over the lettering and, by hell, if he didn't wish
to be one of those damned books so he could be the recipient of
her tender caress.

"Ah," he murmured, stretching out that syllable. He stuffed his
cravat inside his jacket. "But *this* is your library," he reminded her.
Feeling her gaze on his every movement, he strode with languid
steps toward her.

She fiddled with her skirts and when she spoke, her words
brought him to a halt. "It is peculiar," she said softly, running her
palm along the edge of a book. "For months, I have watched creditors enter my home and remove volume after volume that they
deemed valuable."

Nick stiffened, as guilt scrabbled with his conscience. He didn't
want this story from her. He didn't want to see the sadness in her

eyes as she recounted a tale that he'd written, like some kind of master poet of evil.

Alas this was to be a penance of sorts. Her lips tipped up in a sad smile. With her long, elegant fingers, she plucked a volume from the shelf and fanned the pages. "Each time they would come, I would stare out the parlor window, waiting while they entered, and wondered..."

*I do not truly wish to know what thoughts have paraded through her head on those days I carried out my plans of revenge.* "What did you wonder?" he asked quietly, a glutton for self-torture, with her unaware, owning his role in her hurt. And hating himself for her having become a pawn to be used.

Justina dropped her gaze to the title and trailed her fingertips over the gold lettering. "Which books did each auctioneer see of value? It became a game of sorts for me. One that allowed me to move beyond the humiliation and sadness of their visits. First, Shakespeare's works were packed off and I held my breath, until others came and then it was my gothic novels." A humorless laugh fanned her lips. "What use would they have for my novels and, yet, take them they did."

Nay. Take them, *he* had. He'd believed it impossible to feel anything beyond the jaded hatred for her brother-in-law. Had convinced himself that the ends justified the proverbial means, only to bear witness to the effects of his actions against Rutland. "I am sorry, Justina," he said quietly. For so much. She'd deserved far more than he *or* Tennyson. A man who'd come to her of honesty and who had not tricked her from their first meeting with lies and orchestrated exchanges.

She smiled, reassuringly. "So much good came from it, though. With each book taken away, I was forced to expand my mind... to look at new works I would have never plucked from the shelf, unless I'd had no choice but to."

He brushed his knuckles down her cheek, lingering his gaze on the skin he caressed. "How have you remained so hopeful amidst such darkness?" How, when he had been destroyed by it?

Her eyelashes danced wildly as she leaned into his touch. "It is always easy to hope. It is far more difficult to give in to the darkness of life. For then, where would we be?"

Precisely where he already was.

"It has not all been bad," she said softly. She sought to reassure him? When her own existence had been as miserable as his own, in ways? He was humbled by her strength. "My brother-in-law has seen that I and my mother are not destitute."

*Her brother-in-law.* That hated shadow that stood between them.

"He is so good and, yet, he'd allow your belongings to be carted off?" He was unable to keep the vitriolic loathing from his question.

Justina wrinkled her brow. "I don't—"

"He allowed your family to suffer. Allowed your father to sell and scheme so that he was beholden to," *me,* "creditors."

"The only reason I have what I do is because of Edmund," she spoke with such an impassioned defense, Nick gritted his teeth. "He's given me pin money. Funded my wardrobe. When he is in London, he manages to intimidate my father enough to be less reckless." With that, for the first time, she dented the image he had accepted of the man who'd stalked down his hallways, all those years ago. Forced him to see the marquess in a way that was at odds with all he'd come to know, believe, or accept. Her gaze held his. "You do not know it, but my father is a drunkard, Nick. He is a gambler and a whoremonger. His behaviors are a disease that not even a fear of my brother-in-law will stop. Edmund knows that." She lifted her shoulders in a shrug. "As such, he cannot simply turn over a small fortune when it will only be quickly squandered."

"You are too forgiving," he said quietly. Would she be equally so when she discovered his role in her family's ruin? *Tell her. It is time to tell her all. Even as it means she'll likely hate me.* But mayhap she might understand what drove him. *I am deluding myself.* He opened his mouth but Justina lifted her palms up, waving that book in her hand.

"Why should I hold Edmund to blame for my father's vices? I would never dare hold you responsible." She filed the book on the shelf and smiled at him. "As I said, some good came of it."

He cocked his head. Of her miserable state and uncertain future?

She layered her back against the shelving and looked up at him. "If it hadn't been for my books being sold off, I'd not have discovered The Circulating Library. And if I hadn't been there a fortnight earlier, then we'd not have met."

Nick lifted a hand and propped it over her head. "We were destined to meet." Those words came, born of a truth that had brought them together. He'd been so driven in his plans to embroil her in his scheming, he'd have not rested until she, the ultimate pawn, was his.

And in the very greatest irony the Bard himself could not have penned on his pages, Nick had made her his for reasons that had nothing to do with punishing her. In the end, only he could be punished. As her father discovered his true plans and Rutland inevitably returned, this ease between him and Justina, this inexplicable draw would unravel like the seams of a frayed garment. *I will tell her. Eventually. Soon.*

She searched his face with her eyes. "What is it?"

Not wanting this moment mired in guilt and regret, Nick lowered his lips close to her ear. "You are now my duchess and shall want for nothing." He'd see to it that every single title taken from her was restored and filled this very room.

Her breath caught loudly and she angled her head so their gazes met. "You are all I want," she whispered.

With a groan, he covered her mouth. She immediately parted her lips, allowing him entry. He swept his tongue inside and, with their tongues, dueled in a primitive dance. He slid one palm about her nape, angling her to better receive him. With his other hand, he found the lush curve of her hip and sank his fingertips into the soft flesh. His body throbbed with a hungering for her and he moved his hands lower. He cupped her buttocks and dragged her into the vee of his thighs. Rotating his hips against the small of her belly, he ached in a way he never had for any woman. Shock rooted around his chest. He'd resolved to never let anyone inside and, yet, how effortlessly she'd slipped in.

"Nick," she pleaded and her head fell back. Several pins slipped free of her chignon and her long tresses cascaded about them in a shimmery golden waterfall.

Nick tangled his hands in those blonde strands. "Like satin," he rasped as he dragged a trail of kisses from the corner of her mouth, lower, to her neck, gently suckling the place where her pulse pounded. He reached behind her and slipped free button after button, cursing the small pearl pieces that stood as a barrier between them.

After wrenching the garment, he slid it over her arms and lower still, shoving it down her ample hips until it landed in a fluttering heap between them. He drew away from her and hooded his lashes. She stood like that proud Venus, memorialized by Botticelli; golden splendor and cream white flesh.

Her cheeks flushed, Justina fluttered her hands about her breasts and he brought her arms down to her sides. "You are beautiful," he whispered. Then freeing her of her shift, Nick filled his palms of her naked breasts. The abundant flesh spilled over his hands. Shaking with his need for her, he lifted the right mound to his mouth and drew the erect pink bud between his lips and sucked.

She moaned and he caught her against him and the bookshelf, anchoring her so she remained upright. All the while, he continued to worship her perfect breast.

Their chests heaved, with their raspy breaths coming in time. Nick ran a hand caressingly from her breast down to her belly and then he found the soft downy thatch that shielded her womanhood. Touching her as he'd ached to since their earliest meetings.

"Nick," she pleaded, splaying her legs in an invitation that dragged him close to the edge of madness.

A primal growl rumbled in his chest. In one fluid movement, he swept Justina into his arms and carried her to the nearby leather button sofa.

JUSTINA WAS AFIRE. HER BODY thrummed and ached and thrilled with Nick's every touch. His every stroke.

As he settled her on the sofa, she shoved up onto her elbows and watched through heavy lashes as he shed his jacket, tossing it aside so it sailed to the floor in a soft heap. Next, he tugged free his waistcoat. His shirt followed onto that growing pile of garments on the floor.

Justina's mouth went dry. His chiseled form was the kind of beauty those great sculptors could never properly do justice. The light whorls of golden hair on his chest, the tautness of his belly, was male perfection, personified.

Not removing his gaze from hers, Nick yanked off his boots and set them aside. When he placed his hands at the waist of his black breeches, her heart tripled its beat. She'd seen sketches of the ancient Greek gods in paintings housed in museums her sister had dragged her to. Nothing, however, could have prepared her for the moment Nick pushed his breeches down and kicked them aside.

Justina's breath caught as he stood before her in all his naked splendor. He was a beauty to rival that first great male master-piece shaped in Eden. She dipped her eyes lower and then swiftly yanked her gaze up. "You...I..." Her words trailed off as he came down slowly over her.

"Were made to join together," he finished for her in a husky whisper. Then his lips found hers again, melting her reservations, erasing her fears, as she turned herself over to the bliss of simply feeling. He worked a hand between them once more and caressed between her thighs, sliding one finger inside her molten heat. A shuddery hiss burst from her lips as Nick toyed with her nub.

"I have never felt pleasure like this," she whispered. Justina bit her lip hard and undulated into his expert stroking.

"Ah," he enticed, touching his lips against her temple and then trailing a path lower, over her cheek and neck. "'Pleasure is spread through the earth, in stray gifts to be claimed by whoever shall find'," he reminded, calling forth those great words penned by Wordsworth. "Let us find it together," he urged and thrust another finger inside her wet channel. Her head fell back and a scream tore from her throat.

"Nick," she begged, lost in a sea of feeling.

He drew his hand back and she cried out at the loss of him, but he laid himself between her splayed thighs and settled his shaft at her center. "I do not want to hurt you," he said hoarsely, lowering his brow to hers. Beads of perspiration dotted his forehead.

Justina stroked her fingers down his back. The muscles rippled under her caress. "You could never hurt me," she breathed and leaned up, claiming his mouth.

His male groan of approval blended with her breathless pants as he plunged deep. Her body bucked at the stiff intrusion.

She cried out, but he swallowed it with his kiss. Clenching her eyes, Justina went still and held herself motionless. His length stretched her tight walls.

"Justina," he rasped, his breath came hard and fast as he touched his lips to her temple. "I am so sorry."

She forced her eyes open. The angular planes of his face, ravaged, sent love spiraling in her heart. "Shh," she whispered. "I am all right," she promised.

His irises darkened with passion, turning his eyes nearly black. "I have never known a woman like you," he said in gravelly tones. Then he began to move. Slowly. She stiffened. And then the slow drag of him inside her and the pressure eased, leaving in its place a wondrous throbbing.

Her breath hitched and she lifted her hips, meeting his thrusts until all memory of pain receded, leaving nothing in its place but the blissful pleasure of him rocking inside her. And out. Over and over. Justina clung to him, holding tight, as their pace quickened.

She panted as he brought her up to that glorious height again. Their movements took on a frantic, desperate rhythm and she gave herself fully to his mastery. Then he reached between them and found her with his fingers, just as he thrust home once more.

Justina screamed softly as she exploded in a sea of sensations; flecks danced behind her vision. Nick hurtled over that same precipice of wonder on a low, ragged groan that went on forever. He spilled himself inside her, in deep, rippling waves that pulsated through her core.

And then he stilled, collapsing onto his elbows to catch his weight. His breath came in quick, loud exhalations against her temple. A sated smile danced on her lips.

"If I had Shelley or Wordsworth's words, I might be able to capture the wonder of such a moment," she said in sleepy tones.

He quickly shifted them, arranging her atop his chest. She lay there with her ear pressed to the place where his heart loudly pounded. Her hair hung loose and flowing about them. Nick stroked his hand in a slow circle over the small of her back; that gentle caress brought her heavy lids closed. "How could any poet manage to convey in words what we just shared? It is because that moment belonged to only us," he said quietly as his passion-sated baritone washed over her. At the beautiful poignancy of his words, she looked at him. Their gazes collided. "And you are correct. You are not Wordsworth, Byron, Shelley or any other poet."

His words slammed into her with all the same hurt she'd known at her father's derision and the world's opinion of her.

Nick ceased his gentle stroking and moved his hand up to her face. He palmed her cheeks. "You are Justina Tallings. Write your own work."

She drew back and searched his face for any hint that he made light of her. For the whole of her life, her father had spoken of her in disparaging words, as one who saw little use of her or for her. She knew not what to make of a man who spoke about the possibility of her writing anything of import.

"Write your own story, Justina," Nick repeated. "Those passages you began and abandoned. Byron, Shelley, the lecturer at The Circulating Library, none of those men know any more than you... and they certainly do not know how you are feeling," he added.

Her throat worked spasmodically and she swallowed several times, struggling to speak. "I have only ever been an object to my father. A chess piece. He saw me as a means to strengthen his wealth and power. But he never saw *me*. My sister and Andrew and Mother, they love me. They, too, are content to see the same thing Society sees in me." Justina leaned up and captured his face between her palms. "You see me. In ways that I never fully saw myself—until now." And for that, he would own the whole of her heart, forevermore.

Passion clouded Nick's gaze as he claimed her lips in another powerful meeting. She found how wrong she'd been in her love of poetry and gothic novels.

Nothing in those pages could ever compare to the feeling of being in her husband's arms.

# CHAPTER 16

cJUSTINA SNORED.

It was an endearing discovery Nick made when he awakened the following morning with his wife's naked form curled against his side. Her satiny soft hair cascaded about them and he gently brushed the strands from her face, tucking them behind her ears. Another soft, noisy exhalation spilled past her faintly-parted, bow-shaped lips. It was just one more discovery about the woman he'd intended to trap and ruin, and who, in the end, he'd ultimately wed with noble intentions.

*Can there really be noble intentions when I intend to ruin her family, still?*

Guilt needled away at his conscience and cut across the peaceful-ness he'd woken to with her in his arms. There would come time enough for reality later. For now, there was this peace between them; so much so, in fact, that it was so very easy to believe they were any other blissfully wedded couple and not two people brought together by the sins of another man's past.

Nick stroked his hand in a smoothing circle over her generous hip. In her sleep, she nestled against him. How trusting she was… in sleep and waking. The innocence he'd once been in possession of had been so very long ago that he'd believed himself incapable of recognizing it. But Justina's innocence had proven a balm to his wounded soul—healing and, more, a tangible reminder of how it had once been.

And how it could still be, if he abandoned his scheming.

His body stiffened involuntarily against the unwanted weakening and he dragged a hand over his eyes. What was happening to him? Rutland had promised his father two years and ultimately had come in the dark of night and cut those years into a fortnight. For that, Nick should be able to send a bloody note that would beggar the Barrett family.

Needing distance between his wife and his riotous thoughts, he slowly edged away from Justina. Another loud snore escaped her. As she was rolling onto her back, she flung her arms out, baring her naked breasts to his gaze.

Nick swallowed a groan. He wanted her, again. Having known her three times throughout the night, she would be tender this morning. Though he'd proven himself a bastard in many ways, he wasn't a brute who'd slake his lust.

Reluctantly, he pulled the coverlet over his wife's frame, concealing her splendorous nudity, and then swung his legs over the edge of the bed. Quickly retrieving his garments, he dressed and then made for the door separating their chambers. He paused, passing one, lingering, regretful look at his wife. Then left. His valet, Russell, looked over as he entered the room, giving no outward reaction to Nick's sudden presence.

Quietly closing the door behind him, Nick stalked across the room, while Russell hurried to the wardrobe and proceeded to draw out garments for his employer, and help Nick through his ablutions.

Nick's gaze continued to stray to the door separating him from Justina. He caught sight of his grinning visage in the bevel mirror. What hold did the lady have that she should occupy his every thought and deter him in the goal that had sustained him for thirteen years?

Russell came forward with a white cravat. Accepting it in his fingers, Nick waved the servant off and proceeded to arrange the fabric. The young man rushed off to gather a sapphire jacket and as he returned, the garment outstretched, Nick shrugged into it.

A soft rapping at the front door brought his attention swinging forward. "Enter," he called out.

His butler appeared at the entrance. "You've a visitor, Your Grace.

He shot a perplexed look to the ormolu clock atop his mantel. Seven o'clock in the morning. No guest would come to call at such an unfashionable hour. "Who—?"

Thoms cleared his throat. "It is your sister, the Countess of Dunkirk. She demanded to see you. I took the liberty of showing her to your office."

*Bloody hell.* Of course, Cecily would be livid. "I'll be with her shortly," he said curtly. His loyal butler nodded and hurried from the room, closing the door behind him.

With a curse, Nick finished buttoning his jacket and then started for his office. He'd little doubt what brought her 'round this morning. In his haste to secure a special license from the archbishop and marry Justina before her father or Tennyson could act, he'd not given thought to a proper wedding. Rather, he'd convinced himself that the offer he'd made Justina, and her acceptance of it, had been nothing more than a matter of convenience to aid the lady. He reached his office and stopped.

Brandishing a paper in her hands, his sister stood beside the marble chess table. Fury radiated from her slender frame. Not wasting time with Social niceties or familial greetings, she leveled a glare on him. "I've come to speak to you."

"I see that," he drawled. Stepping inside, he closed the door behind them.

By the narrowing of her eyes, his attempt at dry humor was the wrong one. "Well?" she demanded, stalking forward. She stopped several feet away. "What is this?" She hurled a copy of *The Times* at him. It bounced off him and landed in a fluttery heap at his feet. He stared down at the gossip column, his name marked clearly alongside Justina's.

He sighed. "I can explain." Poorly.

"Explain why you were married and I, as your sister, find out in a bloody gossip column." With each word, she took a step closer until her skirts brushed the front of his desk. "And to the Marquess of Rutland's sister-in-law," she hissed. She glanced about. Did she search for the very person in question? "What have you done?"

Of course, she would assume his actions had only to do with Justina's relationship to the man whose happiness he wished to destroy. "It is not as it seems," he said gruffly. Not entirely, anyway. He scrubbed his hands over his face.

"And how does it seem?" she shot back. He let his arms fall to his side. "As though you married the sister-in-law of the man you vowed to destroy."

"Quiet," he bit out, glancing quickly at the door. *Soon, she'll know. She'll learn my connection to Rutland and my vow to destroy her wastrel father and brother.* Guilt settled deep in his belly.

Cecily crossed her arms at her chest. "Very well, then, tell me how it *is*." His sister had long taken her responsibilities as elder sister as seriously as if she'd been eighteen years older and not just one.

With her standing before him, a furious glint in her eyes, such a truth was never truer. Nick stooped and picked up the scandal sheet. "The lady was...compromised."

The ever-narrowing of her eyes hinted at her fury. "By you."

He shook his head once. "By the Marquess of Tennyson."

His sister cocked her head. "But..."

Restless, he stalked over to the chessboard and picked up the marble pawn. How many times had he found purpose and strength on these boards? Plotting. Planning. Scheming. Nick closed his palm briefly around it and proceeded to explain the whole of the evening at Chilton's ball. He took care to leave out the incriminating truths of the original intention for that grand event which had, in fact, included him trapping Justina. Before some inexplicable force had changed his mind.

When he'd finished, Cecily eyed him with a wary skepticism; a cynical jadedness that had not existed before her marriage to the ancient Earl of Dunkirk. "Why did you do it?"

Her question took him aback. "Why did I—?"

"Marry her," she clarified. "Why should you have cared who the lady found herself married to?"

Because it would have destroyed the part of his soul that still lived to know a woman such as Justina was forever bound to the Marquess of Tennyson. That the idea of her in the man's bed, bearing him children, and suffering through his perversions would have haunted him the same way his father's suicide lingered, all these years later. When his sister gave him a probing stare, he cleared his throat. "I could not have seen her marry one such as him." He'd sinned enough by allowing Cecily to marry one of those reprobates.

His sister touched a hand to her chest. "It was because of me," she said quietly, making the same partially accurate supposition Justina had.

"It was because of her…and because *I* failed you," he conceded.

"And what of her brother-in-law? What are your intentions toward that gentleman, now?"

Her words threw a thick blanket of tense silence upon the room. What were his intentions? Still, to ruin him. Only, the major piece of his scheme had hinged on hurting that man through the people who mattered to the marquess. Forcing Rutland to watch his wife suffer as her beloved sister was married to a man on a matter of revenge and beggaring them.

His gut clenched. "What would you have me do?" he asked tiredly.

The fight went out of Cecily as she moved before him. "It is not too late to change, Dominick. You are still the person you once were."

His throat moved. "You're wrong." His voice came as though he'd been dragged down a graveled road. "I've consumed myself in hate and ugliness. It's destroyed all remnants of the brother you remember."

"If that was true, you wouldn't have given a jot if Rutland's sister-in-law married a man like Tennyson," she accurately pointed out. "It is time to let go of your hatred and start again." His sister placed a hand on his shoulder and squeezed.

How could she forgive? How, when she lived with a daily reminder of her hell? The question hung on his lips, unasked, as he stared at the pain in her eyes. She needed no reminder from him of the misery that was her marriage.

He slammed the pawn back into its proper place; the table shook under the force of that movement. "I must do this for our family," he explained, frustration ripping those words from him. Did he will her to understand? Or attempt to convince himself to do this thing?

"No, Dominick," she countered. "You are doing this for you." Her thinly veiled condemnation rang like a shot in the night. "This is not for Papa. Or Mama. Or me and my miserable marriage. Or Felicity. But you. Your hatred will destroy you." She paused and held his gaze squarely. "And if you go forward with this, Justina will be destroyed, as well."

WHEN SHE'D ARISEN, JUSTINA HAD rushed through her morning ablutions. She planned on visiting Gipsy Hill for the lecture at The Circulating Library. It was what she would have done on any other day, during any other week.

Reticule dangling from her fingers, she wound her way through her new home. Except...

*Then, this is not just any other day. I am now a married woman.*

*Married*, she mouthed the word. She'd spent her life both fearing she'd make a miserable match like her mother and dreaming that she'd find that ideal of love, with a respectable, honorable gentleman. And in the end, she'd found her respectable, honorable gentleman. Or rather, they'd found each other in one chance meeting in the streets of Gipsy Hill.

She *intended* to go, until she'd passed the Morning Room and froze.

"...You are doing this for you..."

She hovered outside, an interloper on an exchange she had no place listening in on. She should go. Just as she should have gone. And yet, the angry tones and sharp voices raised while Nick spoke with his sister had held her to this doorway. And wrong or not, she listened still.

"...your hatred will destroy you..."

Those muffled words, a chiding rebuke leveled at Nick, reached through the doorway. Gooseflesh dotted her skin. What hatred did her husband carry that his sister would come here and speak of it now? It gave her pause, a reminder of how much she both knew him and, yet...how little she knew of him, as well. A memory flickered forward. Those cold shadows she'd seen in Nick's eyes...

"...do you think she will not find out who...."

The she and who in question were lost, only stirring Justina's disquiet. Footsteps sounded in the room and she frantically looked about, contemplating escape to avoid discovery. Plastering a smile on her face, she put her fingers on the door handle just as someone within opened it.

Her husband and his sister looked back with equal degrees of shock.

Cheeks warming, Justina cleared her throat. "Forgive me for interrupting," she said weakly. "I was…" Eavesdropping like a naughty child. "I was…" *Inventing cryptic tales within my head about your exchange.* They both continued to stare. She made another clearing noise. "I simply wished to say hello," she finished lamely. She'd little right to be standing outside during their personal discussion.

The young countess smiled gently and stretched her hands out. "Please," she began, taking Justina's spare hand. "I wanted to visit and wish you happiness." Lady Cecily shot a disapproving look back at her brother. "And scold my brother for failing to include his niece or me in the joyous occasion."

The joyous occasion. How hopeful and optimistic and, yet, the other woman could not know her brother had bound himself to Justina, all to save her from marriage to another. "Thank you," she said belatedly. With the woman's unintentional reminder, she reflected on the fact that he'd not included his family. She looked over at her husband, who stood with his face in a smooth mask which revealed nothing of what he was now thinking.

"I do not wish to interrupt you any further on the day after your wedding," the countess said, releasing her hands. "But mayhap you might come and visit with Felicity and me?" Her new sister-in-law gave her a warm smile that reached her pretty blue eyes.

"I would like that very much," Justina said returning her smile.

"If you'll excuse me?" Sparing one last glance for her brother, the countess sailed from the room and Justina was left alone with Nick.

And alone, in light of all they'd shared last evening, left her uncharacteristically silent.

Her husband studied her through thick, golden lashes. "Justina," he greeted on that mellifluous baritone that sent heat rolling through her.

"N-Nick," she greeted. She wet her lips and his eyes went to that subtle, unintentional movement. "I was…" Her words trailed off as he strolled toward her with slow, languid steps.

"You were just…?" he urged huskily as he stopped a hairsbreadth away from her.

She gave her head a shake. How was it possible for a person to so affect her ability to string so much as a proper sentence together? He lowered his mouth to hers and claimed her lips in a hungry kiss that weakened her knees.

But then, as quick as it had begun, he drew back, and she mourned the loss. He brushed his knuckles over her cheek and she leaned into that caress. "You are well this morning?" he murmured. Heat slapped her cheeks behind the question in his eyes.

"I am," she assured him quickly. "Quite fine." Though slightly tender from their lovemaking, he'd awakened her body and left her feeling alive in ways she'd never known. "Are you?" she blurted.

His hard lips twitched. "Indeed." There was a wealth of meaning to that single utterance that sent another round of heat to her cheeks. His gaze went to her reticule. "And were you headed somewhere this day?" His questioning prodded her back to her previously unfinished thought.

"Yes," she said, gesticulating wildly with renewed enthusiasm for the lecture. "There is a lecture this morn on Mrs. Wollstonecraft's works." She held her breath and searched for a hint of disapproval from him on the scandalous enlightened thinker who challenged the place and station of women.

"I see," he said, revealing little with that two-word utterance.

Justina coughed into her spare hand. "Yes, well, then. I shall allow you to your business." She started to turn when he called out, staying her movements.

"Justina?"

"Nick?" she returned.

Her husband folded his arms at his broadly-muscled chest. "Would you rather attend your lecture alone?"

Would she rather attend alone? "Uh…I don't…"

The right corner of his lips quirked up. "If you'd rather I not accompany you?" He stared patiently back.

He wanted to join her. When she'd arrived belowstairs, prepared to leave for her visit to Gipsy Hill, she'd not dared think to so much as ask him to join her. Her heart pounded wildly in her chest. Her parents' marriage was one where two people carried on and conducted their lives entirely separate from one another. And with his request, the remainder of her heart was lost to him. "You can accompany me," she suggested.

"You're certa—"

"I'm certain," she said, her words coming quickly.

He held out his fingers and she slid hers into his. His larger palm immediately swallowed her smaller one, engulfing it with his strength and warmth.

A short while later, they walked through the clogged streets of Lambeth, winding their way between gypsies hawking their wares and patrons in coarse garments. "How often do you visit the lectures?" he asked as they strolled down the pavement.

"Every week. Sometimes more," she added. She stole a sideways peek, searching for a hint of disapproval. Instead, his gaze remained contemplative. "What is it?" she added, when he remained curiously silent.

Nick paused, forcing her to a stop. He gestured down the street to that establishment that had become so important to her. "You sit at the back rows listening to the opinions of others." Her breath caught as he delicately tapped her temple. "What you have to say, Justina. What opinions you have are no less important. You wished for a salon." He held her gaze. "Form your own.

*Form my own.*

As the street continued bustling on around them, they held one another's gazes. She'd once dreamed of love, like her sister knew. Dreamed of a life different than the life her mother lived. And somehow, with the hand of fate, she'd found this man. Where most dukes would demand nothing less than a proper, staid wife, Nick would have her turn their home into a place for scholars to assemble.

A rogue wind whipped about them and tossed a bonnet at her feet, cutting across the beautiful moment. She paused and knelt down to rescue the article. With her gaze, she took in the row of satin roses sewn along the brim, tracing it with her fingertips.

How important those pieces had once been and, yet, even with her love of literature now, the pretty articles still beckoned. A wistful smile played at her lips. Her husband knelt beside her in a moment that felt so reminiscent of their first meeting. Had it really been but a fortnight ago when they'd met in these very streets?

Just as he'd done with that book from this very cart, Nick reached for the bonnet and she handed it over. "It is lovely," he acknowledged.

"Would you like to try it on, my lady?" the gray-haired woman asked, stepping closer.

Justina quickly jumped to her feet. "Oh, no." She held her palms up. "I've no need for a bonnet." She'd long ago forced aside her silly fascination with such fripperies.

"Ah," her husband drawled, shoving lazily up into a stand. "But surely one who once collected them, you would, at the very least, wish to try it on?" he murmured. Her heart beat faster as he removed the satin one currently on and replaced it with the gypsy's. "We will take it," Nick said. Never taking his eyes from her, he removed a heavy purse and handed it over to the old Rom woman.

Justina made a sound of protest, but he touched his fingertips to her lips, silencing her words.

"Do you believe there is something wrong in appreciating literature and admiring a bonnet or a fan?"

How easily he saw her every thought. It was as though their souls had melded on these very roads, all those days ago.

The wind pulled at the strings of the velvet bonnet and whipped them in the air. "For so long, my family and Society saw only a girl who loved baubles and fripperies." Though, her siblings and mother hadn't judged those interests, they'd formed an opinion of her intelligence because of it. She lifted her shoulders in a little shrug. "These," she said, removing the article and holding it up for his inspection. "Came to represent all I was. I wanted to be more than bonnets and baubles," she added, in a bid to make him understand why she'd ceased collecting them.

"And you think because as a girl you collected bonnets, that as a woman you should disdain them?" Her husband carefully disentangled the item in question from her fingers and traced the same path with the tip of his index finger along the brim. "Appreciating a beautiful garment or bonnet does not make you vain. It does not make you less clever than you are. It makes you a woman with varying interests and there is something far more beautiful in a person who appreciates much, than a person afraid to appreciate at all."

Her heart thudded wildly in her chest.

"Come," the gypsy murmured, an indecipherable glint in her eyes. Tucking her recently acquired purse in a pocket sewn within her crimson skirts, she motioned with her hands. "For your generosity, let Bunica look at your palms and see what the future holds."

Nick grinned wryly. "A man makes his own fate."

"Ah," she said in mysterious tones that tempered his cocksure grin. "The fates unfurl many paths...and it is only for you to choose the one to travel." Bunica motioned once more and Justina looked to her husband.

Skepticism marred his sharp, chiseled features.

"Is there not truth that we took different paths a fortnight ago and ultimately found each other?" Justina reminded him. She took the bonnet from his hands, waited.

The woman crooked her fingers. "Surely, my lord wishes to know of life and love...and the children he will one day have."

Nick held Justina's gaze and then with a wink, tugged off his gloves. "Tell me," he said as the old woman took his hands and studied his palms. "Will my daughters have the clever wit of their mama?"

All she'd wanted was a husband who saw past a superficial beauty to the woman she had become inside. Love for this man clogged her throat and made it difficult to swallow.

The gypsy's quiet, self-murmurings pierced the charged moment between her and Nick. "This line runs to your heart and it is full," Bunica said. The gypsy gave a grunt of approval. "You know great love."

Over the old woman's head, Nick's gaze collided with Justina's. For all the searing intensity with which he stared back, Justina could almost believe he did, in fact, love her. The gypsy made a tsking sound. "You also know darkness, my lord."

A harsh glint lit his gaze. At the prophetic words so very close to those uttered by his sister that morning, a chill wracked her spine. She thought of the parts of his past her husband had shared, of his shattered youth and struggle, to the life he now lived.

"See, this line here," Bunica went on, "is the line of *darkness*. But this intersecting one here, the mark of your heart, shows the triumphant power of that emotion."

And in that simple telling, the woman was right. How many times had the love Justina had for her mother and siblings been enough to pull her from the sadness of a heartless father? Did Nick see the strength in that emotion, as well? If he did not, she would show it to him. She would prove that overwhelming strength could blot out all darkness.

"You will know great love and…" Bunica raised his hand closer to her eyes and peered at the skin. "Happiness, with four babes."

Most gentlemen would have pulled their hand back and called the gypsy's words drivel and, yet, her husband stood patiently through her prophecies. Some of the tension went out of Nick as he caught Justina's eye. "As long as they have their mother's spirit, I hardly care if they are boy babes or girl ones." He winked and a tremulous smile pulled at her lips.

The gypsy released his hand. She then held hers out toward Justina.

Swiftly removing her gloves, Justina turned them over to her husband along with the bonnet. She then offered her palms to the old gypsy. Their hands touched. An instant of heat scorched her and she gasped at the stinging warmth. Bunica immediately released her when the gypsy's gaunt cheeks went ashen. A cold chill scraped along Justina's spine. "What is it?" Justina murmured.

The old gypsy scrunched her mouth and then, with a nod, reached out again. This time, when their fingers touched, there was a muted heat to the woman's gnarled hands. Concentrating on Justina's palms, the woman studied them in silence. "I see wickedness and death," Bunica said quietly. Justina's stomach knotted. It was silly to believe in gypsy lore and magic and, yet, she remained transfixed in silent horror. "I see the death of dreams and blood—"

The charged tingling broke as Nick wrenched Justina's hands away from the gypsy's and glared at the old woman. "We make our own fate," he reiterated, fire burning in his eyes. "It is nothing more than a gypsy's game," he bit out.

Of course, it was madness to believe a person could see the future, nonetheless, the cold inside remained. Justina worked a tremulous smile for Nick's benefit, but her lips ached with the forced smile. "I wish to know the rest," she murmured, even as she did not. Over her husband's protestations, she held her palms up.

Bunica studied the lines once more. "There is evil…but there is also light here." She touched a chipped fingernail to the center line intersecting from Justina's wrist to the middle of her palm. "This mark is of far greater strength and has the power to overcome even death. As long as you claim control of your life, my lady, you will know happiness."

Justina stared at that single line from which others connected. There was no talk of love and laughter and babes. How very different a future this woman painted for her than the life Nick would know. By the gypsy's prophecies, it was as though they were two different people, leading entirely opposing lives. "Is that…all?" she asked haltingly.

Bunica nodded and released her for a second time.

"It is rubbish," Nick growled. Reaching for Justina's hand, he collected her fingers and glowered at the gypsy. "I called it rubbish before and it is still *rot*. We make our futures." Angling his shoulder in a dismissive manner, he cut Bunica from Justina's direct line of vision. "*We* will make our future, Justina," he vowed and he spoke as a man who'd taken on the world once and triumphed.

She thought of the story he'd shared of his childhood. Of all he'd endured after his father's death, and the responsibility he'd taken on, and her love for him swelled. He didn't see how, with love, one would always, ultimately triumph. "It is not all darkness, Nick," she reminded him gently. "She saw light." The knowing gypsy's eyes remained on them, blatantly taking in their exchange. "And light and hope has the power to heal all."

Her husband's eyes blazed a path over her face. "You are remarkable, Justina Tallings."

*Tallings.* She belonged to him. Nay, they belonged to one another. It was a bond she'd longed for even before her sister had made a beautiful love match with Edmund. It had sustained Justina when she'd seen the misery that was her mother's cold union. An eerie sense of being gripped her and she glanced about for the invisible foe this gypsy had conjured with her prophesizing.

Forcibly thrusting aside the dark thoughts, Justina turned to thank the woman. Bunica reached inside her pocket and withdrew a ruby and pearl bracelet. Shimmery white pearls lined the gilded band that led to a gold filigree heart at the center with a single ruby in the middle. "It is for you," she murmured, holding it out.

With reverent hands, Justina studied the piece. Her gaze lingering on the single heart so very much like the pendant her sister had once worn and then gave to another. Several semi-precious stones were missing from the piece and, yet, there was a simplicity to the bracelet that made it far more beautiful than the gaudy baubles adorning the necks, wrists, and ears of fashionable ladies.

"It is beautiful," Justina whispered.

"As long as the gild and pearl lie against the wrist, the wearer of the bracelet will forever know that true love doth exists." The whispered prophecy rang loud amidst the mundane street sounds.

Another patron approached the wagon, calling the gypsy's notice away, leaving Justina and Nick alone.

The whispered words of hope, rolling around her head, blended with the ominous future she'd portended for Justina. She started as Nick claimed the bracelet from her fingers. With slow, precise movements, he looped the bauble around her wrist and then pressed the clasp. Then, raising her hand to his mouth, he placed a gentle kiss to the place where her pulse pounded. "I love you," she said softly and he went motionless; unblinking under the weight of her profession.

Nick shook his head once.

"I do," she said to herself with soft surprise, as passersby rushed around them. Andrew and Gillian had spoken with a surety of Justina's love for Nick. They saw the romantic, whirlwind courtship and not much more. Justina's love, however, came not from what he'd done in marrying her. For that, he'd have her gratitude. Rather, she loved Nick Tallings for being a man who urged her to speak her mind and use it without apology. Who believed she had a mind, when not even her family saw her as in possession of a clever wit. She was stronger for his presence in her life. "I'm not asking or expecting you to love me," she assured him, when he still said nothing. Not yet. Mayhap in time, he'd come to feel the same depth of emotion in his heart. "You have given me so much." Her gaze fell involuntarily to the bracelet, lingering on that single heart. "You don't demand or expect me to be a biddable miss." The woman her father had demanded she be. "You applaud me for thinking and using my voice." Which, having borne witness to her own mother's stifled existence, Justina saw that for the gift it was.

He dragged a hand over his mouth and glanced about, but not before she detected the panicky glint in his eyes. "Justina, there is so much…" *There is so much what?* Her mind screamed for the remainder of that unfinished thought. "I…" Her heart hung suspended in a breathless moment of anticipation for those words. Nick cleared his throat. "We will be late for the lecture," he said gruffly and she managed a smile so brittle, her cheeks felt they would shatter.

That is all he would say. "Of course," she murmured. *What did I expect? That I should confess the feelings in my heart and like those gothic tales I once read, he'd drop to a knee and pledge his eternal love?*

As they started across the street, having told herself, in time, he would come to care, disappointment struck painfully in her breast.

# CHAPTER 17

¶IT HAD BEEN INEVITABLE.

Ultimately, all good came to an end. Time had proven as much. For Nick, that good came to an end nearly one week later as he stared blankly down at the note in his hands. He quickly snapped it shut and stuffed it inside his jacket. "When did this arrive?" he demanded of his butler.

"Earlier this morn, Your Grace," Thoms murmured. "A boy came 'round back and wouldn't put it in anyone else's hands."

Dread twisted in his belly and held him frozen behind his desk.

"Do you require anything else, Your Grace?" his butler prodded, bringing him to attention.

Nick gave his head a clearing shake. "Her Grace?"

"She is paying a visit to a Miss Farendale, Your Grace," the man murmured.

"Miss Farendale," he repeated. At the man's nod, Nick consulted his timepiece. He'd but a short while to meet the baroness and then return. Mayhap Justina would not even arrive to find him gone. "See that my mount is readied, immediately," he ordered, stuffing his watch fob inside his jacket.

When the other man rushed off, Nick let fly a string of curses. The problem with a venomous serpent was one could never rid oneself of the poison. And in his case, in Lady Carew, he'd embroiled a lethal creature who would not rest until she spread that venom. Shoving to his feet, he stalked from the room.

A short while later, braced for the impending meeting, Nick guided his mount through the streets of London. The baroness was displeased. And history had proven the perils of a spurned lover. They had been united in their goals for Rutland…and she would expect all the Barretts to suffer for their connection to the marquess. Everything had changed…and yet, at the same time, nothing had.

After a seemingly endless ride through the quiet streets of London, Nick dismounted and motioned over a small boy. The lad sprinted over and collected the reins. "There will be more," he promised handing over a small purse. Then, he bounded up the steps of the museum and entered the soaring main entrance. He blinked, struggling to adjust to the dimly lit space. Once his eyes became accustomed to the faint light, he did a quick survey of the antechambers.

Carefully avoiding the handful of patrons circulating at this unfashionable hour, Nick skirted the perimeter of the museum, reading the antechamber signs. His gaze snagged on the far right corner and he squinted at the sign there. "Egyptian Room". With a sick dread and frustrated anticipation, he made his way forward. The hum of silence rang loudly. He moved slowly, deeper into the room, past a row of cat mummies and Egyptian sculptures of pharaohs. He stopped at the back of the room, amongst the monuments that served as his only company.

A pair of arms snaked around his waist and he jerked erect as the baroness' sultry laugh echoed damningly off the walls. "Caught unawares," she whispered against his neck. She caressed her fingers over the front of his breeches. "Were you thinking of me, Huntly? Is that what has you so distracted? How delicious would it be to rut here amongst the naughty Egyptian art?"

"My lady," he bit out tightly. He removed her hands from his person and turned to face her. How had he ever desired one such as her? Her rouged cheeks and kohl-lined eyes were an overblown false attractiveness that could never rival Justina's effervescent beauty.

She fingered the plunging line of her décolletage. Her large, white breasts nearly spilled from the scandalous garment and distaste soured his mouth at her blatant display. "You've, no doubt, missed a real woman in your bed." She parted her legs slightly, the satin rustling noisily. "Would you like to take me here, hmm?"

How had he ever been attracted to this viper? "Despite Wessex's demands on your family, you've come to London all to have an itch scratched," he said coldly.

A breathy laugh bubbled past her lips. "If ever there was a lover to brave it for, Huntly, it is you."

Panic swelled inside and he fought to battle it down. It had been one thing when the baroness had been shut away in the countryside, afraid to defy the Viscount Wessex. It was an altogether different matter when she was this fearless, determined figure before him. Those who were emboldened could not be contained or controlled.

As such, she'd never be content if she believed he'd formed a real marriage with Rutland's sister-in-law.

"What do you want?" he whispered. If they were discovered together, the gossip would be vicious, and Justina would pay the ultimate price.

"You ask what I want?" Her lips hardened into a brittle line. "It has been a week since you married the mousy chit." An eerie chill skittered along his spine at the maniacal glimmer in her eyes.

Nick swallowed back the stinging words for her disparagement of Justina. With the baroness' blinding jealousy, any words would be wasted. "And?" he snapped.

The lady planted her arms akimbo. "Society is claiming yours is a love match."

His skin pricked with the sense of being studied and he glanced about, finding the room empty still. Nick returned his focus to the vindictive creature flashing hatred from her eyes.

"Lower your bloody voice," he ordered. None of their originally planned goals had been achieved. Nor would they be. It was a truth that had slowly come to him...not simply because of Cecily and Chilton's urging, but rather for an understanding of what he had become and what he didn't wish to be—Rutland.

A shuddery gasp burst from the lady's lips and he looked to her. "Why...why...the gossips are true?" she whispered, her eyebrows shooting to her hairline. "You...you *care* for her."

"My feelings for my wife do not signify," he lied, dusting his gloves together. Nor would he discuss Justina with this viper.

Her catlike eyes formed thin slits. "Then you'll destroy the Barretts."

He let his silence serve as his answer. Having colluded with one such as the baroness, there could be no simple abandonment of his earlier intentions without recompense. His father-in-law and brother-in-law's misery would have to suffice. His man-of-affairs had already begun calling in Andrew Barretts' vowels. Why did that not bring anything more than a deep-seated self-loathing?

*Because I've become Rutland.* Isn't that what he'd wanted? Had worked for.

The lady gave a pleased nod and spoke through his tumultuous musings. "See it through, Huntly. If all of Society isn't abuzz with word of their ruin in five days, I'll see it done." With a promise of retribution in her cold eyes, his former lover marched off.

His mind churned slowly with Lady Carew's pledge. Everything was set. Had been the moment he'd signed those marriage papers in Waters' office. He'd begun shoring up the remaining, outstanding debt belonging to the father. It was everything he'd worked toward. And yet, there was no thrill.

*It's because Rutland has not yet learned what I've done. When he does... when I see the horror and pain in his eyes, I'll find peace at last.* With that hollow assurance ringing in his mind, he left the Egyptian Room. Keeping his head down, he took his leave of the museum.

A short while later, with the duplicitous virago's threat whispering around his mind, he found himself at the back table of Brooke's. He rolled his snifter between his hands and contemplated the amber depths of his brandy.

"You look like hell."

Bleary-eyed, he glanced up from his drink at the owner of that voice.

His friend, Chilton, didn't bother to ask permission, but tugged out a seat. He motioned over a servant. The liveried footman rushed over to set out a glass for him. "Have the reports in the gossip columns been to the contrary then?" he asked after the man had gone.

"I don't attend the gossip columns," he said tersely and took a long swallow. He once had. All to obtain invaluable information about Rutland and those connected to the man. Nick downed his drink.

"The *ton* has remarked on the blissfully wedded union between the Diamond and the duke. Tell me, are you the gloriously happy, lovesick peer Society takes you as?" By the mocking edge to that statement, the baron had already formulated his own opinion on the state of Nick's happiness.

The usually erroneous gossips had proven, for once, correct. He *was* happy. *A lightness within her soul… with the strength to save…* He grimaced and quashed the futile verse. Rather, he had been happy. When previously he'd believed only Rutland's misery could bring him peace. Nick took another sip, waging a war inside that should not exist. That hadn't existed until Justina.

His friend filled his own glass.

"I have to do it," Nick said quietly and Chilton froze mid-pour. The baron glanced over at his friend with surprise in his gaze. "There can be no peace unless Rutland is ruined," Nick repeated. "I vowed to destroy him," he said, his words a hoarse entreaty, needing strength suffused from someone who'd known him through those darkest days.

Chilton leaned forward and shrank the space between them. "And your wife?" His friend eyed him over the rim of his snifter. "I take it you've not yet…told her about your connection to the gentleman."

Nick shook his head once. It hardly mattered, anyway. "Nor do I suspect the lady will forgive such deception on my part," he said, voicing the gripping fear that had kept him awake beside her when they lay twined in one another's arms after they'd made love.

"She certainly won't if you destroy her father and brother." Chilton chuckled, that sound devoid of mirth. He finished his drink and set down his empty snifter. "There will assuredly be no love if you see through your plans." Those matter-of-fact words twisted Nick's stomach in knots. "I would rather wager my happiness in telling her all and hoping she can see that my love proved greater than my hate."

*My love?* Nick opened and closed his mouth several times. "I…" The denial died from his lips. *Love her.* The staggering truth slammed into him with all the force of a fast-moving carriage. *I love her.* He loved her wit and her smile. He loved her ability to hope, despite the ugliness the world had shown her.

"You've known my opinion, all along. You cannot do this." Chilton cut across Nick's whirring thoughts. "Speak to the lady. Tell her all and tell her you love her." Nick's gaze took on a faraway quality. A spark of pain resonated in their depths. "Because if you do not, the regret will someday threaten to destroy you in ways Rutland or no man could."

Nick stared back. His friend spoke as one who knew. They all carried secrets. Which ones belonged to Chilton? A commotion sounded at the front of the club and they both looked to the entrance of the elite establishment as a young gentleman stumbled and staggered through the club. He found a table, collapsing into one of the leather chairs.

His brother-in-law's loud slurring call for a drink roused another flurry of annoyed whispers from the other patrons. He frowned. The young man's misery shouldn't matter. Nick had begun calling in the younger Barrett's vowels. This misery was his doing and he should be reveling in it. *Just leave him there, blubbering into his drink.* But just as Justina had slipped past his defenses and penetrated a wall of hatred, her impressionable, always-grinning brother had, as well. *Bloody hell.* "If you'll excuse me, Chilton?" Nick asked, shoving to his feet.

"Of course. Go. Go," the baron urged, waving a hand. "I suspect you'll have need of my carriage to see the gentleman home."

Murmuring his thanks, Nick made his way over to the man whose vowels he owned in their entirety. "Barrett," he greeted.

Justina's brother lifted his head, revealing bloodshot eyes.

"May I join you?"

Gone was the youthful grin. In its place was a stark emptiness that Nick had learned too young. "Huntly, myyy friend," he slurred. "Care for a driiink?" He swiped a hand about and jostled the decanter of brandy.

Nick quickly rescued it and set it to rights. He sat, at a loss for words since he'd brought about this misery.

Barrett looked like he'd dueled with the Devil and lost. His usually greased and immaculate hair hung tousled. His cravat in disarray. "She ended it." Andrew's voice broke and, with his throat working, he reached inside his jacket and fished around. He withdrew a letter.

The cloying scent of roses slapped at Nick's senses while the younger gentleman rambled on. That was what the man was sobbing over? Not his rapid descent into dun territory, but rather… a young lady. Then, wasn't that the effect a good woman had on a man? They made one forget logic and order and flipped one's world upside down.

"Saaid we couldna ever be and we only lived in a world of pretend." Justina's brother stared at him through bloodshot eyes. "Told her I was going to end up in dun territory, but that we could make our future work togetherrr."

Rutland would be devastated by the young man's suffering. So why then did Nick sit here with this hollow ache, as well? Because he'd been the one to shatter both his youth and his heart. Nick had thieved away Andrew's romantic innocence by breaking his financial standing. *Just as I've ultimately done to Justina's innocence.* "If she loved you enough, it would not matter, Barrett," Nick said quietly. "Your love would be enough." *Will that be the case for Justina?* A slow-building dread twisted in his belly.

Barrett's upper lip peeled in a cynical grin. He'd been forever changed. "It is far more complicated than that. There is another… gentleman and she belongs to him, and always will." His words ended on a whispery hush and he began to weep.

Another round of whispers and censorious stares were cast Barrett's way and Nick frowned. He'd not subject the young man to any further whispers and gossip. *No more than I've already secretly done.* "Come," he urged, taking to his feet once more. "Let me help you home," he said gruffly. Wrapping an arm around Barrett's shoulders, he helped him to a stand.

"Goooddd of you, Huntly," Barrett said, borrowing support from him as they made their way through the club. "It's why you deserve love." Guilt stabbed at Nick like a vicious dagger being plunged inside his person and twisted around. "Where IIIII?" Barrett tripped and Nick quickly righted him. "I've been a lousy sonnn and bruther," he slurred. "Alwayyys asking for Justina's help. And Phoebe's. And Edmund's." Edmund. That name stirred the embers of Nick's hatred. A stark, necessary reminder that he desperately required in this moment.

They reached the front of Brooke's and with a curt order, Nick called for Chilton's carriage. "Yes, I," Barrett continued over the exchange between him and the servant at the front of the establishment. "I was an equally rotted…" He creased his brow. "Rotten?

Rotter?" Justina's brother looked to him. "Is it rotted or rotter?"

"I think either are, in fact, words," Nick mumbled shouldering the tall man outside the front doors and into the streets. "And I'm sure you were neither." He was the ruthless bounder. Bitterness soured his mouth.

"And I'm a rottered suitor..." Barrett's face contorted in a paroxysm of grief.

Chilton's carriage waited twenty paces away and Nick gave silent thanks, as he guided the other man to the conveyance. "In you go," he urged when they'd reached the door.

Barrett lifted one leg up and then promptly tumbled back on his arse. Nick cursed. He swiftly bent and guided the drunken man upright. Perspiring from his efforts, he motioned to the driver and, together, they lifted the younger man inside, settling him on the opposite bench.

After the driver fetched and secured Nick's mount to the carriage, Nick climbed in his friend's conveyance. A moment later, it lurched forward and he was left alone with Justina's brother. The younger man lay huddled in the corner, with the left side of his head pressed against the window. A faint, muffled weeping filled the confines, muted by the rumble of the rapidly churning wheels. Then a bleating snore escaped Barrett.

The young man snored like his sister. That detail only strengthened the connection between those siblings all the more.

Nick stared at the other man. He'd intended to destroy each of the Barretts as a means of hurting Rutland. Staring at his wife's slumbering brother, exposed and vulnerable before him, he searched for the triumph in this. And found none.

Not until Rutland saw those he loved suffering, as Nick's own family had, could he then feel the thrill of victory.

The carriage rolled to a stop outside Viscount Waters' townhouse and Nick shoved the door open. Jumping out, he reached back inside and hefted the future viscount from the conveyance. Chilton's driver rushed over and helped Barrett out of the streets. Grunting under the surprising weight of the young man, Nick started slowly along the pavement and up the front steps.

He raised his hand to rap, but the door was yanked open. The old butler, his face a stark mask of worry, reached past the driver and helped usher Andrew inside. Nick murmured his thanks as a sharp cry went up.

"Andrew!"

A tall, slender woman with auburn hair came rushing down the stairs, tripping over herself in her haste to reach the younger man. She ran frantic eyes over his face and cupped it between her hands. His lashes fluttered.

"Mattther," Barrett slurred. *The mother.* "You've returned. You missed the festivities of Justina's wedding."

*My mother would never dare limit what I read. She has always lived to see her children happy...*

"Myy chum, Huntly here, isss taking wahnderful care of me, isn't that riiiight?"

Some of the panic receded in the older woman's sapphire blue eyes and she blinked slowly. Then she seemed to register Nick's presence. "My lady," he greeted with a bow.

Her lips parted and she dropped her hands from her son's face. "You are Justina's husband." *The rotted one. Or the rotter.* Either worked for him, as well.

"I am, my lady."

She quickly gathered his hands in hers and, with far greater generosity or kindness than he deserved, she smiled at him. "Your Grace, we received word from Justina's friends about my..." Her smile withered and she dropped her voice, speaking in hushed tones. "My husband's intentions for Justina and the Marquess of Tennyson. We came as quickly as we were able." Tears shimmered in her eyes. "Thank you for saving her."

Oh, God. This was his penance; to be ripped apart with the guilt of his own lies. Lies that contained kernels of truth. "Your daughter saved me far more than I ever saved her," he said hoarsely. Justina had rekindled parts of him that he'd believed long dead. She'd reminded him of the joy and wonder he'd found on a printed page and in a lecture hall. He'd repaid those gifts with lies. And would repay that by ruining her family.

*These people before me...*

"Theyyyy're in love," Andrew said loudly, his head lolling against the broad shoulder of the butler.

Nick's face went hot with the younger man's admission. A twinkle lit the lady's kindly eyes. "I must see Andrew taken abovestairs, Your Grace."

With a nod, he turned the future viscount over to several servants who started abovestairs with their drunken master. The viscountess dropped a curtsy and then started up the stairs, pausing on the second step. She glanced back. "Thank you for everything, Your Grace."

"There is nothing to thank me for," he murmured. What hatred would she feel for him if she learned the truth? *When* she learned the truth. She smiled at him once more and followed after her son.

Nick turned on his heel and then stopped. Disquiet spread through him. *We came as quickly as we were able.* The duchess' words rang in the foyer.

*Rutland.*

Heart picking up a maddening beat, Nick rushed to the door, and the servant in wait pulled it open. Nick flew down the steps and bounded for the baron's carriage. Of course, by now, Rutland would have likely received word and made for London. And where he'd once been filled with a breathless anticipation for the inevitable meeting, a sick dread filled him now. He yanked the carriage door open and pulled himself inside. For there was no doubt the relentless marquess would know precisely who he was…and why he'd done what he had.

All guilt and remorse for Justina's unfortunate role in his scheming was briefly obliterated as Nick was filled with a thirst for this long-awaited justice—

for himself, and Cecily, their mother. Father.

A moment later, the carriage rattled along through the crowded streets of London. Frustration gripped him as he looked out the window, cursing the sudden throng of conveyances. After an interminable stretch of time, his townhouse came into view and Nick rapped once on the ceiling. Before the barouche had rocked to a full stop, he yanked the door open and jumped out. A jarring pain shot from his feet up through his legs and, ignoring it, he moved past curious passersby to the front of his residence. He looked back and ordered the carriage driver to see his horse tended.

He pushed through the front door and then stopped. *The Devil is here.* The same way he'd known as a boy of fourteen from the ominous darkness lingering in the air, so, too, did Nick know it now, walking down a different set of hallways. In a different house. A palatial mansion. Possessing a new title and a wife. And a family forever destroyed.

His butler came forward. "You have a visitor, Your Grace." The servant's skin paled. "The Marquess of Rutland arrived a short while ago and insisted on waiting until you'd returned." He gave his employer a pained look. "I took the liberty of showing *him* to your office."

Nick glanced frantically about. "My wife?" he demanded harshly.

"Has still not returned, Your Grace."

Some of the tension left him. He gave thanks that she'd be shielded from this long overdue exchange. Nick stared down the hall. Then feeling not unlike the boy who'd snuck about, seeking a glimpse of the Devil, he prepared to face the demon once more. Dismissing the other man with a curt thank you, Nick made for his office. With each step that brought him closer to the man who'd ruined his family, a vital thrumming surged in his veins. The last he'd seen the marquess, he had been a cowering boy, huddled on the floor at his feet. No longer. Now, he'd become a man of equal stature and power.

He reached the oak panel and stopped, his gaze frozen on the doorway. For years, he'd dreamed of and planned this meeting. Had sustained himself through his grandfather's verbal and physical assaults with the hunger for revenge. *Today, I can have my revenge and let those dreams be at last realized.* Schooling his features into a hardened mask, Nick pressed the handle and stepped inside.

The hated figure standing in the center of his office spun around. *Lord Rutland.*

They assessed one another. Time had aged the marquess. His frame heavier with muscle and, if possible, his eyes harder than they had been thirteen years earlier, Lord Rutland stood before him with several days of growth on his face. His clothes were dusty and wrinkled. In short, a shadow of the smooth, flawless young lord who'd so casually ripped his family asunder.

All the hatred he had built himself up with enlivened him and renewed a long-ago pledge he'd made. Blotting out even the memory of his new wife. For in this brief moment, he was transported to another office. His father's. Where his sire had met with Rutland and then taken his life for the terms put to him. Nick drew the door closed. "Lord Rutland," he said in a silky soft greeting that could rival the smooth edge of a blade.

The marquess glanced him up and down. "Tallings," he said gruffly. That one word, Nick's name, said more than all the volumes in his vast library. The marquess *knew*.

He tamped down a frown. What was the other man feeling? Did he know the same panic and terror that had riddled his once-young self? Or was this jaded beast incapable of those weak sentiments? Yet again, Rutland showed nothing and Nick was shredded, still, on the inside. Determined to elicit some response from his nemesis, Nick widened his cold, practiced smile. "Ah, you remember me, then?"

*...Your family isn't my responsibility, Tallings... Your failings, are...* Those words twisted around his mind like a vicious cancer, destroying him all over again.

"I know who you are." That concession came as though physically pulled from the marquess.

Nick smirked. "I am *honored*. I was but a boy." Did he imagine Rutland flinching? Surely the Devil was incapable of guilt. "After all, what is it you said, hmm?" He creased his brow and then held a finger up with a false dawning. "Of course, I recall." He leveled the Marquess of Rutland with a hard stare. "You said, you would leave this house and my family and never think of us again."

The color seeped from the marquess' skin. Nick found strength in that slight crack in the other man's remarkable composure. His wan complexion made him human. Proved Rutland was, in fact, possessed of the same weaknesses that riddled every man's soul. It made him *human*. Unnerved, Nick glanced away first and tried to reconcile his discovery.

He had sustained himself on the vision of a monster. Monsters, however, were pretend. Reserved for the pages of books and children's inventive imaginations. Seeing him now with this unwanted, powerful lens marked Rutland as a man who experienced compassion...and mayhap love. To hide the faint tremble in his hands, wrought by that realization, Nick clasped them at his back.

Rutland's clever gaze took in that slight movement. Of course, he'd miss nothing. Discomfited by the other man's stony silence, Nick forced a chuckle. "In fairness, it wasn't this house, was it? It was an entirely different one and my father was a mere baronet."

"You do not know all the details of my dealings with your father," Rutland said, his words coated in steel.

"Ah, but I do not need to know all of them. All I need to know is that every member of my family suffered because of you and, now, I will quite gleefully destroy your father-in-law and your brother-in-law." Nick dropped his voice to a low whisper. "And as I do, Rutland, and your wife bears witness to the suffering brought about because of your actions, know that it is because of *you*."

Rutland offered him a pitying smile that sent heat rushing up Nick's neck. Why wasn't the man enraged? Fearful? "You still have not learned, have you?"

Nick fought the question hovering on his lips. It spilled out, anyway. "Learned what?"

"That in our every dealing, *we* are responsible, if at the very least, in some part, for the outcomes. Your father is not free of absolution. And yet, you'd seek to destroy the Barretts in some twisted game of revenge on me." The mask lifted and, at last, that desired regret and shame paraded over Rutland's visage. Only, there was no victory or solace for Nick. Uninvited, the marquess came forward. "I know games of revenge. Better than you ever can." The ghost of an empty grin turned the man's hard lips. "I'd wager I'm the only man you've sought revenge on."

His muscles jumped reflexively inside his coat at that accurate supposition. "It hardly matters how many but, rather, the deservingness of the person you'll exact justice on."

Rutland chuckled. "But that is where you are wrong."

"Regardless, I'll not debate with you," he said dismissively. Nick's teeth set at the audacity of the marquess and his bloody suppositions. "You're out of time here." He took a perverse pleasure in hurling those final words given his father back at the man who'd destroyed him.

Rutland took another step closer until only a handful of paces separated them. When Nick was a boy, the marquess had towered over his small, reed-thin figure. With time, Nick had added nearly the same amount of height and muscle to his frame. They remained locked in a tense battle of silence. The marquess eyed him through razor-sharp slits. "Is that what this is about then, Tallings?"

"Tsk, tsk," Nick chided, mockingly. He spread his arms wide. "It is *Huntly* now." He flashed a hard grin and, with that, Lord Rutland was restored to the unflappable beast that had entered his family's home all those years ago.

"I am too old for games." Lord Rutland seethed. Despite himself, unease skittered along Nick's spine. The marquess' voice, still gravelly and harsh, momentarily froze him, pulled him back to another office, another exchange.

And goddamn Rutland for transforming Nick into that sniveling coward, shaking on the hallway floor. Pointedly ignoring him, Nick wandered over to his fully-stocked sideboard. Feeling the marquess' intent gaze on his every movement, he made a show of studying the decanters the way he might evaluate his estate reports. Then, selecting the finest bottle of French brandy, he poured himself a snifter. Still presenting the other man with his back, he swirled the contents of his glass in a circle, raised it to his lips, and slowly sipped.

All the while, he stared blankly at the gold satin wallpaper.

*...I need more time... You promised I had more time...*

He pressed his eyes closed briefly, blotting out the marquess' mirthless laugh from years ago, but it was futile. The bastard had reentered his life, as planned, and the door had been opened, letting in memories he'd long buried. Behind clenched eyes, his father's lifeless visage danced in the air, suspended on that noose. Bile stung his throat.

"Tallings," the marquess commanded. It spoke levels of the man's conceit and power that he should enter Nick's office, nay, now a duke's office, and issue directives. "Is it money you want?" he asked curtly. "Name your amount."

Nick counted several moments, refusing to allow the black-hearted bastard any control of the exchange. He then wheeled slowly around. "The night you walked out of my father's office, he hanged himself." All the color leeched from the marquess' face. "I cut him down myself," he said, his voice hollow. "Dragged a chair over and sawed the scrap of my mother's curtain he'd used to do it." Lord Rutland's throat muscles moved. Was it fear for what this now meant for the Barretts? Or was it regret? As soon as the thought slid in, he scoffed. Men like Rutland weren't capable of regret. "My mother died shortly thereafter of a broken heart," he continued in a methodical recounting, determined to have this at last said. As much as for him, as the bastard before him. "My sister was forced to wed a doddering lord at fifteen; an old, heartless man who hasn't had the grace to die and, through it, do you know what strengthened me?"

The other man's shoulders went back in the only real indication he'd heard that statement.

*Give me some response. Some bloody reaction.* For then, surely there would be some triumph to this moment. "I was made stronger by the words you gave me, Rutland." Did the bastard even recall that utterance?

The marquess drew in a jagged sigh. All these years, Nick had imagined Rutland to be invincible only to find that the man's armor had also cracked. Then, mayhap that was the sorcery of the Barrett women. It only marked him more like this man he'd long despised. In ways he didn't want to be. In ways they were both men who'd been forever changed by women.

"When my world was crumpling, your words of revenge and hatred were the only ones that sustained me." With Nick's telling, all the old nightmares flared to the surface. Nightmares he'd foolishly believed he'd mastered. "Do you remember what I promised you all those years ago?" he rasped.

The gold flecks in Rutland's eyes glinted with…remorse. So, he was capable of it. The mask lifted and, at last, that desired regret and shame paraded over his visage. Only, there was no victory or solace for Nick. "I do not."

How odd those words had been so formative as to who and what he had become. Yet, this man didn't even so much as recall uttering them. It rekindled his hatred for the marquess. "To destroy all those you loved." *Only now…Justina is one of those people.* He fought through that mocking reminder and fixed on his need to inflict hurt on the ruthless bastard standing before him. "You once told me you didn't love anyone. But by your presence here, well, I'd say that is no longer true, is it?"

Rutland's face contorted. And the absolute desolation and despair stamped in his harsh features should bring the ultimate joy. But Nick stood back, feeling like the bastard he'd spent years professing Rutland to be. "It is why you wed Justina."

It was Nick's turn to register surprise. Of course, word had found its way to the marquess.

"I received mention of your name from the lady's friends," Rutland sneered. "But the missive was delayed."

If not for the lost note, Nick's marriage would never have been.

For Rutland would have ridden his horse to death to stop it. Justina, when learning his connection to the marquess, would have never gone through with it. The thought left him bereft inside. For these weeks with her, she'd reminded him of what it was to laugh again. Had driven back all the darkest nightmares and left in their place this lightness which was at odds with the man he'd thought himself to be. "For years, I vowed to destroy you," he said, more to himself.

"What do you want?" the marquess repeated. There was a faint entreaty there that matched the desperation Nick's father had shown all those years ago.

He found strength in that. "Why, I already have everything I need, Rutland." He motioned to his spacious office that could fit the whole of the Home Office inside it. "I'm obscenely wealthy, not because I bankrupted other families to build my power," A muscle jumped at the right corner of Rutland's jaw, "but because of work I actually did with my hands." He turned his palms up, revealing the callused flesh, marked by years of toil. Nick folded his arms and rested them at his chest. "And do you know what else I have?" He took a perverse delight in taunting the other man with the retribution at his fingertips.

Rutland remained stonily silent. Questions, however, snapped in his brown eyes.

"I have your father-in-law's unentailed properties as well as his son's." The remaining color leeched from Rutland's cheeks. "I own every vowel both men have ever held outstanding. Not a creditor will extend them a line should they sell their soul for that coin." Where was the sense of victory? The thrill of triumph? Everything had changed. A cinch was cutting off his airflow. Making it impossible to draw breath. For not only was there Justina, but also the trusting, always affably smiling Andrew Barrett.

The marquess slid his eyes closed.

*Checkmate.*

Only, with his stomach twisted in agonizing knots, it felt very much like he'd lost everything all over again.

# CHAPTER 18

"I SWEAR YOU ARE THE only newly, *happily* married woman who'd go off to see to matters of business." Gillian's mutterings were nearly lost to the busy Lambeth Streets.

Justina carefully picked her way over a murky puddle. "Ah, but as long as I claim control of my life, I'll always know happiness," she pointed out, echoing the gypsy Bunica.

The cryptic gypsy.

Following her and Nick's visits to Lambeth, she'd alternated between worrying about the eerie prophecy gleaned from her palms and chastising herself for worrying about something that moved far beyond the logical. When Justina prided herself on her clear thinking.

It was that which drove her out into the streets of Lambeth today, with Gillian dragged along for company.

"Will you slow down?" Gillian implored, her breath coming in quick, little gasps.

Justina abruptly stopped and her friend mumbled her thanks. Pushing her bonnet back, she surveyed the shops lining the streets, reading the signs. And then she found it. It was a small sign. Wooden, crooked, and but for that slight tilt, otherwise nondescript. A slow smile pulled her lips at the corners. The sign called her forward. Ignoring Gillian's lamentations, she quickened her pace. For nearly three years, she'd lived in a largely uncertain state. The only freedom she'd known from her father's machinations had come from Edmund's frequent intervention and rescue…and her own furtive attempts to avoid those machinations.

In the weeks she'd known Nick, she'd found not only the ability to use her voice but, now, also the ability to take control of all aspects of her life. She stopped outside the white stucco establishment and peered up at the sign.

"Winslow's?" Gillian read as she stopped at Justina's side. Her friend scratched at her brow. "What is Winslow's?"

Justina pulled her gaze away from that hated name. "They are creditors," she said quietly. Understanding lit the other woman's eyes.

These were the men who'd filed into her home and marched off with their arms filled with her belongings. And her mother's. And Andrew's.

But now, she was no longer Justina Barrett, impoverished daughter of a wastrel. She was a duchess. And with that title came power. With that, Justina pressed the handle and stepped inside.

Sunlight streamed through the two small front windows, bathing the room in light. She wasn't sure what she'd expected of the place. Mayhap because she'd not allowed herself to think of the bounders who made their fortunes off other families' misfortunes. But this was certainly not it. As modest on the inside as the outside, the hardwood floors were coarse and marked, with two desks set almost haphazardly, with no uniformity, at opposite ends of the establishment.

Footsteps sounded at the back entrance of the building and, as one, Justina and Gillian looked over.

Mr. Johnson, with his monocle at his eye and pursed mouth, had the same distasteful look he'd worn each time he'd stepped inside her family's residence. "May I help you?" he asked. By his tone, the only help he wished to render was guidance to the door and out of his establishment.

She tipped her chin up. "My name is Justina Barr—Tallings," she swiftly amended. "The Duchess of Huntly."

The graying proprietor's monocle fell and clattered noisily on the floor. Gillian smothered a giggle in her hand.

Yes, there was something heady and empowering in confronting the beasts who'd made off with her family's most cherished belongings as a woman of power, now.

"Your Grace," Mr. Johnson said quickly, dropping a deep bow.

Did he even remember her as the young lady whose copies of Miss Austen's work he'd made off with? Or did a man such as him never give another thought to those people who dwelled inside the homes he pillaged?

"You have removed numerous articles from my father, Viscount Waters," she said in steely tones as she handed her reticule over to Gillian.

Mr. Johnson flared his eyebrows and they nearly disappeared into his hairline. Yes, what must he think about her changed circumstances? She clenched and unclenched her jaw.

"I've come to see the restoration of my mother's jewelry and my collection of books."

The hated creditor frowned. "I'm afraid that isn't possible." With that dismissive pronouncement, he took up position behind one of the vacant desks and proceeded to study a ledger.

Justina wrinkled her nose. Well, apparently even the title of duchess wasn't enough to impress this stony-faced creditor. She and Gillian exchanged looks. Bringing her shoulders back, Justina stomped over to the desk and placed her palms on the edge. "I'm afraid you did not hear me properly," she said coolly. "I've come to see my family's possessions restored."

Mr. Johnson picked his head up from his book. A muscle ticked at the corner of his mouth. "As I said, I am afraid that is impossible." He made to return his attention to that damned ledger and she shot a hand out, grabbing it. "I beg your pardon?" he cried, hopping to his feet.

Justina snapped the book closed and set it down neatly on the edge of his desk. "Have you already sold those items?" she demanded. It shouldn't matter. Not truly. They were material possessions. And yet, this moved beyond the wealth or cost of those goods. This went to the powerless state she and Phoebe and her mother had all existed in these years. "Have you?" she repeated, when he remained stonily silent.

"I've not."

Some of the tension went out of her. Gillian moved into position at Justina's shoulder; a silent, but powerful show of solidarity. "Very well," Justina said, holding her hand out. Her friend promptly returned her reticule. Fishing around inside, her fingers collided with a folded sheet of velum. She withdrew the note and slid it over the desk, finding a perverse delight in Mr. Johnson's clear discomfiture.

"What is this?" he blurted.

Much the way her own governess had delivered her deportment lessons years ago, Justina spoke in those like tones. "That is a list, Mr. Johnson." She pointed her index finger at the page, bringing his gaze briefly from her to the sheet and then back. "Those are all the items I'd like to purchase on behalf of my family. I'll need the amount and then my husband's man-of-affairs will see to the arrangements."

"I'm afraid I cannot help you, Your Grace," he said tightly, pushing the page back. "I suggest you return home and speak to your husband about...these particular items."

Gillian's gasp resounded around the room.

Fury mingled with annoyance and Justina layered her palms on the desk once more. "Are you saying you'll not deal with me because I am a woman, Mr. Johnson?"

The graying creditor had the ashen hue of one who'd consumed a rancid plate of kippers. "I've strict orders not to release these items for any purpose other than auction."

Justina staggered back. "Auction?" she asked, her voice emerging breathless. She struggled to make sense of what he was saying. What manner of bastard did her father deal with that the man would bar anyone from giving fair coin for those possessions? And fury melded with pain and frustration that she should still be deprived of this control. Powerless once more. "But I can pay," she blurted, hating the plaintive quality to that statement.

She dimly registered Gillian settling a comforting hand on her sleeve. "Come," her friend murmured, giving a slight squeeze.

Justina shrugged off that touch. By God, she'd not leave until this man gave her a bloody answer.

"The *gentleman*," A ruddy blush stained Mr. Johnson's cheeks, "has ordered these items to auction and no one possessing connections to the Barrett family will be permitted to bid."

The air grew sparse in the office and Justina staggered back a step. Then another. And another. Hating herself for that weakness, she forced herself around. With slow, calculated strides, she stalked out of the office.

Gillian followed close at her heels.

Not a word was said between them until Dominick's carriage bore Gillian home. "I am sorry," she said softly, covering Justina's right hand with her own.

"Why would anyone do that?" she implored, when she trusted herself to speak.

Her friend gave her head a slight shake. "Because there is no understanding people; men or women, lords or ladies."

No, there wasn't. And just like that, her legs had been cut out from under her once more by a damned *gentleman*. How different would that meeting with Mr. Johnson have gone if Nick has been at her side? Bitterness soured her mouth. The remaining journey to Gillian's Mayfair residence continued in silence until the well-springed conveyance rocked to a halt outside the Marquess of Ellsworth's townhouse.

Gillian lingered. "There is no shame in asking your husband to aid you in this," she said gently.

No, there was no shame in it. She and Nick would be partners in life. This, however, had been about her seizing that control for herself and righting a wrong done to her and her mother and Phoebe without anyone's influence but her own. "Thank you, Gillian."

Her friend gave her an encouraging smile and then accepted the hand of a footman.

As the carriage took Justina on the remaining trip to her new home, she peeled the curtain back and stared out at the fashionable townhouses. Despite her friend's opinion, it wasn't that she was too proud to seek out help. She'd accepted assistance countless times from her sister and Edmund, and even her husband who'd married her to keep her from the likes of Tennyson. She arrived a short while later and entered the front doors as they were thrown open. She shrugged out of her cloak and turned it over to the servant.

"My husband, Thoms?" she asked, handing off her reticule.

The butler swallowed loudly. "He's in his office, Your Grace."

She took two steps.

"His Grace doesn't welcome interruptions while he's conducting business."

And froze.

Once more, another person ordering her about. Determining for her what she could and could not do. With a winning smile for the old butler, she continued onward, without a word, for Nick's office.

She reached for the handle when two voices carried out into the hall. Both familiar. But it was one that held her frozen. *Edmund.* A loud humming filled her ears. Nothing would take her devoted brother-in-law from his wife's side. Nothing and no one. With trembling fingers, Justina tossed the door open. "Edmund," she managed to squeeze out past the fear holding her in the doorway.

Phoebe's husband blanched. "Justina." Her name emerged as a strangled plea and the sound of his misery propelled her into movement.

Shaking, she pulled the door closed and leaned against it. "Phoebe," she rasped. "Is she...?"

"She is well," Rutland hurried to assure.

She pressed her palms over her eyes and sent a prayer skyward. And yet... what had brought him here in such haste?

NICK HAD GONE FROM COMPLETE control of his fate and future to an outside observer on an intimate exchange between his wife and her brother-in-law.

"You are certain Phoebe is well?" Justina demanded as she came forward.

Phoebe. The sister. Odd, until now, he'd not allowed himself to think of the woman Rutland had bound himself to. The woman he'd come to love who'd cracked his armor and made Nick's plan all too easy. Until Justina. She' thrown it all into upheaval.

Rutland gave his head a forceful shake. "Phoebe is well," he repeated gruffly.

"Garrick?" Justina asked on a rush.

"The babe is doing well."

Some of the tension left his wife's shoulders. *Garrick.* Lord Rutland's son. A little babe. Fragile and frail and dependent upon Justina's sister and this man he had dedicated his life to hating. Once again, that small detail made Rutland more man than monster.

Nick stood behind his desk, removed from the exchange, an observer to a discourse between family members. And worse, in a way that spoke to the forged bond between his wife and the man before him. A bond that would not be severed.

*Only mine will be.*

He struggled to draw in a breath, staggered by that truth.

Justina worried her lower lip. "Truly?"

The marquess glanced over the top of her golden curls. "*I'd* not lie to you."

Of course, his clever wife would detect that slight emphasis placed there. Her brow creased. "Edmund, why *are* you here?" she asked slowly.

Silent as the grave, Lord Rutland looked to Nick. At last, with the black rage radiating from his brown irises, the marquess was transformed back to the same ruthless, lethal predator in Nick's family's cottage.

Despite himself, he flinched at that slight, mocking gleam in his brother-in-law's eyes. *Oh, God, he is now my brother-in-law.* It had been his original intention to link them for life and, yet, this again moved them into a new, unfamiliar sphere. "The marquess was just leaving," Nick said curtly.

His wife rotated her gaze between Nick and Lord Rutland. "What?" she blurted.

Except, the marquess remained fixed to the floor in a blatant display of insolence and arrogance.

Nick ignored his wife's perplexed inquiry. "Lord Rutland was just leaving," he said, his command coming out clipped, while frustration gripped at him. How eerily empty he felt with this bloody exchange. Where was the thrill of his victory? Where was his promised reward?

Justina moved in a whir of satin skirts, coming behind his desk. "Don't be silly, Nick. Edmund has just arrived. We cannot be so rude as to send him away." Not allowing him a reply, she looked to her brother-in-law. "Why are you here, Edmund?" She gave her head a shake. "Not because I'm not pleased to see you. I am. I…"

Over the top of her head, he and Rutland exchanged another lengthy stare. Which Justina, this time, saw.

"What is it?" Uncertainty laced that question.

Before either gentleman could respond, a commotion sounded

in the hallway. The furious bellowing of Viscount Waters muffled through the door.

"I don't care if he's in with the goddamned King of England," the man thundered. "I'll knock down every bloody door until I see the bastard."

Justina took a hurried step closer to Nick. That subtly trusting movement wrenched somewhere inside where his heart beat. That trust would die. As it should. He'd set out to beggar her family. Even as he'd saved her from a miserable fate as Tennyson's wife, she was now bound to him, forever reminded of his treachery.

The marquess gave him a long, sad look and shook his head; that gesture pitying and knowing. Knowing that Nick's tenuous and fleeting grasp on happiness had seconds left to live before Nick lost everything that truly mattered. The only thing that had ever really mattered—Justina's love.

Viscount Waters hurled the door open and Nick shot his focus to the front of the room. His father-in-law's bulging eyes did an inventory of the room, lingering briefly on Lord Rutland. Fear flashed in those blue depths and then he briefly shifted them over to Nick. Before settling on Justina. "You goddamned bloody twit," he bellowed and she jumped. The viscount thrust a finger in her direction.

An unholy, red rage clouded Nick's vision, as a primal growl rumbled low in his chest. "Shut your bloody mouth or I will do it for you," he snapped.

Fear bled briefly from the viscount's eyes, but then he looked again to his daughter. "This is your fault," he seethed and charged forward.

The marquess quickly placed himself between the viscount and Nick's desk, cutting off the path to Justina. "Shut your fool mouth, Waters," the marquess commanded, squeezing the older man's forearm. The viscount cried out.

For the first time, he saw that since Rutland had wed her sister, Justina had known some security because of his presence in her life. If it hadn't been for the marquess, she would, no doubt, be wed to another man, sold off by her father. Who would have believed Nick would have felt anything other than disdain for the all-powerful Lord Rutland?

"You did this, gel," Waters continued, surprisingly relentless in the face of his son-in-law's fury. But then, financial ruin made a man do maddening things, like hang himself at the end of a rope or challenge a beast like the Marquess of Rutland.

His wife proved her strength, once more, and she stepped out of his protective shadow. "I have no idea what you are talking about." She looked between the gentlemen assembled.

Words stuck in his throat. The revelation that had been inevitable. The truth that could no longer be hidden. Nor should he want it hidden. But the minute the admission was breathed to life, every moment before with Justina would ring as hollow moments built on deception and treachery. Agony brought his eyes briefly closed.

In the end, it was the viscount who stole the response for him. "Your *husband* is going to beggar me, Andrew, and your entire family. You whored yourself to a man who will ruin us."

# CHAPTER 19

W̶HEN ᴊUSTINA WAS A GIRL just learning to swim, with
Andrew instructing her in the lake outside their cottage in Leeds,
she'd fallen into the water and sank to the bottom. The world had
existed as a swishing of muted noise and sound from the depths.

Just now, with her father's words ringing in her ears, it felt
remarkably like that long-ago day. Shouts erupted as Edmund
gripped her father in a punishing hold. At her father's sharp yelp,
she broke the surface, once more.

Justina gave her head a clearing shake as guilt took hold. How
quickly she'd doubted him. "Nick would not do that." She leveled the outraged charge at her miserable sire, hating herself for
allowing her reprobate father to plant the seeds of doubt against
her husband; the one man who'd appreciated her for more than
an empty beauty.

"He did do it," her father spat. His fleshy lip peeled back in a
snarl, he'd the look of a stuffed orangutan she'd once seen in her
visits to the Royal Museum with Phoebe. Something in that connection settled her jittery nerves, sorted her tumultuous thoughts.

"Do not come here," she began. "And spread your lies about my
husband." She looked to Nick for strength, but he remained coolly
unflappable, his chiseled features carved of stone.

"Lies?" her father barked. He ambled his corpulent frame around
Edmund and stopped so he had her in his direct vision. "Your *hus-*

*band* offered for you and asked me to name all those holding my vowels." Spittle formed in the corners of his mouth as he spewed his fury. "And he sent his creditors to collect."

"That's not possible," she said, her voice coming as though down a long hall.

"The very same men who've collected all our possessions arrived this morn to take the rest."

Justina looked frantically to her husband. His skin was an ashen hue, like one who'd boarded a ship and been cast out into a violent storm. "Tell him he's wrong, Nick." He met her request with silence. "Tell him," she cried, her voice pitching to the ceiling, and he winced.

"I cannot do that," he said quietly.

*No.* Her knees went weak and she shot her hands out, seeking purchase.

"Yes," her father replied and she started, unaware she'd spoken aloud.

Nick turned his palms up and came forward. "Justina," he implored. Just that. Her name. No assurances. No denials. Why? Why was he not denying all these heinous charges?

She stared blankly at those hands that had so lovingly stroked her. His words muted and muffled in her ears.

"It is true, Justina," Rutland confirmed.

She touched her fingertips to her mouth. "That is why you are here." Her voice emerged as a threadbare whisper. Her brother-in-law's statement, confirmed in Nick's silence, ripped a hole inside her chest and she struggled for words.

Angling his body in a dismissive manner, the marquess looked to her. "Notes were discovered, from a former maid," he grimaced. "Apparently your...husband's plans had been in the making for awhile."

"Notes?" she echoed dumbly.

Splotches of color marred her brother-in-law's cheeks. "She was providing information between your husband and his lover."

His words sucked all the air from the room. Justina stilled, unable to draw in a single gasping breath. His lover. *Not* his former lover. Given her own parents' miserable union, she'd not been naïve to the reality that many men took lovers, but the image painted of her husband with another was crushing. Another woman whose body he'd stroked and who'd known his tender caress and the feel of him as he moved deep inside her. A tortured moan lodged in her throat and she choked on it.

"Justina, let me explain," Nick entreated. "She is no longer my lover. I ended it with her before I even met you."

She tried to make sense of that admission. What was truth and what was just another lie?

"My maid was gathering details about our family and giving them to…" Rutland motioned to Nick. "…this one," he added with more gentleness than she ever remembered in him.

No. It could not be. That was a ruthlessness her husband was incapable of. Except… The earth dipped and swayed and she steadied herself against the nearest seat. "I never told you I collected bonnets." Her voice came as though down a long corridor. It was an insignificant detail, but his gleaning of it was more telling than anything.

Her husband closed his eyes and she *knew*. Knew by the tight corners drawn at his lips. *No. No. No.* It was a litany that screamed around the chambers of her mind until she thought she'd go mad from it. Everything could not have been a lie. She'd trusted him. "Nick," she pleaded hoarsely. "Please say something."

His mouth moved, but no words came out.

Justina dug her fingertips into her temples. Every moment they'd shared had been meant to deceive and trap. Falsehoods. Lies. Her feet twitched with the need to flee and escape the new reality of her existence. She curled her toes into the soles of her slippers anchoring herself to the spot. There was no running from this. What was there then? For her? For them?

*Nothing. There is nothing…*

"I don't give a jot about his lover," her father whined. He jerked his chin at a pallid and unmoving Nick. "He is going to call in my vowels." Her heart thudded hard against her ribcage. "See me and Andrew work on a turnip farm." He sneered. "The same damned anonymous man collecting my debt this Season is none other than your husband." The viscount lunged forward but, once again, Edmund caught him, staying his attack.

Justina fluttered a hand to her throat as her mind sought to keep up with the rapidly spinning out of control thoughts. "No," she whispered and yanked her gaze over to Nick. "Tell them they are wrong, Nick." *Tell me they are wrong.* "Tell them there is a misunderstanding. You would not do these things. Not to my family." Yes, there was evil in her father, but there was only good in her mother and brother. He'd not repay that kindness with destruction.

Skin ashen, her husband stared at her. His eyes filled with such grief that her gut clenched. Why would he say nothing?

At last, he spoke. "I would speak to you…" He glanced briefly at the others present. "alone," he amended hoarsely.

"Speak to me alone," she repeated, a panicky edge to her tone. "Simply tell me they are incorrect." Her body shook until she feared she'd snap under the weight of it. She hugged herself to stave off the chill. "Tell me," she pleaded.

Nick hesitated and then slowly shook his head. "I cannot do that."

At his quiet admission, all the breath left her on a loud exhale. *Oh, God.* Her mind resisted what her heart already knew. "*Why* can't you do that?" she demanded. Her sharp-pitched cry pealed around the office.

Something raw glinted in the silvery flecks in his blue eyes. His Adam's apple bobbed. "Because it is true."

*Because it is true.*

Hurt, panic, and despair melded inside, as pieces of her heart cracked and broke. Justina staggered away from him. "No." That one word, built on a desperate need to believe in him—in them— and the good she'd always longed for in an honorable husband. "Did you seek to beggar my family?" She closed her eyes, recalling the pain and shame as strangers entered her home and carted off her mother's most cherished possessions. *My* books. "Did you?" she cried out when he said nothing.

"That was…is my intention."

Is. Not was. And so wholly, flatly delivered as though she were a stranger he'd not even passed in the street. Justina covered her face with her hands and fought to breathe.

*…The gentleman has ordered these items to auction and no one possessing connections to the Barrett family will be permitted to bid…*

It was why the creditor suggested she speak to her husband that morn. Of course. It made sense. A panicky, half-mad giggle spilled past her lips. *What a fool I've been.* And how neatly she'd stepped into his trap. He'd only met and married her to ruin her family.

Every beautiful word, every *chance* meeting, had been no game of fate as he'd claimed…but something sinister. Her shoulders sagged with the weight of her agony and shame. It did not make sense. What reason had he to hate her family that he'd so ruthlessly ensnare her in this twisted scheme?

"Justina, let us speak alone," Nick repeated gruffly. He stretched a palm toward hers. "I can explain."

"Explain, Your Grace?" she hissed, slapping at his hand. He let it fall to his side. "What is there to explain?" Feeling like a cornered cat she'd once spied at her family's country cottage, she flinched and hurriedly backed away, moving closer to Edmund. With ever-narrowing eyes, her husband followed her each movement. She stopped so that she was side-by-side with her brother-in-law.

Edmund immediately took one of her hands and gave it a firm squeeze. "Come with me," he offered, his guttural baritone harsh with regret.

Nick moved with the speed of a black panther as he came around the desk. "Please," he entreated. "If you wish to leave after I explain everything, I will not stop you."

Coward that she was, Justina longed to run, as her brother-in-law urged. And yet, for years, she'd wanted to be valued as a woman capable of making her own decisions and speaking for herself. If she walked out now or ever with Edmund or anyone else, she'd be surrendering all her long-sought after self-control. Justina took a deep breath. "My husband wishes to speak to me," she said. Nick looked to her with hope in his eyes. "Please leave, so we might *talk*." What could he possibly say? Nothing could right these wrongs. It had all been a lie.

Her brother-in-law ran pained eyes over her face. "I am so sorry," he said softly, the gruff words so faint, she struggled to hear. "Speak to your…" He blanched. "…husband. And after, know you may come to me. Any time." He directed that last piece to Nick.

The viscount grunted. "I'm not going anywhere until Huntly forgives my debt." His words ended on a cry as the marquess gripped him by the arm and steered him from the office. Then, the door closed behind them, leaving her and Nick—alone.

Tension hung heavy in the room, thick like a London fog.

With stiff movements, her husband made his way over to the sideboard and poured himself a drink. Justina blinked rapidly. A bloody drink? Her father and brother-in-law had come in here and shattered her happiness with accusations Nick hadn't denied, and now he'd pour himself a bloody drink? She was tired of every male in her life turning to drink for strength. "What do you have to say?" she demanded, proud of that steady deliverance when inside she was shaking. With fear. Anger. And a numbing despair.

He turned around and, in one long, slow swallow, finished his drink. Did he seek resolve in the bottom of his snifter? "I once you told you about my childhood."

At the abrupt shift in discourse, she shook her head. "I don't—"

"There was a man," he said with a somber matter-of-factness that frayed her tightly coiled nerves. "A man who ruined my family. Destroyed my father." He perched his hip on the edge of the Chippendale piece and stared expectantly back.

Instead, she shook her head once more in befuddlement. "What does that have to do with *me*?" she asked, hating the threadbare plea there. "With us?" she amended. This was now their life— together.

"That man was the Marquess of Rutland."

"The Marquess—" The air left her on a shuddery hiss as his words hurled her out into a turbulent sea of confusion. Her brother-in-law, Edmund, Phoebe's hero, her family's champion had been the person who'd destroyed Nick's family? That accusation went against everything she knew of Edmund and everything she'd come to believe about this man before her. A stranger.

*Impossible.*

Nick dragged his spare hand through his hair. "Oh, I assure you, quite possible."

Unaware she'd spoken aloud, she stared at him, this gentleman, who'd only fed her half-truths. This man, who by her father's words, intended to ruin her family. Nick could not see, the Barretts had been ruined long, long ago financially by Justina's wastrel father. This was just one more act that would see Justina's mother hurt, once more. Only this time, by another man—Justina's husband, now. Bile stung the back of her throat and she choked it back.

"I vowed revenge and, yet, Rutland cared for no one. Until your family. Until…" *Me.* His gaze held hers. The weight and wealth of meaning behind the glimmer in his blue depths and the unfinished admission stole the life from her legs. Justina gripped the top of the leather winged back chair.

Honoria's warnings flickered forward. "Why were you at Gipsy Hill?" She wetted her lips. Both needing an answer from him and never wanting to know. He said nothing. "And Lady Wessex's gardens and Lord Chilton's hall?" Her voice climbed in volume, shaking under the weight of her fear.

"You were Rutland's beloved sister-in-law. His wife's dearest friend," Nick said quietly and his words sent ice coursing through her veins. "It was my plan to win your heart and break it."

"But you are the *Darling* Duke, Nick," she whispered. Society, however, had proven wrong about so many others before. "I believed you wanted to c-court me." Her voice cracked. For still, with everything revealed in these moments, she wanted him to still be the man *she* had taken him for.

"Everything changed," he said on a rush. Abandoning his glass, Nick came over and settled his hands on her shoulders. She forced herself to look into the eyes of this liar she'd married and the agony in his gaze ripped another hole in her already desperately splintered heart. "The more I knew you, I could not ruin you."

And he hadn't. Lord Tennyson had. And Nick simply stepped in and claimed his just reward.

Shrugging off his touch, she moved away, needing space between them. "But you did ruin me," she whispered. Nausea roiled in her belly as the full truth at last sank in her slow to comprehend mind. She lifted her gaze to his, not wanting to see her reality laid out within his eyes, but needing to know the truth. Needing to see what her mind continued to reject. Surely, she could not have been so very wrong. Surely, she could not have been such a fool. "You sought me out, courted me, married me, all to punish Edmund?" Her question emerged hesitant, riddled with her own disbelief. "Surely, one person could not have planned out revenge against an entire family." She touched a finger to her chest. "Me, included."

And she *knew*. Knew by the regret that paraded over his harsh, angular features. A tortured moan stuck in her throat, choking her, and she glanced frantically about.

"I need you to understand," Nick implored. He came toward her, hands turned up in supplication. "It began as such." With his tousled golden hair and flawlessly beautiful features, he'd the face the Devil had surely donned when he'd come to Earth to tempt, taint, and ruin. "Somewhere along the way, it all changed. Your spirit, your strength, your wit," She winced. "All captivated me."

*Oh, God.* For all Honoria's warnings and Justina's family's worry that her romantic spirit would be her downfall, she'd believed herself stronger. Capable of both seeing and knowing the good in people. She caught her head in her hands. How bloody foolish she'd been....and how very desperate for love. In that, she had been the silly romantic with stars in her eyes. "Lies," she whispered. "Everything was a lie." She yanked her neck up suddenly and met his gaze. "Tell me, was your love of poetry even real?" Or was that one more orchestrated trickery meant to deceive.

"That was real," he said, his voice hollow.

And she was to believe that? With this stranger before her, staring on, her world came apart slowly like the seams being torn from a gown until all that was left was a wilted pile on the floor. She clutched at her throat. "I gave you my mind, my dreams, my..." Her voice caught. "Body," she whispered. Nick went whipcord straight. "All of who I was and wanted to be and you used that against me."

The muscles of his face spasmed. "Yes." Nick dragged a hand through his unkempt tresses. "No." He drew in a slow breath through his tightly pressed lips.

"Which is it?" she cried.

"It is both," he said and her eyes slid involuntarily closed.

She'd dreamed of a marriage based on love. Searched for a husband who valued her mind. She cringed. In the end, she'd proven to be the empty-headed fool her father had accused her of being. The shame of that was nothing compared to the aching sorrow for the dying dream she'd carried for a life with Nick. Justina choked and staggered back, away from him. She'd taken a magical meeting on the streets of Lambeth and shaped them into the romantic exchange she'd always yearned for. "Tell me, Your Grace. Did you and your lover have a good laugh at my expense?" She hurled that question at him, finding strength in her fury. "Did you practice all your pretty words on her?" *Do you love her?*

Pain stabbed at her breast.

"The moment I met you," he said somberly. "I couldn't see any other woman but you." He paused and his features set in a mask of ravaged pain. "There was…and will only ever be, you."

Tears welled in her eyes, blurring his visage before her. She despised herself for her weakness in clinging to that pledge as much as she hated her husband for this betrayal. It was too much. This moment. All of it. She lifted her hem and bolted.

Nick moved quickly, and she stumbled over herself in her bid to escape him. Justina raced behind his desk, placing the mahogany piece between them. The distance small and, yet, the gulf dividing them was greater than the whole of the Thames. "Listen to me, Justina." He jerked to a halt at the opposite side of the desk. "Please."

TODAY SHOULD HAVE BEEN THE culmination of every dream he'd carried. Dreams that had sustained him through darkness. Yet he stood here, with Justina eyeing him—a viselike pressure strangled off his airflow—the same way he'd looked upon the Marquess of Rutland.

Now the pity and regret in Lord Rutland's eyes made sense. It had been the gaze of a man who'd known the implications of Nick's actions far better than Nick himself.

*Because that is what I allowed myself to become.* Just as his sister had predicted and accused, he had taken on the other man's form. In a bid to make himself stronger. Standing here, with Justina's heart-shaped face pale as the parchment on his desk and tears streaming down her cheeks, he didn't feel strong. He felt as if he'd been flayed open with a dull blade and left exposed and broken.

Nick drew in a ragged breath and let it out slowly. "It was initially my intention to…" *trap.* "…marry you." The greatest crimes he'd once spoken freely about with Lady Carew slithered around his mind. Justina had always deserved more. Than him. Tennyson. Or any other bloody toff in London.

Her expressive eyes revealed nothing but a blank emptiness that slammed into him. "Marry me," she repeated.

"I could not do it," he confessed, his voice hoarsened.

His wife eyed him as though he'd descended into the depths of madness. Mayhap he had. Because when presented with Justina's suffering, Rutland, the one man who'd occupied Nick's sole thoughts and efforts for thirteen years, didn't matter a jot. "But you *did* do it," she whispered.

He briefly dusted a hand over his eyes. "Trap you," he amended through gritted teeth. She recoiled, horror spilling from her eyes.

"Our meeting at Gipsy Hill?" Her arms hung loosely at her sides.

Heat scorched his neck. She'd force him to breathe that truth and she was deserving of it. "I intended to coordinate our meeting that day, but that loose horse bolted down the road, changing my plans."

"Your plans." Justina peeled her lip back in a cynical sneer that had the same effect as a dagger being put in his belly. "How was our first meeting to go, Your Grace?"

His chest spasmed. *Your Grace.* That formal title that stripped away all intimacy of their given names.

"How was it to go?" she demanded again. The high-pitched timbre of her voice hinted at her rapid loss of control.

"I had orchestrated a runaway phaeton," he said quietly. Shame filled him. How had he intended those ruthless plans for her? "There was no need for it because of the wild horse."

"My God," she breathed and skittered her agonized gaze about.

His insides twisted in vicious knots. He could not allow her to believe it had all been a lie. Along the way, everything had changed. She'd reminded him what it was to enjoy anything outside of his plans for Rutland. She'd reawakened his love of poetry and taught him how to smile again. "After meeting you, Justina, I realized I could not embroil you in my plans for Rutland."

His insistent profession brought her head swinging back straight, so their stares met. "That is why you stopped calling," she said softly, the words spoken more to herself.

Nonetheless, Nick nodded. *Make her see reason. Make her understand.*

*I've already lost her.*

Battling back panic, he explained. "Your father was going to sell you to Tennyson without the benefit of marriage." All the same fury, as potent and raw as when he'd learned it from the marquess' mouth, burned hot in his veins.

She cocked her head. Those tears glittering in her eyes slipped down her cheeks, leaving silent marks of her despair that ravaged him. Encouraged by her silence, he continued.

"I secured your dowry and your family's property, in your name. That is no lie." So she could have some control of her future. Even as with this, she'd likely leave and take every happiness he'd known in these miserable thirteen years.

"Am I supposed to find honor in that, Your Grace?" she spat. Justina gave him a long, sad look. "Should I admire you for so graciously *sparing* me?" She jerked her chin up. "The moment you decided to hurt my family as a means to hurt Edmund, you embroiled me in your plan." She gave her head a sad, pitying shake. "You are no different from Tennyson or any other gentleman my father kept company with. You are the same."

Her stinging words struck in his chest. "Yes," he said, his voice deadened to his own ears. That was who he was.

Justina firmed her mouth. "Do you care for me?"

Care for her? He loved her. Had loved her since she'd blurted out a challenge to a stodgy scholar in The Circulating Library on Lambeth Street. He could not give her those words now. They'd ring as hollow and false; a desperate maneuver to break past the wary guard that had gone up about her. Yet, he needed to say them anyway. Needed her to know those words were, in fact, true.

"If you have to think so long, then I have my answer," she said tiredly and made to step around him.

Nick swiftly placed himself between her and the doorway, halting her retreat. He needed her to understand. "I love you," he confessed in solemn tones, willing her to see that.

An empty laugh bubbled from her lips. "You *love* me?"

He drew in a steadying breath. She was entitled to her hatred. He'd known all along she would despise him once his plan came to light but he hadn't expected it to hurt this much. "I do not expect you to forgive what I've done—"

"What business did you see to this morn?" she interrupted.

That abrupt shift knocked him off-kilter. *Oh, God, she knows.* For a brief moment, he considered lying, but he could not allow any more falsities between them. "Justina," he entreated.

"Who. Did. You. See?" she clipped out in coolly emotionless tones. The icy steel so at odds with the carefree lady he'd sat beside in The Circulating Library and he slowly died inside at her transformation. "It was your lover, wasn't i-it?"

"How—?"

She jerked as though he'd struck her.

"I did not lie to you before. She is my *former* lover," he said around a tight throat. "I ended it before I even met you."

"I see." Those two words, which both said everything and nothing all at the same time, cleaved at his insides. He was losing her. With every question and every revelation, she slipped further and further away.

*Nay, I already lost her. I lost her the minute I knocked into her on the streets of Lambeth.* Nick gathered her hands and squeezed. "I was a miserable, rotted bounder before you. A rogue. Ruthless. Driven by evil. I am not that man. Not anymore. Because of you."

She lifted her chin, a sad smile hanging on her lips. "When did you intend to tell me that we exist because of nothing more than your twisted plans for revenge?"

*I waited too long.* "The timing certainly seems damning," he conceded gruffly. "But after I met with…" She recoiled. "…after my meeting," he swiftly substituted. "I pledged to speak to you but found your brother at his club and in his cups and returned him home to your mother."

A brittle laugh exploded from her lips. "My, how very gallant you are. Helping my brother who you beggared at the gaming tables."

Nick flinched. "What would you have me do? Leave him there, heartbroken so the gossips could tear him down?"

"You already did that enough on your own."

"Your brother and father wagered away their wealth," he snapped. "I'm deserving of your resentment, but do not make either of the Barrett males out as paragons. Not when they've also wronged you and your kin."

By the white lines at the corners of her mouth, she knew he was right on that score. Again, he attempted to make her see that she was all he wanted. "I am deserving of your anger." And more. "But know," he continued in somber tones, "you are all I ever wanted. All I ever needed that I believed myself—"

"Stop!" Justina cried out. She yanked free of him and hugged her arms close to her chest in a sad, lonely embrace. "You told me everything I wished to hear. Praised my mind," she cringed. "Because that is all I wanted. For a gentleman to see me for something other than the label of Diamond I'd been given." Tears flooded her eyes and a lone crystalline drop streaked down her cheek. She angrily swiped at it. "But you didn't even see that in me, Nick. You saw me as an object to exact your revenge." The sight of her proud grief ravaged him.

Nick claimed her face between his hands and forced her gaze to his, willing her to see. "It all *changed*. From the moment you threw yourself into the street to save a poor child, my world was flipped upside down." And it would never, ever be righted. "I wanted to tell you. In the library, I tried to."

"Let me go, Your Grace," she ordered. His arms fell useless to his sides.

Justina started around him and, this time, he proved a coward, yet again. For he let her go. His wife lingered at the front of the room, her fingers on the door handle. She angled her head around. "Was any of it real?"

From the moment he'd knocked her to the ground and stared into her expressive eyes, he'd been forever lost. "Would you believe me if I said from the moment I sat beside you in that lecture hall, all of it was?"

Her even, white teeth sank into her lower lip and tears welled afresh in her eyes. She gave her head a jerky shake. "No. I would not." Justina glanced down at her hands, silently studying the creases on her palms. "When we met in Lady Wessex's gardens, I saw something dark in your eyes. Something I couldn't identify," she whispered. She raised her gaze to his. "Now I know. It was hatred. And I didn't see it before because I was blind to those sentiments. But now I know." Her words hit him like a kick to the gut. His heart contracted, making words and thoughts impossible.

With that, she pressed the handle, opened the door, and closed it behind her with a quiet, damning click.

Nick stood there long after she'd gone, staring at the oak panel. At last, he conceded how wrong Rutland had been in the lessons he'd imparted. Revenge and hatred hadn't made him stronger. For, with the room ringing with the memory of his wife's quiet despair and her father's thunderous charges, Nick had never felt weaker than he did in this moment.

For even as he loved her now, she'd begun as a pawn whose family he'd sought to destroy…and that could never be undone.

*…You have an entire lifetime to show her who you are…*

With a curse, Nick sprinted from his office and bounded through the halls. Chilton's words echoed around his mind and, with his pulse pounding loudly in his ears, he took the stairs two at a time. "Justina," he called out hoarsely as she reached her rooms.

She paused with her fingers on the handle, but did not look back.

He held his palms up in supplication. "I…" He glanced up and down the hallway. "I would speak to you," his words emerged as an entreaty.

She faced him. "There is nothing more to say."

Some dark, hardened emotion glinted in her blue eyes, freezing him in his spot. For it was a sentiment he knew. One he recognized.

*Hatred.*

Just as she'd said. Bile stung his throat and he swallowed it. "Please," he panted, out of breath from his race to meet her. There was no pride where this woman was concerned. From the moment she'd risked her life to save a child in the street, she'd forever won his heart.

She shoved her door open and when she said nothing, he followed inside behind her. Nick braced for the stinging vitriol of her outrage. Instead, she stared back at him with tired eyes. "What do you want, Your Grace?"

*Your Grace.* Again, that barrier of propriety erected between them that shattered the intimacy they'd shared these past weeks. *I want it back. I want us as we were for the brief time we shared.* "I cannot atone for my crimes against you," he began, taking a step toward her. For, ultimately, he'd wronged all the Barretts. She stiffened, but remained fixed to the floor. Encouraged when she did not retreat, he continued coming. "But I would explain myself." Where he could do so better than he'd done in his office. Not so she would forgive him but, rather, so mayhap she'd at least understand.

Wordlessly, she tipped her chin up, urging him on.

His tongue felt heavy in his mouth and he waged war to keep this secret from her, still. He owed her every truth. "Long ago, my father owed a debt to Lord Rutland. A business debt."

"You said as much," she said, her voice so eerily emotionless, a chill ran along his spine. This was not who she was. This jaded, wary figure bore no resemblance to the vibrant, smiling woman who'd broken down his every defense.

He nodded jerkily. "Yes, I told you that much." Still, he could not get the words out. For the whole of his life, he'd lived a lie. A secret shared with no one…and only suspicious servants the wiser. "Lord Rutland called that debt in early." For no reason, other than to destroy. And ultimately, he'd proven successful in that endeavor. "My father killed himself," he said quietly, for the second time giving those words life.

Justina gasped. She stared at him with round eyes. Yes, for in their Society, the ultimate crime would forever be a man's suicide.

Unable to meet her gaze for fear of what he might see there, he looked beyond her shoulder. "Following his meeting with the marquess, I entered Papa's office and found him." All the oldest horrors and memories came rushing forward and he concentrated on his emotionless telling to keep from descending into madness. "A man never forgets the sight of a body, dangling, in death." His voice grew hoarse. "It is silent. Morbid. It destroyed me," he whispered, that part to himself.

The floorboards creaked, indicating she'd moved.

A soft, unexpected touch landed on his arm and, blinking slowly, he looked at her. She said nothing. Offered no words. Offered nothing, other than that silent, unspoken show of support. Support he didn't deserve. The blade twisted all the deeper in his chest. "I allowed my hatred for your brother-in-law to sustain me," he continued hoarsely. "I found purpose in that hatred. I didn't believe I was capable of feeling anything beyond it." His throat worked. "Until *you*." She'd made him feel again. Forced him, too. Despite every vow he'd taken to be ruthless and unfeeling. She'd restored light when there had only been darkness.

Her fingers tensed on his sleeve. Then she lowered her hand slowly, falteringly to her side and he mourned the loss of that connection. "It was all pretend, Nick," she said so softly, her words were nearly lost to him. "Everything from your actions to your words to me about poetry and literature—"

"It wasn't," he entreated, gathering her hands. Willing her to see. To know that it had only ever been her. "That is who I once was. I was a boy who found happiness in books and poems and I forgot all that." After he'd discovered his father, his life had descended into such hell that all those words and verses had seemed like useless inanities. Justina had reminded him what it was to feel something other than hatred and to yearn for those pleasures he'd once known. "But for the handful of verses I wrote for my niece, I've not so much as thought of putting pen to paper or reading poetry again—until you. From the moment you threw yourself into the street to save a child, you captivated me. You made me forget my hate and made me…feel again." He held her gaze, willing her to see. "I love you."

His words were met with an endless silence, punctuated by the ticking clock. His heart constricted painfully. *Did I truly believe I could so easily convince her of my love?*

Justina hugged her arms close in a lonely embrace. "I don't know what we do from here, Nick," she confessed.

"I want to begin again with you." He took another step closer. "And I want you to want to begin again with me," he said and stopped. He wanted her to come to him, because she wished it, not because he forced his presence upon her.

"Do you intend to destroy my family?"

Her question brought him up short. How could he not? It was the goal that had sustained him through the nightmares and the misery and the hell. It had given him purpose. What was he without vengeance on Rutland?

*What am I without her?*

"What choice do I have?" he pleaded, wanting her to show him how he could attain both—closure on his past and her love. Odd, in the beginning he'd viewed Justina as a pawn. Yet, his existence had morphed into a complicated chessboard and he was trapped in the corner. "There is no other move to make," he finally said, accepting that truth.

Justina gave him a long, sad smile. "There is always another move to make, Nick. It is about making the right one." She inhaled quietly; that wispy sound contradictory to the storm raging inside him. "You say you want to begin again. But you don't. Not truly." He opened his mouth to speak but she continued over him. "You see, you ask me to forgive you. You ask to begin again." She slashed a hand between them. "And yet, you are so stuck in the past, hating Edmund. You are unable to forgive. I don't know if I can forgive you," she admitted with her usual forthrightness. Only this time, those words speared him. "But I know, as long as you intend to destroy those I love, we can't even begin to try." She smoothed her palms along her skirts. "If you'll excuse me?"

"Of course," he said hollowly, backing up. They were all polite formality, even as a pressure was weighting his chest, crushing his heart, and cracking an organ he'd believed incapable of further hurt. Just another thing he'd been wrong on. "I will allow you to your thoughts." He sketched a bow and with each step that carried him to the door, he braced for words from her—

Words that did not come.

# CHAPTER 20

*A*FTER *N*ICK HAD TAKEN HIS leave, Justina remained in her chambers sitting on the edge of the bed with Wordsworth's complete works on her lap.

As she'd been sitting for the better part of an hour. Numb, staring blankly at the empty hearth, she was afraid to move. Afraid to breathe. For if she did, she'd surely shatter into a million shards.

The weight of the volume resting on her legs brought her gaze, unbidden, downward to a specific verse, one that made a mockery of everything she'd believed—her lips twisted in a pained smile—everything she'd hoped for. Like one of those master poets they had bonded over, he'd fed her pretty little lies that had drawn her further and further down the path of ruin.

*Pleasure is spread through the earth, in stray gifts to be claimed by whoever shall find it…*

Her throat worked painfully and she slid her eyes closed to blot out the inked lines. Except they lingered in her mind, whispering around the chambers breathed in the husky timbre of her husband's voice as he'd made love to her. Forcing her eyes open, she snapped the book closed. With a sharp cry, she hurled it across the room where it hit the door with a soft thump and then sailed to the floor, landing indignantly on its spine.

The childlike display did nothing to alleviate the agony sluicing away at her insides. Instead, it only served as a reminder of every mistake she'd made, that now saw her married to a man who despised her brother-in-law and who'd destroy her mother as well as Andrew.

*I returned him home to your mother…*

Nick had seen her mother. He'd stepped inside her family's household. The same household he intended to destroy. It wasn't how she'd thought her mother's first meeting with him was to go. It was to be joyous and filled with laughter, with the only regret there being that Viscountess Waters had not been able to attend the unexpected wedding.

Oh, God, what was to become of her mother? Of course, Edmund would never see either her or Andrew destitute. But neither could he protect them from Society's scorn and shame if and when the Barrett males ended up on a turnip farm, as her father had raged.

With a shuddery sob, Justina dropped her face into her hands. The rub of it was, she had not been naïve to the manner of men her brother and father were and always had been. With their wicked activities, they would have ultimately led the family to total financial ruin. The viscount had transferred to Andrew an addiction to those gaming tables. But this…this scheme carried out by Nick had been a carefully orchestrated plan to knock her family down, so that they could never recover. It was an act perpetrated in hate and she'd been nothing more than a chess piece being shifted about a board he'd created.

She leapt to her feet.

Suddenly, sitting here in this home, the home of the man who intended to destroy them, she saw herself for the coward she was. She needed to face her mother and Andrew. Justina lurched to her feet. With wooden steps, she found her way to the foyer.

The butler materialized from the corner. "Your Grace?" There was concern stamped in his wrinkled features.

"I would have the carriage readied," she ordered.

He hesitated and looked about with a strain in his eyes. She curled her fingers into tight fists. Did he seek his employer's permission and approval?

Oh, God. *I am no different than property.* With one faulty and costly misstep, she'd become—her mother. Would her husband carry on with other women and reduce her to the same miserable state her father had done with the viscountess? *Your dowry is yours, as is your family's property.* She stopped with her gaze fixed on the double doors. Why would Nick do that? If she were simply another piece of his plan to inflict hurt upon Edmund, why had he put those gifts in her name, allowing her that vital control? "I want my carriage readied," she said in firm tones that sprung the butler into motion.

After an endlessly infernal stretch, the butler reappeared, opening the door for her.

Not bothering with her cloak, Justina rushed outside and, accepting the driver's proffered hand, allowed him to hand her inside the elegant black barouche. With the fresh paint of the seal and smoothness of the lacquer, the carriage stood as a testament to Nick's wealth in the face of her own abject circumstances, until now.

As the driver closed the door behind her, she huddled against the side of the carriage. His wealth, however, had never mattered. Who he'd been and how he'd treated her had mattered more than anything. Through all of it, the sale of her family's belongings, even the books, she'd not mourned the material. She'd, instead, sustained herself with the dream of what her sister knew. The love penned on the pages of those sonnets discovered only this Season. The carriage lurched into motion and Justina bit the inside of her cheek hard.

Everything had been a lie. *You made me forget my hate and made me…feel again.* Except, once more, those pleas, the emotion bleeding from his eyes had told a different tale than that of revenge. She knocked her head against the back of her seat. "You are trying to see only what you want," she muttered into the confines of the coach. She'd had her foolish dreams of love and desires to be seen as more than a Diamond. But in the end, she'd been less than that useless Diamond to Nick. She'd been a pawn. A piece he'd manipulated and maneuvered upon the chessboard of life, a game which could never be replayed.

And once again, she gave herself over to tears. She buried her face into her hands and wept.

She cried for the death of her dreams.

She cried for a love she'd so desperately wanted and believed she'd found with Nick.

She cried for the boy he had been who'd been so brutally destroyed by his hate and thirst for revenge.

And more, she cried for what they would never have together. That beautiful love known between Phoebe and Edmund. For her, that emotion would remain nothing more than a dream upon a page. She cried until her eyes ached and there wasn't another tear to shed. With a shuddery hiccup, she rubbed the tears from her cheeks.

The carriage rolled to a halt before a familiar townhouse. Suddenly, she was very much like the small girl who'd scraped her knees and sought out her mother. Not waiting for the driver, Justina shoved the door open and leapt from the conveyance. With a grunt, she landed hard on the pavement. She shot her arms out to steady herself.

Aware of the blatant stares from passersby, she kept her gaze trained forward. Manfred, God love him, stood in loyal wait. He opened the door, allowing her entry.

"Miss…" Pain bled from the man's eyes. "Your Grace."

He knew. Of course, he'd know. Her father would not be able to contain his vitriolic outbursts. Gossip would spread. By the stares in the street, it already had. The gossips could all go hang. None of their opinions mattered. "M–My mother?"

"Is in his lordship's office."

*Oh, God.* The viscountess would pay the price for her husband's fury. As she always did.

Quickening her strides, Justina rushed down the hall. Unbidden, she took in details she'd come to accept as part of her existence; the diminishing wealth, the bare places where paintings had once hung…all gone…claimed by Nick. … *Your brother and father wagered away their wealth…* She slowed her steps. Because they'd allowed it. Nick may have tricked and trapped them, but had it not been him, they would have lost all to Tennyson or some other bounder. *…he intended to sell you without the benefit of marriage…*

Thunderous shouting reached down the hall and her stomach pitched. Her mother's answering cry filled the corridor. With all the secrets revealed this day, she wanted to lay this all at Nick's feet. But God help her—she could not. Just as he'd been wrong to lay blame solely at Edmund's feet for his father's folly, so, too, could she not put this all on her husband. Squaring her shoulders, she turned to go and intervene on her mother's behalf when a faint sniffling from within the library froze her steps.

Justina turned and opened the door. Pain struck her heart once more. Andrew sat on the leather button sofa with his head buried in his hands. His usually greased and immaculate hair hung tousled over his fingers. His cravat lay at his feet. Just another suffering Barrett. "Andrew," she whispered and he raised his head slowly.

His eyes, ravaged by tears, may as well have been mirrors of her own grief. "'Stina," he greeted hoarsely. That childhood moniker he'd assigned her as a girl wrenched at her heart.

What was there to say? He had been fooled just as much as she'd been. They'd both committed a great folly in how they'd played fast and loose with information and trust. "I'm—"

"She ended it." Andrew's voice broke. With his throat bobbing up and down, he held out a letter.

His unexpected pronouncement cut across her agony. With a welcome confusion, she walked over and accepted the ivory velum. The cloying scent of roses slapped at her senses as she read.

*My Love,*

*We could never have been. We both always knew that. We just allowed ourselves that dream. Alas, with all dreams come awakenings. I can no longer see you. Please do not contact me. It would only bring me greater suffering. You will live in my heart.*

*With love and devotion,*

*Your Heart*

Justina read those beautiful words etched in parting and her heart hurt all over for different reasons. "Oh, Andrew," she said softly, sinking to a knee beside him. She reached for his hand and took it in hers, crushing the letter.

Her brother stared through bloodshot eyes at their connected fingers. "She must know, I gather. Must know about my debts and that Huntly will see me on a turnip farm."

"Don't you see, Andrew? If she loved you, it would not matter. Your love would be enough." She squeezed his hand. Just as she was not enough for Nick. His twisted revenge had always mattered more. If he'd chosen them, then mayhap they could begin again. But how could they, when he was determined to hurt those she loved? Justina damned the tears that stung her vision.

Andrew peeled his lip back in a cynical grin that gutted her.

He'd been forever changed. "You believe that still after Huntly?"

She released his hand and let her arms fall to her sides. "I have to." For if there wasn't love for at least some fortunate souls like her sister, what was there in the world but darkness and despair?

"It is far more complicated than that. There is another…gentleman and she belongs to him and always will." His words ended on a whispery hush.

A booming shout reached into the library and they both looked to the doorway, recalling Justina to her own misery. She briefly closed her eyes. Sucking in a shallow breath, she shoved to her feet. "I must go see to Mama."

"I've been a lousy son," Andrew said quietly. "I have," he said over her sound of protest. "I was an equally rotted suitor." His face contorted in a paroxysm of grief and he coughed into his hand. "But my greatest regret is that I was a terrible brother. I was so bloody self-absorbed that I allowed that bastard to trap you…" He scoffed. "And all along, I took drinks with the chap and joined him at his gaming tables."

"We were all deceived," she insisted, not making excuses for her traitorous husband's actions. "My willingness to believe the lies he fed me, that is not your fault, Andrew. It is mine," she said, willing him to see the truth there. Willing herself to start seeing it.

Another distant shout went up, recalling her to the upheaval their mother now faced. Spinning on her heel, she hurried from the sparse library to her father's office. She reached for the handle and stopped.

"You encouraged her bloody foolish dreams," he cried.

"I encouraged her to believe in love." The viscountess' words rang with a sharp rebuke which set off another bevy of cursing from her pitiful husband.

"We are ruined," her father thundered. "Ruined. It is all the stupid chit's fault." He dissolved into a noisy round of tears.

And perhaps she *was* a wicked daughter, but the evidence of his despair did not bring her any proper sadness. Since she was a girl, she'd borne witness to how those gaming hells proved more valuable and important than even his own kin. If it hadn't been Nick, it would have been someone else. She knew that. Knew he would have done just as her husband had said and sold her off to settle a debt.

Certainly not to a man who'd allow her the keys to her dowry and a prosperous landholding. Whereas Nick's devotion to his family had turned him into a figure bent on revenge, Justina's own father had never been driven by anything more than his own material wants. Even her brother was guilty of that charge.

"By God, she has far more intelligence in the whole of her hand than you do in your entire person." Love for a mother, who'd always defended her, filled her. Despite the misery that came with being married to Viscount Waters, she'd always sought to show her children laughter and happiness. "*You* are the one who beggared this family. Not me. Not Justina. Not Phoebe. You. And *you* poisoned Andrew into believing your love of whores and cards is the way to live."

Crystal shattered and with her mother's gasp penetrating the doorway, Justina quickly shoved the door open and stepped inside. Her parents swiveled their stares in her direction. She quickly took in the punishing grip her father had on his wife's delicate wrist and fury sent her surging forward. "Release her," she seethed, quaking inside at his violence. He'd been a diffident father. A disloyal husband. But he'd never been violent. Until now. Whereas Nick had taken every word she'd thrown at him and never laid a hand upon her. Had allowed her the right to her feelings without attempting to oppress her.

"You'd come in here and order me about?" he boomed, his large belly shaking with the force of his yell. "Do you see what you've wrought upon this family? You couldn't have just spread your legs for Tennyson."

*Not married*...spread her legs for. That pointed reminder of a truth Nick had given her. Justina gritted her teeth. "I said release her," she ordered, rushing forward. He'd never feared her, his wife, Phoebe. The only things he responded to were power and influence. To him, a woman would never be anything more than just that, a woman. "If you do not release her," she threatened, "I will tell my husband." As hurt as she'd been by Nick's machinations, he'd granted her great power with the name and title she now invoked.

That penetrated whatever mad haze consumed the viscount. He released his wife and wheeled around. His large frame shook with his desperate, mirthless laugh. "Do you truly believe your husband cares what happens to a single member of this family?"

*I love you.*

"Yes," she said quietly. For there was no reason for him to lie. With calm and logic restored, she could admit that he may have deceived her, but somewhere along the way he had come to...love *her*. There was a calm, graceful healing in that. "I believe he does." He simply loved his plans for Edmund more.

Her father's deep, belly laugh shook his frame. "You've always been a fool."

Nor would her husband call her names and seek to belittle her. He'd wanted to shame her but, by his admission and then his actions, had been incapable of it. "You are a vile bully," she said, taking delight in the way his eyes bulged in shock. "You are a coward. My husband may have exacted his revenge upon Edmund, using our family, but *you* allowed it," she said in a calm matter-of-factness. With each true admission, a further weight was lifted, setting her free. "*You* were the person who sat down with countless men for countless wagers. *You* were the man who kept on with whores and mistresses." She jabbed a finger at him. "*You* were the one who was going to sell me to Tennyson without the benefit of marriage."

Her mother gasped and alternated her horrified stare between her husband and daughter. Yes, because ultimately Mother had forever been silenced by the man she'd had the misfortune of marrying. He'd never allowed her the freedom of her mind.

The viscount sputtered. "You mouthy chit. I will—"

"You will do nothing," she said calmly, plastering on a cold smile. And with each bold challenge, strength infused her spine—and something more—pride. For the whole of her life, she'd been the dutiful daughter. Silent. *Silenced*. She may resent Nick for having lied and deceived her, but he'd at least given her one gift—he'd set her free from those constraints and she'd not be quiet, anymore. "And you will not put your hands on her again."

Her father ambled over and Justina locked her feet to the floor, holding firm. "You'll not give me directives, you stupid chit."

She'd not allow him to cow her. Not anymore.

"If you say so much as another word or touch either one of them again, I'll see you dead." That quietly spoken utterance brought their gazes to the door.

Justina looked to her brother who stood in the frame, his face flushed with rage.

"Don't you dare…" Her father's blustering words died on a whimper as Andrew strode across the room. Hands outstretched, he gripped the viscount about the neck and drove him against the wall. A golden-framed portrait shook under the force of the movement.

"If you touch them again, I will end you," he whispered. Andrew squeezed his father's neck tighter.

Justina stared, frozen, as their father choked and gasped. His face turned red as he pried at his son's hand. Spittle formed in the corners of his lips.

In the end, it was not their father's certain death that penetrated Andrew's efforts, but the touch of his mother's hand on his arm. "Andrew," she said, between tears, a plea in her voice.

He stopped and blinked slowly. Then with alacrity, he released his father.

The viscount collapsed in a sobbing, gasping heap at his feet.

Yes, Justina, Andrew, their mother had all been deceived by Nick. But with his actions, he'd helped them all: her, Andrew, and their mother, find their voices and stand up to the jailer who'd held them captive. She stared at her cold-eyed brother, her cowering father, and her quietly weeping mother.

Now, what would Nick do with the chains that bound the Barretts to him?

# CHAPTER 21

"UNCLE DOMINICK."

Nick tossed his arms wide and Felicity charged into them. Surely, the sole person in the whole of the kingdom happy to see him since he'd brought his life crashing down yesterday.

Shoving aside his misery, he hefted her into his arms and staggered back. "You must have grown at least four stone since last we met."

"And grown a foot?" Felicity piped in.

"I was going to say two feet." At her innocent giggle, he managed his first smile of the day. And he imagined a world with he and Justina having a child of their own. With her wit and spirit and—

"Are you going to cry, Uncle Dominick?" his niece asked, jerking him back from a precipice of yearning for that vision of a babe born of him and Justina. "Your eyes have gone all sad like Mama's."

Sad like Mama's. His chest pulled. For that was who Cecily had been for so very long. A young, sad mother marred by life. Unhappy almost as many years as she'd been happy. It had been just one more resentment he'd heaped at Rutland's feet. But that blame was more his and their evil grandfather's than the marquess'. That realization struck him, belated and true.

"Uncle Dominick?" Felicity tugged at his lapel.

"How can I be sad when I'm here with you?" he countered,

forcing another grin. He gave Felicity a light squeeze and set her down. Nick glanced about for a glaringly absent mama and governess. "Shouldn't you be in a lesson?" he quizzed.

He may as well have committed treason against the king for the outrage in her wide eyes. "Shh," she hissed, slapping a finger against her lips. His niece stole another furtive glance about. In her bid to escape nursemaids and governesses, how very much she was like Cecily.

"Mama is not home?" he surmised.

"She's not." He fought his disappointment. As much as he loved his niece, it had been Cecily's company he sought. "Will you play chess with me until she returns?" Without awaiting an answer, she grabbed his hand, and began tugging him along. When they'd reached the modest library, Nick and Felicity claimed their usual seats behind the ivory chessboard and proceeded to play in their customary quiet.

Following the tumult of Rutland's return yesterday afternoon and Justina's rightful hurt and accusations that had robbed him of sleep, there was something calming in the silence. The calm after the storm where a person could think through all that had come to pass.

He studied Felicity's bent head as she puzzled over the board. How innocent she was. She saw a chessboard and saw a game. Whereas, he had allowed even that simple pleasure to be perverted by his warped need for revenge. His niece tapped her fingertips distractedly on the edge of the table. After a long stretch, she emitted a sigh.

"What is it?" he asked, shifting in his chair.

"The pawn is useless." She motioned to the move that she was considering.

His gaze fell to the small ivory pawn. He picked it up and turned it over in his hand. All along, in his scheming, he'd believed Justina was his ultimate pawn. She had even likened herself to that piece. "That isn't true," he said quietly. Felicity looked up, befuddlement in her eyes.

"But you *always* said," she cleared her voice and spoke in a deeper voice, in imitation of his own. "'The pawn is the least valuable piece.'"

Yes, he had. "Because I'm a rotted teacher," he muttered. Just as he'd been a rotted husband. Andrew Barrett's slurred ramblings ricocheted around his mind. Now, because of his wife, he saw even this small token in a whole new light. "The pawn is the only piece that can promote to any other piece once it reaches the eighth rank." He paused, looking to the most powerful on the table. "Even queen," he said softly. With her spirit and valor, Justina could never have been just a pawn. Her sense of justice and right marked her far stronger than him or Rutland, or any other person he'd ever known.

Felicity continued to drum her fingertips. "My only move is to claim your pawn," she said in beleaguered tones.

"There is always another move." He stilled. *There is always another move to make, Nick. It is about making the right one.*

*I cannot do it...* Not if he wanted a future with her. And he did. He wanted them to be a family who loved and laughed, and found strength in those freeing sentiments. He could not. Mayhap he'd known that all along.

Nick came to his feet.

Felicity looked up. "Uncle Dominick?"

He reached over the table and hefted her into his arms, giving her a quick squeeze. "Thank you," he whispered.

"Your..." She wrinkled her pert nose. "What did I do?"

"You helped me see my move." When he'd been too blind to see anything past his own foolishness and obstinacy. "Promise to return?" he echoed their familiar phrase.

"Permission to leave granted," she said and pressed a kiss against his cheek.

He set her down quickly. Grabbing two pieces from the chessboard, he pocketed them and sprinted from the room. Heart thundering against his ribcage, Nick raced down the corridors.

What a bloody mess he'd made of his life. There could be no undoing the wrongs but, as Chilton had said, there could be a moving forward. And ironically, the path forward required a reconciliation with his past.

He reached the foyer just as his sister entered.

As she handed her bonnet over to a servant, surprise rounded out her eyes. "Nick?"

He quickly caught her by the shoulders. "You were right," he rasped, earning curious looks from the servants. "I cannot do it. I wanted to do this for you and..." He swallowed hard, taking ownership of that at last. "It was for me," he whispered. "It was always for me. And I cannot do it. I love her." Lightness suffused his chest.

A slow, smile, the first real one he remembered from his sister in more years than he cared to count, met her eyes. "I am so very proud of you, Dominick." Cecily swatted at his arm. "Now, go. Go to her."

He would. But first, there was a matter of business he had to see to. Following a long visit with his man-of-affairs, Nick found himself climbing the steps of a different townhouse.

He came to a stop, staring at the black door. A door he'd once sooner have burned down than visit. Nick briefly closed his eyes. *I have to do this.* There had never been a choice where Justina was concerned. He knocked.

The door was immediately opened by an aged butler who gave him a quick once-over.

"I am here to see his lordship," Nick said quickly, fishing out a card.

The older man studied it a moment, his expression revealing nothing. He stepped back and motioned Nick inside. Then, without waiting to see if he followed, the old servant started down the corridor.

Nick adjusted his longer stride behind the slow, shuffling steps of the butler. As he walked, he distracted himself by looking about the walls of the man who lived here. A man he'd spent years hating. And yet, if it hadn't been for him, he would have never met Justina.

As he moved deeper and deeper into the townhouse, the gilt frames revealed portraits of a smiling, dark-haired lady with two babies on her lap. Nick paused, drawn to that painting. For the man who stood, smiling at her side, his gaze reserved for the top of that painted lady's head, was not the Devil who'd haunted him all these years...but, rather, just a man. A father.

He peered at Lord Rutland's softened visage. Mayhap that was the power the Barrett women had. They shattered hatred and left in its place this healing love.

"Your Grace?"

The wizened tones of the butler snapped him back to the moment. Nick continued on until they reached a closed door.

The butler rapped once and pushed the door open. Lord Rutland yanked his head up from the papers at his desk. Surprise flared in his eyes, mixed with a burning hatred. "His Grace, the Duke of Huntly, to see you, my lord."

The marquess didn't bother to rise. There was no hint of pleasantries or greetings as he entered and the door was closed behind him. Once he'd built this man out to be a beast. Only to find…he was very human. Just flawed and broken—as Nick was. That silent reminder forced his legs into movement. He came to a stop before Rutland's desk. His gaze fell to the balled-up sheets and then lingered on the clean paper but for three words.

*My dearest Phoebe…*

Rutland seethed. "What do you want?" he demanded, bracing his palms on the smooth, mahogany surface.

Nick forced his attention away from that private missive. Reaching inside his cloak, he fished out a large stack of bound notes. Wordlessly, he tossed them atop the desk. The crumpled sheets fluttered, with one drifting over the edge.

Rutland looked questioningly at him.

He jerked his chin at the stack. "Take them," he said tightly.

Eyeing him warily, the marquess collected the sheets. Not taking his gaze from Nick as he slipped the ribbon off, Rutland at last attended the pages. "What is this?" he asked cautiously.

"It is everything," he said quietly. "They are the younger Barrett's vowels. The properties. The viscount's debt. They are yours. Everything except Justina's dowry and a landed property." The other man lifted his shock-filled gaze.

For a lifetime, Nick had strengthened himself by dreaming of the demise of this man and his in-laws. As such, there should be a pained regret in giving everything over to this bastard. And yet… A great pressure eased in his chest, filling him with a remarkable calm. "I wanted to destroy you," he managed, his throat working. A broken, empty laugh spilled from his lips. "I wanted to return to London and prove I was stronger than you. Wanted to destroy everyone you loved." His lips twisted in a sad smile. "In the end, I fell in love with Justina. Somewhere along the way, my plan became twisted." His gaze traveled involuntarily to those notes. "I'd have you set the funds aside for Andrew for when he's older. He'll just go through them now at the gaming tables if you turn them over to him. And the rest…I thought you might set it aside and allow the viscountess to come to you when she is of need of those funds."

Rutland shuffled through the pages and then looked up, again. "Why have me do it?" he shot back. "If you're determined to win your wife's heart, why not do this as the ultimate gesture of your regard?" Of course, men such as them would be forever wary and jaded...of all offerings.

"I'm not doing this to win her," he said quietly. "I am doing this because it is the right thing to do." When he'd awakened this morn, Lord Rutland's opinion was the last thing he had cared about or worried over. Now, he'd have Justina's brother-in-law, this man who'd protected his wife these past two years when she'd needed that protection, know all. "May I sit?"

Rutland jerked his chin at one of the vacant leather wing back chairs.

He settled onto the edge and turned his palms up. "I have been gripped by nothing these past thirteen years but my quest for revenge," he said quietly. "It sustained me through the misery that had become my life."

His brother-in-law went motionless.

Nick glanced around the immaculate office. His gaze lingered on a map of Wales that hung above the marquess' desk. .... *She had dreams of traveling to Wales... And eventually, with Edmund, found her way there...* He yearned for those still yet unknown and undecided dreams with Justina. He forced his gaze back to Rutland's. "I have been a shell of the person I once was." Just as his sister had rightfully pronounced. "Until Justina," he quietly added.

Rutland set down the documents and leaned back in his chair.

"She taught me how to smile again." And read books he'd abandoned. Nick's throat worked. "I lived again. Because of her." Yet, in the end, he'd repaid those gifts with nothing but heartache. His stomach muscles clenched and he dusted a shaky hand over his face.

"Now, you have an entire lifetime to show her who you really are."

Nick dropped his arm in surprise. He searched his brother-in-law for a hint of mockery and found none. A ragged, broken laugh burst from his lips, echoing around the office. "There can be no undoing what I've done."

"No," Rutland agreed. There was no accusation there. "But you can move forward and learn to trust and love together."

*Trust?* His face spasmed and he looked away. How did one go about rebuilding a fragile gift that had been shattered by one's own careless hand? "She hates me," he said, squeezing those words out past a tight throat.

The marquess stretched his legs out before him. "Yes, but there is a delicate line between hate and love. Have you told her?"

Had anyone told him he would have been sitting down, accepting advice and guidance and forgiveness from the Marquess of Rutland, he'd have called them mad and bound for Bedlam. "I have." She, of course, saw that pledge as only one more lie. He cursed. What a blunder he'd made of it all.

"It will not be an easy task to win her heart," his brother-in-law conceded and there was something calming in that direct honesty.

Through the haze of his own misery, Nick looked at him, staggered by the truth. "You know something of it?" he asked hesitantly. This relationship with Rutland was a new one. A cautious one forged by the love they had for women born to the same family. Mayhap in time, there could be complete healing here, as well.

Rutland gave a nearly imperceptible nod. "I do. We're speaking of you," the other man added, gruffly. As one who'd shut everyone out about the hell that haunted him, he recognized that protective attempt in another. "You are married to Justina." The marquess narrowed his eyes, transformed, once again, into the dark scoundrel all feared. "It would be wrong of me to pass judgment on you when I was guilty of the same crimes against my own wife. Whatever I had hoped for in a husband for Justina, you are the man she married...and I would see her happy. If she can be," he tacked that last part on as a chilly reminder. The marquess came to his feet and stretched a hand out.

Nick stared at those fingers. ...*as long as you intend to destroy those I love, we can't even begin to try...* The seconds ticked by and then he slowly stood and placed his palm in the marquess' hand. They shook.

It was a new beginning.

His brother-in-law drew his arm back, lowering it to his side. Nick made to go when Rutland stayed him. "Huntly?"

He glanced back.

"I was wrong. Revenge and hatred only weaken you."

He started. Rutland did recall those words he'd tossed out to him all those years ago. Regardless, it was a truth he'd learned too late. Nick gave a brusque nod. "I know that, now. I spent years blaming you for my father's mistakes. He was wrong." They'd all been. Papa, Rutland—*me*.

"I was, as well," the marquess conceded. "I was angry and hollow and broken." Grief ravaged his features. "And I am so very sorry for what I did to your family. I can never atone for that crime." His gaze darkened. "Or so many of my others. I can only try to be a better man now."

That was all they could do. Both of them.

Nick firmed his jaw. And he was determined to spend the rest of his life earning Justina's trust and love.

With that, he took his leave of Rutland and started toward his future.

# CHAPTER 22

THINGS WERE AS THEY'D BEEN three weeks earlier.

Honoria, following Nick's revelation and Edmund's arrival in London, had returned from visiting Phoebe and now sat loyally at Justina's side in The Circulating Library. Gillian occupied the other seat. Andrew strolled the streets of Lambeth. For all intents and purposes, everything was the same.

Only, while Justina sat waiting for the lecture to begin, the room filled with just a smattering of guests, she accepted the truth. Life would never return to the way it had been.

Three weeks ago, she'd been a naïve miss dreaming of love and hiding in a lecture hall, afraid to so much as utter her own opinion. Now, she was a woman married, awakened to the darkness that existed in a person's soul. Only, it was not solely Nick who'd opened her eyes to the truth of the world around her—but the truth of who and what Edmund had been, as well. She'd spent the whole of her life escaping from her own father's ugliness with dreams of perfection. She was to have found a loving, devoted husband, larger than life, who didn't seek to silence her, as her own mother had been. In the end, she'd lifted Nick upon a pedestal which only a fictional figure could dare attain.

"I'm sorry," Honoria said in hushed tones. She stretched a hand out, covering Justina's gloved fingers.

God, how she despised being this object of pity. From the

moment her friends had arrived that morning and insisted on accompanying her to a lecture, she'd met nothing more than sad looks and stilted silence. In the end, she'd proven Honoria's jaded cynicism about a gentleman and his intentions—correct.

There was no "I-told-you-so", however. Rather, there was a devoted friendship that she'd be forever grateful for.

She had no illusions that her timely appearance was anything more than deliberate; a request from Phoebe. Because, ultimately, she had always been the girl in need of care. Only Nick had treated her as a woman in possession of her own mind and a woman who should speak freely for it. Trusted in her enough that he'd given her one of the most prosperous landholdings her father had held—and lost. What did that say about her husband?

While Gillian and Honoria conversed, Justina glanced several rows ahead to the empty chairs she and Nick had occupied a few weeks ago. This same room he had stolen into and whispered all the words she'd hoped to hear from a suitor; of shared interests and dreams. But then, could he really feign that appreciation for literature? That niggling voice continued. How, when all of Society knew nothing of her interests and desires, would he have not only gleaned that information, but then memorized verses?

It wasn't all a lie. After the shock and agony of yesterday's revelations, she could, in this new day, see that there had been more between them. But was it enough? She nibbled at her lower lip.

"I know you'll both call me a romantic," Gillian said softly, interrupting her thoughts and calling her attention. "But sometimes, gentlemen do horrid things. And make rotten choices that hurt a person. Phoebe," she reminded them, looking back and forth between her friends. "My sister. But then they'll have these moments," she clasped her hands to her chest. "These grand gestures that prove their love and worth."

Honoria snorted. "What are you saying?" she asked, just as the lecturer, an old bewigged gentleman, took his place at the podium.

Scowling, Gillian dropped her hands to her lap. "I am saying that just because His Grace intended something awful and hurt Justina, that there can still be love."

A long groan burst from Honoria, earning several silencing whispers and frowns from the patrons scattered about the room. "Do you think Huntly, who intended to break her heart, is going to suddenly change and be..." She swatted the air. "...a hero charging in on a noble steed?"

"Is Phoebe not hopelessly in love with the marquess?" Gillian challenged, going toe-to-toe with their cynical friend. "And my sister with Cedric? Hmm?"

While they quarreled, Justina's heart thudded hard. It was silly to cling to Gillian's reminder and yet...

*You made me forget my hate and made me...feel again... I love you...*

He'd already had her heart. What reason had he to lie now?

"Shelley once wrote, 'First our pleasures die—and then our hopes, and then our fears—and when these are dead, the debt is due dust claims dust—and we die too.'"

Her heart constricted.

"My goodness that is horrid," Gillian whispered loudly, ignoring the long looks sent her way. "Whyever would anyone dare call that romantic?"

Honoria rustled through the program detailing the discussions for the lecture. "*This* is what you'd come to?" she asked, waving the page at Justina. "A discussion on Shelley, sorrow and sadness?" In hindsight, it had been a rather rot idea to come here for that reason, as well.

"It is redundant," Gillian agreed.

"Ahem," the lecturer paused in his speaking and fixed their trio with a glare. Contented with their silence, he continued on. "As I was saying. Shelley writes of sadness and sorrow. It is a theme that is—"

*Real.*

"Depressing," Gillian muttered under her breath. "There is far more than enough treachery and misery that one can do without this gentleman's woeful musings."

As the lecturer droned on at the front of the hall, Justina stared past him. How much of her life had she possessed a preconceived dream and notion of what love and happiness were? She'd aspired to that emotion and looked upon life in shades of blacks and whites. There had never been grays. Her mother's marriage was a miserable one and had served as the basis for everything she never wanted. Yet, in Phoebe's, she had seen the love...and not the process to that great emotion. In her naivety, Justina hadn't delved into the details of how Edmund had once hurt her sister.

She'd only focused on Phoebe's suffering and eventual happiness. Now she wished to know. As a woman. For mayhap if Phoebe and Edmund had found forgiveness and love, that gift could exist for her and Nick.

How very foolish she'd been. She'd seen him in one light, not allowing herself to linger on the darker pieces he'd revealed. *I didn't want to see anything else...* She'd been content with the dream. The problem with dreams is that they invariably ended and left one with the cold reality that was life.

*What is my reality?*

She'd resolved to never be her mother, but had never given proper thought to who she did wish to be and, more, how to shape herself into that person. Nick's words rang in her ears.

*...You come here weekly, and you sit at the back rows listening to the opinions of others... What you have to say, Justina. What opinions you have are no less important...*

She blinked slowly, staring at the gentleman droning on and on, with his own opinions and the truth slid forward. She didn't want to simply sit and listen anymore. She wanted a voice, but one she was unafraid to use. Nick had helped her realize that. In coming here and hiding in a lecture hall, she was hiding from her husband and the future that was now theirs. In that, she may as well be the same girl hiding from Tennyson. She needed to fight for him and for their future—together. A lightness filled her chest and she shoved back her chair to stand when whispers rent the monotony of the lecture.

The steady tread of a footfall brought her attention sideways and her heart squeezed. Gaze trained forward, Nick strode down the narrow aisle toward the front podium. His eyes briefly found hers. He was here. *Why is he here?* Emotion clogged her throat and she struggled to swallow past the hope there.

"What is he doing here?" Honoria whispered, echoing Justina's thoughts as he stopped at the front of the room and proceeded to exchange hushed words with the lecturer.

With a final nod, Nick claimed a place behind the podium. Reaching inside his jacket, he withdrew his spectacles and placed them on. Then he fished out a piece of white parchment.

Justina cocked her head.

"The autumn winds carpet the earth in deadened leaves, ush–

ering in winter's cold." His quietly spoken words filled the hall, raising whispers from the gathered gentlemen.

"He writes poetry," Gillian said, widening her eyes.

"Yes." No. He hadn't. She slid back into her seat and clung to the edge.

"The season lasts eternal, freezing, destroying in its hold." Nick lifted his gaze from the page. From across the hall, his gaze locked with hers. In his eyes, the love and regret there stole her breath. "But with her love, spring returns and slowly the chill recedes. Bringing forth hope, and laughter, and everything that can be." The column of his throat moved.

Tears welled in her eyes and his face blurred. She frantically wiped at them. Needing to see him.

Gillian sighed. "His grand moment."

Justina bit hard on her lower lip. He'd put pen to parchment— for her.

"You were my spring. You awakened me in ways I'd believed myself long dead. You filled me with joy," he said, hoarsely. "Life may change, but it may fly not; Hope may vanish, but can die not—" *Oh, God.* She touched quivering fingers to her lips. "Truth be veiled, but still it burneth; Love repulsed—" Nick held her stare, waiting. His meaning clear.

A teardrop spiraled down her cheek. She let her hand fall to her lap. "But it returneth," she whispered. It did. Because as long as forgiveness and redemption existed, so, too, did love.

Her husband touched his hand to his heart. "I made a blunder of it all, Justina," he called out. His voice trembled with the weight of emotion underlining that pronouncement. His words filled the hall, raising whispers as wide-eyed stares moved between him and her.

The small gathering of gentlemen swiveled their heads to where she sat.

"That you did," Honoria groused, earning an elbow in the side from Gillian.

Nick continued over that interruption. "I do not seek to pretend that I can ever be worthy of you." He would humble himself in this way for her? A man who'd shared nothing of himself all these years. "But I am selfish enough to want you anyway." Clearing his throat, he folded his parchment and stuffed it back inside his jacket. "If you'll have me." And then started the same path down the aisle.

She sat frozen, her throat working painfully, and the lecturer reclaimed his spot as though it was every day a powerful duke entered his hall and read a poem before a crowd of strangers. He'd not force her hand. Where so many husbands, like her father, would demand submission and order their wives about.

"Surely you aren't going to simply let him go?" Gillian whispered.

Justina swung her gaze to the back of the hall just as Nick departed. She pressed her eyes closed. Mayhap she was weak. Or ten times the fool again. Shoving back her chair she sprang to her feet and sprinted from the room. But she wanted to at least try with him.

Her skirts whipped noisily at her ankles as she rushed for the door. She stumbled against it, then righting herself, pulled it open. Breathless, she stepped outside and searched the crowded streets. She located him ten paces ahead, making for his mount. Cursing his longer strides, she cupped her hands about her mouth. "Dominick Tallings," she cried and he spun about.

Shock and hope mingled in his features.

She raced after him and then skidded to a stop.

"I could not do it," he blurted.

She cocked her head.

The wind whipped about them, tossing the fabric of their cloaks together in a noisy whir. "I cannot destroy your father or brother." He paused. "Or Rutland." Her heart caught. "I paid him a visit this morn." His words came rapidly, rolling into one another. So at odds with his usual calm and ease. "Your father's vowels. Andrew's. All of it, I've given it over to Rutland. Now you may trust that no harm will ever come to your family at my hands."

Her heart squeezed and she touched a hand to her lips. He'd not only abandoned his vow for revenge but had sought out Edmund, giving all her family's possessions over to him.

"I know you cannot forgive what I've done, Justina, but—"

She leaned up and pressed her mouth to his in a brief meeting, silencing his words, then sank back on her heels. "I love you." Hope lit his eyes. "Not because of any material gift you've given or for what you've given my family back but because of what you let go."

He dropped his brow to hers. Whatever words he opened his mouth to speak were cut into by a sharp voice, coated in fury.

"How very touching, Your Grace," a voice chimed close. They both whipped around.

The woman, a striking stranger with hardened eyes, stared back. "What a beautiful display from the Darling Duke for his fool wife. A wealthy, powerful husband who also writes poems? Tsk, tsk, my how fortunate you are, Your Grace." She flashed a small gun. A maniacal glint burned from the depths of the woman's eyes, hinting at her madness.

Justina's mouth went dry. She stole a look back for Nick, whose skin matched the stark white of his cravat.

"Come, nothing to say? No greeting? No invitation to tea? I expect we should be good friends," the woman said, turning to Justina. "After all we've shared?"

All they'd shared. The cold-eyed stranger scraped a ruthless stare over her. Then it registered. This was Nick's former lover. Fear turned over in her belly when the lady waved her weapon in their direction.

Tension spilled from Nick's frame. "Lady Carew," Nick said slowly, as though handling a fractious mare. "Set your weapon down," he urged, guiding Justina behind him.

"Stop," the woman cried, her voice taking on a high-pitched tenor that hinted at her rapidly receding control. He immediately stilled.

Justina's pulse thudded loudly in her ears, muffling the street sounds. She looked about frantically at the passersby for assistance. They may as well have been any other trio gathered for tea and pastries for all the attention paid them.

"This did not go as I had planned," Lady Carew explained in eerie tones that hinted at her madness. "Huntly and I had crafted everything so beautifully. Your brother-in-law was to be devastated. You were to be miserable." Her face contorted, transforming her lovely features into something macabre. "I was to have Huntly as a lover. But you could not be deterred by the note Tennyson delivered to you. Instead, you landed the duke," she spat. The hatred in that charge raised the gooseflesh on Justina's arms. It had been *her*. The note Lord Tennyson had forced into her hand had come from this mercenary creature.

"What do you want?" she asked quietly, ignoring the silencing look Nick shot her.

"You abandoned all our plans for this one, Huntly." Lady Carew's voice shook.

Nick took another small step, angling his body between Justina and the incensed woman.

"Surely you don't intend to kill a duke and a duchess in the middle of Lambeth Street?" Justina compelled.

From the corner of his eye, Nick caught her gaze and gave a slight shake of his head.

"Come, Your Grace, do you truly believe me so gauche as to kill you?" the lady asked with a little giggle. "I merely wish to meet the woman Huntly threw me over for."

"Marianne?" The shocked inquiry cut into the lady's tirade and they glanced down the alley to where Andrew stood. Confusion spilled from his eyes as he took in the woman wielding a weapon.

Her arm wavered between Justina and Nick. "Andrew," she greeted as if they met at Almack's.

His confused gaze went to the weapon trained on his sister. "What are you doing?" His whispered query, laced with disbelief, cracked Justina's heart open. Her hopeful brother would never be the same after this treachery.

"She is my husband's former lover," Justina quietly supplied.

"What?" That word ripped from him as Andrew took a slow step forward. "You are wrong." Shock bled from his eyes and he touched a hand to his chest. "Huntly, old chap?"

Nick turned his palm up. "I—"

"Shut up," the viper hissed, jabbing her pistol in Nick's direction. "Surely you did not think I could ever love a boy like you?" the lady cackled. "How free you were with information about your family."

All the color leeched from Andrew's cheeks and he shook his head in mute silence. "You are mad," he whispered and took a step forward.

"Stop!" The faint tremor to that command hinted at the lady's thin grasp on control as she swung the gun in his direction.

Justina shot a fist out, catching the mad woman hard in the stomach. The weapon sailed through the air, landing with a noisy jingle on the cobblestones at Andrew's feet. Nick rushed the lady, knocking her down.

"No," Lady Carew wailed as he pulled her wrists hard behind her, looking around.

Several constables came running to gather the screaming madwoman. She was forcibly dragged off, legs flailing, curses on her lips.

Justina stared after the young lady, not many years older than herself. In a bid to drive back the tremble in her arms, she folded them close to her midsection. This was the woman who'd known Nick in the most intimate of ways. Who'd schemed and plotted with him. Until she drew her last breath she would regret his connection to that viper but, mayhap, he'd not have come into her life without it?

She lifted her gaze to her husband's face. Searching for some response. Yet, he studiously avoided her eyes. What was he thinking?

IT WAS DONE, AND YET it wasn't.

As Lady Carew's screams faded to a distant hum and then to nothing at all, horror turned in his belly. *I brought this about.* With his dark, twisted plans for revenge, he'd bound himself to people of true evil and it had nearly cost him his wife. Nick briefly closed his eyes. Until he drew his last breath, he'd see that gun trained on Justina's chest. A gun in the hand of a mad-woman who, at any moment, would have pulled that trigger and—

His wife slid her fingers into his. Those long digits trembling, marking her own tumult, forced his eyes open and he suddenly registered the sea of strangers staring on.

Men and women who gaped and gawked, and didn't give a jot that this was, in fact, his and Justina's and Andrew Barrett's life.

A large hand settled on his shoulder and gave it a slight squeeze. "Come." Andrew's uncharacteristically gruff voice, devoid of its usual cheer and also newly hollow, twisted the blade of guilt. "Take my sister from here," he urged with the same control of a skilled military commander.

Giving his head a jerky shake, Nick guided Justina to the carriage with Andrew trailing close behind. As they walked briskly along the streets of Lambeth, he felt her gaze on his face. What was she thinking? He tried to swallow past the lump of regret and anguish clogging his throat.

*No doubt the folly it was in ever trusting herself to me. In marrying me.*

They reached the black conveyance. Numb, he went to help Justina up but she ignored his hand and turned to Andrew.

Feeling like an interloper, he retreated several steps while brother and sister spoke in hushed tones. Scraps of their conversation drifted over.

"...I'm so very sorry, Andrew..."

Andrew's reply was lost to him and Nick swallowed hard. His wife said something else that earned a pained smile from her brother. Going up on tiptoe, Justina pressed a kiss on his cheek. He glanced in Nick's direction and then over to his sister. "Do you need me to stay with you?" he asked loudly, his meaning clear. He'd battle Nick in these very streets if she asked it.

Justina looked at Nick and he stiffened. Braced for her rejection. Deserving of it. Expecting it. Even as she was entitled to her resentment and hatred of him, he wanted her forgiveness. Wanted to prove he could be better for her...not because of her. He searched for a hint of what she was thinking and feeling but her expression gave no indications. "No," she said quietly. "I would speak with my husband."

His brother-in-law flexed his jaw. "I'll return home and see Mother is cared for. If you need me, though, Justina, send word," he ordered, sparing another hard look at Nick.

Guilt sluicing away at him, he forced himself to meet that direct stare. What did one say to the man one had set out to ruin? Who'd become embroiled with a viper because of one's planning and plotting? Who'd had his heart and innocence shattered in the streets of London, no less? "Barrett," he began in solemn tones.

Andrew stuck a hand out and Nick started. "I am trusting you with my sister, Huntly." His brother-in-law glowered. "Do not make me regret it or I will see that you do."

He immediately placed his hand in the other man's. That truce undeserved and speaking volumes of Andrew Barrett's character. Then, life changed them all. Sometimes for the better. "I won't," he pledged.

Justina lingered. "Gillian and Honoria—"

"Go," Barrett urged. "I will see they are returned home safely."

She nodded and, this time, allowed Nick to hand her inside the carriage. He climbed in after her.

Long after the conveyance rolled on through the streets of London, silence hung heavy between them. He contemplated all Cecily and Chilton had said these years. They had both proved correct—inflicting pain on Rutland would never have undone the years of misery he and his family had known. Since Justina, he'd proven a man capable of love and goodness. Also a man with flaws and failings.

The slight weight of two chess pieces inside his jacket called him.

Nick reached inside, feeling his wife's gaze taking in his movements as he withdrew one of the ivory pawns. He held it out and she stared at a moment before accepting the small piece.

"After my father's death, I saw life like a game board." He gestured to that symbolic object in her hold and she moved her keen gaze from it to Nick. "It was easier that way," he went on quietly. "I saw the boy I'd been, my father, even my sister and mother, as those weak, powerless figures. I never wanted to be that man." A sad chuckle rumbled in his chest. "Oh, I never wanted to be king, but I wanted to be master over myself. But more, I wanted to be what my father was not. A hero." His throat constricted. How very pathetic and small he'd been. He appreciated that now, as a man who'd lived life.

Setting the pawn down on the bench, Justina claimed the spot beside Nick. She reached up and, with a delicate butterfly caress, angled his face toward hers. "Oh, Nick," she said softly, running her eyes over his face. "You still don't see, do you? You'll continue to make mistakes. We *both* will." Her lips turned up in a tender smile. "But I do not want a hero from the gothic novels I'd read. I want *you*."

"I love you," he rasped. "Justina…"

She captured his face in her hands and held his gaze. "Take

me home," she urged with a gentle smile, palming his cheek. "With *you*. Where I belong."

And at long last, the thread binding him to his darkened past snapped.

He was free.

# EPILOGUE

*One Fortnight Later*
*London, England*

NICK HAD SPENT THE PAST thirteen years mired in hatred. Seeking revenge. Bitter. Hurting. Justina had shown him there was something far more powerful, beautiful and healing—love.

There would always be regret. For who he'd been. What he'd done...to himself, to Justina. Her family. His own kin. But as she'd promised, they'd moved on together.

"Oomph," she grunted as Nick inadvertently steered his blindfolded wife too close to the wall.

He brought them to a stop and whispered into her ear. The hint of honeysuckle on her skin wafted about his nose, intoxicating like fine brandy. "My apologies."

Justina angled her head back. "A visit from Byron?" she ventured.

Nick laughed, the mirth real and full as it rumbled in his chest. "You are relentless, love."

"Determined," she corrected. "And Byron?"

"Relentless and determined," he allotted, as she was in every aspect of life. Through the folded satin cravat covering her eyes, he tweaked her nose. "Sir Byron would have to return from Ravenna," he pointed out.

His wife searched a hand about and found his nose, returning the measure. "Ahh, but then wouldn't that be the surprise?"

"Indeed, you're correct. It would." He gripped her by the shoulders and directed her forward. "But that's still not it," he whispered into her ear.

Her breathy laughter flitted off the hallway walls as she allowed him to steer her onward. "Shelley?"

A grin tugged at his lips. "You guessed that already." As she'd been guessing since he'd escorted her from their chambers earlier that morn with mention of a surprise waiting.

"Him," his wife corrected. "I guessed him. Not that."

"Very well. Him. And no, Mr. Shelley is not paying a visit." He paused. "Perhaps someday." He brought them to a stop. "Here," he murmured, positioning her in the center of the doorway. Reaching behind her, he slowly loosened the knot holding the cloth in place. It fell with a fluttery wisp to the floor.

Justina blinked slowly. "Here," she breathed. She took a tentative step forward and then paused mid-movement. Her keen gaze touched on every aspect of the former parlor. From the gilded chairs in their neat rows, to the white satin upholstered sofas arranged in each corner of the room, to the lectern at the very center of the room. Wordlessly, his wife wandered inside. At the protracted silence, he shifted on his feet.

He'd wanted to give her a place where she was in control. Where the topics and discussion could be guided by her and her clever intellect. She trailed her fingertips along the back of one of the gold chairs. Suddenly, uncertain, Nick cleared his throat. "It is a salon," he said lamely, when she wheeled back to face him. "Or that is what I'd hoped. Or intended. Or thought." Stop rambling. He compressed his lips into a line. And yet, it mattered to him that this mattered to her.

"I see that," she whispered, returning her attention to the converted space.

"I want you to have a place that is yours," he explained, needing her to understand. "Where no pompous man presumes to dictate your thoughts. I thought it could be a place where you encourage other young women to—*oomph.*" He staggered back as she charged over.

Quickly righting them, Nick immediately folded her in his

arms. Happiness shone bright in her eyes, blending with so much love that it filled every corner of his being, making him all the stronger for it. "You like it, then, Your Grace?" he asked, brushing the pad of his thumb along her lower lip.

"I adore it, Nick," she returned.

"You are free to invite anyone you wish. You do not have to have me in attendance. I—"

"I want you at my side," she said solemnly, collecting his hands in her own. "Always and everywhere. Forever."

He had lived in a state of hatred and ugliness for so long, he'd once believed his soul was dead. Incapable of light or goodness. She'd saved him. Set him free and restored him to the person he'd once been. "Forever," he pledged and claimed her mouth in a kiss that promised that very gift.

## The End

# OTHER BOOKS BY CHRISTI CALDWELL

## TO ENCHANT A WICKED DUKE
*Book 13 in the "Heart of a Duke" Series by Christi Caldwell*

*A Devil in Disguise*

Years ago, when Nick Tallings, the recent Duke of Huntly, watched his family destroyed at the hands of a merciless nobleman, he vowed revenge. But his efforts had been futile, as his enemy, Lord Rutland is without weakness.

Until now...

With his rival finally happily married, Nick is able to set his ruthless scheme into motion. His plot hinges upon Lord Rutland's innocent, empty-headed sister-in-law, Justina Barrett. Nick will ruin her, marry her, and then leave her brokenhearted.

*A Lady Dreaming of Love*

From the moment Justina Barrett makes her Come Out, she is labeled a Diamond. Even with her ruthless father determined to sell her off to the highest bidder, Justina never gives up on her hope for a good, honorable gentleman who values her wit more than her looks.

*A Not-So-Chance Meeting*

Nick's ploy to ensnare Justina falls neatly into place in the streets of London. With each carefully orchestrated encounter, he slips further and further inside the lady's heart, never anticipating that Justina, with her quick wit and strength, will break down his own defenses. As Nick's plans begins to unravel, he's left to determine which is more important—Justina's love or his vow for vengeance. But can Justina ever forgive the duke who deceived her?

## ONE WINTER WITH A BARON
*Book 12 in the "Heart of a Duke" Series by Christi Caldwell*

*A clever spinster:*
Content with her spinster lifestyle, Miss Sybil Cunning wants to prove that a future as an unmarried woman is the only life for her. As a bluestocking who values hard, empirical data, Sybil needs help with her research. Nolan Pratt, Baron Webb, one of society's most scandalous rakes, is the perfect gentleman to help her. After all, he inspires fear in proper mothers and desire within their daughters.
*A notorious rake:*
Society may be aware of Nolan Pratt, Baron's Webb's wicked ways, but what he has carefully hidden is his miserable handling of his family's finances. When Sybil presents him the opportunity to earn much-needed funds, he can't refuse.
*A winter to remember:*
However, what begins as a business arrangement becomes something more and with every meeting, Sybil slips inside his heart. Can this clever woman look beneath the veneer of a coldhearted rake to see the man Nolan truly is?

## TO REDEEM A RAKE
*Book 11 in the "Heart of a Duke" Series by Christi Caldwell*

*He's spent years scandalizing society.*
*Now, this rake must change his ways.*

Society's most infamous scoundrel, Daniel Winterbourne, the Earl of Montfort, has been promised a small fortune if he can relinquish his wayward, carousing lifestyle. And behaving means he must also help find a respectable companion for his youngest sister—someone who will guide her and whom she can emulate. However, Daniel knows no such woman. But when he encounters a childhood friend, Daniel believes she may just be the answer to all of his problems.

Having been secretly humiliated by an unscrupulous blackguard years earlier, Miss Daphne Smith dreams of finding work at Ladies of Hope, an institution that provides an education for disabled women. With her sordid past and a disfigured leg, few opportunities arise for a woman such as she. Knowing Daniel's history, she wishes to avoid him, but working for his sister is exactly the stepping stone she needs.

Their attraction intensifies as Daniel and Daphne grow closer, preparing his sister for the London Season. But Daniel must resist his desire for a woman tarnished by scandal while Daphne is reminded of the boy she once knew. Can society's most notorious rake redeem his reputation and become the man Daphne deserves?

# TO WOO A WIDOW
*Book 10 in the "Heart of a Duke" Series by Christi Caldwell*

*They see a brokenhearted widow.*
*She's far from shattered.*

Lady Philippa Winston is never marrying again. After her late husband's cruelty that she kept so well hidden, she has no desire to search for love.

Years ago, Miles Brookfield, the Marquess of Guilford, made a frivolous vow he never thought would come to fruition—he promised to marry his mother's goddaughter if he was unwed by the age of thirty. Now, to his dismay, he's faced with honoring that pledge. But when he encounters the beautiful and intriguing Lady Philippa, Miles knows his true path in life. It's up to him to break down every belief Philippa carries about gentlemen, proving that not only is love real, but that he is the man deserving of her sheltered heart.

Will Philippa let down her guard and allow Miles to woo a widow in desperate need of his love?

## THE LURE OF A RAKE
*Book 9 in the "Heart of a Duke" Series by Christi Caldwell*

*A Lady Dreaming of Love*

Lady Genevieve Farendale has a scandalous past. Jilted at the altar years earlier and exiled by her family, she's now returned to London to prove she can be a proper lady. Even though she's not given up on the hope of marrying for love, she's wary of trusting again. Then she meets Cedric Falcot, the Marquess of St. Albans whose seductive ways set her heart aflutter. But with her sordid history, Genevieve knows a rake can also easily destroy her.

*An Unlikely Pairing*

What begins as a chance encounter between Cedric and Genevieve becomes something more. As they continue to meet, passions stir. But with Genevieve's hope for true love, she fears Cedric will be unable to give up his wayward lifestyle. After all, Cedric has spent years protecting his heart, and keeping everyone out. Slowly, she chips away at all the walls he's built, but when he falters, Genevieve can't offer him redemption. Now, it's up to Cedric to prove to Genevieve that the love of a man is far more powerful than the lure of a rake.

## TO TRUST A ROGUE
*Book 8 in the "Heart of a Duke" Series by Christi Caldwell*

*A rogue*

Marcus, the Viscount Wessex has carefully crafted the image of rogue and charmer for Polite Society. Under that façade, however, dwells a man whose dreams were shattered almost eight years earlier by a young lady who captured his heart, pledged her love, and then left him, with nothing more than a curt note.

*A widow*

Eight years earlier, faced with no other choice, Mrs. Eleanor Collins, fled London and the only man she ever loved, Marcus, Viscount Wessex. She has now returned to serve as a companion for her elderly aunt with a daughter in tow. Even though they're next door neighbors, there is little reason for her to move in the same circles as Marcus, just in case, she vows to avoid him, for he reminds her of all she lost when she left.

*Reunited*

As their paths continue to cross, Marcus finds his desire for Eleanor just as strong, but he learned long ago she's not to be trusted. He will offer her a place in his bed, but not anything more. Only, Eleanor has no interest in this new, roguish man. The more time they spend together, the protective wall they've constructed to keep the other out, begin to break. With all the betrayals and secrets between them, Marcus has to open his heart again. And Eleanor must decide if it's ever safe to trust a rogue.

# To Wed His Christmas Lady
*Book 7 in the "Heart of a Duke" Series by Christi Caldwell*

*She's longing to be loved:*

Lady Cara Falcot has only served one purpose to her loathsome father—to increase his power through a marriage to the future Duke of Billingsley. As such, she's built protective walls about her heart, and presents an icy facade to the world around her. Journeying home from her finishing school for the Christmas holidays, Cara's carriage is stranded during a winter storm. She's forced to tarry at a ramshackle inn, where she immediately antagonizes another patron—William.

*He's avoiding his duty in favor of one last adventure:*

William Hargrove, the Marquess of Grafton has wanted only one thing in life—to avoid the future match his parents would have him make to a cold, duke's daughter. He's returning home from a blissful eight years of traveling the world to see to his responsibilities. But when a winter storm interrupts his trip and lands him at a falling-down inn, he's forced to share company with a commanding Lady Cara who initially reminds him exactly of the woman he so desperately wants to avoid.

A Christmas snowstorm ushers in the spirit of the season:

At the holiday time, these two people who despise each other due to first perceptions are offered renewed beginnings and fresh starts. As this gruff stranger breaks down the walls she's built about herself, Cara has to determine whether she can truly open her heart to trusting that any man is capable of good and that she herself is capable of love. And William has to set aside all previous thoughts he's carried of the polished ladies like Cara, to be the man to show her that love.

# THE HEART OF A SCOUNDREL
*Book 6 in the "Heart of a Duke" Series by Christi Caldwell*

Ruthless, wicked, and dark, the Marquess of Rutland rouses terror in the breast of ladies and nobleman alike. All Edmund wants in life is power. After he was publically humiliated by his one love Lady Margaret, he vowed vengeance, using Margaret's niece, as his pawn. Except, he's thwarted by another, more enticing target—Miss Phoebe Barrett.

Miss Phoebe Barrett knows precisely the shame she's been born to. Because her father is a shocking letch she's learned to form her own opinions on a person's worth. After a chance meeting with the Marquess of Rutland, she is captivated by the mysterious man. He, too, is a victim of society's scorn, but the more encounters she has with Edmund, the more she knows there is powerful depth and emotion to the jaded marquess.

The lady wreaks havoc on Edmund's plans for revenge and he finds he wants Phoebe, at all costs. As she's drawn into the darkness of his world, Phoebe risks being destroyed by Edmund's ruthlessness. And Phoebe who desires love at all costs, has to determine if she can ever truly trust the heart of a scoundrel.

# TO LOVE A LORD
*Book 5 in the "Heart of a Duke" Series by Christi Caldwell*

*All she wants is security:*
The last place finishing school instructor Mrs. Jane Munroe belongs, is in polite Society. Vowing to never wed, she's been scuttled around from post to post. Now she finds herself in the Marquess of Waverly's household. She's never met a nobleman she liked, and when she meets the pompous, arrogant marquess, she remembers why. But soon, she discovers Gabriel is unlike any gentleman she's ever known.

*All he wants is a companion for his sister:*
What Gabriel finds himself with instead, is a fiery spirited, bespectacled woman who entices him at every corner and challenges his age-old vow to never trust his heart to a woman. But… there is something suspicious about his sister's companion. And he is determined to find out just what it is.

*All they need is each other:*
As Gabriel and Jane confront the truth of their feelings, the lies and secrets between them begin to unravel. And Jane is left to decide whether or not it is ever truly safe to love a lord.

# LOVED BY A DUKE
*Book 4 in the "Heart of a Duke" Series by Christi Caldwell*

For ten years, Lady Daisy Meadows has been in love with Auric, the Duke of Crawford. Ever since his gallant rescue years earlier, Daisy knew she was destined to be his Duchess. Unfortunately, Auric sees her as his best friend's sister and nothing more. But perhaps, if she can manage to find the fabled heart of a duke pendant, she will win over the heart of her duke.

Auric, the Duke of Crawford enjoys Daisy's company. The last thing he is interested in however, is pursuing a romance with a woman he's known since she was in leading strings. This season, Daisy is turning up in the oddest places and he cannot help but notice that she is no longer a girl. But Auric wouldn't do something as foolhardy as to fall in love with Daisy. He couldn't. Not with the guilt he carries over his past sins... Not when he has no right to her heart...But perhaps, just perhaps, she can forgive the past and trust that he'd forever cherish her heart—but will she let him?

# THE LOVE OF A ROGUE
*Book 3 in the "Heart of a Duke" Series by Christi Caldwell*

Lady Imogen Moore hasn't had an easy time of it since she made her Come Out. With her betrothed, a powerful duke breaking it off to wed her sister, she's become the *tons* favorite piece of gossip. Never again wanting to experience the pain of a broken heart, she's resolved to make a match with a polite, respectable gentleman. The last thing she wants is another reckless rogue.

Lord Alex Edgerton has a problem. His brother, tired of Alex's carousing has charged him with chaperoning their remaining, unwed sister about *ton* events. Shopping? No, thank you. Attending the theatre? He'd rather be at Forbidden Pleasures with a scantily clad beauty upon his lap. The task of *chaperone* becomes even more of a bother when his sister drags along her dearest friend, Lady Imogen to social functions. The last thing he wants in his life is a young, innocent English miss.

Except, as Alex and Imogen are thrown together, passions flare and Alex comes to find he not only wants Imogen in his bed, but also in his heart. Yet now he must convince Imogen to risk all, on the heart of a rogue.

# MORE THAN A DUKE
*Book 2 in the "Heart of a Duke" Series by Christi Caldwell*

Polite Society doesn't take Lady Anne Adamson seriously. However, Anne isn't just another pretty young miss. When she discovers her father betrayed her mother's love and her family descended into poverty, Anne comes up with a plan to marry a respectable, powerful, and honorable gentleman—a man nothing like her philandering father.

Armed with the heart of a duke pendant, fabled to land the wearer a duke's heart, she decides to enlist the aid of the notorious Harry, 6th Earl of Stanhope. A scoundrel with a scandalous past, he is the last gentleman she'd ever wed…however, his reputation marks him the perfect man to school her in the art of seduction so she might ensnare the illustrious Duke of Crawford.

Harry, the Earl of Stanhope is a jaded, cynical rogue who lives for his own pleasures. Having been thrown over by the only woman he ever loved so she could wed a duke, he's not at all surprised when Lady Anne approaches him with her scheme to capture another duke's affection. He's come to appreciate that all women are in fact greedy, title-grasping, self-indulgent creatures. And with Anne's history of grating on his every last nerve, she is the last woman he'd ever agree to school in the art of seduction. Only his friendship with the lady's sister compels him to help.

What begins as a pretend courtship, born of lessons on seduction, becomes something more leaving Anne to decide if she can give her heart to a reckless rogue, and Harry must decide if he's willing to again trust in a lady's love.

# FOR LOVE OF THE DUKE
*First Full-Length Book in the "Heart of a Duke" Series*
*by Christi Caldwell*

After the tragic death of his wife, Jasper, the 8th Duke of Bainbridge buried himself away in the dark cold walls of his home, Castle Blackwood. When he's coaxed out of his self-imposed exile to attend the amusements of the Frost Fair, his life is irrevocably changed by his fateful meeting with Lady Katherine Adamson.

With her tight brown ringlets and silly white-ruffled gowns, Lady Katherine Adamson has found her dance card empty for two Seasons. After her father's passing, Katherine learned the unreliability of men, and is determined to depend on no one, except herself. Until she meets Jasper...

In a desperate bid to avoid a match arranged by her family, Katherine makes the Duke of Bainbridge a shocking proposition—one that he accepts.

Only, as Katherine begins to love Jasper, she finds the arrangement agreed upon is not enough. And Jasper is left to decide if protecting his heart is more important than fighting for Katherine's love.

# IN NEED OF A DUKE
*A Prequel Novella to "The Heart of a Duke" Series*
*by Christi Caldwell*

In Need of a Duke: (Author's Note: This is a prequel novella to "The Heart of a Duke" series by Christi Caldwell. It was originally available in "The Heart of a Duke" Collection and is now being published as an individual novella.

~★~

It features a new prologue and epilogue.

Years earlier, a gypsy woman passed to Lady Aldora Adamson and her friends a heart pendant that promised them each the heart of a duke.

Now, a young lady, with her family facing ruin and scandal, Lady Aldora doesn't have time for mythical stories about cheap baubles. She needs to save her sisters and brother by marrying a titled gentleman with wealth and power to his name. She sets her bespectacled sights upon the Marquess of St. James.

Turned out by his father after a tragic scandal, Lord Michael Knightly has grown into a powerful, but self-made man. With the whispers and stares that still follow him, he would rather be anywhere but London…

Until he meets Lady Aldora, a young woman who mistakes him for his brother, the Marquess of St. James. The connection between Aldora and Michael is immediate and as they come to know one another, Aldora's feelings for Michael war with her sisterly responsibilities. With her family's dire situation, a man of Michael's scandalous past will never do.

Ultimately, Aldora must choose between her responsibilities as a sister and her love for Michael.

## ONCE A WALLFLOWER, AT LAST HIS LOVE
### Book 6 in the Scandalous Seasons Series

Responsible, practical Miss Hermione Rogers, has been crafting stories as the notorious Mr. Michael Michaelmas and selling them for a meager wage to support her siblings. The only real way to ensure her family's ruinous debts are paid, however, is to marry. Tall, thin, and plain, she has no expectation of success. In London for her first Season she seizes the chance to write the tale of a brooding duke. In her research, she finds Sebastian Fitzhugh, the 5th Duke of Mallen, who unfortunately is perfectly affable, charming, and so nicely… configured… he takes her breath away. He lacks all the character traits she needs for her story, but alas, any duke will have to do.

Sebastian Fitzhugh, the 5th Duke of Mallen has been deceived so many times during the high-stakes game of courtship, he's lost faith in Society women. Yet, after a chance encounter with Hermione, he finds himself intrigued. Not a woman he'd normally consider beautiful, the young lady's practical bent, her forthright nature and her tendency to turn up in the oddest places has his interests... roused. He'd like to trust her, he'd like to do a whole lot more with her too, but should he?

## A Marquess For Christmas
*Book 5 in the Scandalous Seasons Series*

Lady Patrina Tidemore gave up on the ridiculous notion of true love after having her heart shattered and her trust destroyed by a black-hearted cad. Used as a pawn in a game of revenge against her brother, Patrina returns to London from a failed elopement with a tattered reputation and little hope for a respectable match. The only peace she finds is in her solitude on the cold winter days at Hyde Park. And even that is yanked from her by two little hellions who just happen to have a devastatingly handsome, but coldly aloof father, the Marquess of Beaufort. Something about the lord stirs the dreams she'd once carried for an honorable gentleman's love.

Weston Aldridge, the 4th Marquess of Beaufort was deceived and betrayed by his late wife. In her faithlessness, he's come to view women as self-serving, indulgent creatures. Except, after a series of chance encounters with Patrina, he comes to appreciate how uniquely different she is than all women he's ever known.

At the Christmastide season, a time of hope and new beginnings, Patrina and Weston, unexpectedly learn true love in one another. However, as Patrina's scandalous past threatens their future and the happiness of his children, they are both left to determine if love is enough.

## Always a Rogue, Forever Her Love
*Book 4 in the Scandalous Seasons Series*

Miss Juliet Marshville is spitting mad. With one guardian missing, and the other singularly uninterested in her fate, she is at the mercy of her wastrel brother who loses her beloved childhood home to a man known as Sin. Determined to reclaim control of Rosecliff Cottage and her own fate, Juliet arranges a meeting with the notorious rogue and demands the return of her property.

Jonathan Tidemore, 5th Earl of Sinclair, known to the *ton* as Sin, is exceptionally lucky in life and at the gaming tables. He has just one problem. Well…four, really. His incorrigible sisters have driven off yet another governess. This time, however, his mother demands he find an appropriate replacement.

When Miss Juliet Marshville boldly demands the return of her precious cottage, he takes advantage of his sudden good fortune and puts an offer to her; turn his sisters into proper English ladies, and he'll return Rosecliff Cottage to Juliet's possession.

Jonathan comes to appreciate Juliet's spirit, courage, and clever wit, and decides to claim the fiery beauty as his mistress. Juliet, however, will be mistress for no man. Nor could she ever love a man who callously stole her home in a game of cards. As Jonathan begins to see Juliet as more than a spirited beauty to warm his bed, he realizes she could be a lady he could love the rest of his life, if only he can convince the proud Juliet that he's worthy of her hand and heart.

## Always Proper, Suddenly Scandalous
*Book 3 in the Scandalous Seasons Series*

Geoffrey Winters, Viscount Redbrooke was not always the hard, unrelenting lord driven by propriety. After a tragic mistake, he resolved to honor his responsibility to the Redbrooke line and live a life, free of scandal. Knowing his duty is to wed a proper, respectable English miss, he selects Lady Beatrice Dennington, daughter of the Duke of Somerset, the perfect woman for him. Until he meets Miss Abigail Stone…

To distance herself from a personal scandal, Abigail Stone flees America to visit her uncle, the Duke of Somerset. Determined to never trust a man again, she is helplessly intrigued by the hard, too-proper Geoffrey. With his strict appreciation for decorum and order, he is nothing like the man' she's always dreamed of.

Abigail is everything Geoffrey does not need. She upends his carefully ordered world at every encounter. As they begin to care for one another, Abigail carefully guards the secret that resulted in her journey to England.

Only, if Geoffrey learns the truth about Abigail, he must decide which he holds most dear: his place in Society or Abigail's place in his heart.

# NEVER COURTED, SUDDENLY WED
*Book 2 in the Scandalous Seasons Series*

Christopher Ansley, Earl of Waxham, has constructed a perfect image for the *ton*–the ladies love him and his company is desired by all. Only two people know the truth about Waxham's secret. Unfortunately, one of them is Miss Sophie Winters.

Sophie Winters has known Christopher since she was in leading strings. As children, they delighted in tormenting each other. Now at two and twenty, she still has a tendency to find herself in scrapes, and her marital prospects are slim.

When his father threatens to expose his shame to the *ton*, unless he weds Sophie for her dowry, Christopher concocts a plan to remain a bachelor. What he didn't plan on was falling in love with the lively, impetuous Sophie. As secrets are exposed, will Christopher's love be enough when she discovers his role in his father's scheme?

# FOREVER BETROTHED, NEVER THE BRIDE
### Book 1 in the Scandalous Seasons Series

Hopeless romantic Lady Emmaline Fitzhugh is tired of sitting with the wallflowers, waiting for her betrothed to come to his senses and marry her. When Emmaline reads one too many reports of his scandalous liaisons in the gossip rags, she takes matters into her own hands.

War-torn veteran Lord Drake devotes himself to forgetting his days on the Peninsula through an endless round of meaningless associations. He no longer wants to feel anything, but Lady Emmaline is making it hard to maintain a state of numbness. With her zest for life, she awakens his passion and desire for love.

The one woman Drake has spent the better part of his life avoiding is now the only woman he needs, but he is no longer a man worthy of his Emmaline. It is up to her to show him the healing power of love.

## A SEASON OF HOPE
### A Danby Novella

Five years ago when her love, Marcus Wheatley, failed to return from fighting Napoleon's forces, Lady Olivia Foster buried her heart. Unable to betray Marcus's memory, Olivia has gone out of her way to run off prospective suitors. At three and twenty she considers herself firmly on the shelf. Her father, however, disagrees and accepts an offer for Olivia's hand in marriage. Yet it's Christmas, when anything can happen…

Olivia receives a well-timed summons from her grandfather, the Duke of Danby, and eagerly embraces the reprieve from her betrothal.

Only, when Olivia arrives at Danby Castle she realizes the Christmas season represents hope, second chances, and even miracles.

# "WINNING A LADY'S HEART"
## A Danby Novella

Author's Note: This is a novella that was originally available in A Summons From The Castle (The Regency Christmas Summons Collection). It is being published as an individual novella.

~★~

For Lady Alexandra, being the source of a cold, calculated wager is bad enough…but when it is waged by Nathaniel Michael Winters, 5th Earl of Pembroke, the man she's in love with, it results in a broken heart, the scandal of the season, and a summons from her grandfather – the Duke of Danby.

To escape Society's gossip, she hurries to her meeting with the duke, determined to put memories of the earl far behind. Except the duke has other plans for Alexandra…plans which include the 5th Earl of Pembroke!

# TEMPTED BY A LADY'S SMILE
## Book 4 in the "Lords of Honor" Series

Richard Jonas has loved but one woman—a woman who belongs to his brother. Refusing to suffer any longer, he evades his family in order to barricade his heart from unrequited love. While attending a friend's summer party, Richard's approach to love is changed after sharing a passionate and life-altering kiss with a vibrant and mysterious woman. Believing he was incapable of loving again, Richard finds himself tempted by a young lady determined to marry his best friend.

Gemma Reed has not been treated kindly by the *ton*. Often disregarded for her appearance and interests unlike those of a proper lady, Gemma heads to house party to win the heart of Lord Westfield, the man she's loved for years. But her plan is set off course by the tempting and intriguing, Richard Jonas.

A chance meeting creates a new path for Richard and Gemma to forage—but can two people, scorned and shunned by those they've loved from afar, let down their guards to find true happiness?

## RESCUED BY A LADY'S LOVE

*Book 3 in the "Lords of Honor" Series*

Destitute and determined to finally be free of any man's shackles, Lily Benedict sets out to salvage her honor. With no choice but to commit a crime that will save her from her past, she enters the home of the recluse, Derek Winters, the new Duke of Blackthorne. But entering the "Beast of Blackthorne's" lair proves more threatening than she ever imagined.

With half a face and a mangled leg, Derek—once rugged and charming—only exists within the confines of his home. Shunned by society, Derek is leery of the hauntingly beautiful Lily Benedict. As time passes, she slips past his defenses, reminding him how to live again. But when Lily's sordid past comes back, threatening her life, it's up to Derek to find the strength to become the hero he once was. Can they overcome the darkness of their sins to find a life of love and redemption?

## CAPTIVATED BY A LADY'S CHARM

*Book 2 in the "Lords of Honor" Series*

*In need of a wife…*

Christian Villiers, the Marquess of St. Cyr, despises the role he's been cast into as fortune hunter but requires the funds to keep his marquisate solvent. Yet, the sins of his past cloud his future, preventing him from seeing beyond his fateful actions at the Battle of Toulouse. For he knows inevitably it will catch up with him, and everyone will remember his actions on the battlefield that cost so many so much—particularly his best friend.

*In want of a husband…*

Lady Prudence Tidemore's life is plagued by familial scandals, which makes her own marital prospects rather grim. Surely there is one gentleman of the ton who can look past her family and see just her and all she has to offer?

When Prudence runs into Christian on a London street, the charming, roguish gentleman immediately captures her attention. But then a chance meeting becomes a waltz, and now…

*A Perfect Match…*

All she must do is convince Christian to forget the cold requirements he has for his future marchioness. But the demons in his past prevent him from turning himself over to love. One thing is certain—Prudence wants the marquess and is determined to have him in her life, now and forever. It's just a matter of convincing Christian he wants the same.

## SEDUCED BY A LADY'S HEART
*Book 1 in the "Lords of Honor" Series*

*You met Lieutenant Lucien Jones in "Forever Betrothed, Never the Bride" when he was a broken soldier returned from fighting Boney's forces. This is his story of triumph and happily-ever-after!*

~★~

Lieutenant Lucien Jones, son of a viscount, returned from war, to find his wife and child dead. Blaming his father for the commission that sent him off to fight Boney's forces, he was content to languish at London Hospital… until offered employment on the Marquess of Drake's staff. Through his position, Lucien found purpose in life and is content to keep his past buried.

Lady Eloise Yardley has loved Lucien since they were children. Having long ago given up on the dream of him, she married another. Years later, she is a young, lonely widow who does not fit in with the ton. When Lucien's family enlists her aid to reunite father and son, she leaps at the opportunity to not only aid her former friend, but to also escape London.

Lucien doesn't know what scheme Eloise has concocted, but

knowing her as he does, when she pays a visit to his employer, he knows she's up to something. The last thing he wants is the temptation that this new, older, mature Eloise presents; a tantalizing reminder of happier times and peace.

Yet Eloise is determined to win Lucien's love once and for all... if only Lucien can set aside the pain of his past and risk all on a lady's heart.

# ᴏɴʟʏ Fᴏʀ Tʜᴇɪʀ Lᴏᴠᴇ
*Book 3 in the "The Theodosia Sword" Series*

Miss Carol Cresswall bore witness to her parents' loveless union and is determined to avoid that same miserable fate. Her mother has altogether different plans—plans that include a match between Carol and Lord Gregory Renshaw. Despite his wealth and power, Carol has no interest in marrying a pompous man who goes out of his way to ignore her. Now, with their families coming together for the Christmastide season it's her mother's last-ditch effort to get them together. And Carol plans to avoid Gregory at all costs.

Lord Gregory Renshaw has no intentions of falling prey to his mother's schemes to marry him off to a proper debutante she's picked out. Over the years, he has carefully sidestepped all endeavors to be matched with any of the grasping ladies.

But a sudden Christmastide Scandal has the potential show Carol and Gregory that they've spent years running from the one thing they've always needed.

# ᴄᴏɴʟʏ ᶠᴏʀ ᴅᴇʀ ᴅᴏɴᴏʀ
*Book 2 in the "The Theodosia Sword" Series*

*A wounded soldier:*

When Captain Lucas Rayne returned from fighting Boney's forces, he was a shell of a man. A recluse who doesn't leave his family's estate, he's content to shut himself away. Until he meets Eve...

*A woman alone in the world:*

Eve Ormond spent most of her life following the drum alongside her late father. When his shameful actions bring death and pain to English soldiers, Eve is forced back to England, an outcast. With no family or marital prospects she needs employment and finds it in Captain Lucas Rayne's home. A man whose life was ruined by her father, Eve has no place inside his household. With few options available, however, Eve takes the post. What she never anticipates is how with their every meeting, this honorable, hurting soldier slips inside her heart.

*The Secrets Between Them:*

The more time Lucas spends with Eve, he remembers what it is to be alive and he lets the walls protecting his heart down. When the secrets between them come to light will their love be enough? Or are they two destined for heartbreak?

# ᴄᴏɴʟʏ ᶠᴏʀ ᴅɪꜱ ᴌᴀᴅʏ
*Book 1 in the "The Theodosia Sword" Series*

*A curse. A sword. And the thief who stole her heart.*

The Rayne family is trapped in a rut of bad luck. And now, it's up to Lady Theodosia Rayne to steal back the Theodosia sword, a gladius that was pilfered by the rival, loathed Renshaw family. Hopefully, recovering the stolen sword will break the cycle and reverse her family's fate.

Damian Renshaw, the Duke of Devlin, is feared by all—all, that is, except Lady Theodosia, the brazen spitfire who enters his home and wrestles an ancient relic from his wall. Intrigued by the vivacious woman, Devlin has no intentions of relinquishing the sword to her.

As Theodosia and Damian battle for ownership, passion ignites. Now, they are torn between their age-old feud and the fire that burns between them. Can two forbidden lovers find a way to make amends before their families' war tears them apart?

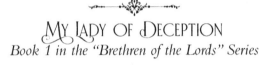

## MY LADY OF DECEPTION
*Book 1 in the "Brethren of the Lords" Series*

*This dark, sweeping Regency novel was previously only offered as part of the limited edition box sets: "From the Ballroom and Beyond", "Romancing the Rogue", and "Dark Deceptions". Now, available for the first time on its own, exclusively through Amazon is "My Lady of Deception".*

~*~

Everybody has a secret. Some are more dangerous than others.

For Georgina Wilcox, only child of the notorious traitor known as "The Fox", there are too many secrets to count. However, after her interference results in great tragedy, she resolves to never help another… until she meets Adam Markham.

Lord Adam Markham is captured by The Fox. Imprisoned, Adam loses everything he holds dear. As his days in captivity grow, he finds himself fascinated by the young maid, Georgina, who cares for him.

When the carefully crafted lies she's built between them begin to crumble, Georgina realizes she will do anything to prove her love and loyalty to Adam—even it means at the expense of her own life.

# NON-FICTION WORKS BY
# CHRISTI CALDWELL

**Uninterrupted Joy: Memoir: My Journey through
Infertility, Pregnancy, and Special Needs**

The following journey was never intended for publication.
It was written from a mother, to her unborn child. The words
detailed her struggle through infertility and the joy of finally being
pregnant. A stunning revelation at her son's birth opened a world
of both fear and discovery. This is the story of one mother's love
and hope and…her quest for uninterrupted joy.

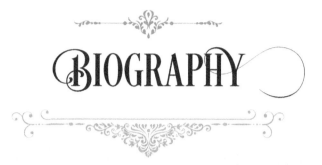

# BIOGRAPHY

Christi Caldwell is the bestselling author of historical romance novels set in the Regency era. Christi blames Judith McNaught's "Whitney, My Love," for luring her into the world of historical romance. While sitting in her graduate school apartment at the University of Connecticut, Christi decided to set aside her notes and try her hand at writing romance. She believes the most perfect heroes and heroines have imperfections and rather enjoys tormenting them before crafting a well-deserved happily ever after!

When Christi isn't writing the stories of flawed heroes and heroines, she can be found in her Southern Connecticut home chasing around her eight-year-old son, and caring for twin princesses-in-training!

Visit *www.christicaldwellauthor.com* to learn more about what Christi is working on, or join her on Facebook at Christi Caldwell Author, and Twitter *@ChristiCaldwell*

Made in United States
North Haven, CT
16 January 2025